W9-BGK-237

THE CREEPS

#1

NIGHT OF THE FRANKENFROGS

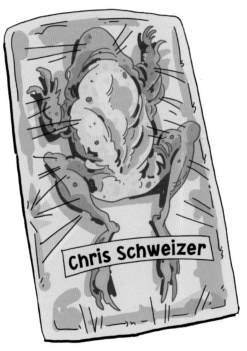

Chris Schweizer

AMULET BOOKS
NEW YORK

PUBLISHER'S NOTE:
This is a work of fiction. Names, characters, places, and incidents are either the product of the author's imagination or used fictitiously, and any resemblance to actual persons, living or dead, business establishments, events, or locales is entirely coincidental.

Library of Congress Control Number: 2014955691

Hardcover ISBN: 978-1-4197-1379-8
Paperback ISBN: 978-1-4197-1766-6

Text and illustrations copyright © 2015 Chris Schweizer
Book design by Pamela Notarantonio

Published in 2015 by Amulet Books, an imprint of ABRAMS. All rights reserved. No portion of this book may be reproduced, stored in a retrieval system, or transmitted in any form or by any means, mechanical, electronic, photocopying, recording, or otherwise, without written permission from the publisher.

Amulet Books and Amulet Paperbacks are registered trademarks of Harry N. Abrams, Inc.

Printed and bound in China
10 9 8 7 6 5 4 3 2 1

Amulet Books are available at special discounts when purchased in quantity for premiums and promotions as well as fundraising or educational use. Special editions can also be created to specification. For details, contact specialsales@abramsbooks.com or the address below.

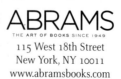

ABRAMS
THE ART OF BOOKS SINCE 1949
115 West 18th Street
New York, NY 10011
www.abramsbooks.com

TO PENNY, MY FAVORITE READER

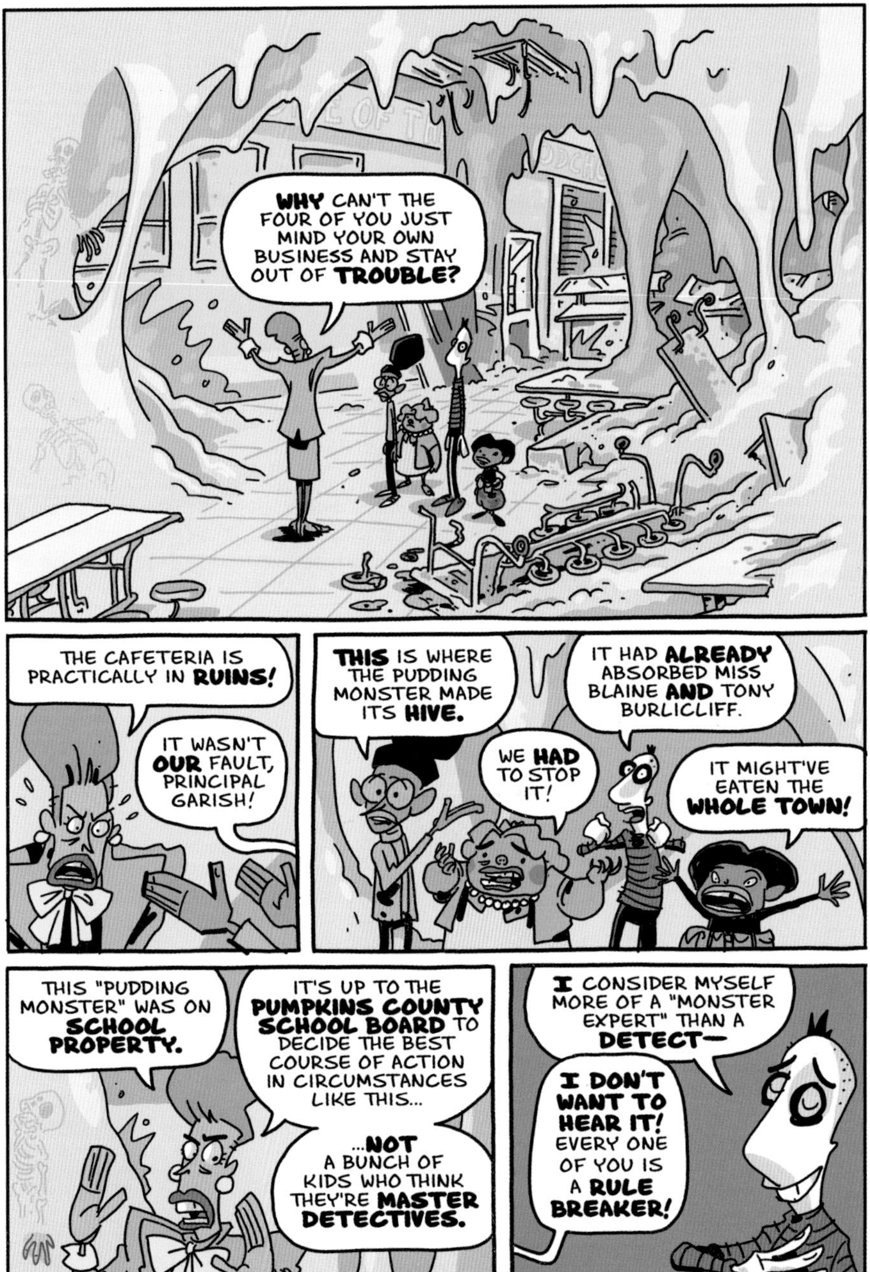

WHY CAN'T THE FOUR OF YOU JUST MIND YOUR OWN BUSINESS AND STAY OUT OF TROUBLE?
THE CAFETERIA IS PRACTICALLY IN RUINS!
IT WASN'T OUR FAULT, PRINCIPAL GARISH!
THIS IS WHERE THE PUDDING MONSTER MADE ITS HIVE.
WE HAD TO STOP IT!
IT HAD ALREADY ABSORBED MISS BLAINE AND TONY BURLICLIFF.
IT MIGHT'VE EATEN THE WHOLE TOWN!
THIS "PUDDING MONSTER" WAS ON SCHOOL PROPERTY.
IT'S UP TO THE PUMPKINS COUNTY SCHOOL BOARD TO DECIDE THE BEST COURSE OF ACTION IN CIRCUMSTANCES LIKE THIS...
...NOT A BUNCH OF KIDS WHO THINK THEY'RE MASTER DETECTIVES.
I CONSIDER MYSELF MORE OF A "MONSTER EXPERT" THAN A DETECT—
I DON'T WANT TO HEAR IT! EVERY ONE OF YOU IS A RULE BREAKER!

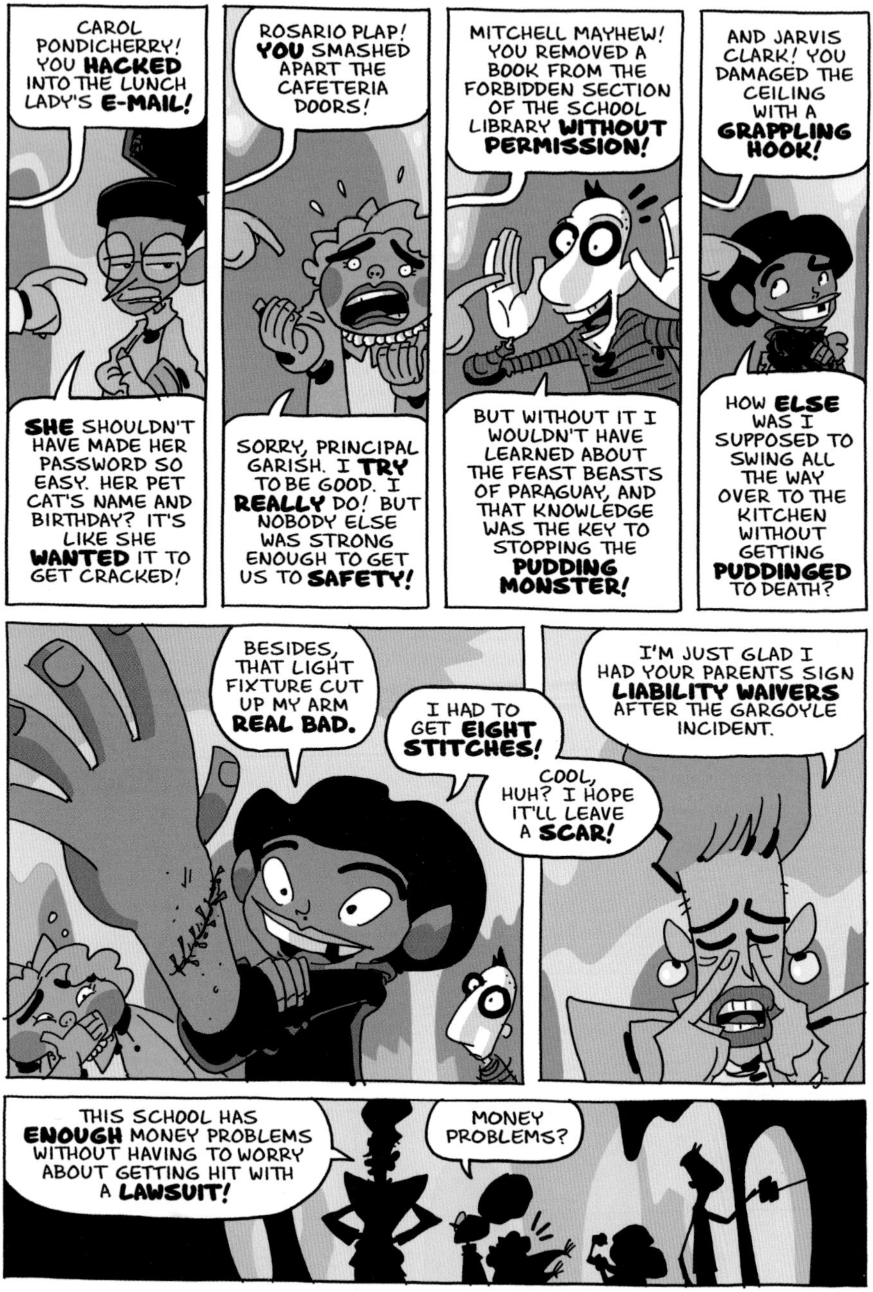
CAROL PONDICHERRY! YOU **HACKED** INTO THE LUNCH LADY'S **E-MAIL!**
SHE SHOULDN'T HAVE MADE HER PASSWORD SO EASY. HER PET CAT'S NAME AND BIRTHDAY? IT'S LIKE SHE **WANTED** IT TO GET CRACKED!
ROSARIO PLAP! **YOU** SMASHED APART THE CAFETERIA DOORS!
SORRY, PRINCIPAL GARISH. I **TRY** TO BE GOOD. I **REALLY** DO! BUT NOBODY ELSE WAS STRONG ENOUGH TO GET US TO **SAFETY!**
MITCHELL MAYHEW! YOU REMOVED A BOOK FROM THE FORBIDDEN SECTION OF THE SCHOOL LIBRARY **WITHOUT PERMISSION!**
BUT WITHOUT IT I WOULDN'T HAVE LEARNED ABOUT THE FEAST BEASTS OF PARAGUAY, AND THAT KNOWLEDGE WAS THE KEY TO STOPPING THE **PUDDING MONSTER!**
AND JARVIS CLARK! YOU DAMAGED THE CEILING WITH A **GRAPPLING HOOK!**
HOW **ELSE** WAS I SUPPOSED TO SWING ALL THE WAY OVER TO THE KITCHEN WITHOUT GETTING **PUDDINGED** TO DEATH?
BESIDES, THAT LIGHT FIXTURE CUT UP MY ARM **REAL BAD.**
I HAD TO GET **EIGHT STITCHES!**
COOL, HUH? I HOPE IT'LL LEAVE A **SCAR!**
I'M JUST GLAD I HAD YOUR PARENTS SIGN **LIABILITY WAIVERS** AFTER THE GARGOYLE INCIDENT.
THIS SCHOOL HAS **ENOUGH** MONEY PROBLEMS WITHOUT HAVING TO WORRY ABOUT GETTING HIT WITH A **LAWSUIT!**
MONEY PROBLEMS?

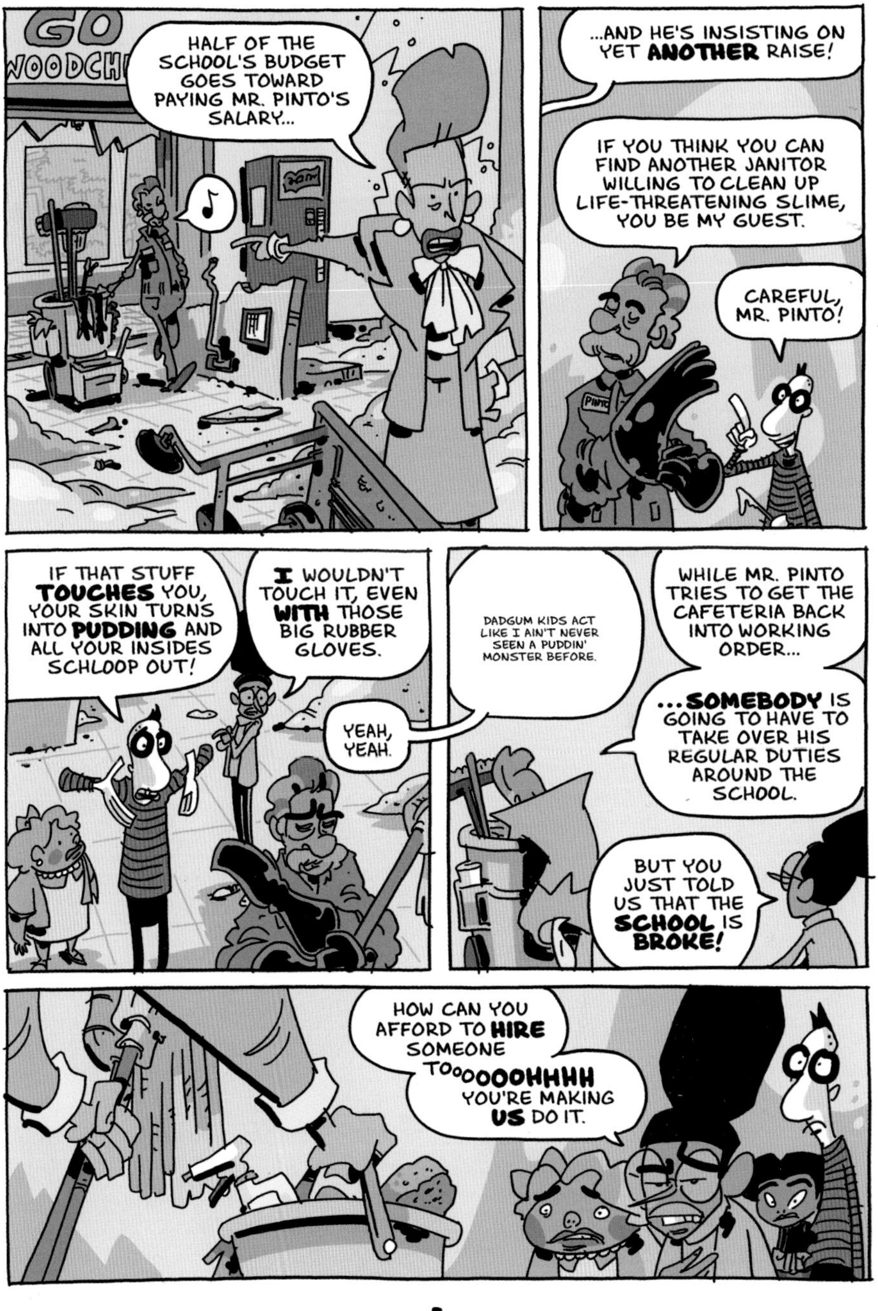
GO WOODCH
HALF OF THE SCHOOL'S BUDGET GOES TOWARD PAYING MR. PINTO'S SALARY...
...AND HE'S INSISTING ON YET ANOTHER RAISE!
IF YOU THINK YOU CAN FIND ANOTHER JANITOR WILLING TO CLEAN UP LIFE-THREATENING SLIME, YOU BE MY GUEST.
CAREFUL, MR. PINTO!
IF THAT STUFF TOUCHES YOU, YOUR SKIN TURNS INTO PUDDING AND ALL YOUR INSIDES SCHLOOP OUT!
I WOULDN'T TOUCH IT, EVEN WITH THOSE BIG RUBBER GLOVES.
YEAH, YEAH.
DADGUM KIDS ACT LIKE I AIN'T NEVER SEEN A PUDDIN' MONSTER BEFORE.
WHILE MR. PINTO TRIES TO GET THE CAFETERIA BACK INTO WORKING ORDER...
...SOMEBODY IS GOING TO HAVE TO TAKE OVER HIS REGULAR DUTIES AROUND THE SCHOOL.
BUT YOU JUST TOLD US THAT THE SCHOOL IS BROKE!
HOW CAN YOU AFFORD TO HIRE SOMEONE TOoooOOOHHHH YOU'RE MAKING US DO IT.

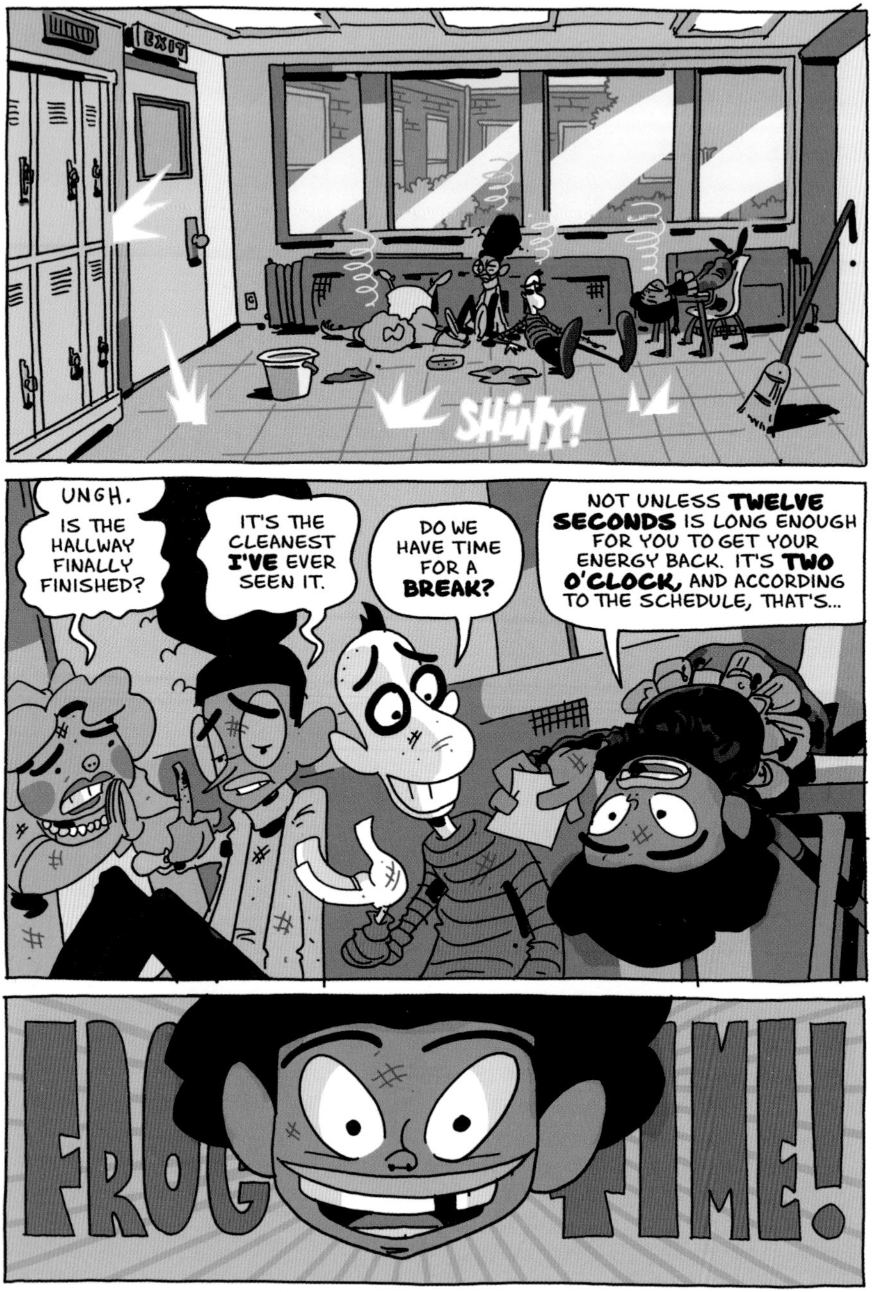
EXIT
SHINY!
UNGH. IS THE HALLWAY FINALLY FINISHED?
IT'S THE CLEANEST I'VE EVER SEEN IT.
DO WE HAVE TIME FOR A BREAK?
NOT UNLESS TWELVE SECONDS IS LONG ENOUGH FOR YOU TO GET YOUR ENERGY BACK. IT'S TWO O'CLOCK, AND ACCORDING TO THE SCHEDULE, THAT'S...
FROG TIME!

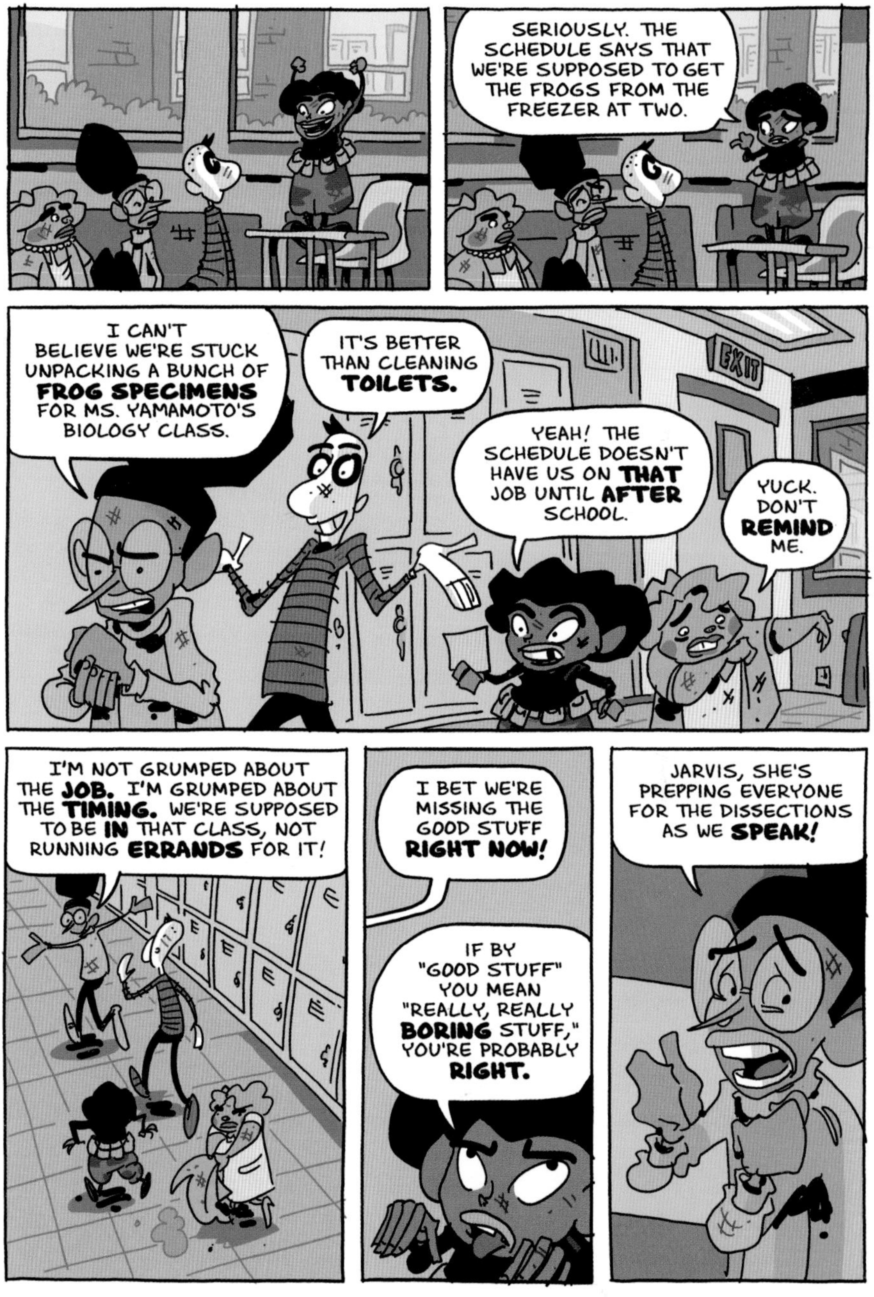
SERIOUSLY. THE SCHEDULE SAYS THAT WE'RE SUPPOSED TO GET THE FROGS FROM THE FREEZER AT TWO.
I CAN'T BELIEVE WE'RE STUCK UNPACKING A BUNCH OF **FROG SPECIMENS** FOR MS. YAMAMOTO'S BIOLOGY CLASS.
IT'S BETTER THAN CLEANING **TOILETS.**
YEAH! THE SCHEDULE DOESN'T HAVE US ON **THAT** JOB UNTIL **AFTER** SCHOOL.
YUCK. DON'T **REMIND** ME.
EXIT
I'M NOT GRUMPED ABOUT THE **JOB.** I'M GRUMPED ABOUT THE **TIMING.** WE'RE SUPPOSED TO BE **IN** THAT CLASS, NOT RUNNING **ERRANDS** FOR IT!
I BET WE'RE MISSING THE GOOD STUFF **RIGHT NOW!**
IF BY "GOOD STUFF" YOU MEAN "REALLY, REALLY **BORING** STUFF," YOU'RE PROBABLY **RIGHT.**
JARVIS, SHE'S PREPPING EVERYONE FOR THE DISSECTIONS AS WE **SPEAK!**

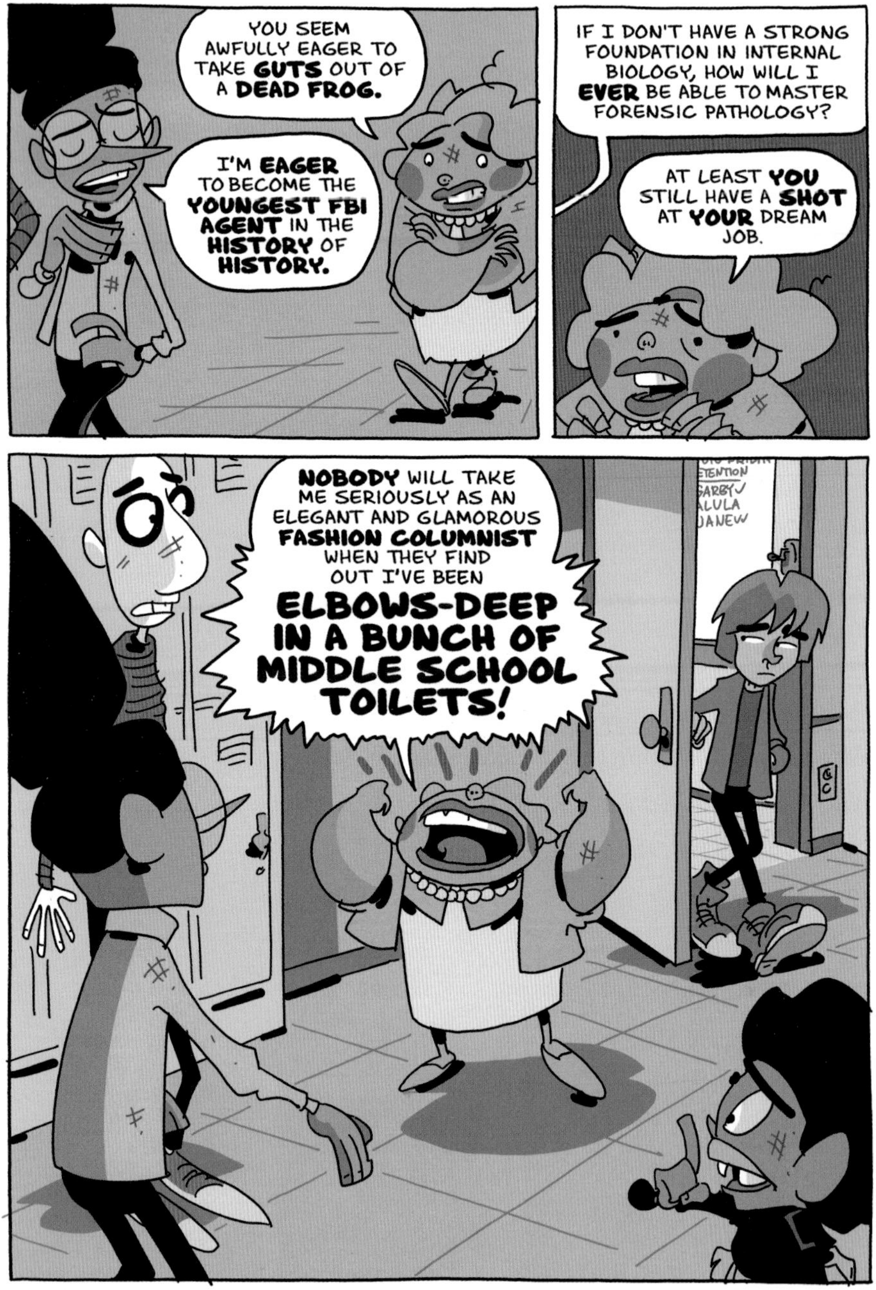
YOU SEEM AWFULLY EAGER TO TAKE **GUTS** OUT OF A **DEAD FROG.**
I'M **EAGER** TO BECOME THE **YOUNGEST FBI AGENT** IN THE **HISTORY** OF **HISTORY.**
IF I DON'T HAVE A STRONG FOUNDATION IN INTERNAL BIOLOGY, HOW WILL I **EVER** BE ABLE TO MASTER FORENSIC PATHOLOGY?
AT LEAST **YOU** STILL HAVE A **SHOT** AT **YOUR** DREAM JOB.
NOBODY WILL TAKE ME SERIOUSLY AS AN ELEGANT AND GLAMOROUS **FASHION COLUMNIST** WHEN THEY FIND OUT I'VE BEEN
ELBOWS-DEEP IN A BUNCH OF MIDDLE SCHOOL TOILETS!

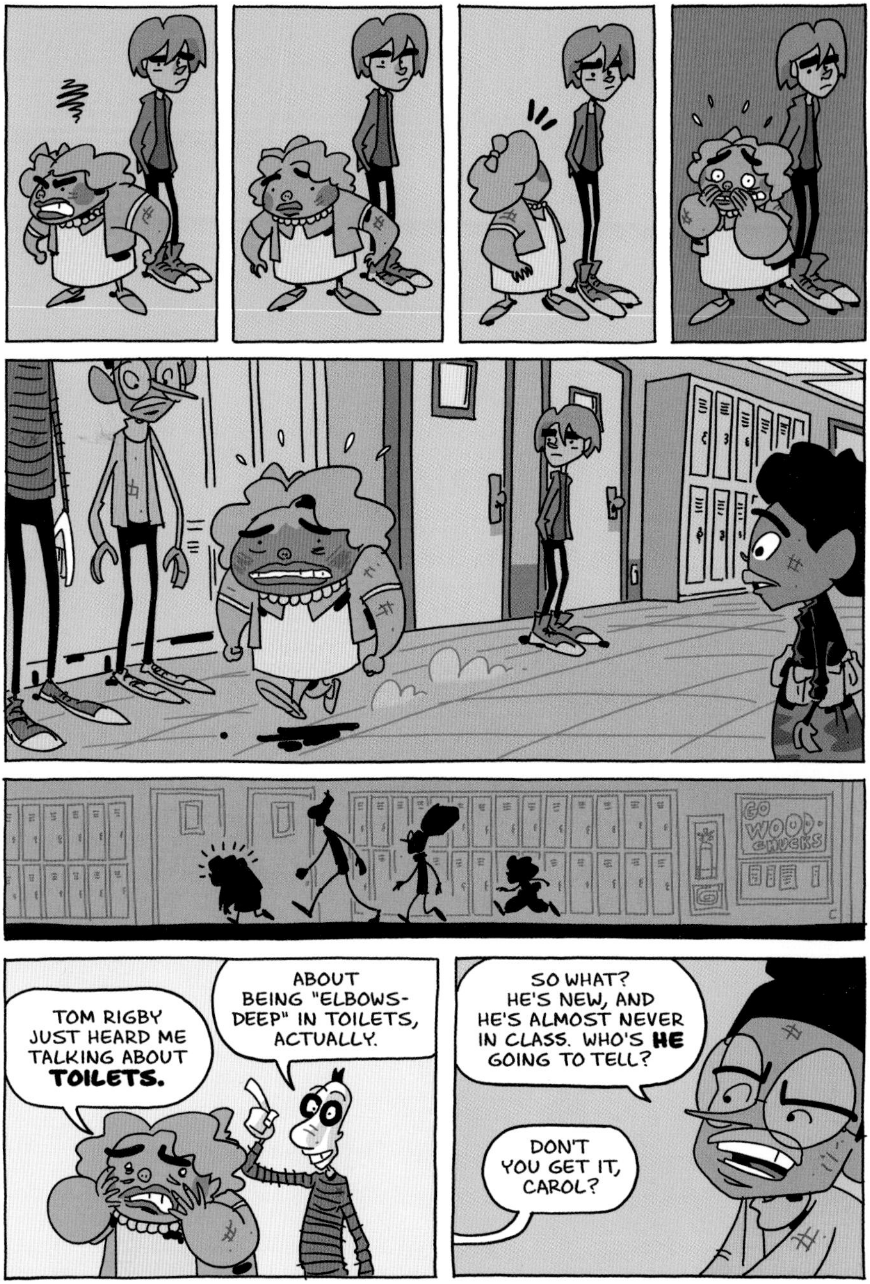
GO WOOD-CHUCKS
TOM RIGBY JUST HEARD ME TALKING ABOUT **TOILETS.**
ABOUT BEING "ELBOWS-DEEP" IN TOILETS, ACTUALLY.
SO WHAT? HE'S NEW, AND HE'S ALMOST NEVER IN CLASS. WHO'S **HE** GOING TO TELL?
DON'T YOU GET IT, CAROL?

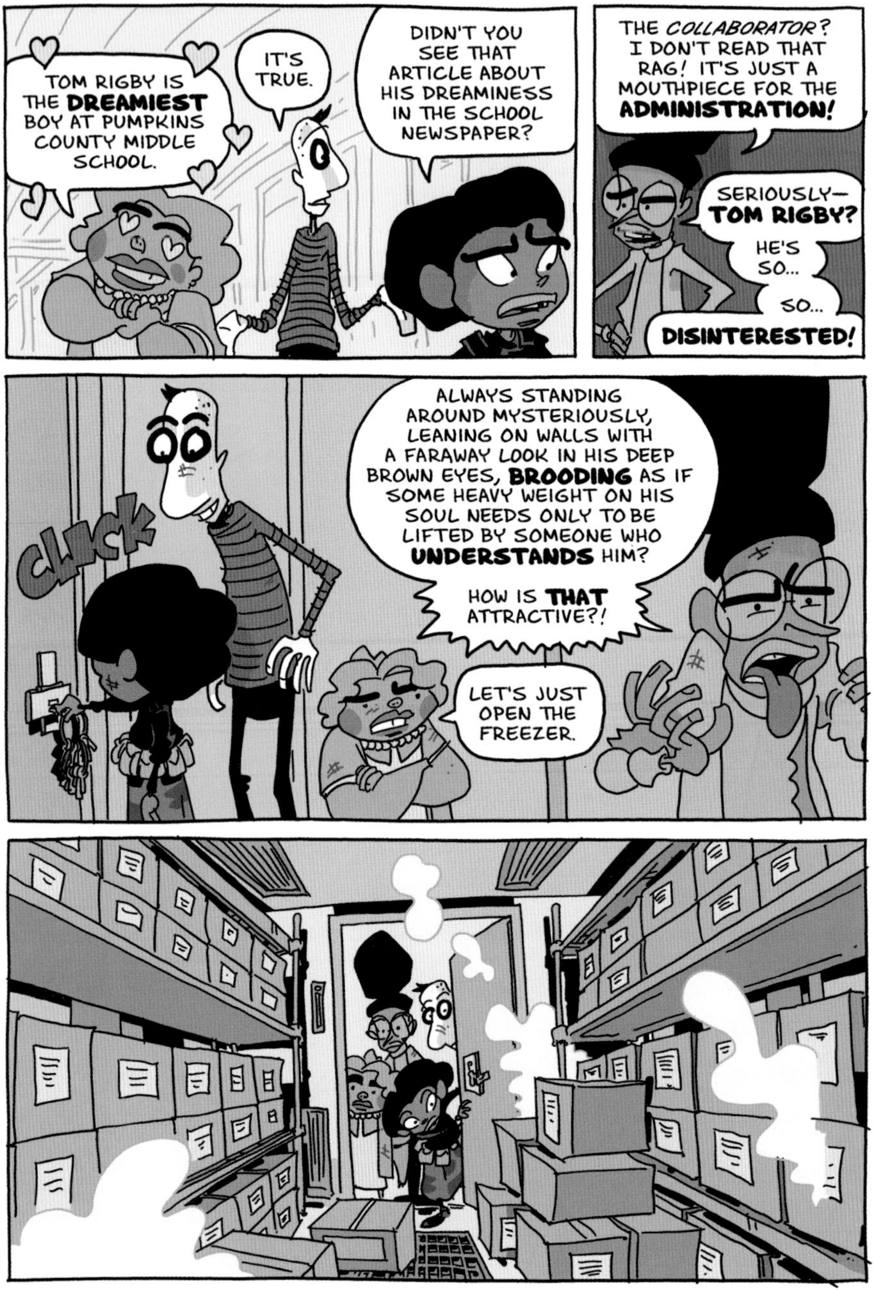
TOM RIGBY IS THE **DREAMIEST** BOY AT PUMPKINS COUNTY MIDDLE SCHOOL.
IT'S TRUE.
DIDN'T YOU SEE THAT ARTICLE ABOUT HIS DREAMINESS IN THE SCHOOL NEWSPAPER?
THE *COLLABORATOR*? I DON'T READ THAT RAG! IT'S JUST A MOUTHPIECE FOR THE **ADMINISTRATION!**
SERIOUSLY— **TOM RIGBY?**
HE'S SO...
SO...
DISINTERESTED!
CLICK
ALWAYS STANDING AROUND MYSTERIOUSLY, LEANING ON WALLS WITH A FARAWAY LOOK IN HIS DEEP BROWN EYES, **BROODING** AS IF SOME HEAVY WEIGHT ON HIS SOUL NEEDS ONLY TO BE LIFTED BY SOMEONE WHO **UNDERSTANDS** HIM?
HOW IS **THAT** ATTRACTIVE?!
LET'S JUST OPEN THE FREEZER.

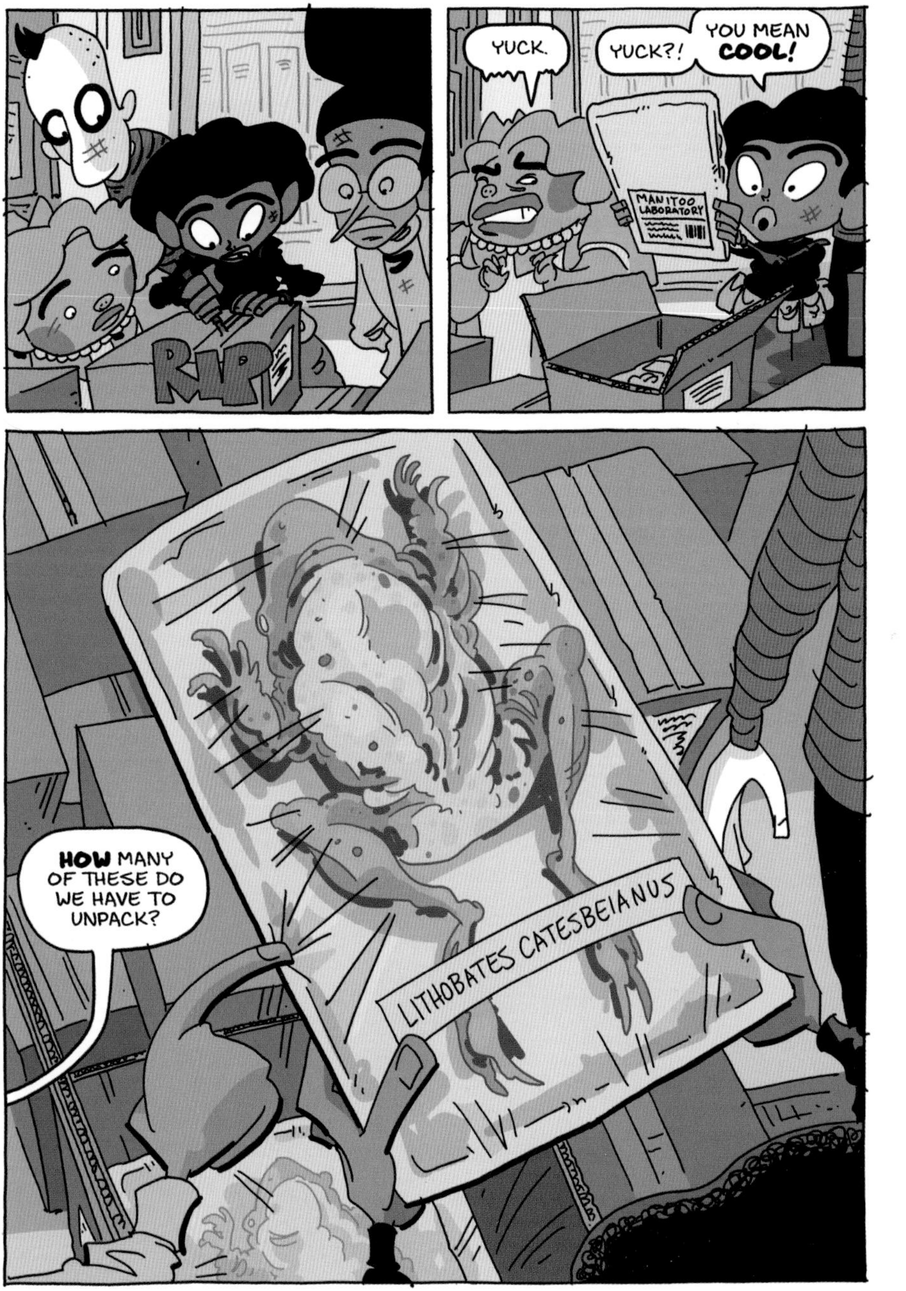
RIP
YUCK.
YUCK?!
YOU MEAN COOL!
MANITOO LABORATORY
HOW MANY OF THESE DO WE HAVE TO UNPACK?
LITHOBATES CATESBEIANUS

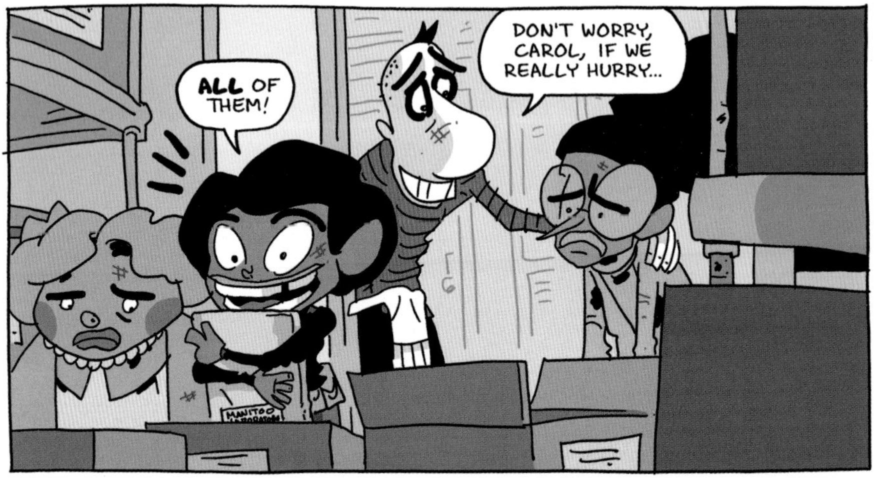
ALL OF THEM!
DON'T WORRY, CAROL, IF WE REALLY HURRY...

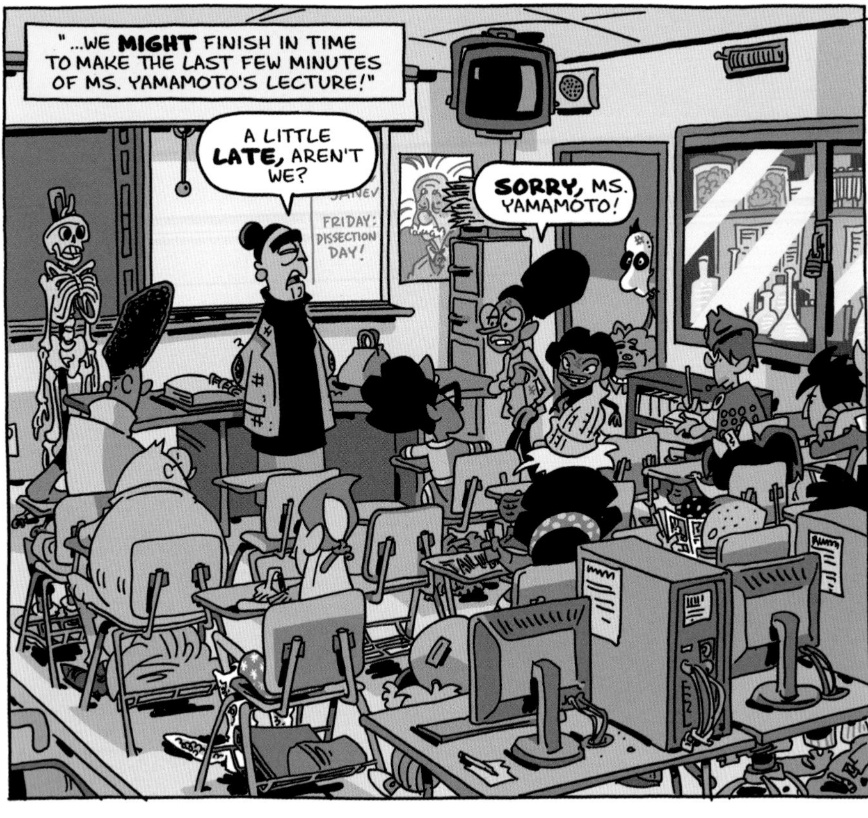
"...WE MIGHT FINISH IN TIME TO MAKE THE LAST FEW MINUTES OF MS. YAMAMOTO'S LECTURE!"
A LITTLE LATE, AREN'T WE?
SORRY, MS. YAMAMOTO!
FRIDAY: DISSECTION DAY!

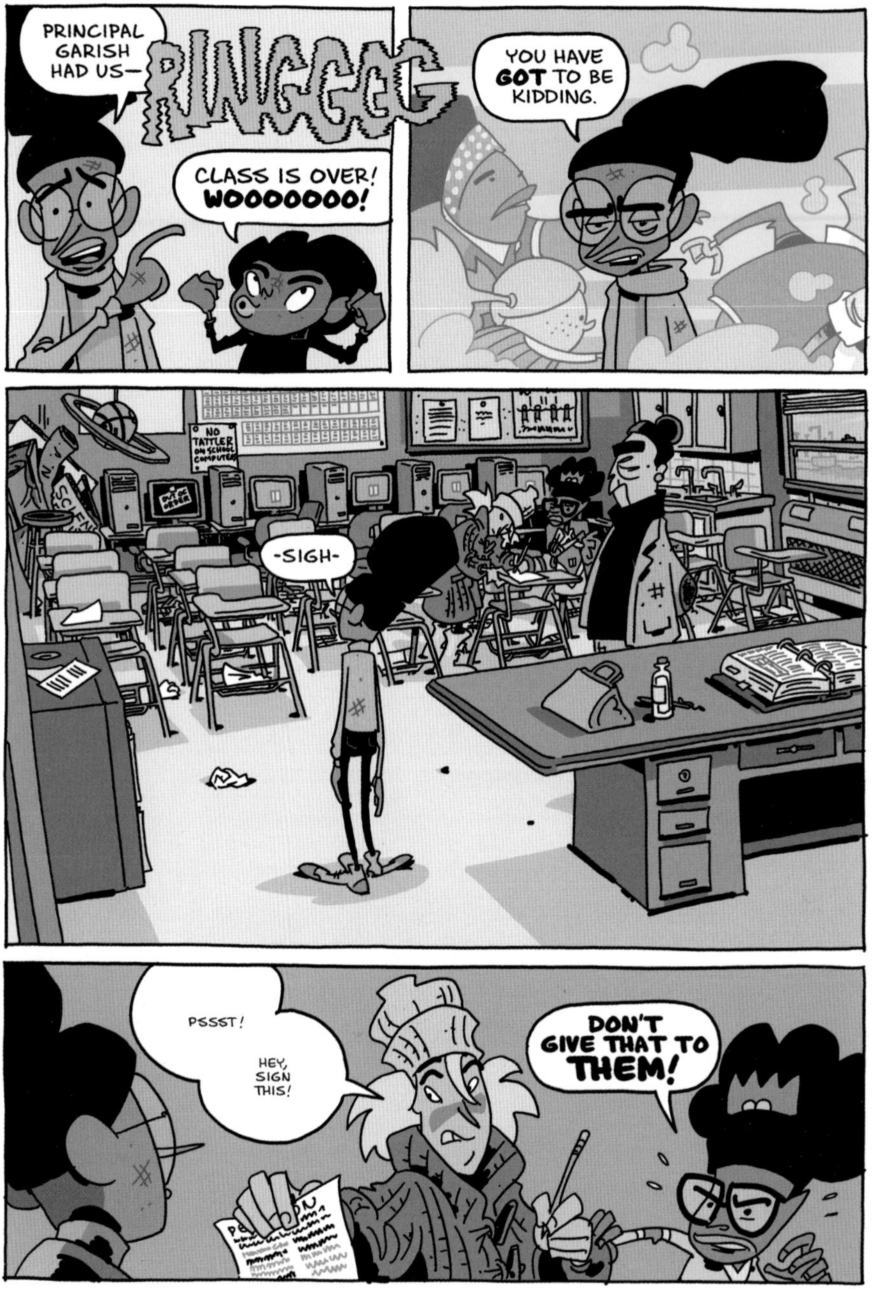
PRINCIPAL GARISH HAD US—
RINGGGG
CLASS IS OVER! WOOOOOOO!
YOU HAVE GOT TO BE KIDDING.
NO TATTLER ON SCHOOL COMPUTERS
-SIGH-
PSSST!
HEY, SIGN THIS!
DON'T GIVE THAT TO THEM!

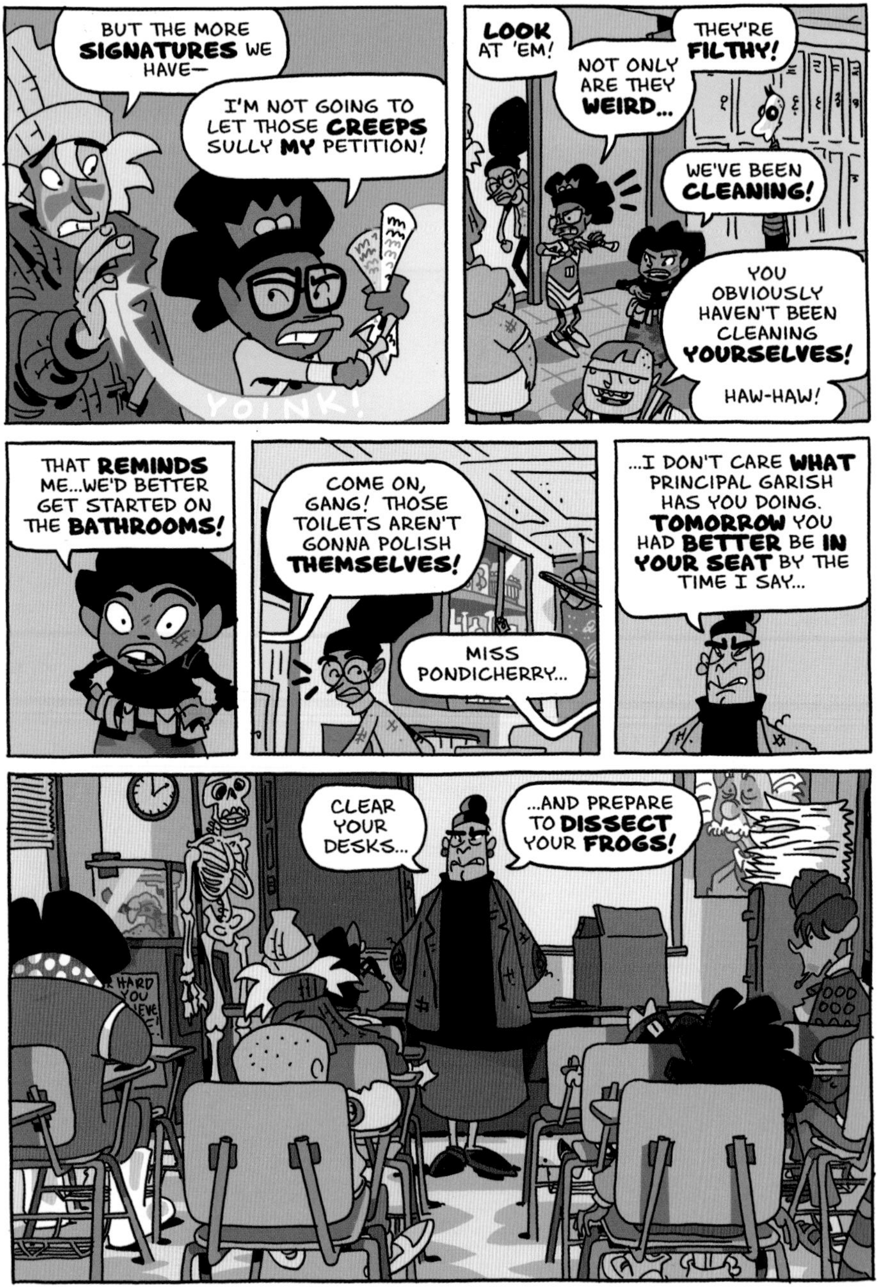
BUT THE MORE SIGNATURES WE HAVE—
I'M NOT GOING TO LET THOSE CREEPS SULLY MY PETITION!
YOINK!
LOOK AT 'EM!
NOT ONLY ARE THEY WEIRD...
THEY'RE FILTHY!
WE'VE BEEN CLEANING!
YOU OBVIOUSLY HAVEN'T BEEN CLEANING YOURSELVES!
HAW-HAW!
THAT REMINDS ME...WE'D BETTER GET STARTED ON THE BATHROOMS!
COME ON, GANG! THOSE TOILETS AREN'T GONNA POLISH THEMSELVES!
MISS PONDICHERRY...
...I DON'T CARE WHAT PRINCIPAL GARISH HAS YOU DOING. TOMORROW YOU HAD BETTER BE IN YOUR SEAT BY THE TIME I SAY...
CLEAR YOUR DESKS...
...AND PREPARE TO DISSECT YOUR FROGS!

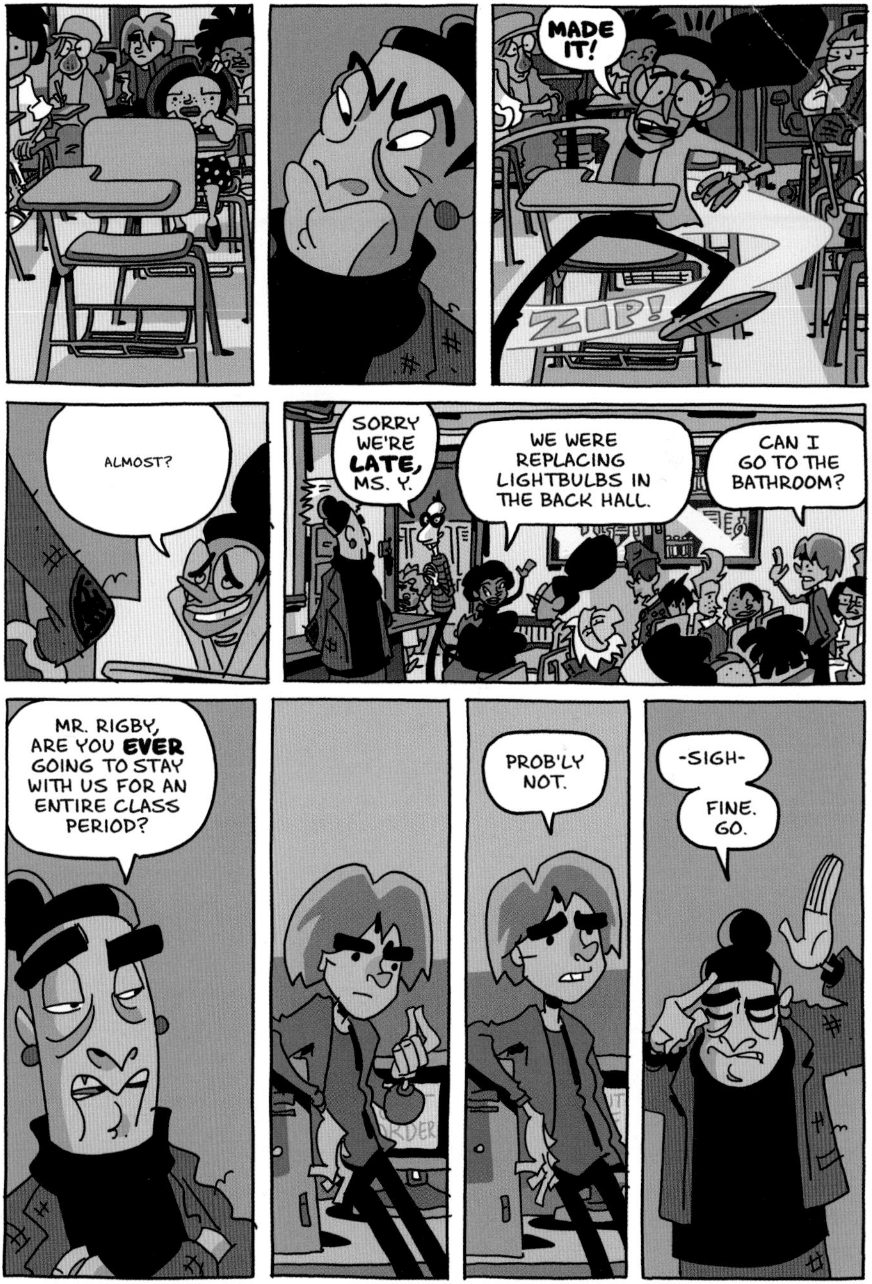
MADE IT!
ZIP!
ALMOST?
SORRY WE'RE LATE, MS. Y.
WE WERE REPLACING LIGHTBULBS IN THE BACK HALL.
CAN I GO TO THE BATHROOM?
MR. RIGBY, ARE YOU EVER GOING TO STAY WITH US FOR AN ENTIRE CLASS PERIOD?
PROB'LY NOT.
-SIGH-
FINE. GO.

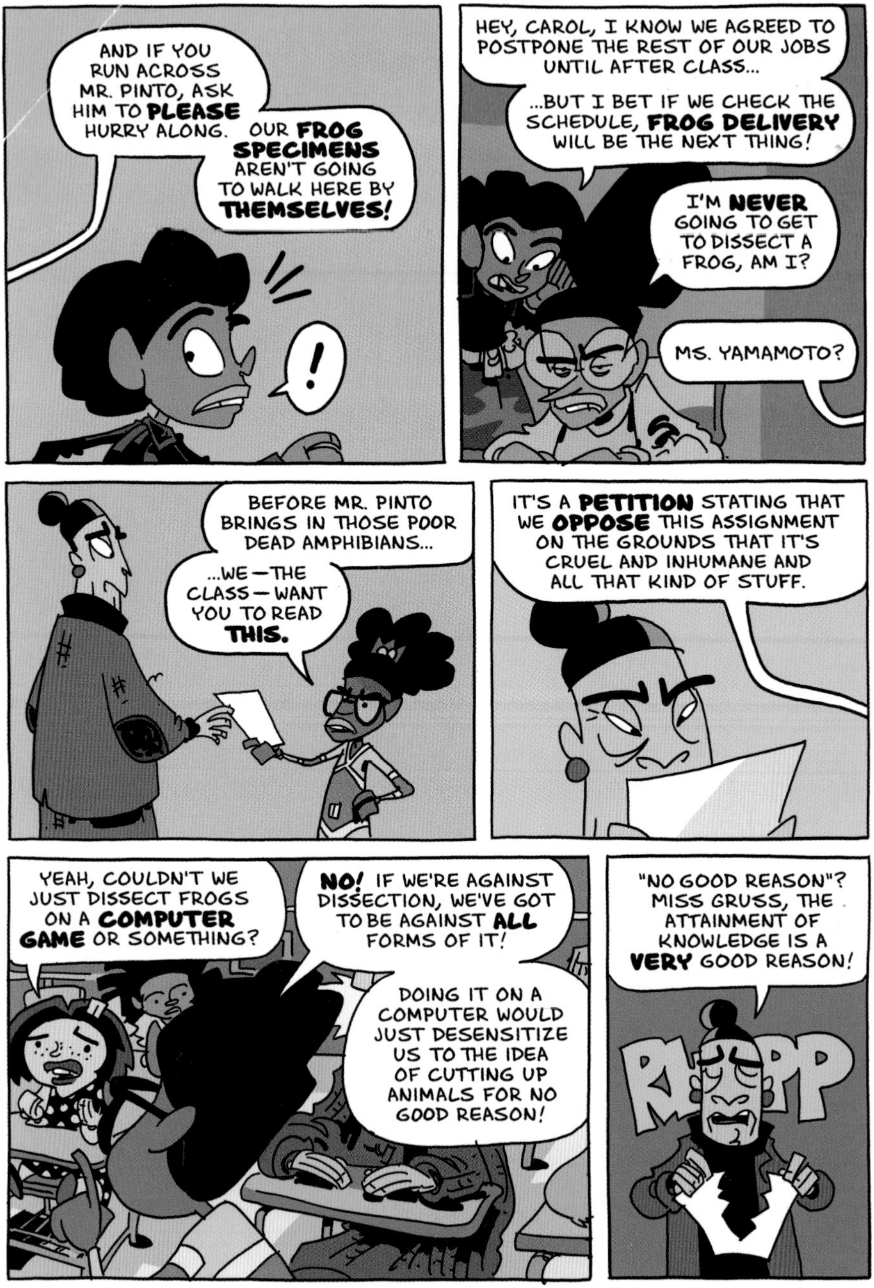
AND IF YOU RUN ACROSS MR. PINTO, ASK HIM TO PLEASE HURRY ALONG.
OUR FROG SPECIMENS AREN'T GOING TO WALK HERE BY THEMSELVES!
!
HEY, CAROL, I KNOW WE AGREED TO POSTPONE THE REST OF OUR JOBS UNTIL AFTER CLASS...
...BUT I BET IF WE CHECK THE SCHEDULE, FROG DELIVERY WILL BE THE NEXT THING!
I'M NEVER GOING TO GET TO DISSECT A FROG, AM I?
MS. YAMAMOTO?
BEFORE MR. PINTO BRINGS IN THOSE POOR DEAD AMPHIBIANS...
...WE—THE CLASS—WANT YOU TO READ THIS.
IT'S A PETITION STATING THAT WE OPPOSE THIS ASSIGNMENT ON THE GROUNDS THAT IT'S CRUEL AND INHUMANE AND ALL THAT KIND OF STUFF.
YEAH, COULDN'T WE JUST DISSECT FROGS ON A COMPUTER GAME OR SOMETHING?
NO! IF WE'RE AGAINST DISSECTION, WE'VE GOT TO BE AGAINST ALL FORMS OF IT!
DOING IT ON A COMPUTER WOULD JUST DESENSITIZE US TO THE IDEA OF CUTTING UP ANIMALS FOR NO GOOD REASON!
"NO GOOD REASON"? MISS GRUSS, THE ATTAINMENT OF KNOWLEDGE IS A VERY GOOD REASON!
RIPP

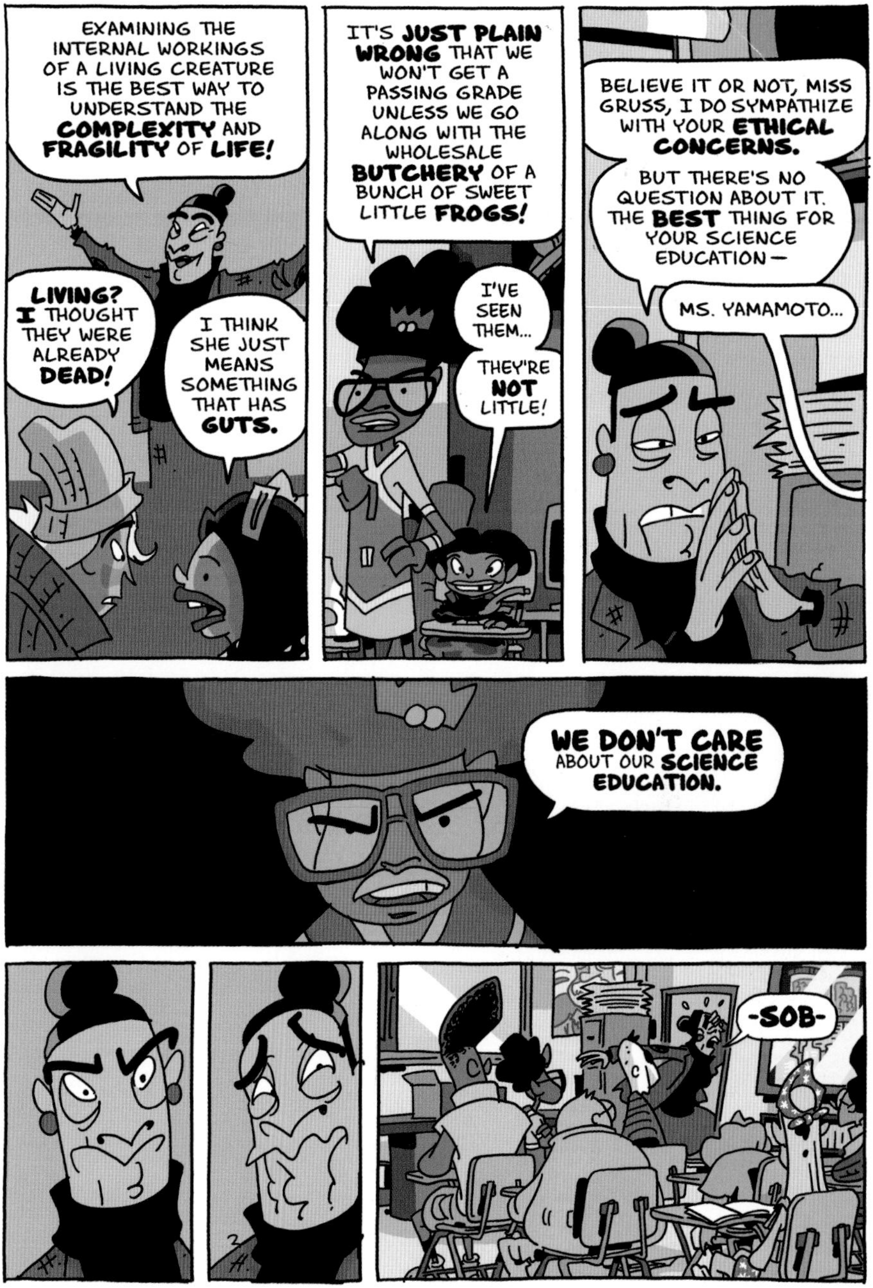
EXAMINING THE INTERNAL WORKINGS OF A LIVING CREATURE IS THE BEST WAY TO UNDERSTAND THE COMPLEXITY AND FRAGILITY OF LIFE!
LIVING? I THOUGHT THEY WERE ALREADY DEAD!
I THINK SHE JUST MEANS SOMETHING THAT HAS GUTS.
IT'S JUST PLAIN WRONG THAT WE WON'T GET A PASSING GRADE UNLESS WE GO ALONG WITH THE WHOLESALE BUTCHERY OF A BUNCH OF SWEET LITTLE FROGS!
I'VE SEEN THEM...
THEY'RE NOT LITTLE!
BELIEVE IT OR NOT, MISS GRUSS, I DO SYMPATHIZE WITH YOUR ETHICAL CONCERNS.
BUT THERE'S NO QUESTION ABOUT IT. THE BEST THING FOR YOUR SCIENCE EDUCATION—
MS. YAMAMOTO...
WE DON'T CARE ABOUT OUR SCIENCE EDUCATION.
-SOB-

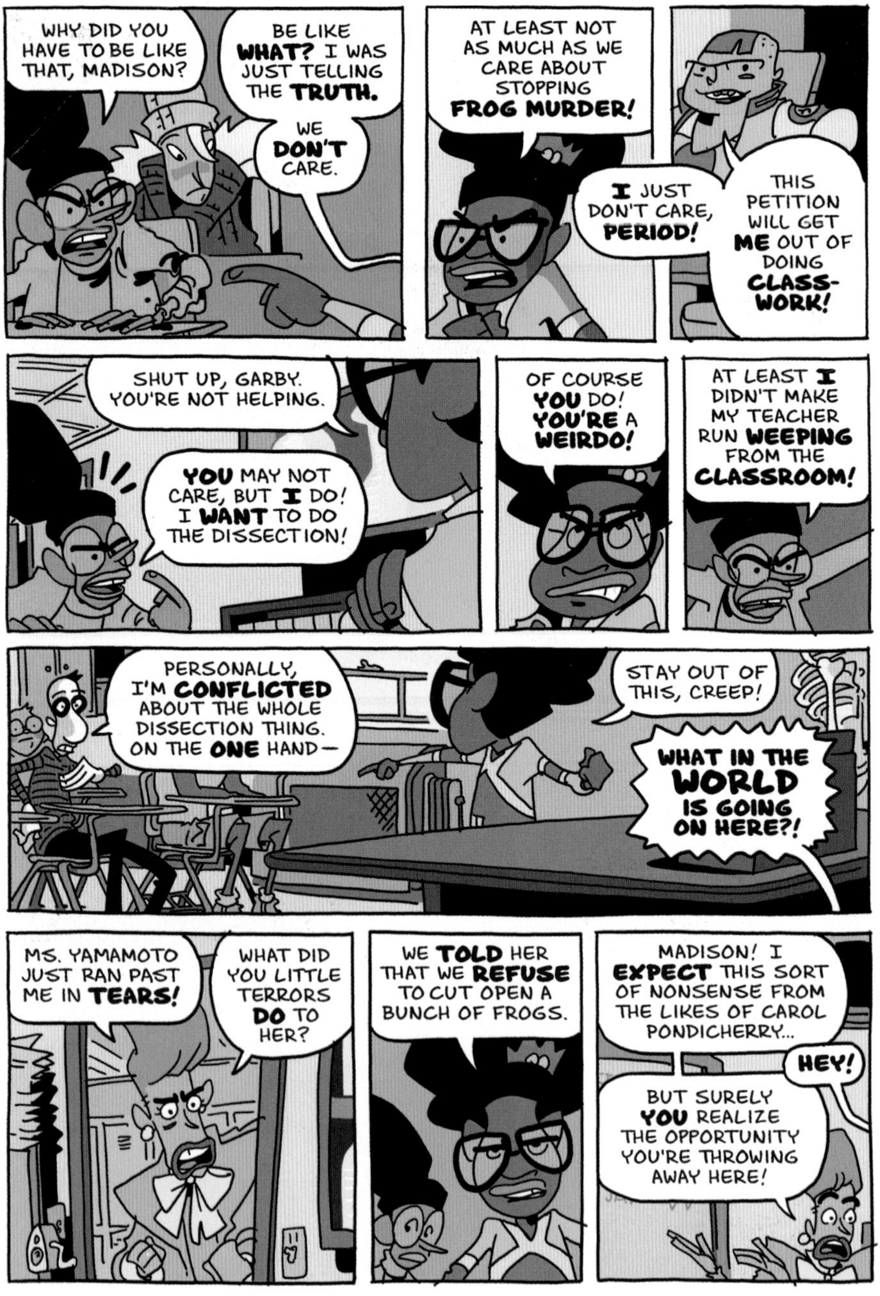
WHY DID YOU HAVE TO BE LIKE THAT, MADISON?
BE LIKE **WHAT?** I WAS JUST TELLING THE **TRUTH.**
WE **DON'T** CARE.
AT LEAST NOT AS MUCH AS WE CARE ABOUT STOPPING **FROG MURDER!**
I JUST DON'T CARE, **PERIOD!**
THIS PETITION WILL GET **ME** OUT OF DOING **CLASS-WORK!**
SHUT UP, GARBY. YOU'RE NOT HELPING.
YOU MAY NOT CARE, BUT **I** DO! I **WANT** TO DO THE DISSECTION!
OF COURSE **YOU** DO! **YOU'RE** A **WEIRDO!**
AT LEAST **I** DIDN'T MAKE MY TEACHER RUN **WEEPING** FROM THE **CLASSROOM!**
PERSONALLY, I'M **CONFLICTED** ABOUT THE WHOLE DISSECTION THING. ON THE **ONE** HAND—
STAY OUT OF THIS, CREEP!
WHAT IN THE WORLD IS GOING ON HERE?!
MS. YAMAMOTO JUST RAN PAST ME IN **TEARS!**
WHAT DID YOU LITTLE TERRORS **DO** TO HER?
WE **TOLD** HER THAT WE **REFUSE** TO CUT OPEN A BUNCH OF FROGS.
MADISON! I **EXPECT** THIS SORT OF NONSENSE FROM THE LIKES OF CAROL PONDICHERRY...
HEY!
BUT SURELY **YOU** REALIZE THE OPPORTUNITY YOU'RE THROWING AWAY HERE!

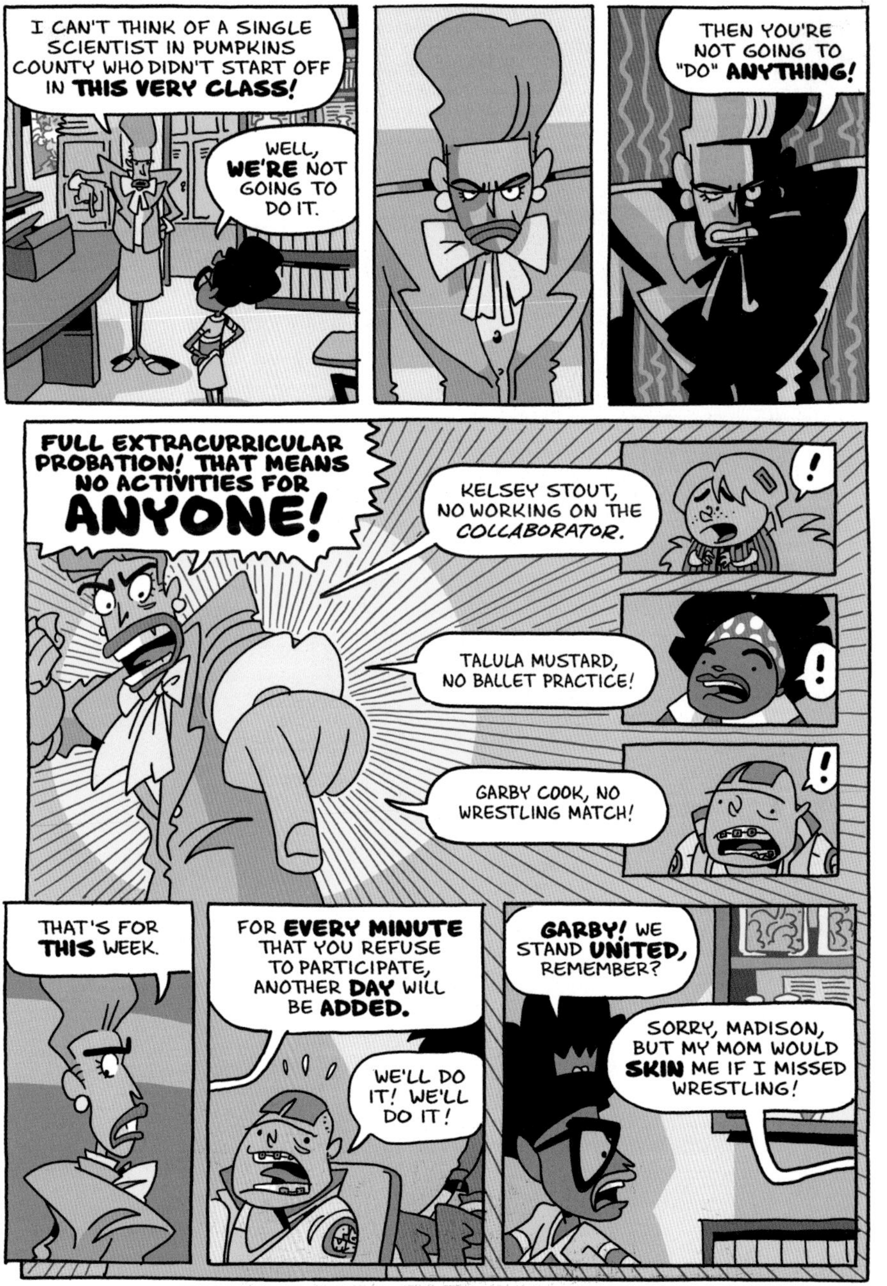
I CAN'T THINK OF A SINGLE SCIENTIST IN PUMPKINS COUNTY WHO DIDN'T START OFF IN THIS VERY CLASS!
WELL, WE'RE NOT GOING TO DO IT.
THEN YOU'RE NOT GOING TO "DO" ANYTHING!
FULL EXTRACURRICULAR PROBATION! THAT MEANS NO ACTIVITIES FOR ANYONE!
KELSEY STOUT, NO WORKING ON THE COLLABORATOR.
!
TALULA MUSTARD, NO BALLET PRACTICE!
!
GARBY COOK, NO WRESTLING MATCH!
!
THAT'S FOR THIS WEEK.
FOR EVERY MINUTE THAT YOU REFUSE TO PARTICIPATE, ANOTHER DAY WILL BE ADDED.
WE'LL DO IT! WE'LL DO IT!
GARBY! WE STAND UNITED, REMEMBER?
SORRY, MADISON, BUT MY MOM WOULD SKIN ME IF I MISSED WRESTLING!

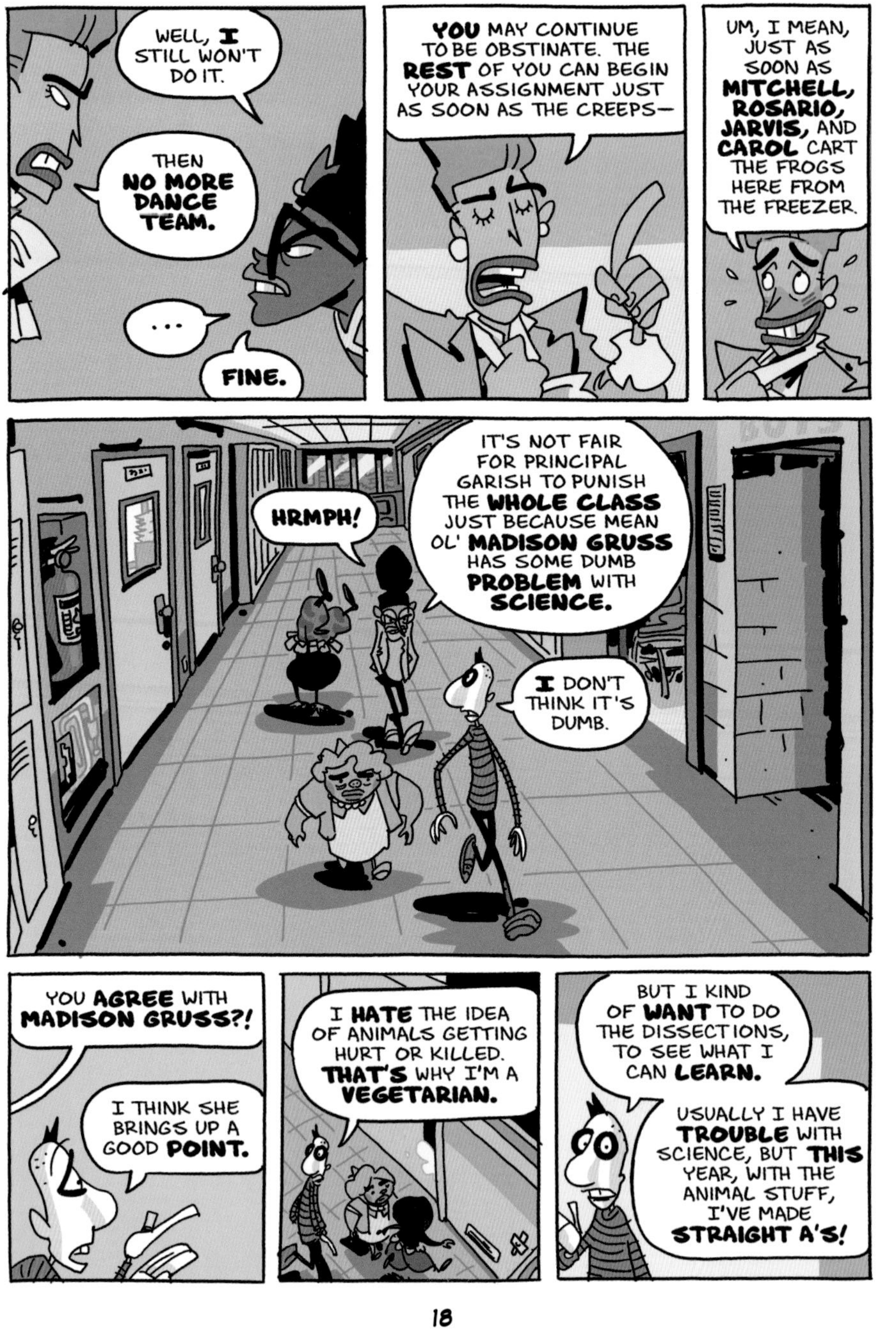
WELL, I STILL WON'T DO IT.
THEN NO MORE DANCE TEAM.
...
FINE.
YOU MAY CONTINUE TO BE OBSTINATE. THE REST OF YOU CAN BEGIN YOUR ASSIGNMENT JUST AS SOON AS THE CREEPS—
UM, I MEAN, JUST AS SOON AS MITCHELL, ROSARIO, JARVIS, AND CAROL CART THE FROGS HERE FROM THE FREEZER.
HRMPH!
IT'S NOT FAIR FOR PRINCIPAL GARISH TO PUNISH THE WHOLE CLASS JUST BECAUSE MEAN OL' MADISON GRUSS HAS SOME DUMB PROBLEM WITH SCIENCE.
I DON'T THINK IT'S DUMB.
YOU AGREE WITH MADISON GRUSS?!
I THINK SHE BRINGS UP A GOOD POINT.
I HATE THE IDEA OF ANIMALS GETTING HURT OR KILLED. THAT'S WHY I'M A VEGETARIAN.
BUT I KIND OF WANT TO DO THE DISSECTIONS, TO SEE WHAT I CAN LEARN.
USUALLY I HAVE TROUBLE WITH SCIENCE, BUT THIS YEAR, WITH THE ANIMAL STUFF, I'VE MADE STRAIGHT A'S!

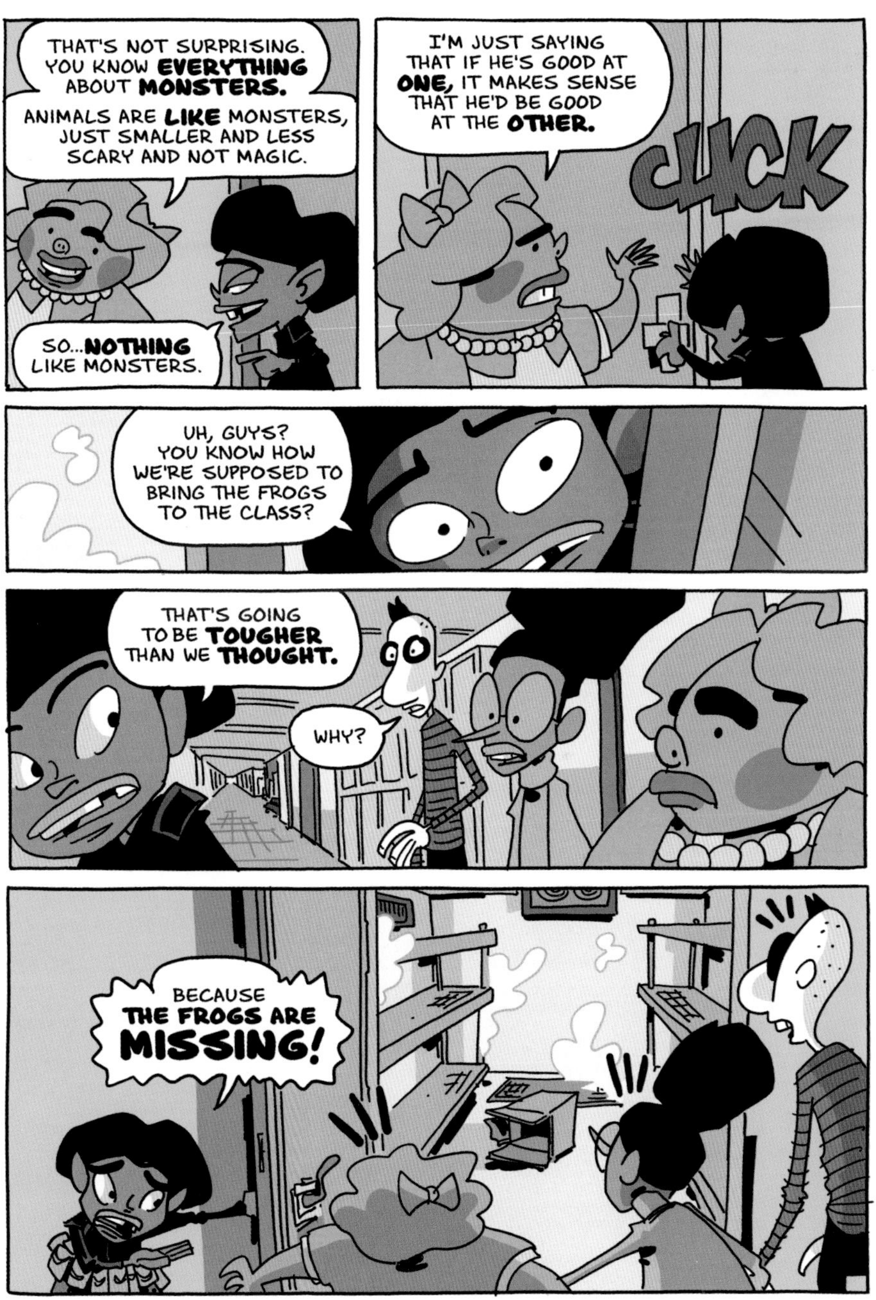
THAT'S NOT SURPRISING. YOU KNOW **EVERYTHING** ABOUT **MONSTERS.**
ANIMALS ARE **LIKE** MONSTERS, JUST SMALLER AND LESS SCARY AND NOT MAGIC.
SO...**NOTHING** LIKE MONSTERS.
I'M JUST SAYING THAT IF HE'S GOOD AT **ONE,** IT MAKES SENSE THAT HE'D BE GOOD AT THE **OTHER.**
CLICK
UH, GUYS? YOU KNOW HOW WE'RE SUPPOSED TO BRING THE FROGS TO THE CLASS?
THAT'S GOING TO BE **TOUGHER** THAN WE **THOUGHT.**
WHY?
BECAUSE **THE FROGS ARE MISSING!**

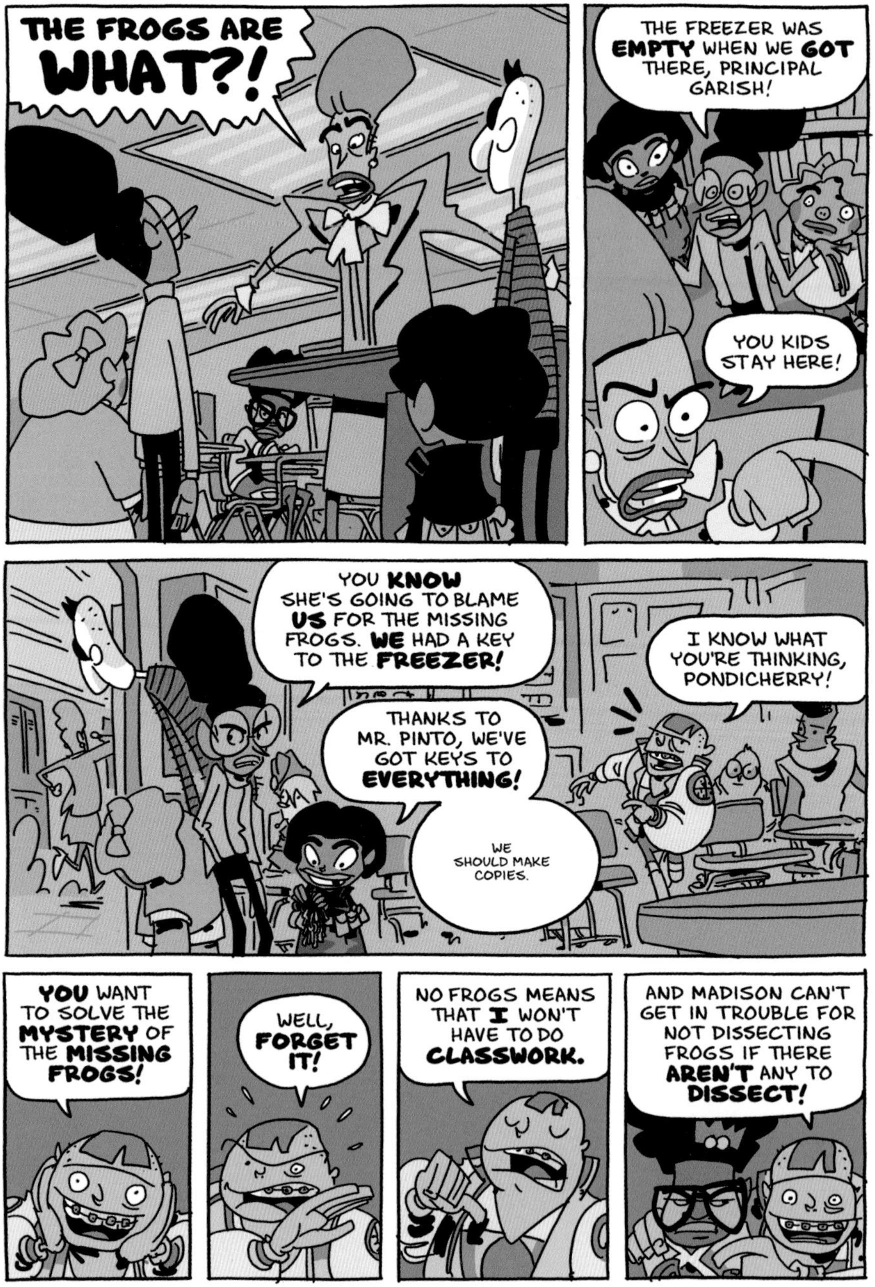
THE FROGS ARE WHAT?!
THE FREEZER WAS EMPTY WHEN WE GOT THERE, PRINCIPAL GARISH!
YOU KIDS STAY HERE!
YOU KNOW SHE'S GOING TO BLAME US FOR THE MISSING FROGS. WE HAD A KEY TO THE FREEZER!
THANKS TO MR. PINTO, WE'VE GOT KEYS TO EVERYTHING!
WE SHOULD MAKE COPIES.
I KNOW WHAT YOU'RE THINKING, PONDICHERRY!
YOU WANT TO SOLVE THE MYSTERY OF THE MISSING FROGS!
WELL, FORGET IT!
NO FROGS MEANS THAT I WON'T HAVE TO DO CLASSWORK.
AND MADISON CAN'T GET IN TROUBLE FOR NOT DISSECTING FROGS IF THERE AREN'T ANY TO DISSECT!

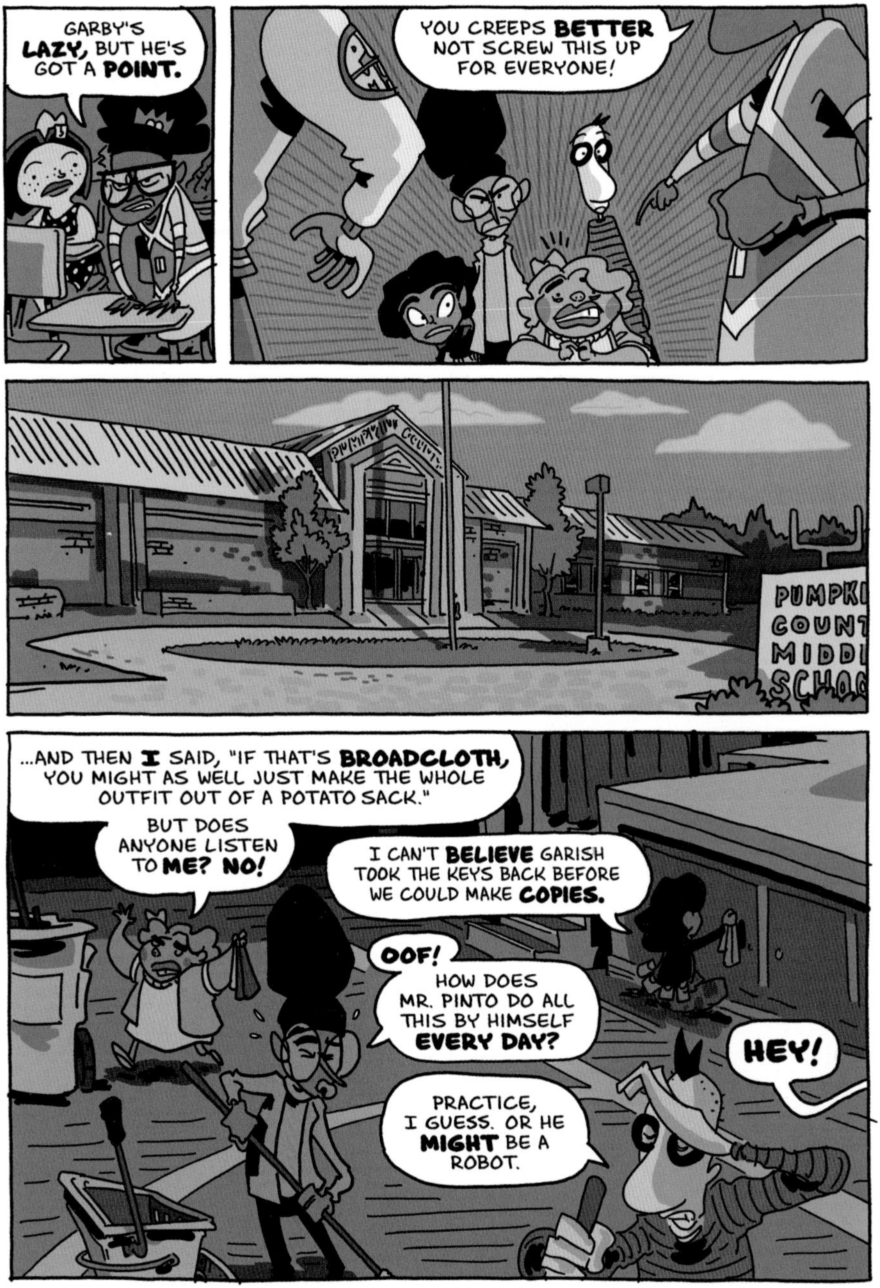
GARBY'S **LAZY,** BUT HE'S GOT A **POINT.**
YOU CREEPS **BETTER** NOT SCREW THIS UP FOR EVERYONE!
PUMPKIN COUNTY
PUMPKI COUNT MIDDL SCHOO
...AND THEN **I** SAID, "IF THAT'S **BROADCLOTH,** YOU MIGHT AS WELL JUST MAKE THE WHOLE OUTFIT OUT OF A POTATO SACK."
BUT DOES ANYONE LISTEN TO **ME? NO!**
I CAN'T **BELIEVE** GARISH TOOK THE KEYS BACK BEFORE WE COULD MAKE **COPIES.**
OOF!
HOW DOES MR. PINTO DO ALL THIS BY HIMSELF **EVERY DAY?**
HEY!
PRACTICE, I GUESS. OR HE **MIGHT** BE A ROBOT.

WHAT ARE YOU CREEPS DOING IN THE **GYM?**

WE DIDN'T FINISH CLEANING BEFORE SCHOOL ENDED, SO WE'RE STUCK HERE EVEN THOUGH WE **STILL** HAVE TO MAKE UP ALL THE CLASSWORK WE MISSED!

THE BETTER QUESTION IS, WHY ARE **YOU** IN THE GYM?

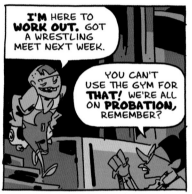

I'M HERE TO **WORK OUT.** GOT A WRESTLING MEET NEXT WEEK.

YOU CAN'T USE THE GYM FOR **THAT!** WE'RE ALL ON **PROBATION,** REMEMBER?

WHAT GARISH DOESN'T **KNOW** WON'T HURT HER.

AND YOU'D **BETTER** NOT **TELL** ON ME, CREEPS!

WE'RE NOT SCARED OF **YOU!**

WRESTLER OR NOT, **ROSARIO** COULD SQUISH YOU LIKE A **BUG!**

BUT I **WOULDN'T,** OF COURSE.

I'M A **DELICATE CREATURE.**

"CREATURE" IS RIGHT! HAW-HAW!

COME ON, GANG. **NO** AMOUNT OF CLEANING WILL GET RID OF THE **TERRIBLE STAIN** THAT JUST SHOWED UP.

HAW-HAW-HAW!

BOYS LOCKER ROOM

ONE!

TWO!

THREE!

FOUR!

22

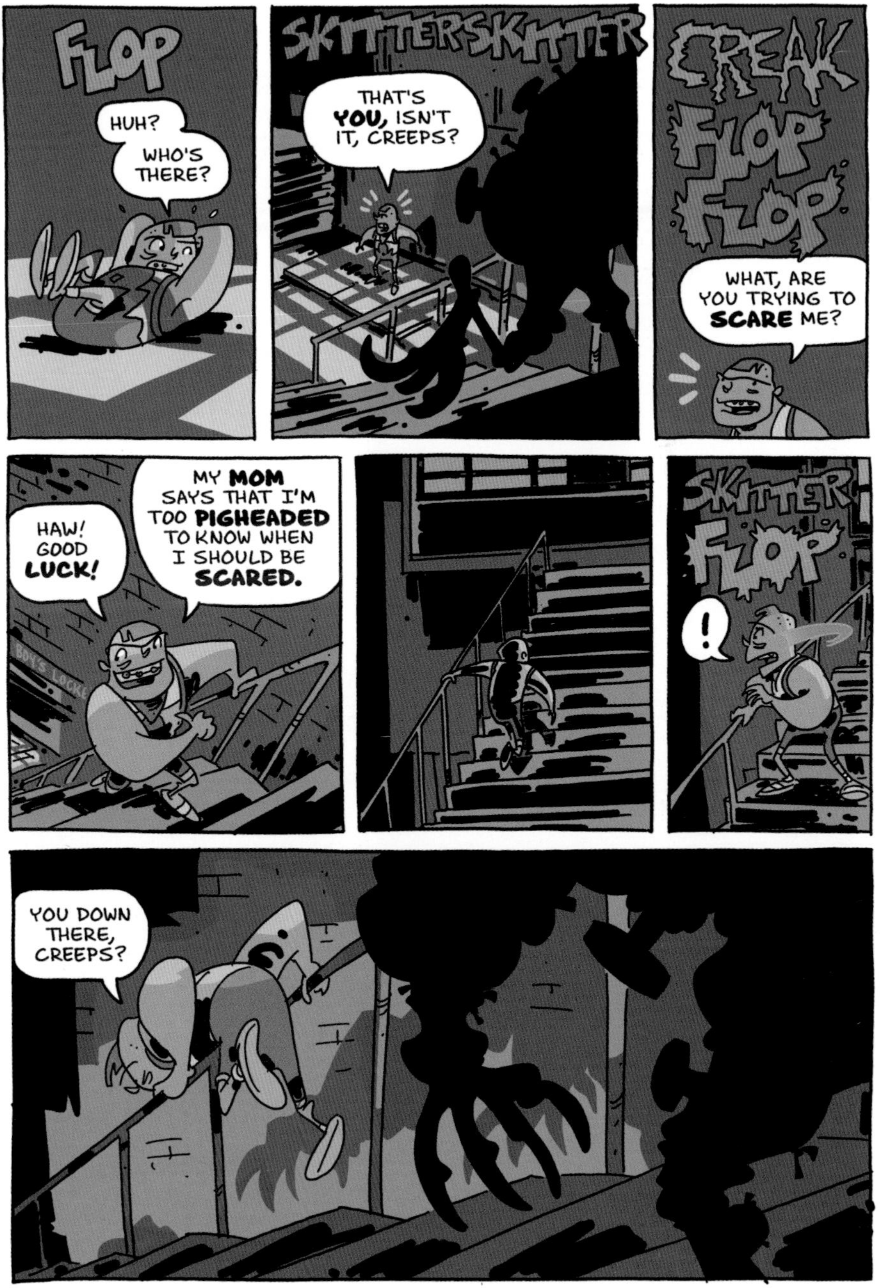
FLOP
HUH?
WHO'S THERE?
SKITTERSKITTER
THAT'S YOU, ISN'T IT, CREEPS?
CREAK
FLOP
FLOP
WHAT, ARE YOU TRYING TO SCARE ME?
HAW! GOOD LUCK!
MY MOM SAYS THAT I'M TOO PIGHEADED TO KNOW WHEN I SHOULD BE SCARED.
BOY'S LOCKE
SKITTER
FLOP
!
YOU DOWN THERE, CREEPS?

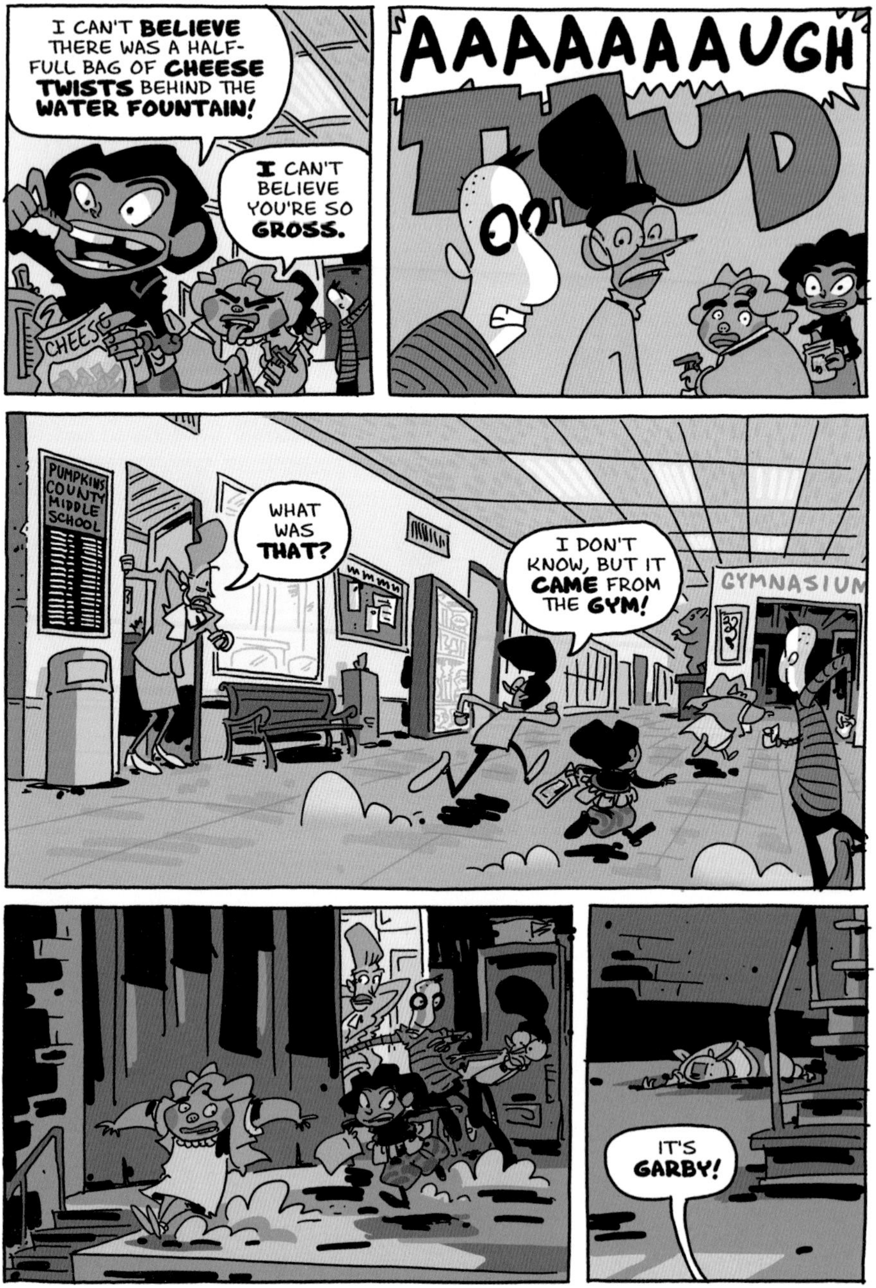
I CAN'T **BELIEVE** THERE WAS A HALF-FULL BAG OF **CHEESE TWISTS** BEHIND THE **WATER FOUNTAIN!**
I CAN'T BELIEVE YOU'RE SO **GROSS.**
CHEESE
AAAAAAAAUGH
THUD
PUMPKINS COUNTY MIDDLE SCHOOL
WHAT WAS **THAT?**
I DON'T KNOW, BUT IT **CAME** FROM THE **GYM!**
GYMNASIUM
IT'S **GARBY!**

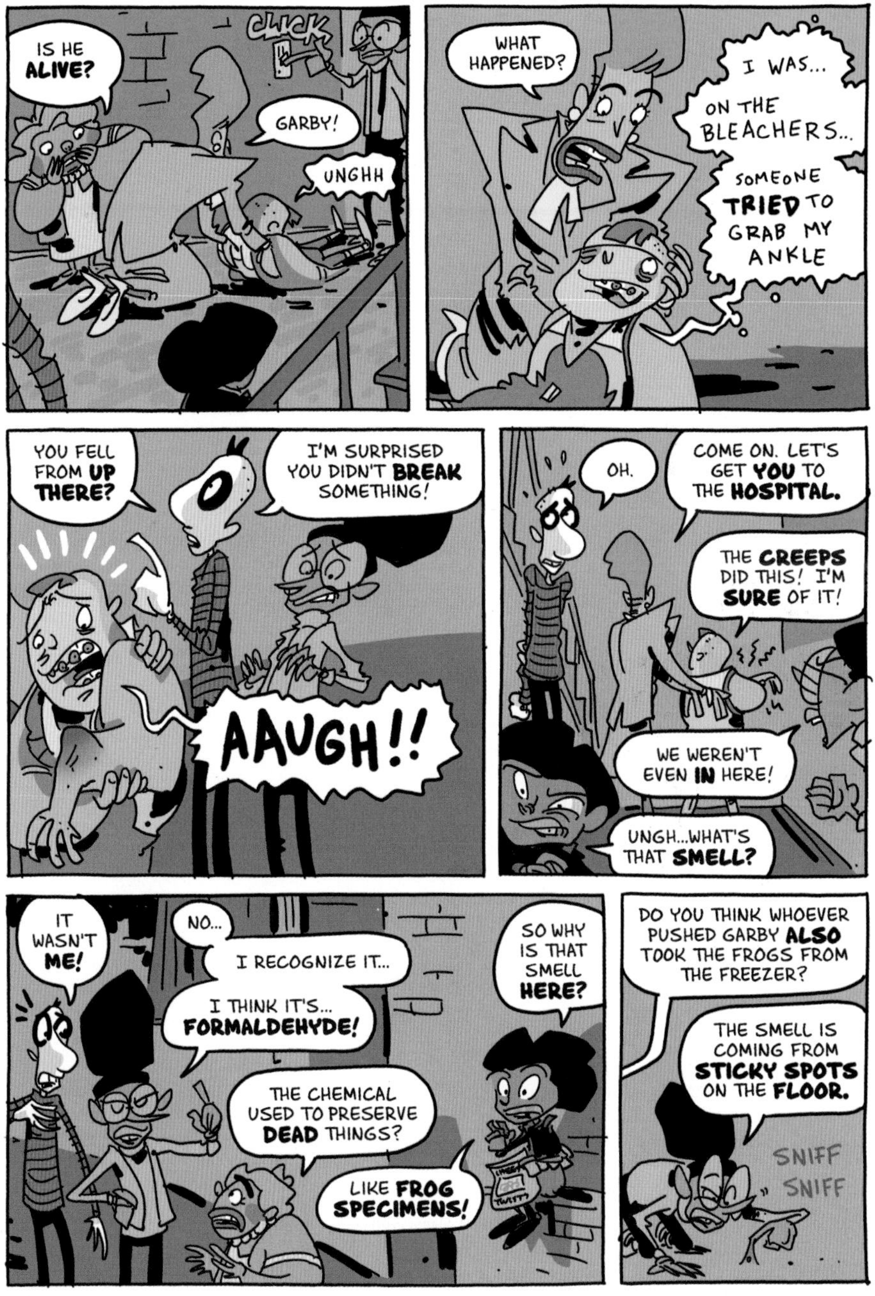
CLICK
IS HE ALIVE?
GARBY!
UNGHH
WHAT HAPPENED?
I WAS... ON THE BLEACHERS... SOMEONE TRIED TO GRAB MY ANKLE
YOU FELL FROM UP THERE?
I'M SURPRISED YOU DIDN'T BREAK SOMETHING!
AAUGH!!
OH.
COME ON. LET'S GET YOU TO THE HOSPITAL.
THE CREEPS DID THIS! I'M SURE OF IT!
WE WEREN'T EVEN IN HERE!
UNGH...WHAT'S THAT SMELL?
IT WASN'T ME!
NO...
I RECOGNIZE IT...
I THINK IT'S... FORMALDEHYDE!
THE CHEMICAL USED TO PRESERVE DEAD THINGS?
LIKE FROG SPECIMENS!
SO WHY IS THAT SMELL HERE?
DO YOU THINK WHOEVER PUSHED GARBY ALSO TOOK THE FROGS FROM THE FREEZER?
THE SMELL IS COMING FROM STICKY SPOTS ON THE FLOOR.
SNIFF SNIFF

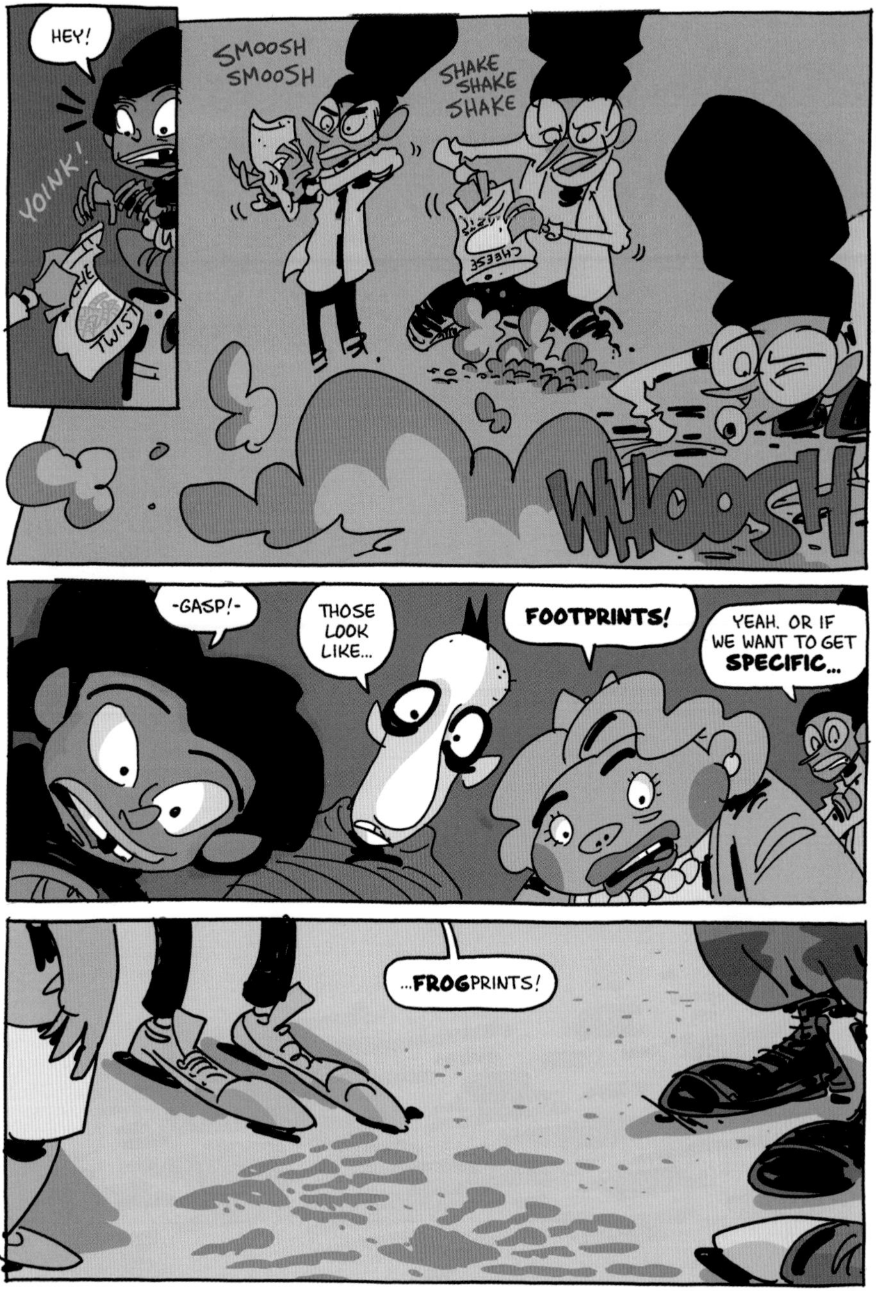
HEY!
YOINK!
SMOOSH SMOOSH
SHAKE SHAKE SHAKE
CHEESE
WHOOSH
-GASP!-
THOSE LOOK LIKE...
FOOTPRINTS!
YEAH. OR IF WE WANT TO GET SPECIFIC...
...FROGPRINTS!

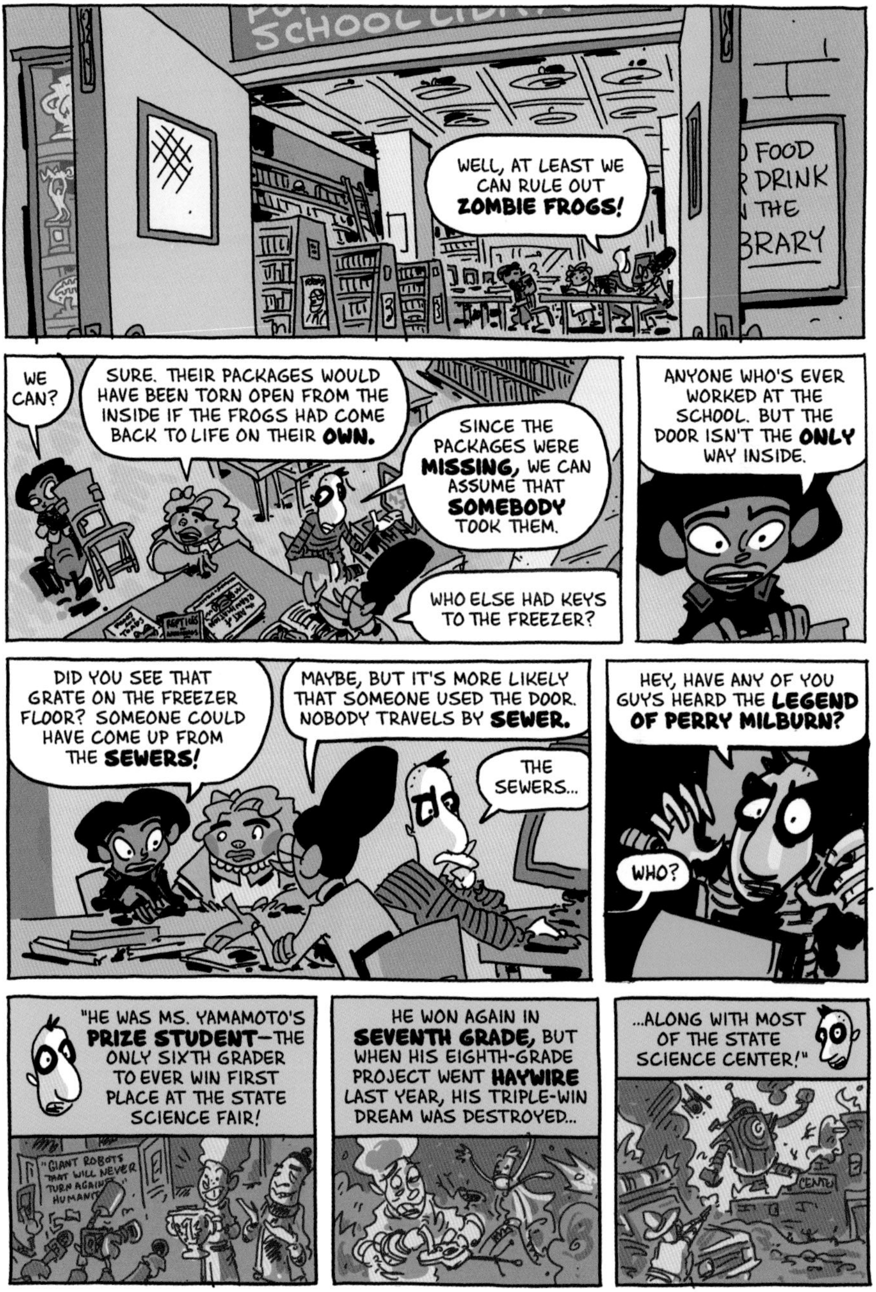
SCHOOL LIBRARY
WELL, AT LEAST WE CAN RULE OUT **ZOMBIE FROGS!**
NO FOOD OR DRINK IN THE LIBRARY
WE CAN?
SURE. THEIR PACKAGES WOULD HAVE BEEN TORN OPEN FROM THE INSIDE IF THE FROGS HAD COME BACK TO LIFE ON THEIR **OWN.**
SINCE THE PACKAGES WERE **MISSING,** WE CAN ASSUME THAT **SOMEBODY** TOOK THEM.
WHO ELSE HAD KEYS TO THE FREEZER?
ANYONE WHO'S EVER WORKED AT THE SCHOOL. BUT THE DOOR ISN'T THE **ONLY** WAY INSIDE.
DID YOU SEE THAT GRATE ON THE FREEZER FLOOR? SOMEONE COULD HAVE COME UP FROM THE **SEWERS!**
MAYBE, BUT IT'S MORE LIKELY THAT SOMEONE USED THE DOOR. NOBODY TRAVELS BY **SEWER.**
THE SEWERS...
HEY, HAVE ANY OF YOU GUYS HEARD THE **LEGEND OF PERRY MILBURN?**
WHO?
"HE WAS MS. YAMAMOTO'S **PRIZE STUDENT**—THE ONLY SIXTH GRADER TO EVER WIN FIRST PLACE AT THE STATE SCIENCE FAIR!
"GIANT ROBOTS THAT WILL NEVER TURN AGAINST HUMANITY"
HE WON AGAIN IN **SEVENTH GRADE,** BUT WHEN HIS EIGHTH-GRADE PROJECT WENT **HAYWIRE** LAST YEAR, HIS TRIPLE-WIN DREAM WAS DESTROYED...
...ALONG WITH MOST OF THE STATE SCIENCE CENTER!"

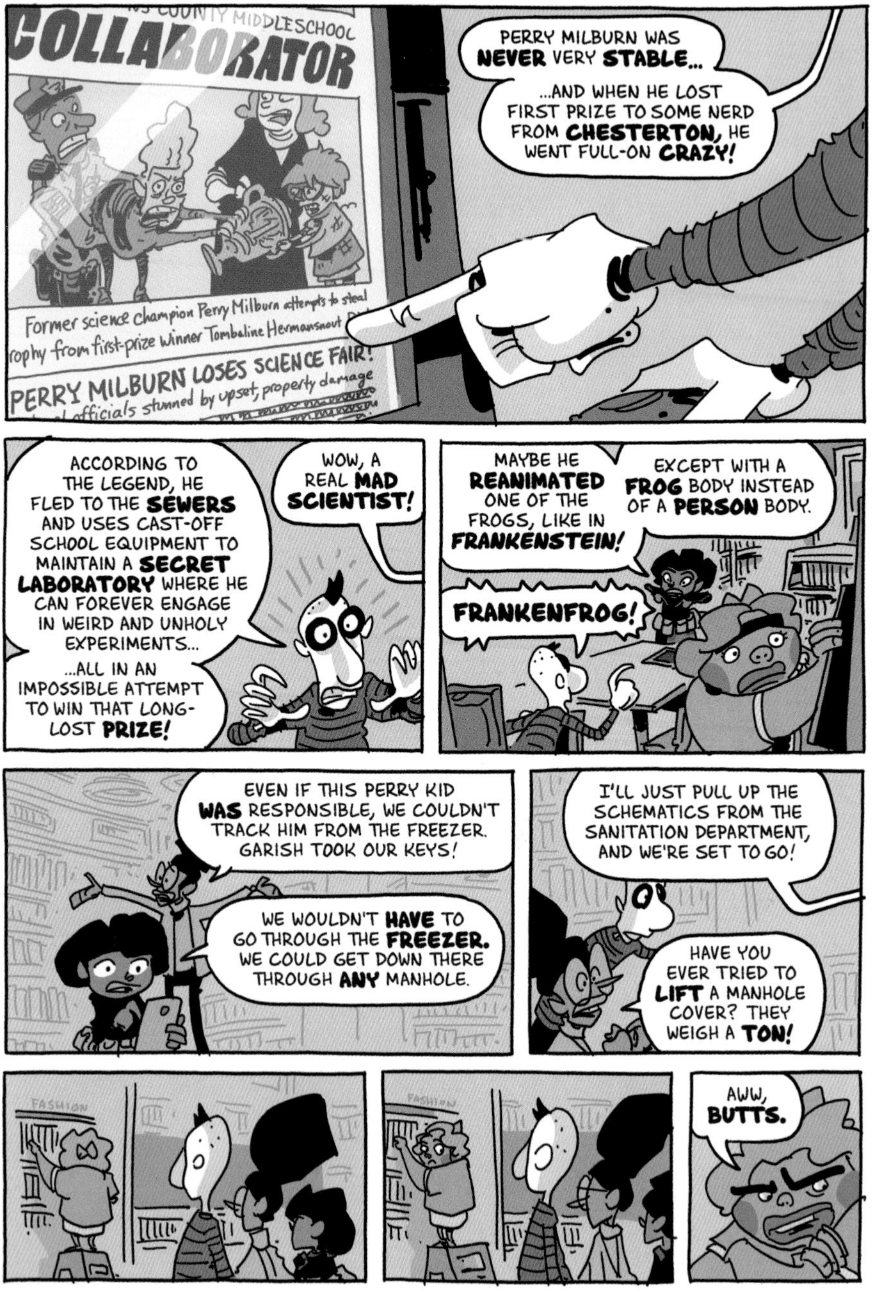
COUNTY MIDDLESCHOOL
COLLABORATOR
Former science champion Perry Milburn attempts to steal trophy from first-prize winner Tombaline Hermansnout
PERRY MILBURN LOSES SCIENCE FAIR!
Perry Milburn loses to upset, property damage
officials stunned by upset, property damage
PERRY MILBURN WAS NEVER VERY STABLE...
...AND WHEN HE LOST FIRST PRIZE TO SOME NERD FROM CHESTERTON, HE WENT FULL-ON CRAZY!
ACCORDING TO THE LEGEND, HE FLED TO THE SEWERS AND USES CAST-OFF SCHOOL EQUIPMENT TO MAINTAIN A SECRET LABORATORY WHERE HE CAN FOREVER ENGAGE IN WEIRD AND UNHOLY EXPERIMENTS...
...ALL IN AN IMPOSSIBLE ATTEMPT TO WIN THAT LONG-LOST PRIZE!
WOW, A REAL MAD SCIENTIST!
MAYBE HE REANIMATED ONE OF THE FROGS, LIKE IN FRANKENSTEIN!
EXCEPT WITH A FROG BODY INSTEAD OF A PERSON BODY.
FRANKENFROG!
EVEN IF THIS PERRY KID WAS RESPONSIBLE, WE COULDN'T TRACK HIM FROM THE FREEZER. GARISH TOOK OUR KEYS!
WE WOULDN'T HAVE TO GO THROUGH THE FREEZER. WE COULD GET DOWN THERE THROUGH ANY MANHOLE.
I'LL JUST PULL UP THE SCHEMATICS FROM THE SANITATION DEPARTMENT, AND WE'RE SET TO GO!
HAVE YOU EVER TRIED TO LIFT A MANHOLE COVER? THEY WEIGH A TON!
FASHION
FASHION
AWW, BUTTS.

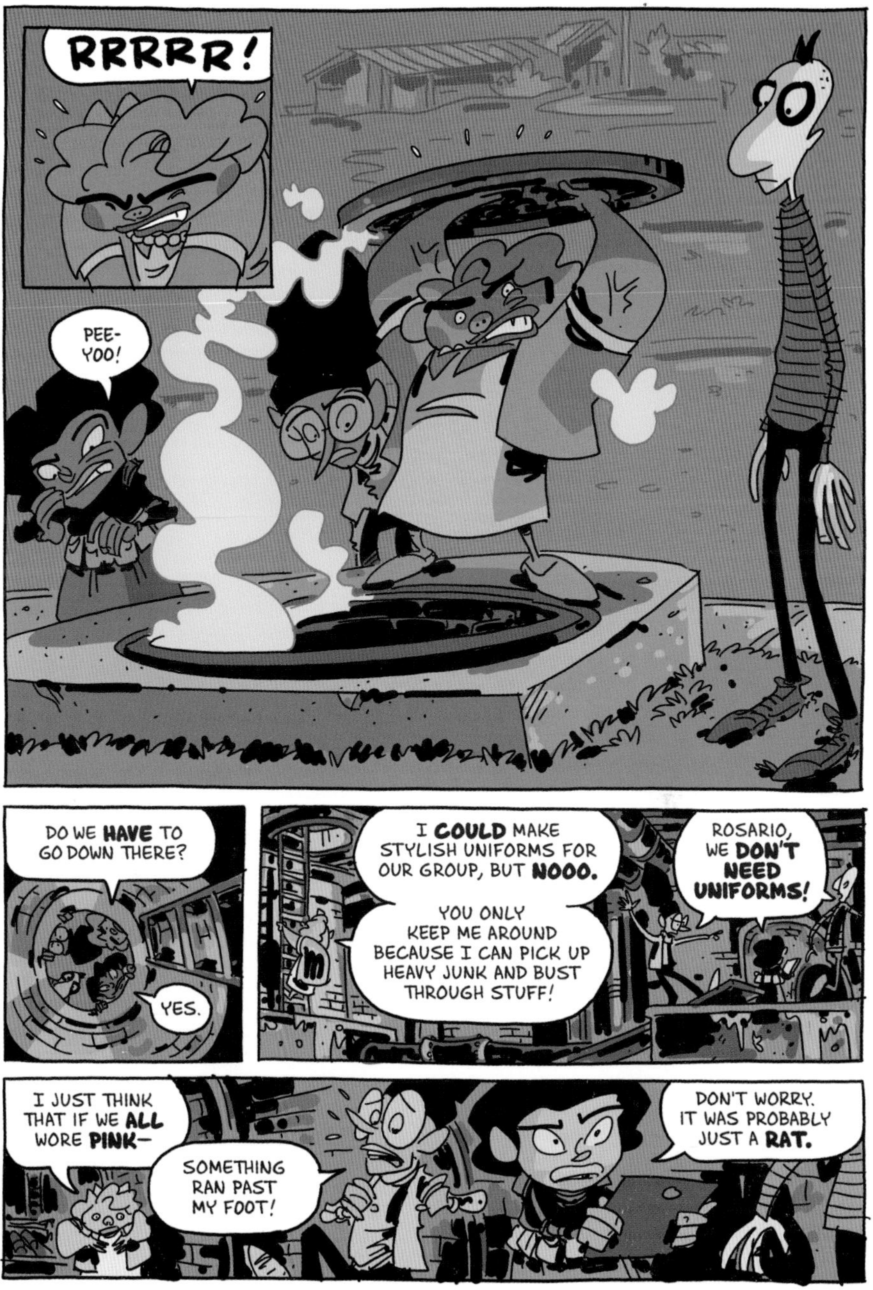
RRRRR!
PEE-YOO!
DO WE **HAVE** TO GO DOWN THERE?
YES.
I **COULD** MAKE STYLISH UNIFORMS FOR OUR GROUP, BUT **NOOO.**
YOU ONLY KEEP ME AROUND BECAUSE I CAN PICK UP HEAVY JUNK AND BUST THROUGH STUFF!
ROSARIO, WE **DON'T NEED UNIFORMS!**
I JUST THINK THAT IF WE **ALL** WORE **PINK**—
SOMETHING RAN PAST MY FOOT!
DON'T WORRY. IT WAS PROBABLY JUST A **RAT.**

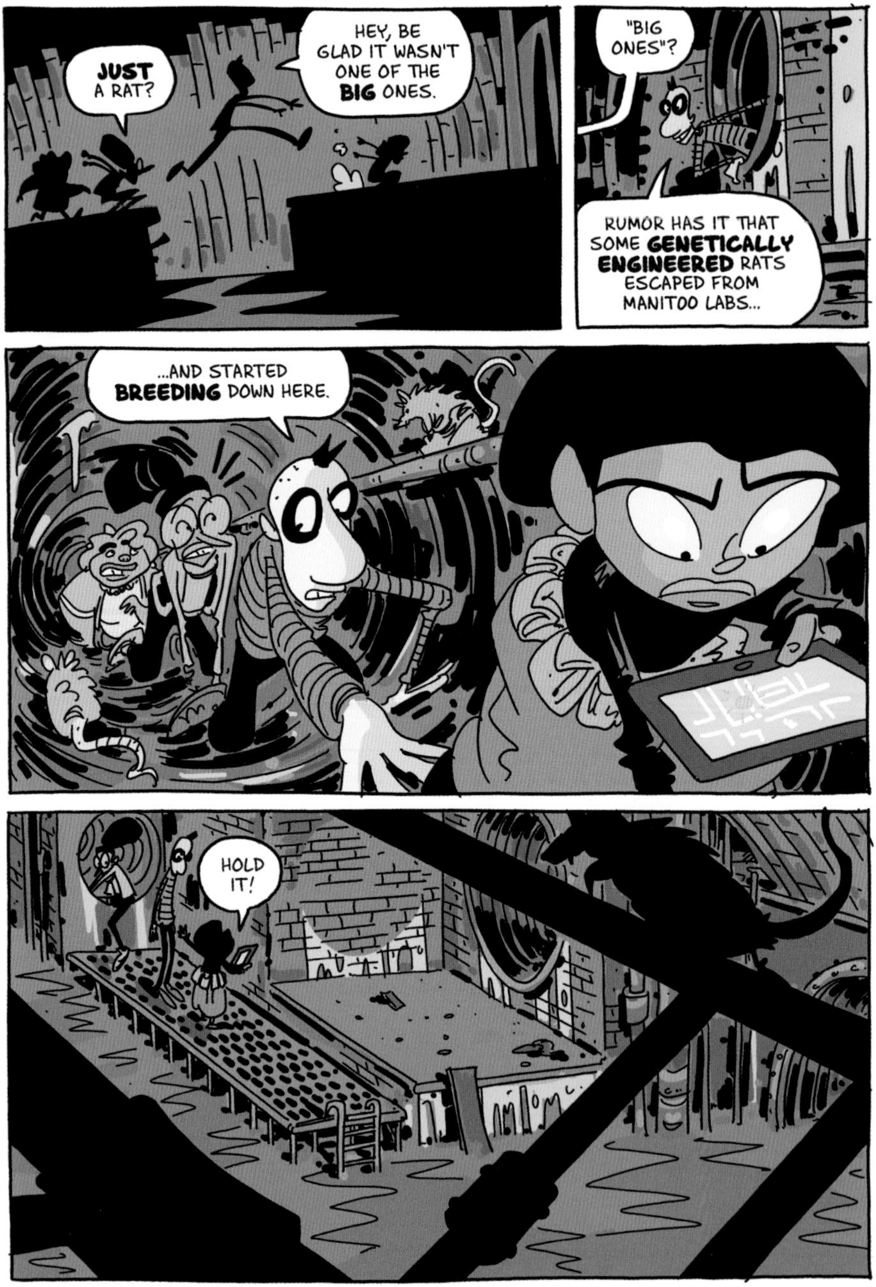
JUST A RAT?
HEY, BE GLAD IT WASN'T ONE OF THE BIG ONES.
"BIG ONES"?
RUMOR HAS IT THAT SOME GENETICALLY ENGINEERED RATS ESCAPED FROM MANITOO LABS...
...AND STARTED BREEDING DOWN HERE.
HOLD IT!

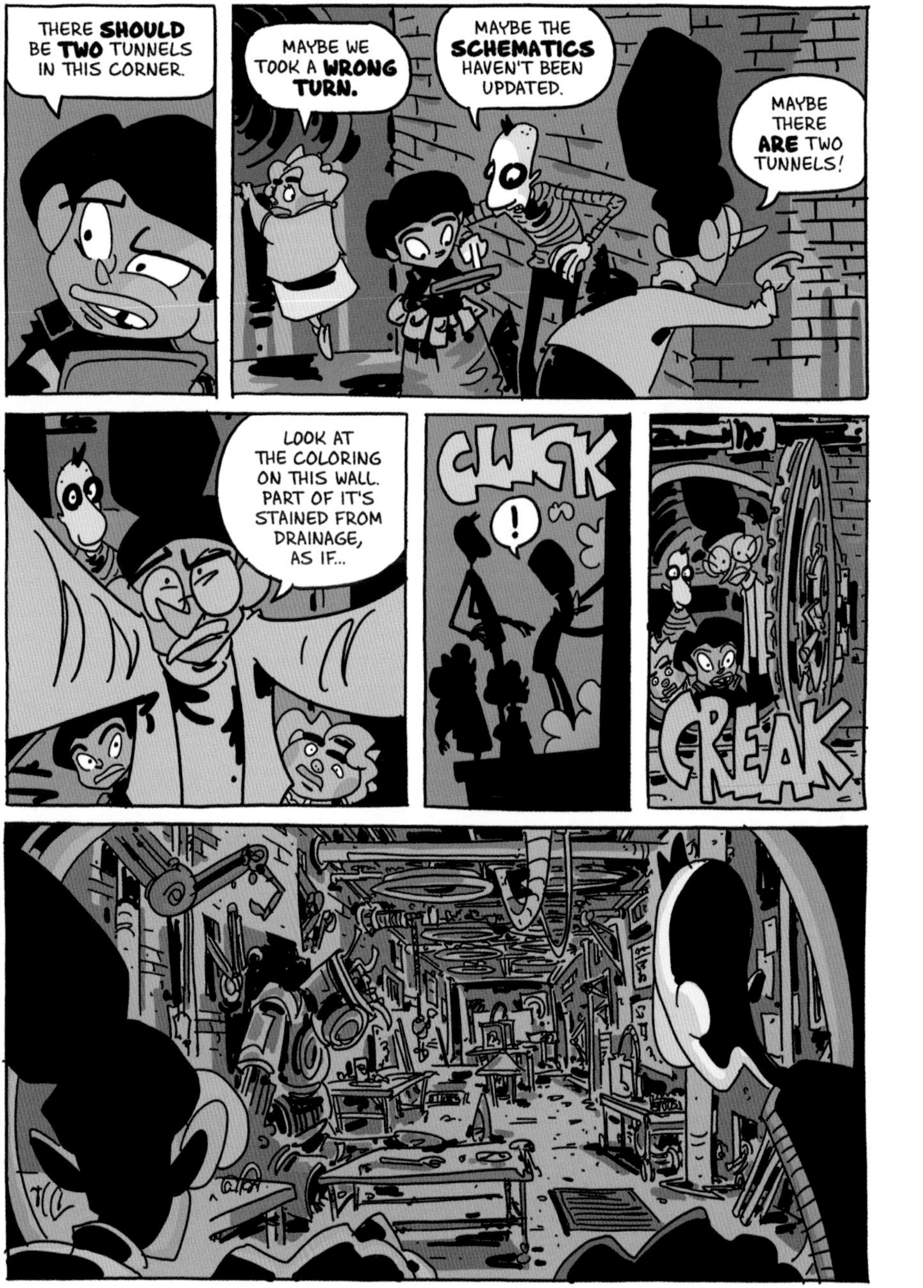
THERE **SHOULD** BE **TWO** TUNNELS IN THIS CORNER.
MAYBE WE TOOK A **WRONG TURN.**
MAYBE THE **SCHEMATICS** HAVEN'T BEEN UPDATED.
MAYBE THERE **ARE** TWO TUNNELS!
LOOK AT THE COLORING ON THIS WALL. PART OF IT'S STAINED FROM DRAINAGE, AS IF...
CLICK
!
CREAK

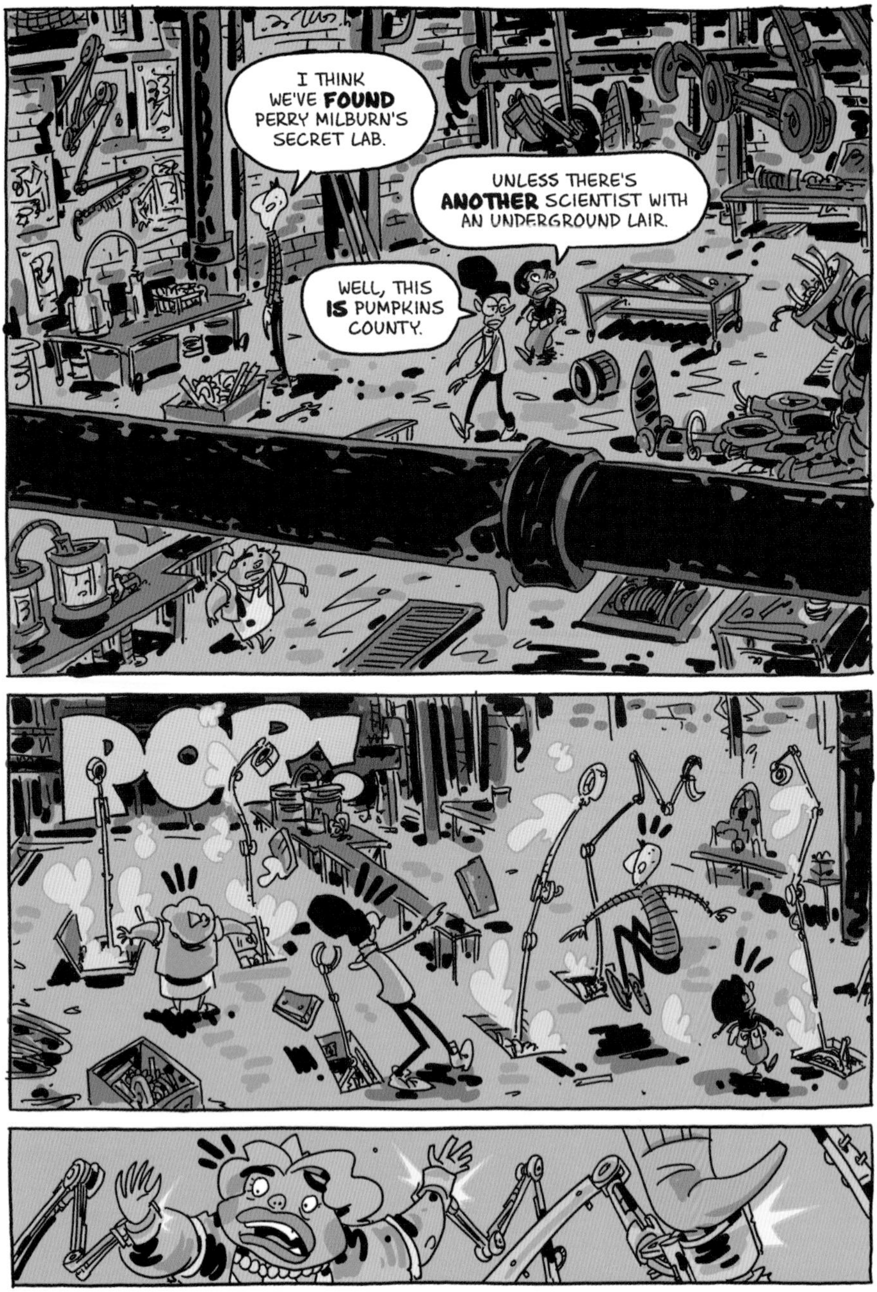
I THINK WE'VE **FOUND** PERRY MILBURN'S SECRET LAB.
UNLESS THERE'S **ANOTHER** SCIENTIST WITH AN UNDERGROUND LAIR.
WELL, THIS **IS** PUMPKINS COUNTY.
POP

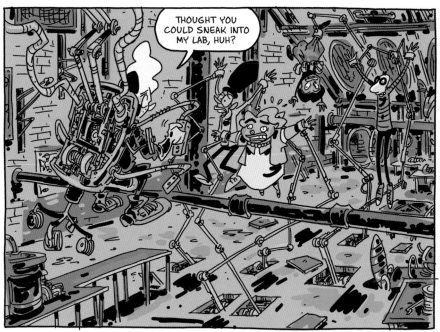

THOUGHT YOU COULD SNEAK INTO MY LAB, HUH?

I KNOW WHY YOU'RE HERE.

YOU'RE TRYING TO STEAL A LOOK AT MY PROJECT FOR THIS YEAR'S SCIENCE FAIR!

YOU'RE PERRY MILBURN, RIGHT?

AREN'T YOU INELIGIBLE FOR THE SCIENCE FAIR?

I NEVER FINISHED THE SCHOOL YEAR, SO TECHNICALLY I'M STILL IN EIGHTH GRADE.

WHICH MEANS I CAN **STILL** RECLAIM MY RIGHTFUL PLACE AS THE **MIDDLE SCHOOL SCIENCE CHAMPION!**

AND **YOU**, I EXPECT, ARE MY **COMPETITION**, TRYING TO DISCOVER THE DETAILS OF MY **SECRET PROJECT!**

THIS "SECRET PROJECT" OF YOURS...

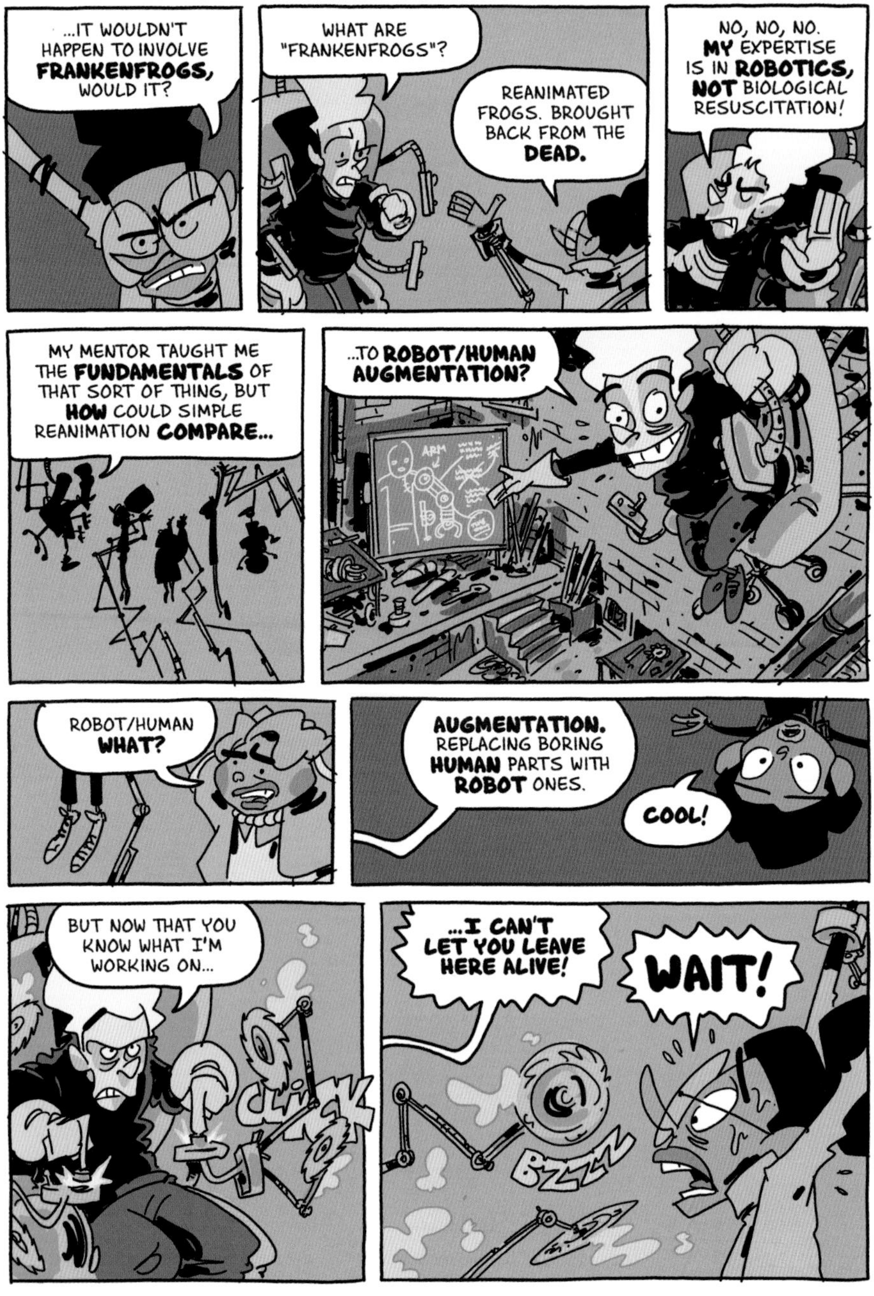
...IT WOULDN'T HAPPEN TO INVOLVE FRANKENFROGS, WOULD IT?
WHAT ARE "FRANKENFROGS"?
REANIMATED FROGS. BROUGHT BACK FROM THE DEAD.
NO, NO, NO. MY EXPERTISE IS IN ROBOTICS, NOT BIOLOGICAL RESUSCITATION!
MY MENTOR TAUGHT ME THE FUNDAMENTALS OF THAT SORT OF THING, BUT HOW COULD SIMPLE REANIMATION COMPARE...
...TO ROBOT/HUMAN AUGMENTATION?
ARM
ROBOT/HUMAN WHAT?
AUGMENTATION. REPLACING BORING HUMAN PARTS WITH ROBOT ONES.
COOL!
BUT NOW THAT YOU KNOW WHAT I'M WORKING ON...
CLICK
...I CAN'T LET YOU LEAVE HERE ALIVE!
WAIT!
BZZZ

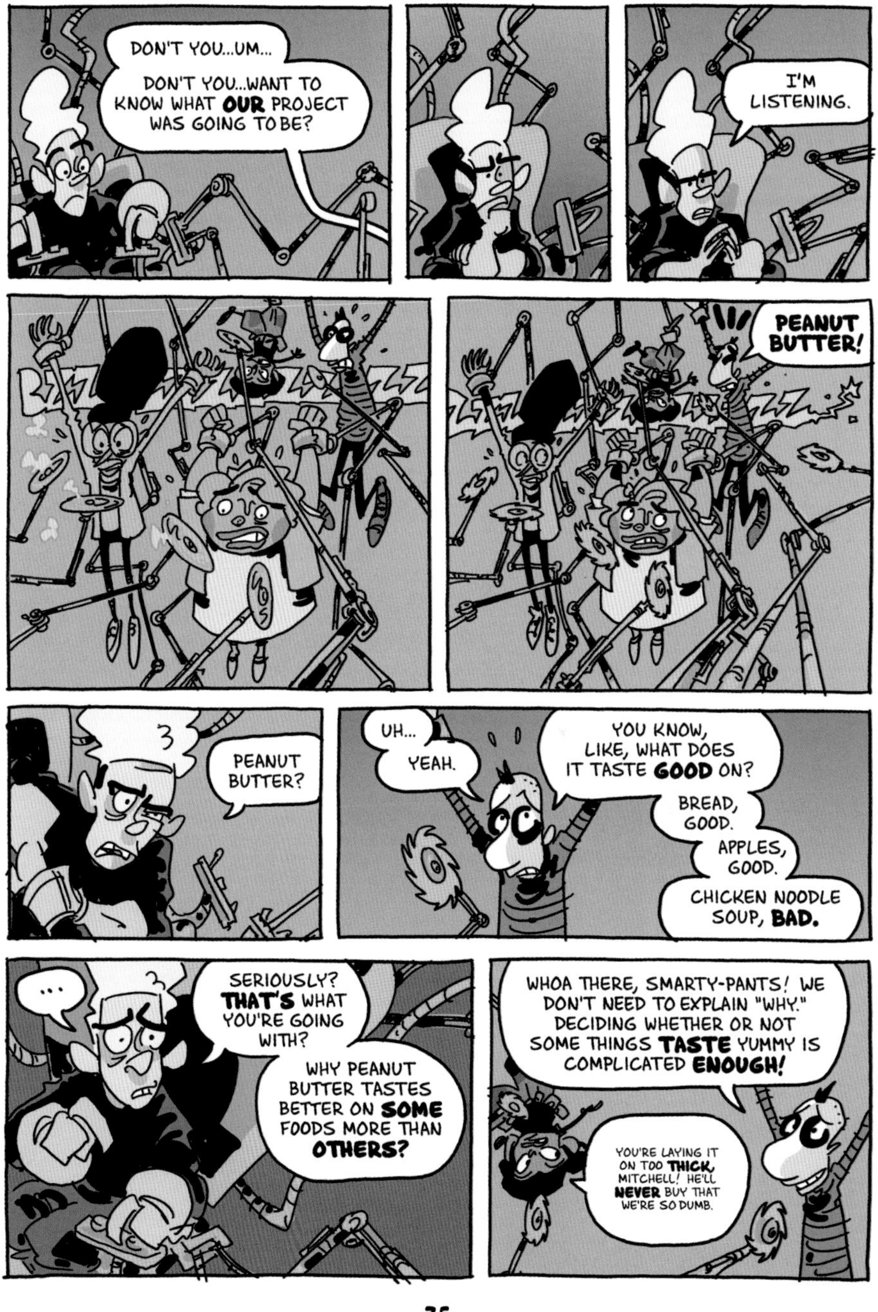
DON'T YOU...UM...
DON'T YOU...WANT TO KNOW WHAT **OUR** PROJECT WAS GOING TO BE?
I'M LISTENING.
PEANUT BUTTER!
PEANUT BUTTER?
UH...
YEAH.
YOU KNOW, LIKE, WHAT DOES IT TASTE **GOOD** ON?
BREAD, GOOD.
APPLES, GOOD.
CHICKEN NOODLE SOUP, **BAD.**
...
SERIOUSLY? **THAT'S** WHAT YOU'RE GOING WITH?
WHY PEANUT BUTTER TASTES BETTER ON **SOME** FOODS MORE THAN **OTHERS?**
WHOA THERE, SMARTY-PANTS! WE DON'T NEED TO EXPLAIN "WHY." DECIDING WHETHER OR NOT SOME THINGS **TASTE** YUMMY IS COMPLICATED **ENOUGH!**
YOU'RE LAYING IT ON TOO **THICK,** MITCHELL! HE'LL **NEVER** BUY THAT WE'RE SO DUMB.

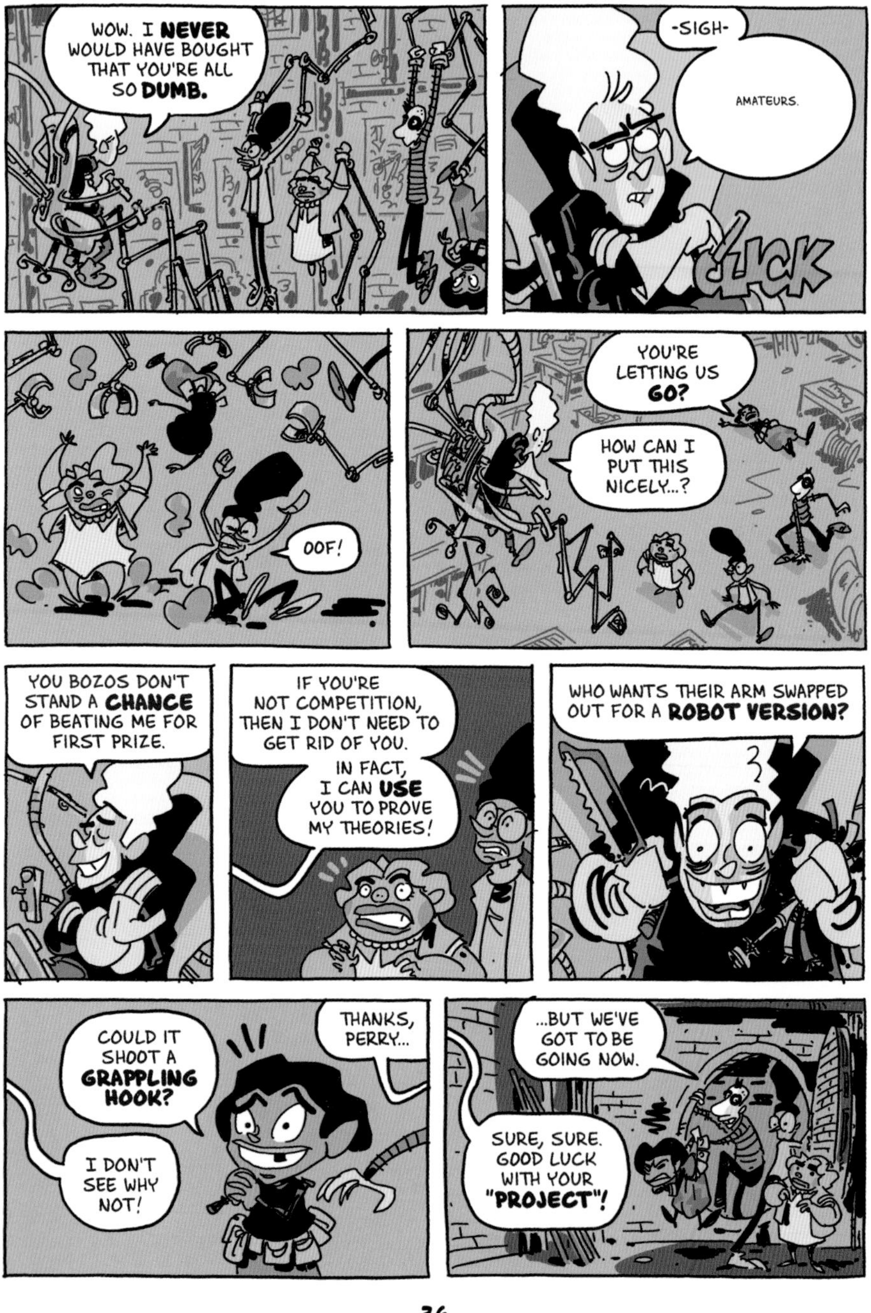
WOW. I NEVER WOULD HAVE BOUGHT THAT YOU'RE ALL SO DUMB.
-SIGH-
AMATEURS.
CLICK
OOF!
YOU'RE LETTING US GO?
HOW CAN I PUT THIS NICELY...?
YOU BOZOS DON'T STAND A CHANCE OF BEATING ME FOR FIRST PRIZE.
IF YOU'RE NOT COMPETITION, THEN I DON'T NEED TO GET RID OF YOU.
IN FACT, I CAN USE YOU TO PROVE MY THEORIES!
WHO WANTS THEIR ARM SWAPPED OUT FOR A ROBOT VERSION?
COULD IT SHOOT A GRAPPLING HOOK?
I DON'T SEE WHY NOT!
THANKS, PERRY...
...BUT WE'VE GOT TO BE GOING NOW.
SURE, SURE. GOOD LUCK WITH YOUR "PROJECT"!

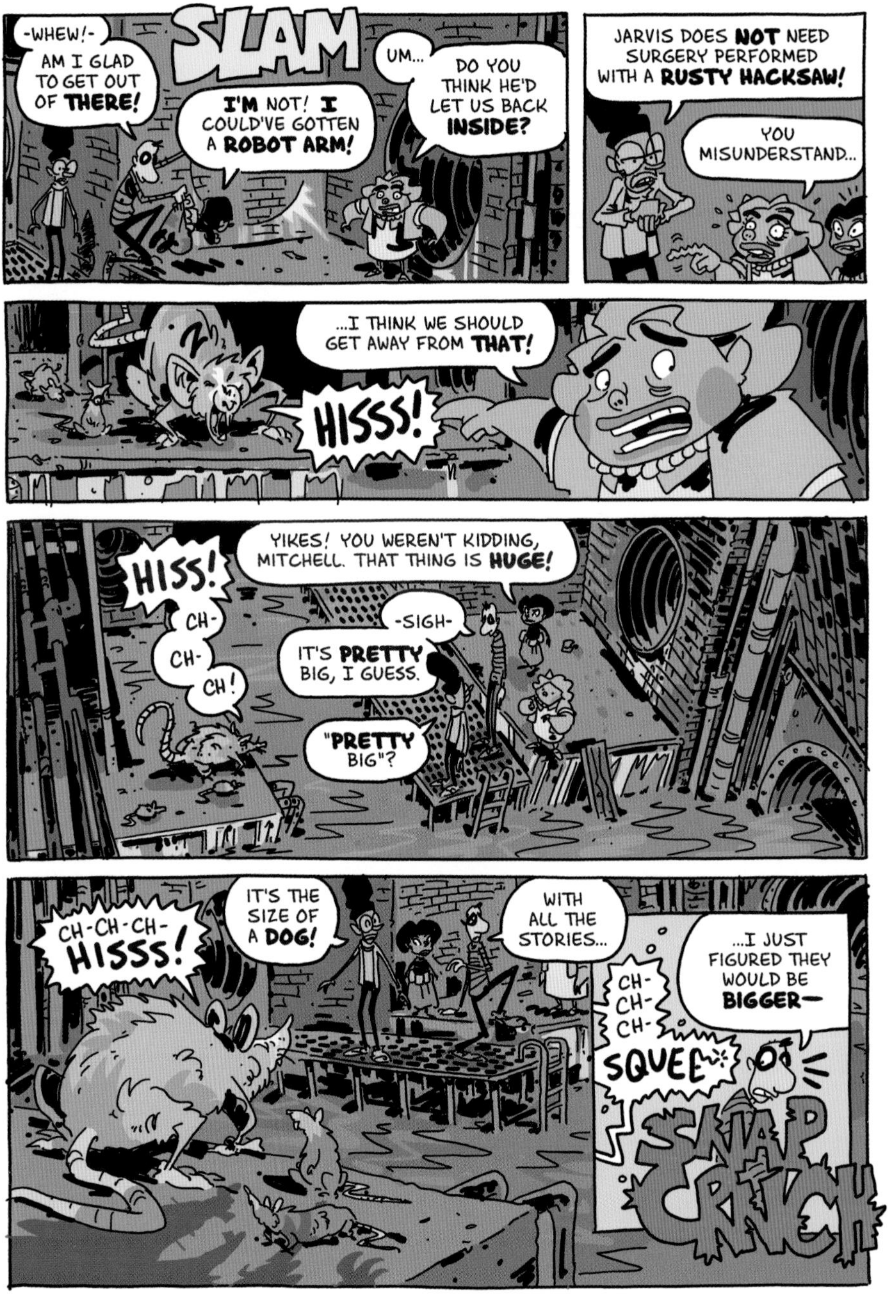

SLAM
-WHEW!-
AM I GLAD TO GET OUT OF THERE!
I'M NOT! I COULD'VE GOTTEN A ROBOT ARM!
UM...
DO YOU THINK HE'D LET US BACK INSIDE?
JARVIS DOES NOT NEED SURGERY PERFORMED WITH A RUSTY HACKSAW!
YOU MISUNDERSTAND...
...I THINK WE SHOULD GET AWAY FROM THAT!
HISSS!
HISS!
CH-
CH-
CH!
YIKES! YOU WEREN'T KIDDING, MITCHELL. THAT THING IS HUGE!
-SIGH-
IT'S PRETTY BIG, I GUESS.
"PRETTY BIG"?
CH-CH-CH-HISSS!
IT'S THE SIZE OF A DOG!
WITH ALL THE STORIES...
...I JUST FIGURED THEY WOULD BE BIGGER—
CH-
CH-
CH-
SQUEE
SNAP
CRUNCH

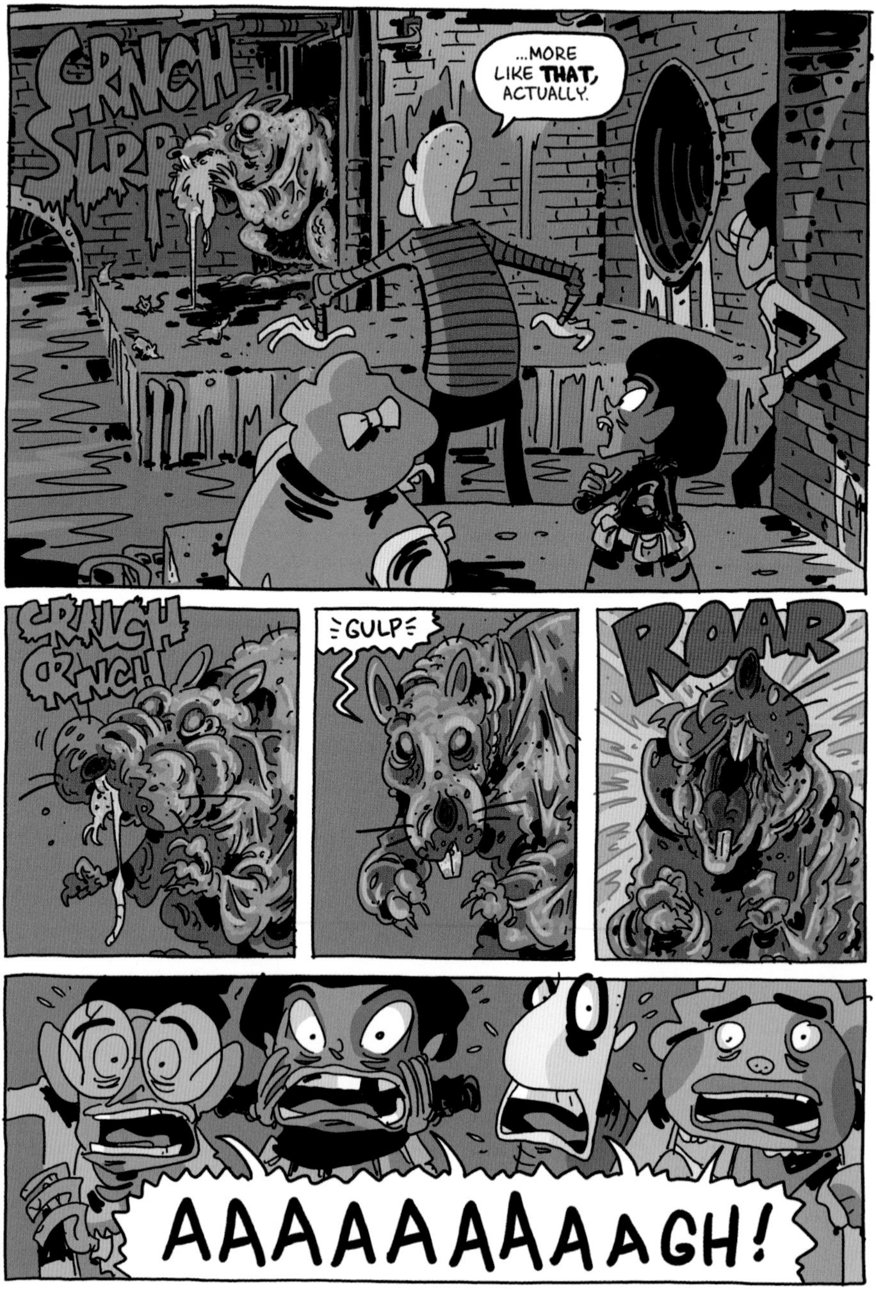
CRNCH
SLRP
...MORE LIKE THAT, ACTUALLY.
CRNCH CRNCH
GULP
ROAR
AAAAAAAAAAGH!

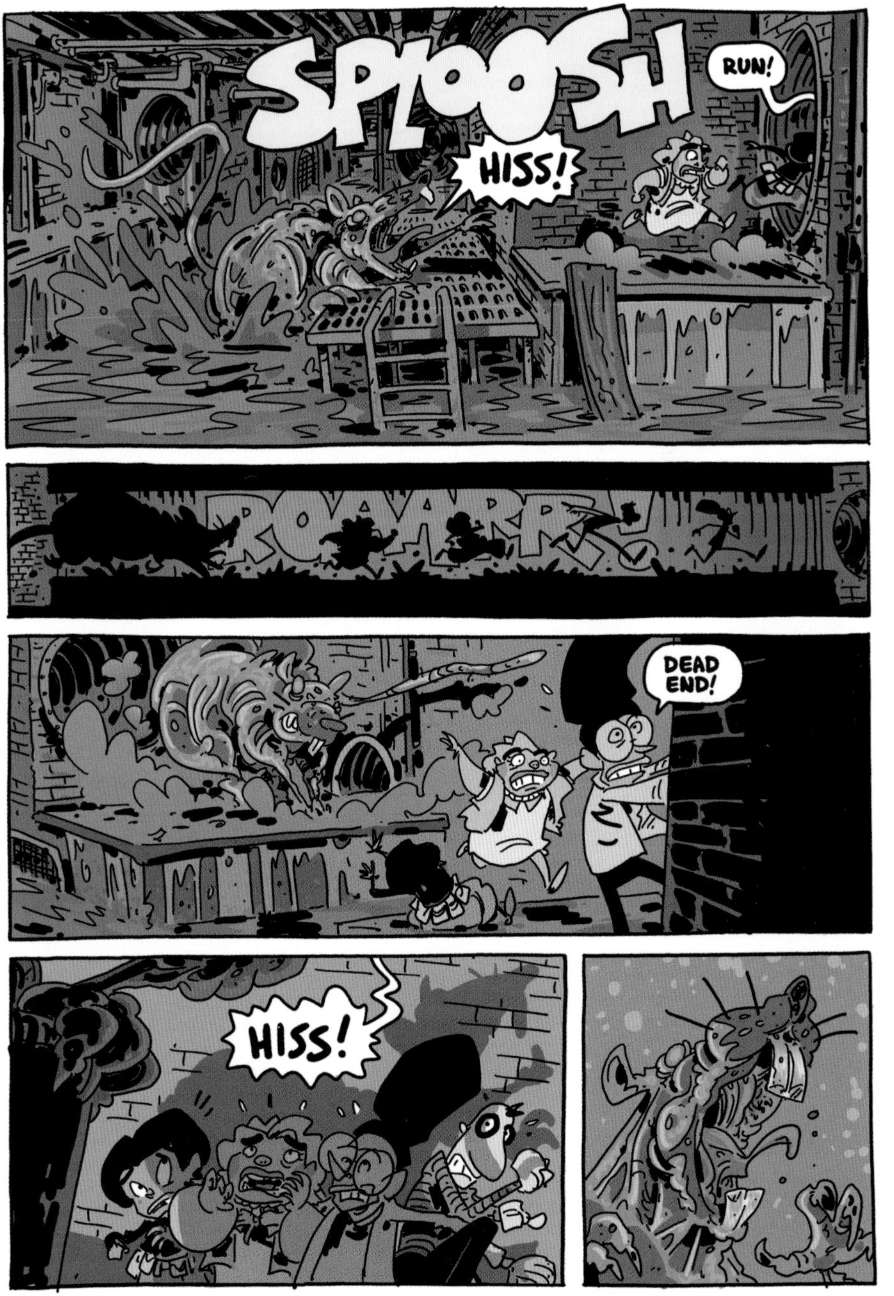
SPLOOSH
RUN!
HISS!
ROAARR!
DEAD END!
HISS!

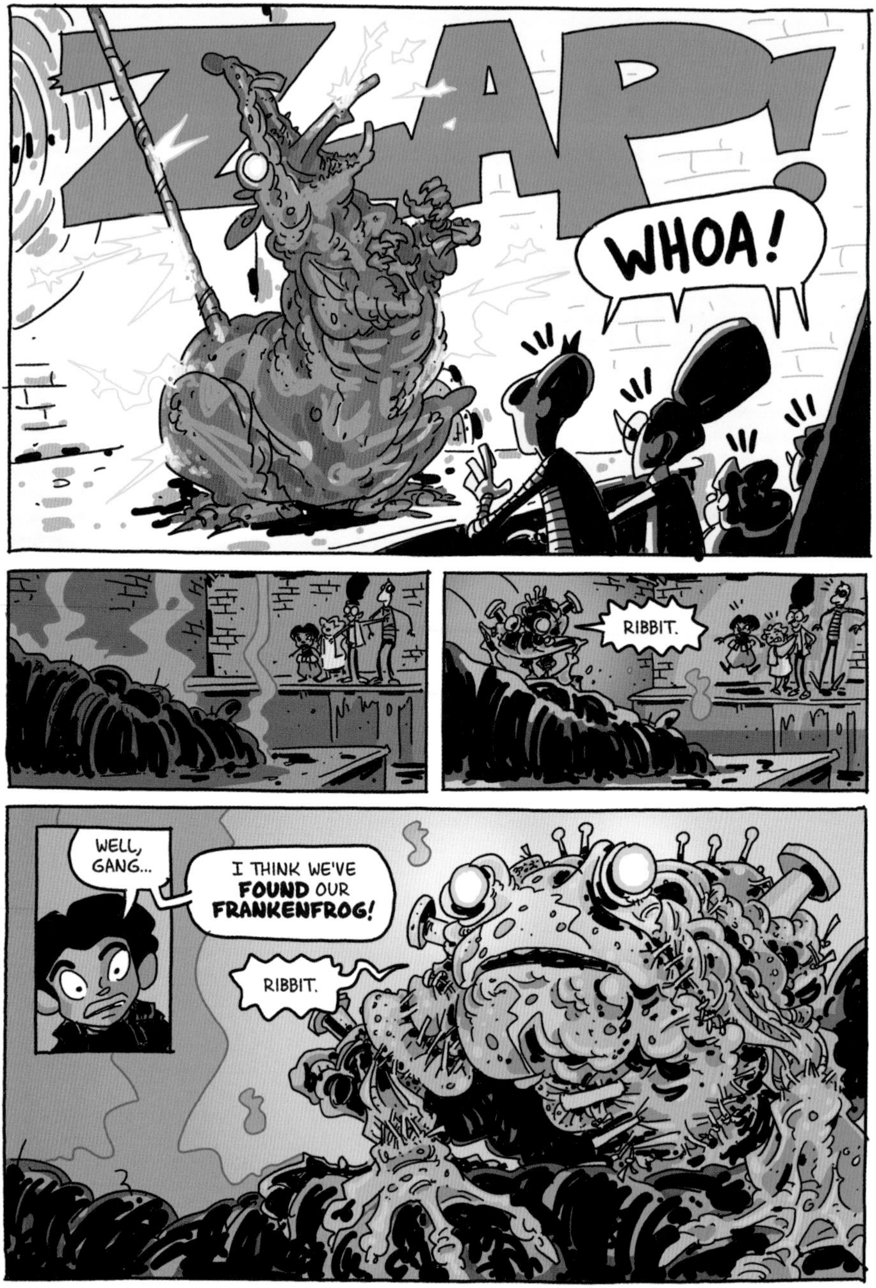
ZZAP!
WHOA!
RIBBIT.
WELL, GANG...
I THINK WE'VE **FOUND** OUR **FRANKENFROG!**
RIBBIT.

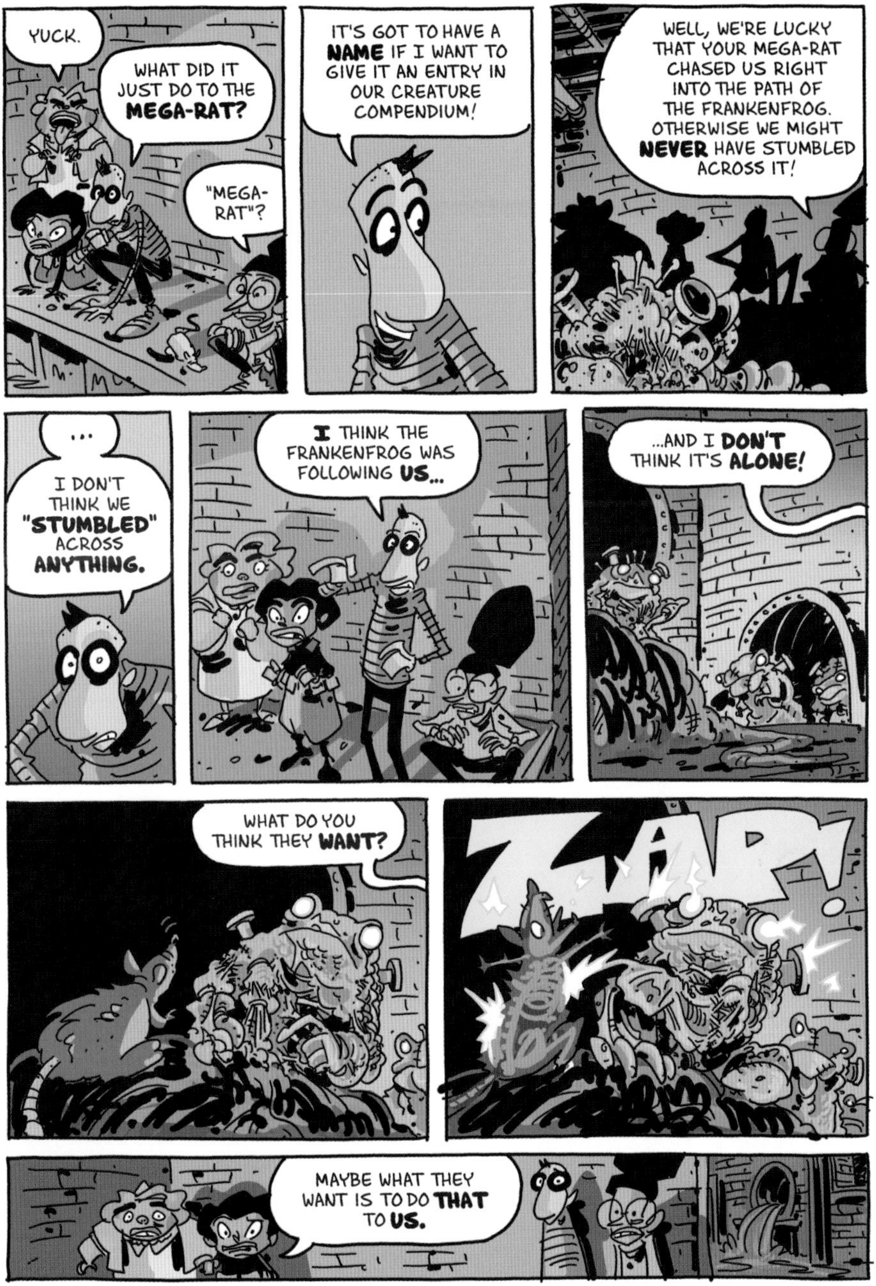
YUCK.
WHAT DID IT JUST DO TO THE **MEGA-RAT?**
"MEGA-RAT"?
IT'S GOT TO HAVE A **NAME** IF I WANT TO GIVE IT AN ENTRY IN OUR CREATURE COMPENDIUM!
WELL, WE'RE LUCKY THAT YOUR MEGA-RAT CHASED US RIGHT INTO THE PATH OF THE FRANKENFROG. OTHERWISE WE MIGHT **NEVER** HAVE STUMBLED ACROSS IT!
...
I DON'T THINK WE **"STUMBLED"** ACROSS **ANYTHING.**
I THINK THE FRANKENFROG WAS FOLLOWING **US...**
...AND I **DON'T** THINK IT'S **ALONE!**
WHAT DO YOU THINK THEY **WANT?**
ZAP!
MAYBE WHAT THEY WANT IS TO DO **THAT** TO **US.**

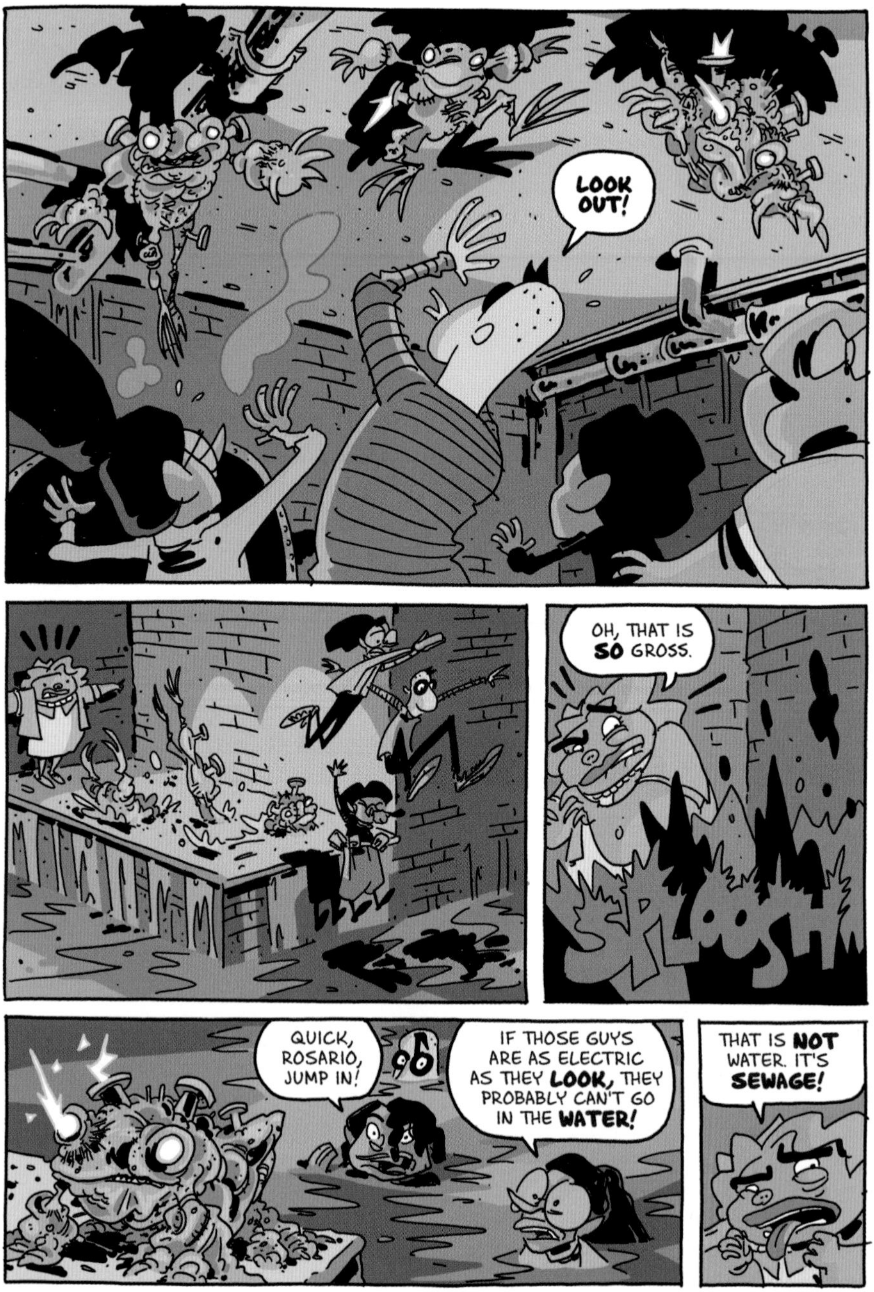
LOOK OUT!
OH, THAT IS **SO** GROSS.
SPLOOSH
QUICK, ROSARIO, JUMP IN!
IF THOSE GUYS ARE AS ELECTRIC AS THEY **LOOK,** THEY PROBABLY CAN'T GO IN THE **WATER!**
THAT IS **NOT** WATER. IT'S **SEWAGE!**

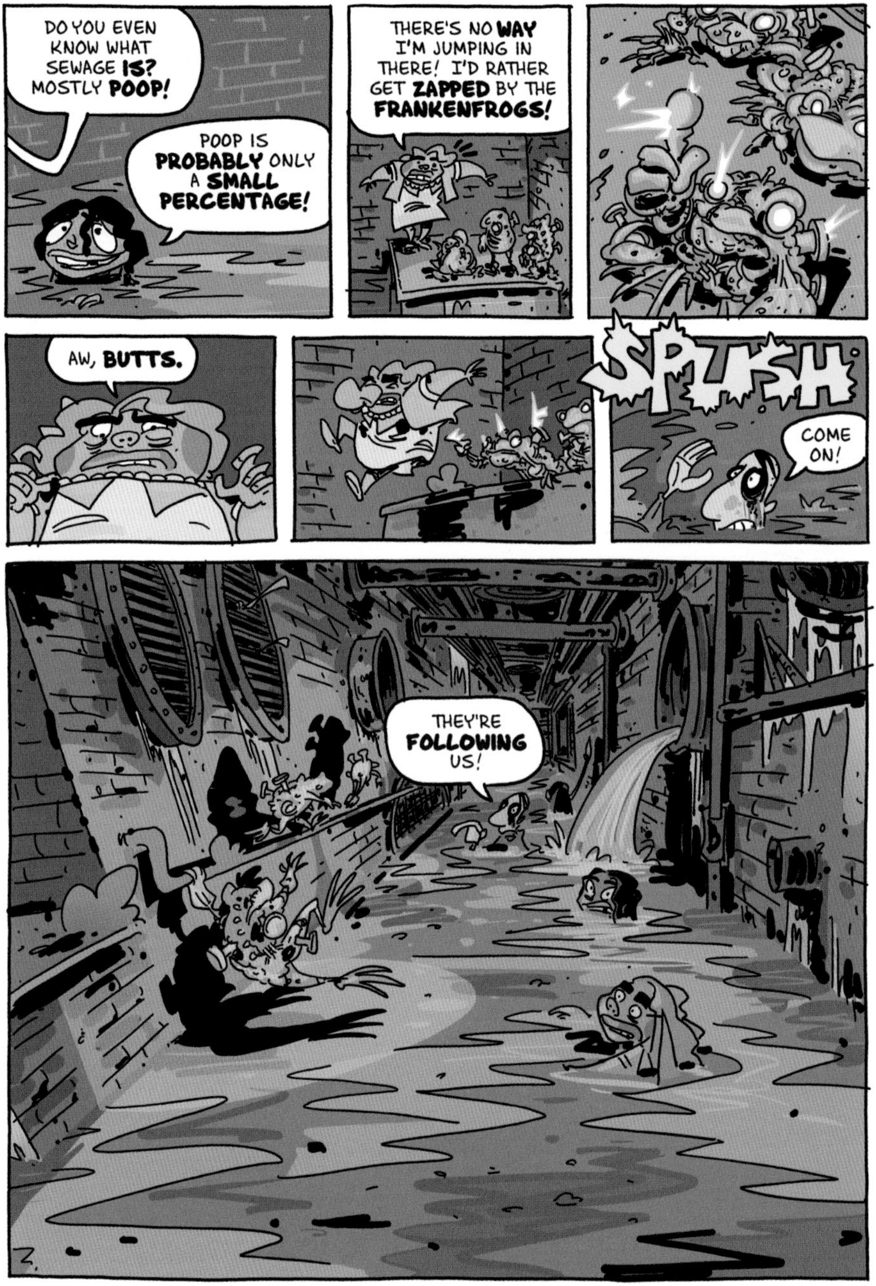
DO YOU EVEN KNOW WHAT SEWAGE IS? MOSTLY POOP!
POOP IS PROBABLY ONLY A SMALL PERCENTAGE!
THERE'S NO WAY I'M JUMPING IN THERE! I'D RATHER GET ZAPPED BY THE FRANKENFROGS!
AW, BUTTS.
SPLUSH
COME ON!
THEY'RE FOLLOWING US!

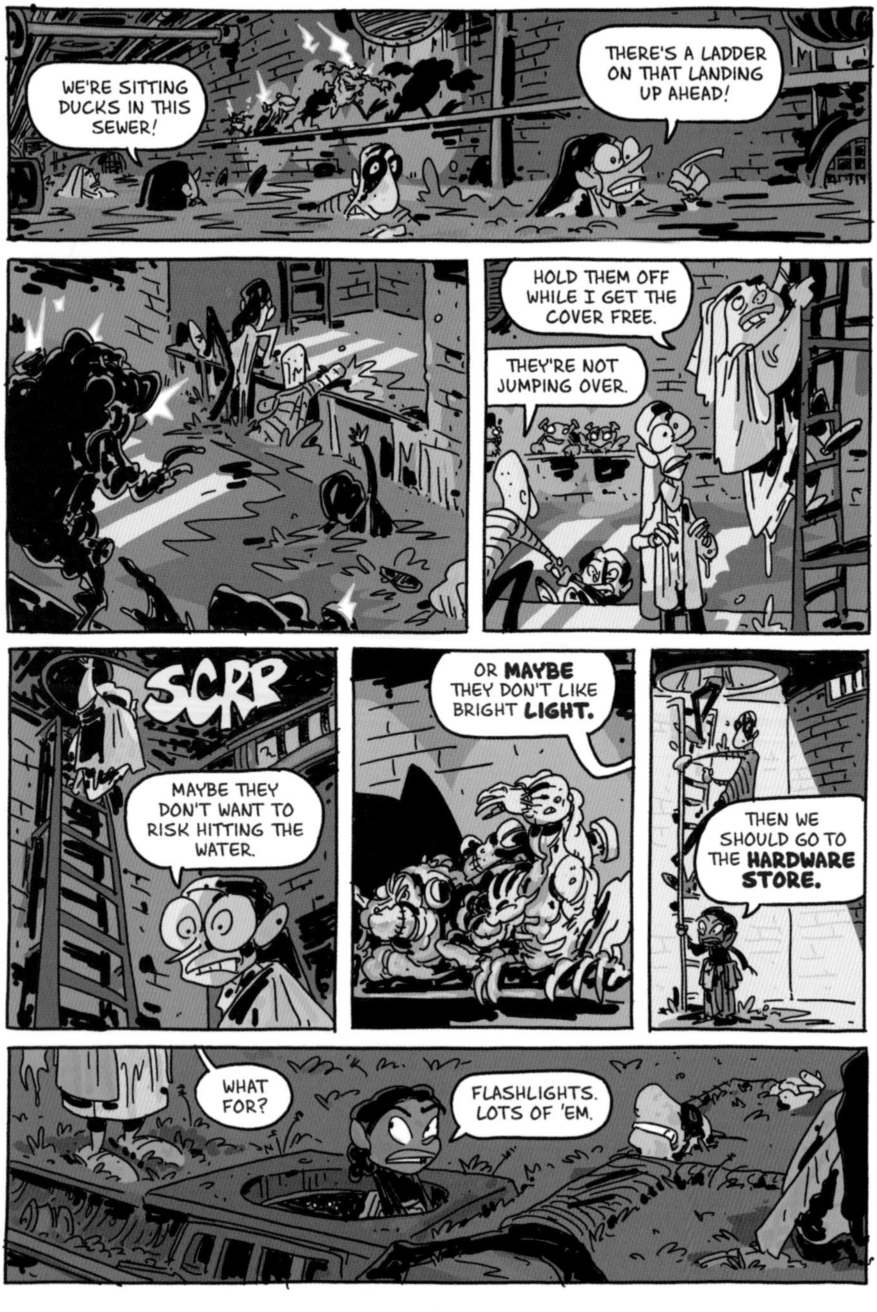
WE'RE SITTING DUCKS IN THIS SEWER!
THERE'S A LADDER ON THAT LANDING UP AHEAD!
HOLD THEM OFF WHILE I GET THE COVER FREE.
THEY'RE NOT JUMPING OVER.
SCRP
MAYBE THEY DON'T WANT TO RISK HITTING THE WATER.
OR **MAYBE** THEY DON'T LIKE BRIGHT **LIGHT.**
THEN WE SHOULD GO TO THE **HARDWARE STORE.**
WHAT FOR?
FLASHLIGHTS. LOTS OF 'EM.

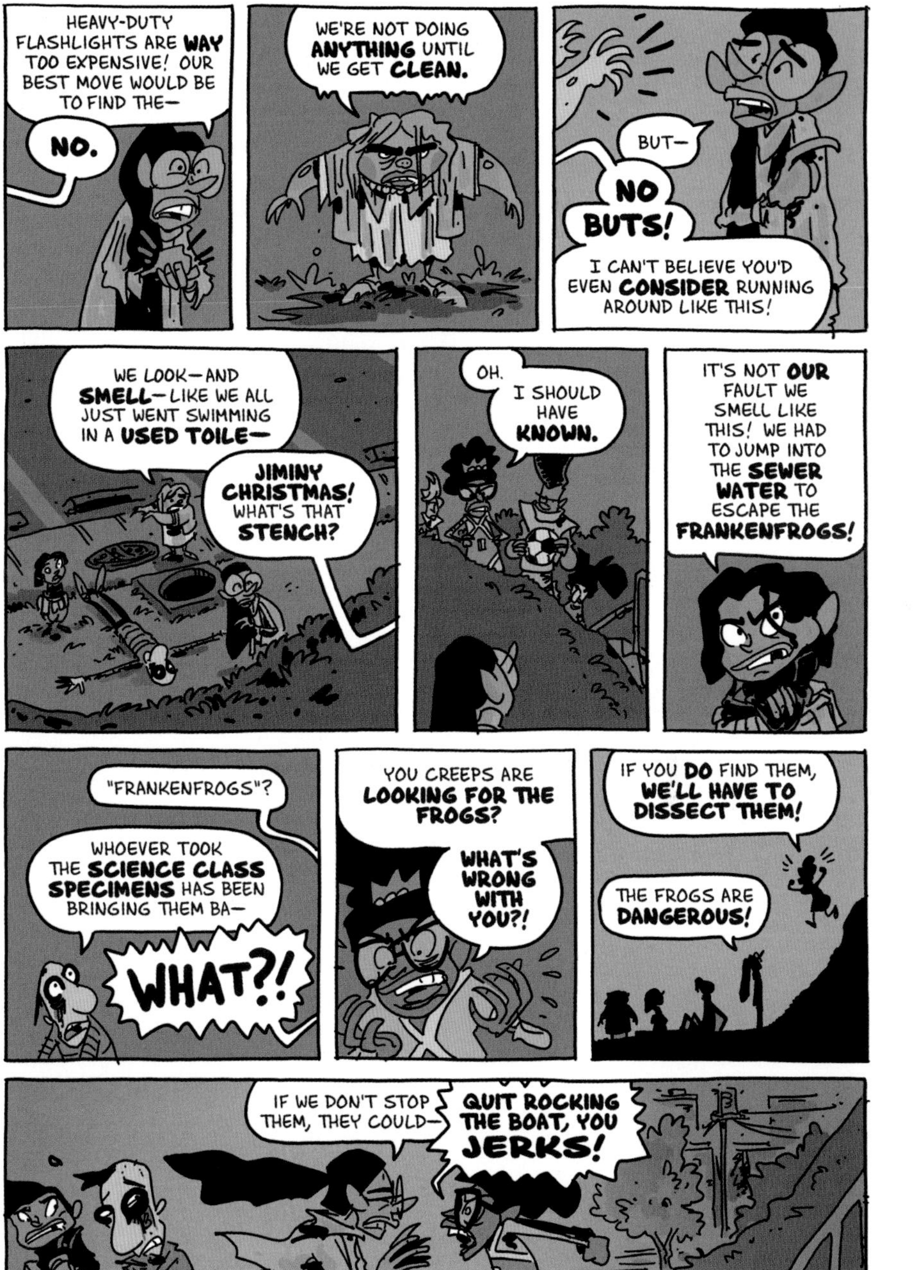
HEAVY-DUTY FLASHLIGHTS ARE WAY TOO EXPENSIVE! OUR BEST MOVE WOULD BE TO FIND THE—
NO.
WE'RE NOT DOING ANYTHING UNTIL WE GET CLEAN.
BUT—
NO BUTS!
I CAN'T BELIEVE YOU'D EVEN CONSIDER RUNNING AROUND LIKE THIS!
WE LOOK—AND SMELL—LIKE WE ALL JUST WENT SWIMMING IN A USED TOILE—
JIMINY CHRISTMAS! WHAT'S THAT STENCH?
OH.
I SHOULD HAVE KNOWN.
IT'S NOT OUR FAULT WE SMELL LIKE THIS! WE HAD TO JUMP INTO THE SEWER WATER TO ESCAPE THE FRANKENFROGS!
"FRANKENFROGS"?
WHOEVER TOOK THE SCIENCE CLASS SPECIMENS HAS BEEN BRINGING THEM BA—
WHAT?!
YOU CREEPS ARE LOOKING FOR THE FROGS?
WHAT'S WRONG WITH YOU?!
IF YOU DO FIND THEM, WE'LL HAVE TO DISSECT THEM!
THE FROGS ARE DANGEROUS!
IF WE DON'T STOP THEM, THEY COULD—
QUIT ROCKING THE BOAT, YOU JERKS!

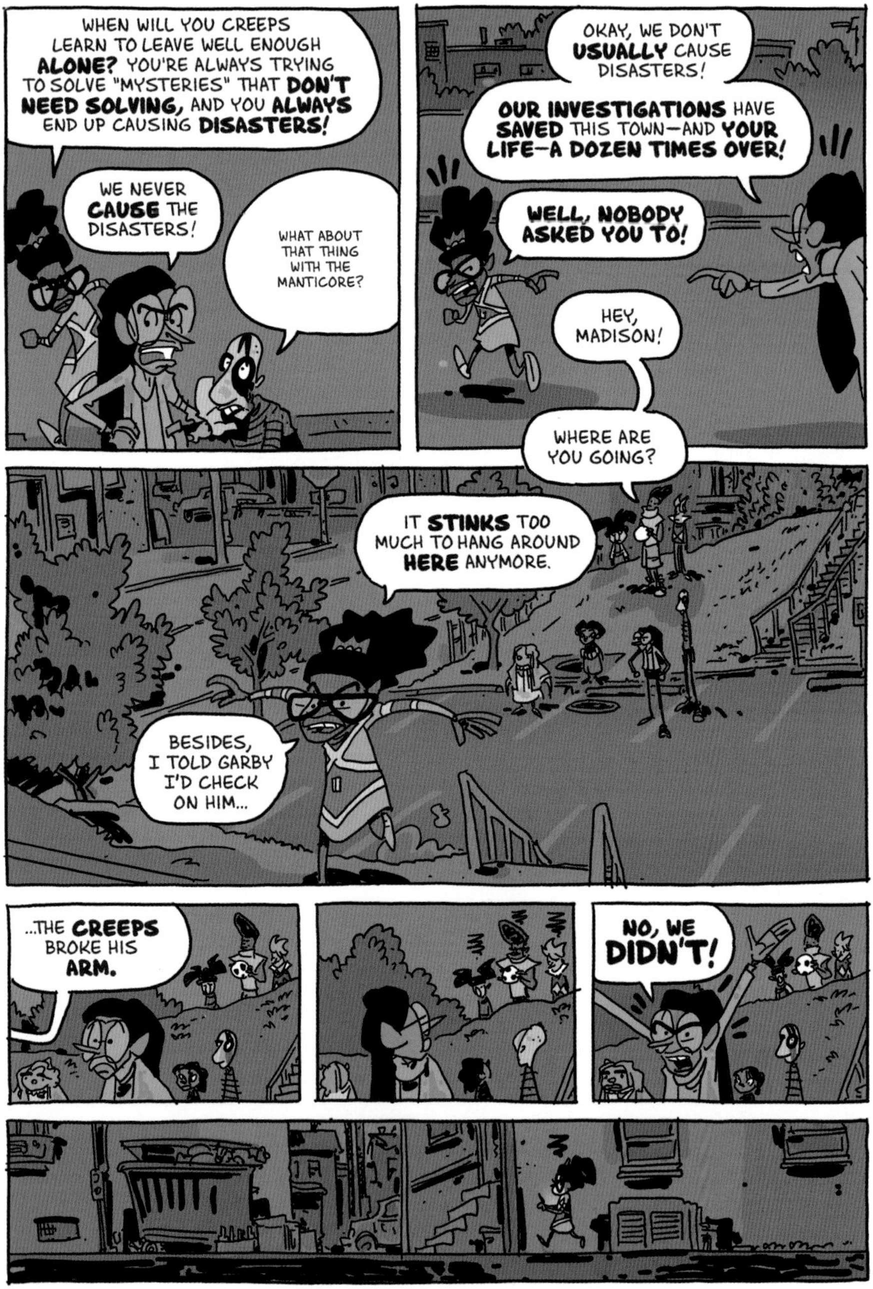
WHEN WILL YOU CREEPS LEARN TO LEAVE WELL ENOUGH **ALONE?** YOU'RE ALWAYS TRYING TO SOLVE "MYSTERIES" THAT **DON'T NEED SOLVING,** AND YOU **ALWAYS** END UP CAUSING **DISASTERS!**
WE NEVER **CAUSE** THE DISASTERS!
WHAT ABOUT THAT THING WITH THE MANTICORE?
OKAY, WE DON'T **USUALLY** CAUSE DISASTERS!
OUR INVESTIGATIONS HAVE **SAVED** THIS TOWN—AND **YOUR LIFE—A DOZEN TIMES OVER!**
WELL, NOBODY ASKED YOU TO!
HEY, MADISON!
WHERE ARE YOU GOING?
IT **STINKS** TOO MUCH TO HANG AROUND **HERE** ANYMORE.
BESIDES, I TOLD GARBY I'D CHECK ON HIM...
...THE **CREEPS** BROKE HIS **ARM.**
NO, WE DIDN'T!

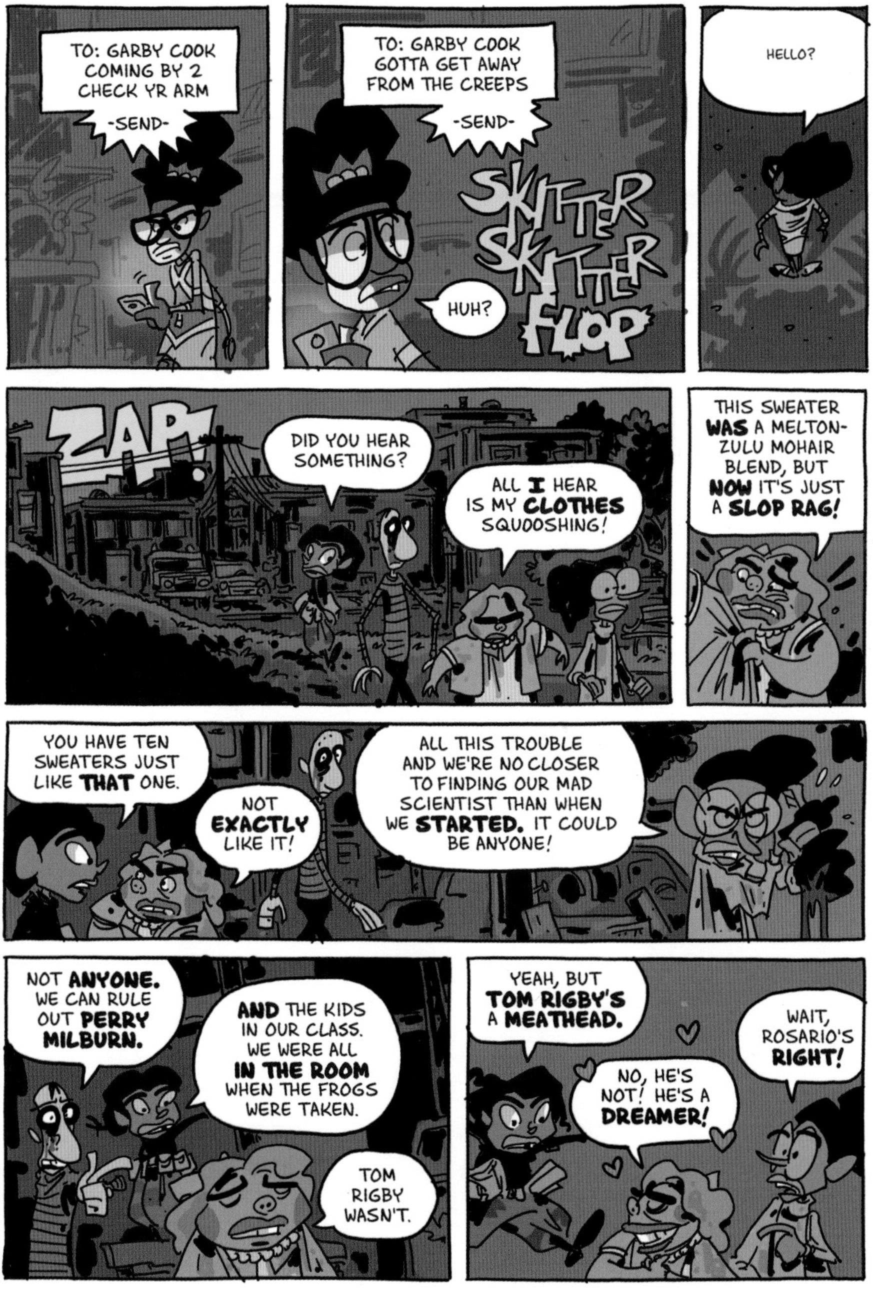
TO: GARBY COOK
COMING BY 2
CHECK YR ARM
-SEND-
TO: GARBY COOK
GOTTA GET AWAY
FROM THE CREEPS
-SEND-
SKITTER SKITTER FLOP
HUH?
HELLO?
ZAP
DID YOU HEAR SOMETHING?
ALL I HEAR IS MY CLOTHES SQUOOSHING!
THIS SWEATER WAS A MELTON-ZULU MOHAIR BLEND, BUT NOW IT'S JUST A SLOP RAG!
YOU HAVE TEN SWEATERS JUST LIKE THAT ONE.
NOT EXACTLY LIKE IT!
ALL THIS TROUBLE AND WE'RE NO CLOSER TO FINDING OUR MAD SCIENTIST THAN WHEN WE STARTED. IT COULD BE ANYONE!
NOT ANYONE. WE CAN RULE OUT PERRY MILBURN.
AND THE KIDS IN OUR CLASS. WE WERE ALL IN THE ROOM WHEN THE FROGS WERE TAKEN.
TOM RIGBY WASN'T.
YEAH, BUT TOM RIGBY'S A MEATHEAD.
NO, HE'S NOT! HE'S A DREAMER!
WAIT, ROSARIO'S RIGHT!

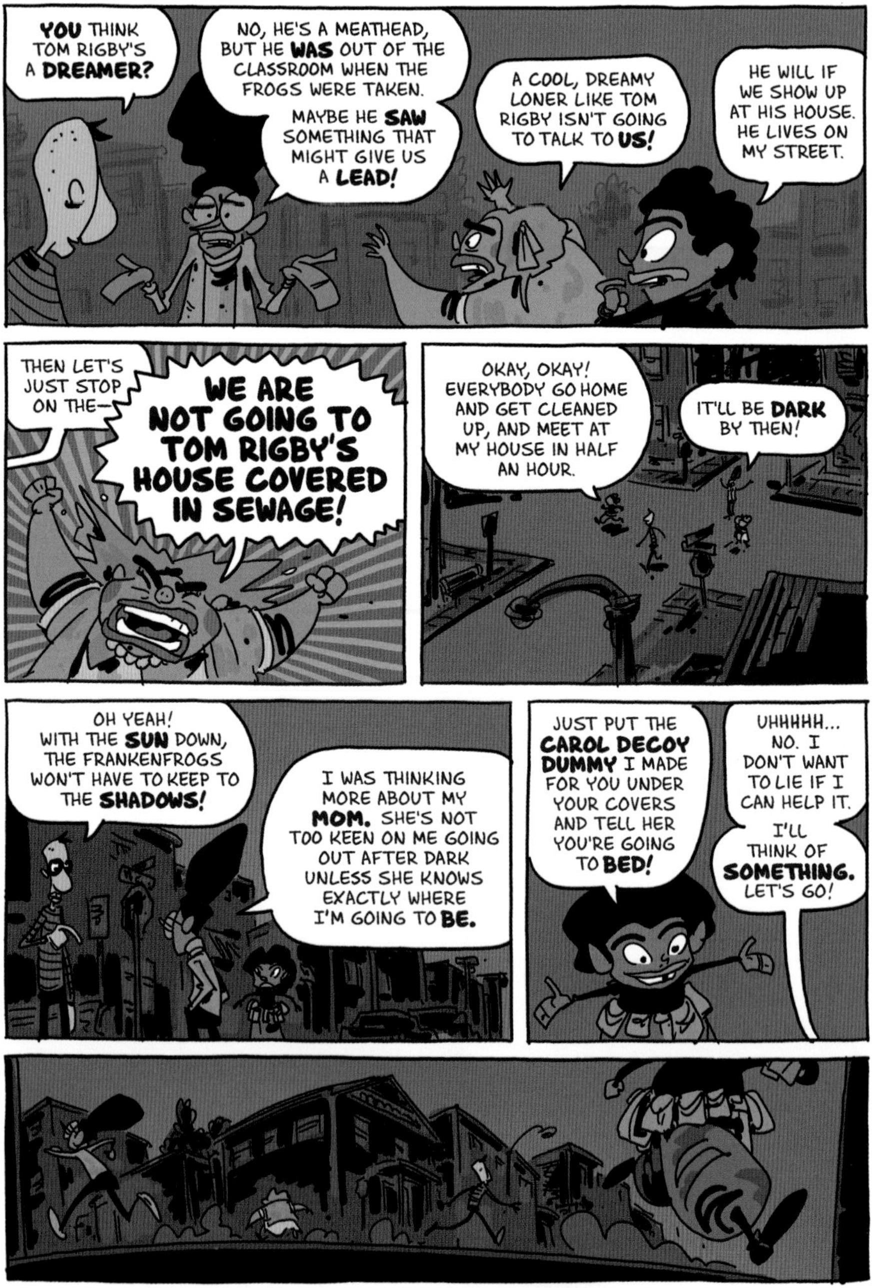
YOU THINK TOM RIGBY'S A DREAMER?
NO, HE'S A MEATHEAD, BUT HE WAS OUT OF THE CLASSROOM WHEN THE FROGS WERE TAKEN.
MAYBE HE SAW SOMETHING THAT MIGHT GIVE US A LEAD!
A COOL, DREAMY LONER LIKE TOM RIGBY ISN'T GOING TO TALK TO US!
HE WILL IF WE SHOW UP AT HIS HOUSE. HE LIVES ON MY STREET.
THEN LET'S JUST STOP ON THE—
WE ARE NOT GOING TO TOM RIGBY'S HOUSE COVERED IN SEWAGE!
OKAY, OKAY! EVERYBODY GO HOME AND GET CLEANED UP, AND MEET AT MY HOUSE IN HALF AN HOUR.
IT'LL BE DARK BY THEN!
OH YEAH! WITH THE SUN DOWN, THE FRANKENFROGS WON'T HAVE TO KEEP TO THE SHADOWS!
I WAS THINKING MORE ABOUT MY MOM. SHE'S NOT TOO KEEN ON ME GOING OUT AFTER DARK UNLESS SHE KNOWS EXACTLY WHERE I'M GOING TO BE.
JUST PUT THE CAROL DECOY DUMMY I MADE FOR YOU UNDER YOUR COVERS AND TELL HER YOU'RE GOING TO BED!
UHHHHH... NO. I DON'T WANT TO LIE IF I CAN HELP IT.
I'LL THINK OF SOMETHING. LET'S GO!

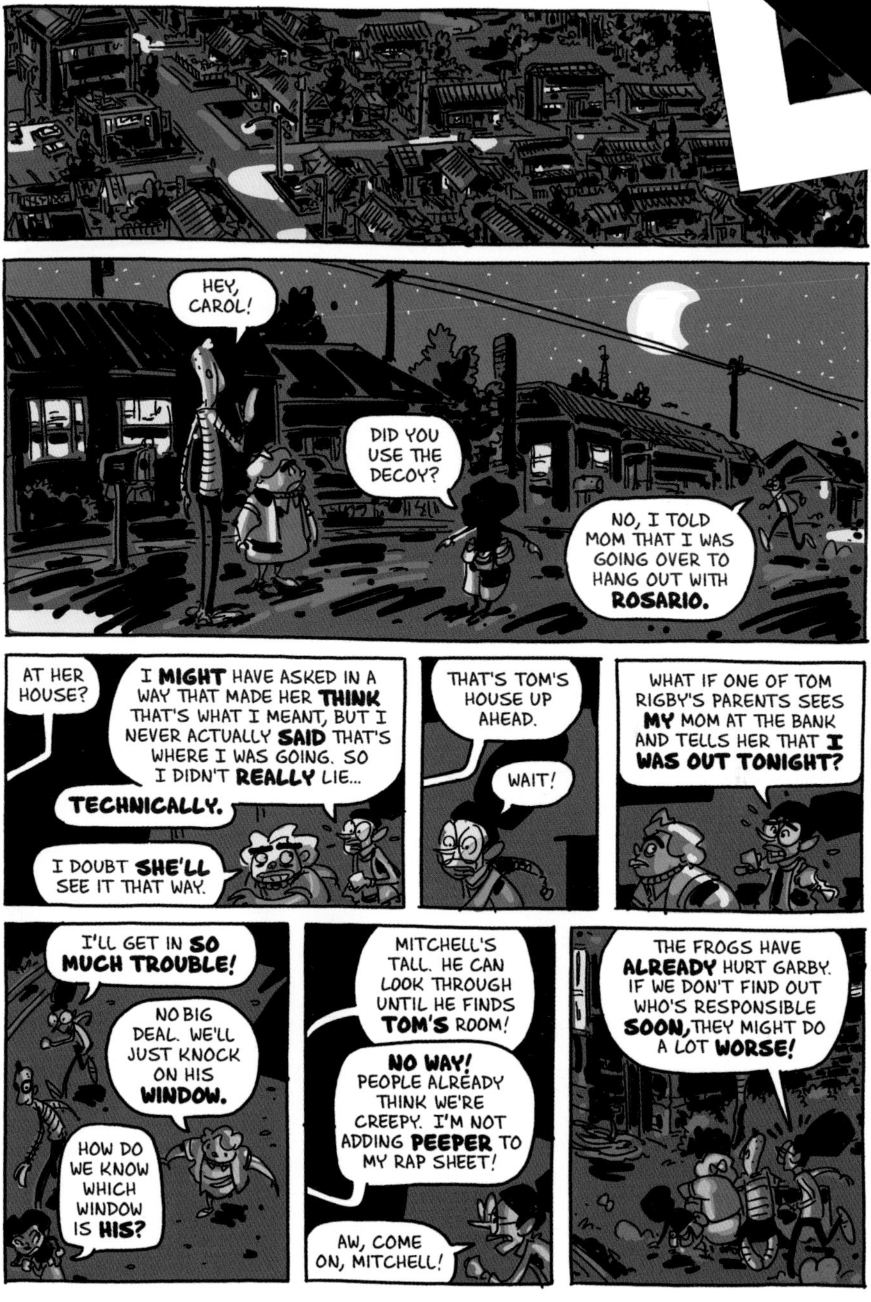
HEY, CAROL!
DID YOU USE THE DECOY?
NO, I TOLD MOM THAT I WAS GOING OVER TO HANG OUT WITH **ROSARIO.**
AT HER HOUSE?
I **MIGHT** HAVE ASKED IN A WAY THAT MADE HER **THINK** THAT'S WHAT I MEANT, BUT I NEVER ACTUALLY **SAID** THAT'S WHERE I WAS GOING. SO I DIDN'T **REALLY** LIE...
TECHNICALLY.
I DOUBT **SHE'LL** SEE IT THAT WAY.
THAT'S TOM'S HOUSE UP AHEAD.
WAIT!
WHAT IF ONE OF TOM RIGBY'S PARENTS SEES **MY** MOM AT THE BANK AND TELLS HER THAT **I WAS OUT TONIGHT?**
I'LL GET IN **SO MUCH TROUBLE!**
NO BIG DEAL. WE'LL JUST KNOCK ON HIS **WINDOW.**
HOW DO WE KNOW WHICH WINDOW IS **HIS?**
MITCHELL'S TALL. HE CAN LOOK THROUGH UNTIL HE FINDS **TOM'S** ROOM!
NO WAY! PEOPLE ALREADY THINK WE'RE CREEPY. I'M NOT ADDING **PEEPER** TO MY RAP SHEET!
AW, COME ON, MITCHELL!
THE FROGS HAVE **ALREADY** HURT GARBY. IF WE DON'T FIND OUT WHO'S RESPONSIBLE **SOON,** THEY MIGHT DO A LOT **WORSE!**

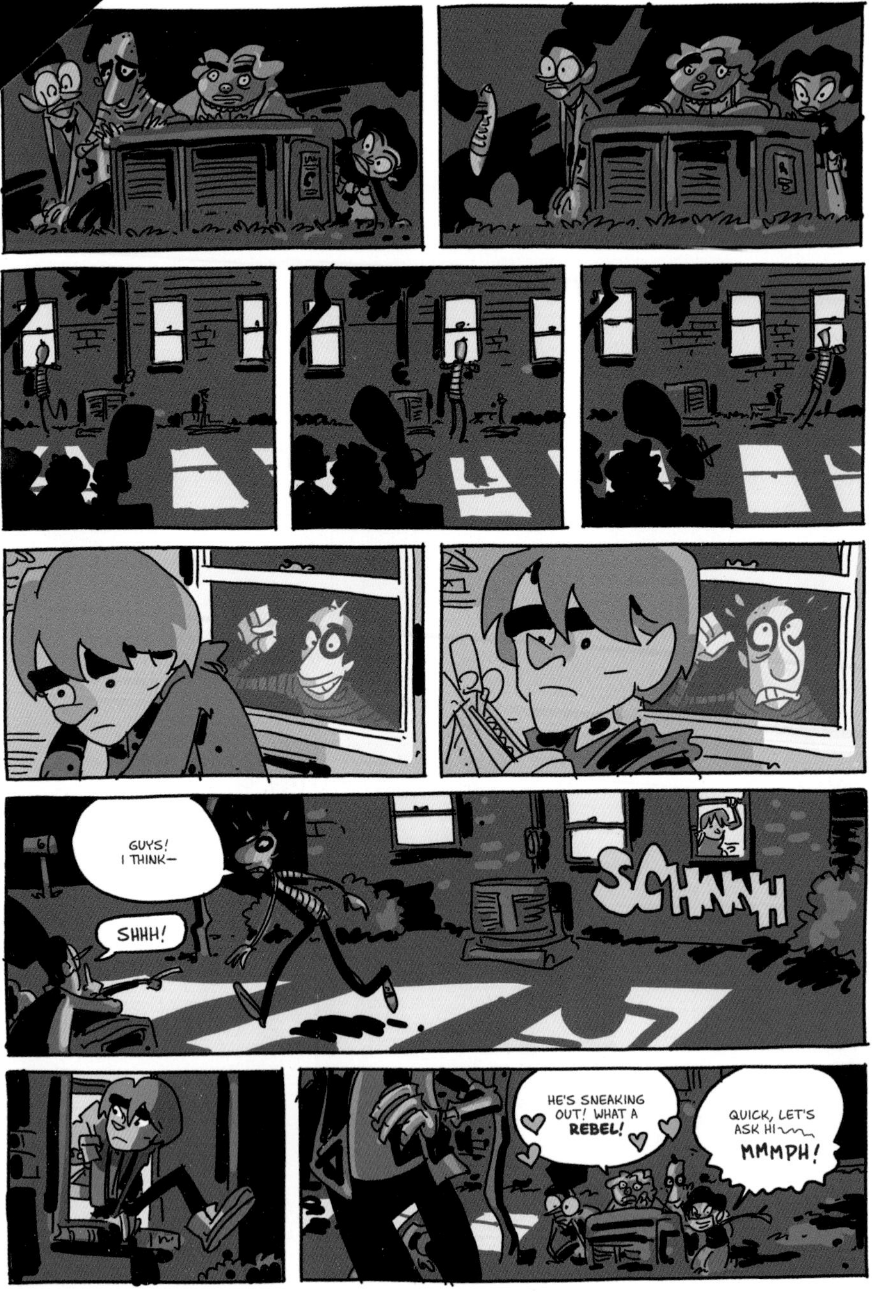
GUYS! I THINK—
SHHH!
SCHNNNH
HE'S SNEAKING OUT! WHAT A REBEL!
QUICK, LET'S ASK HI
MMMPH!

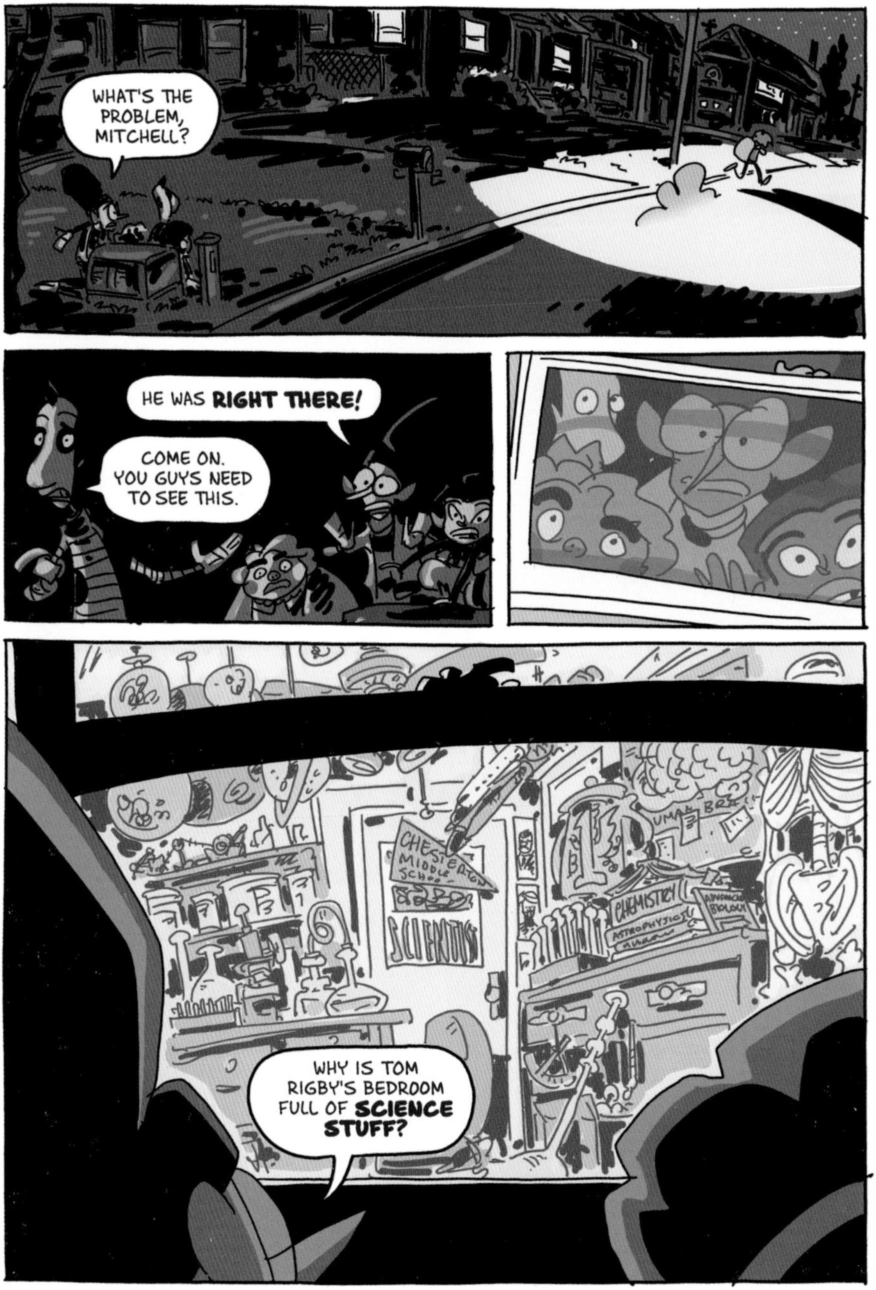
WHAT'S THE PROBLEM, MITCHELL?
HE WAS **RIGHT THERE!**
COME ON. YOU GUYS NEED TO SEE THIS.
CHEMISTRY
WHY IS TOM RIGBY'S BEDROOM FULL OF **SCIENCE STUFF?**

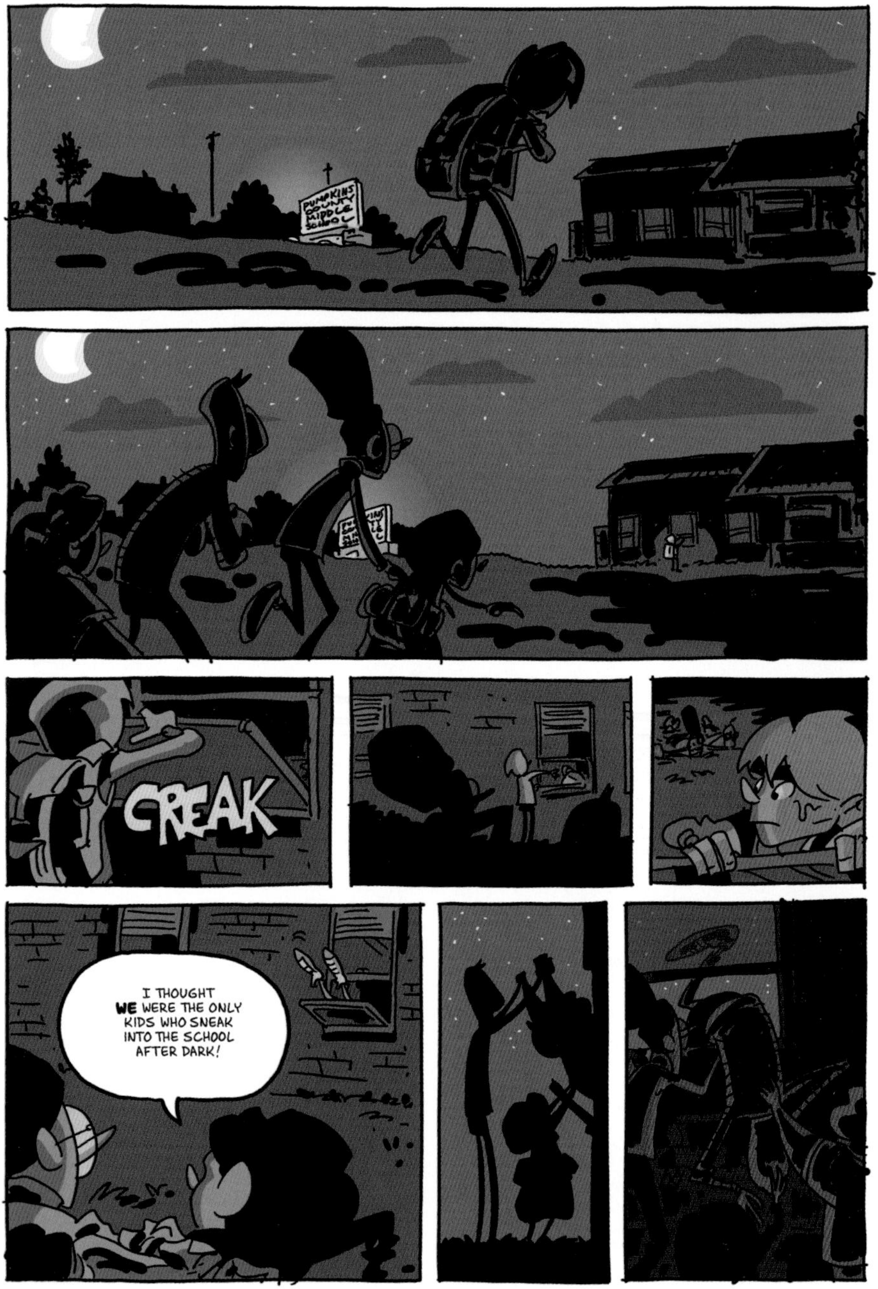
PUMPKINS COUNTY MIDDLE SCHOOL
CREAK
I THOUGHT **WE** WERE THE ONLY KIDS WHO SNEAK INTO THE SCHOOL AFTER DARK!

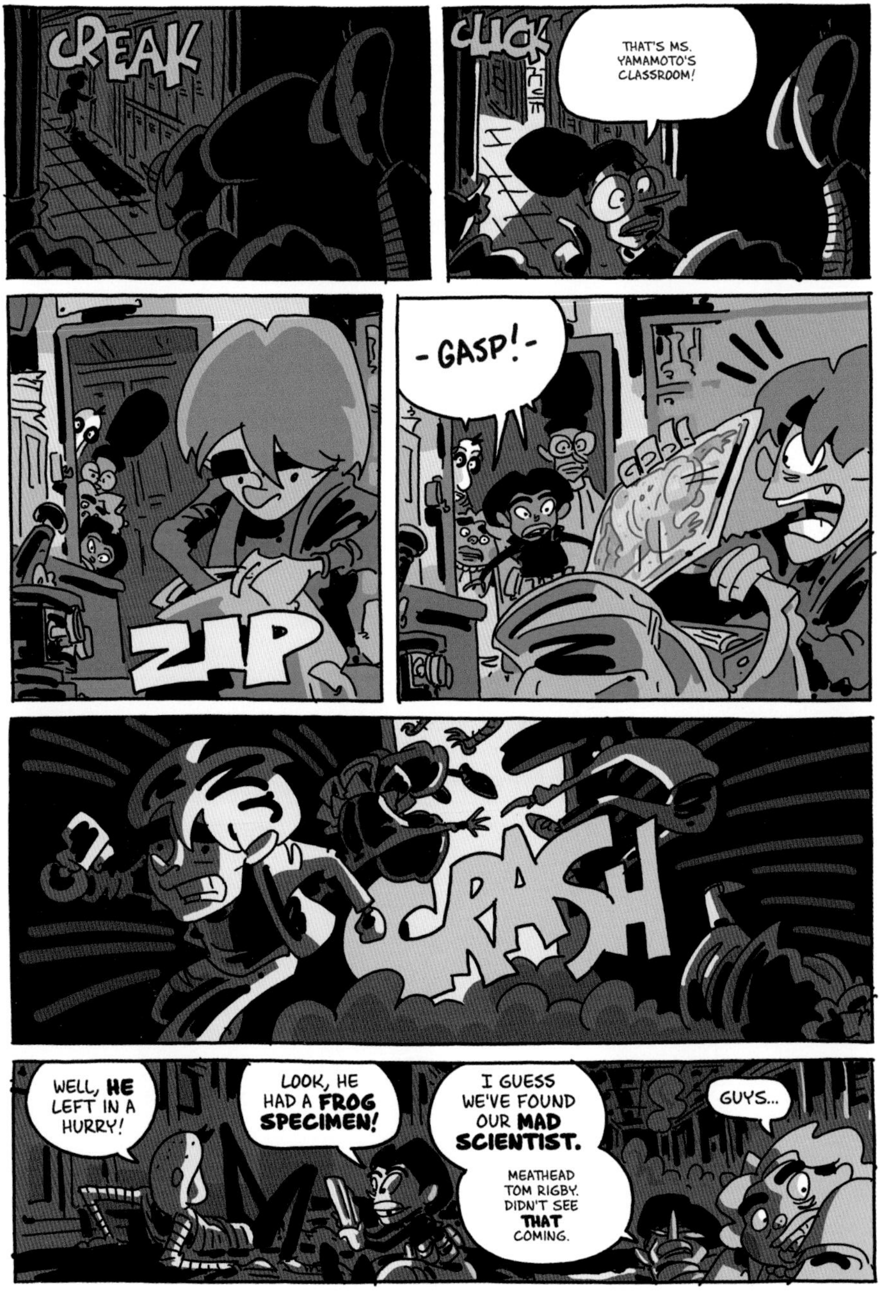
CREAK
CLICK
THAT'S MS. YAMAMOTO'S CLASSROOM!
ZIP
- GASP! -
CRASH
WELL, HE LEFT IN A HURRY!
LOOK, HE HAD A FROG SPECIMEN!
I GUESS WE'VE FOUND OUR MAD SCIENTIST.
MEATHEAD TOM RIGBY. DIDN'T SEE THAT COMING.
GUYS...

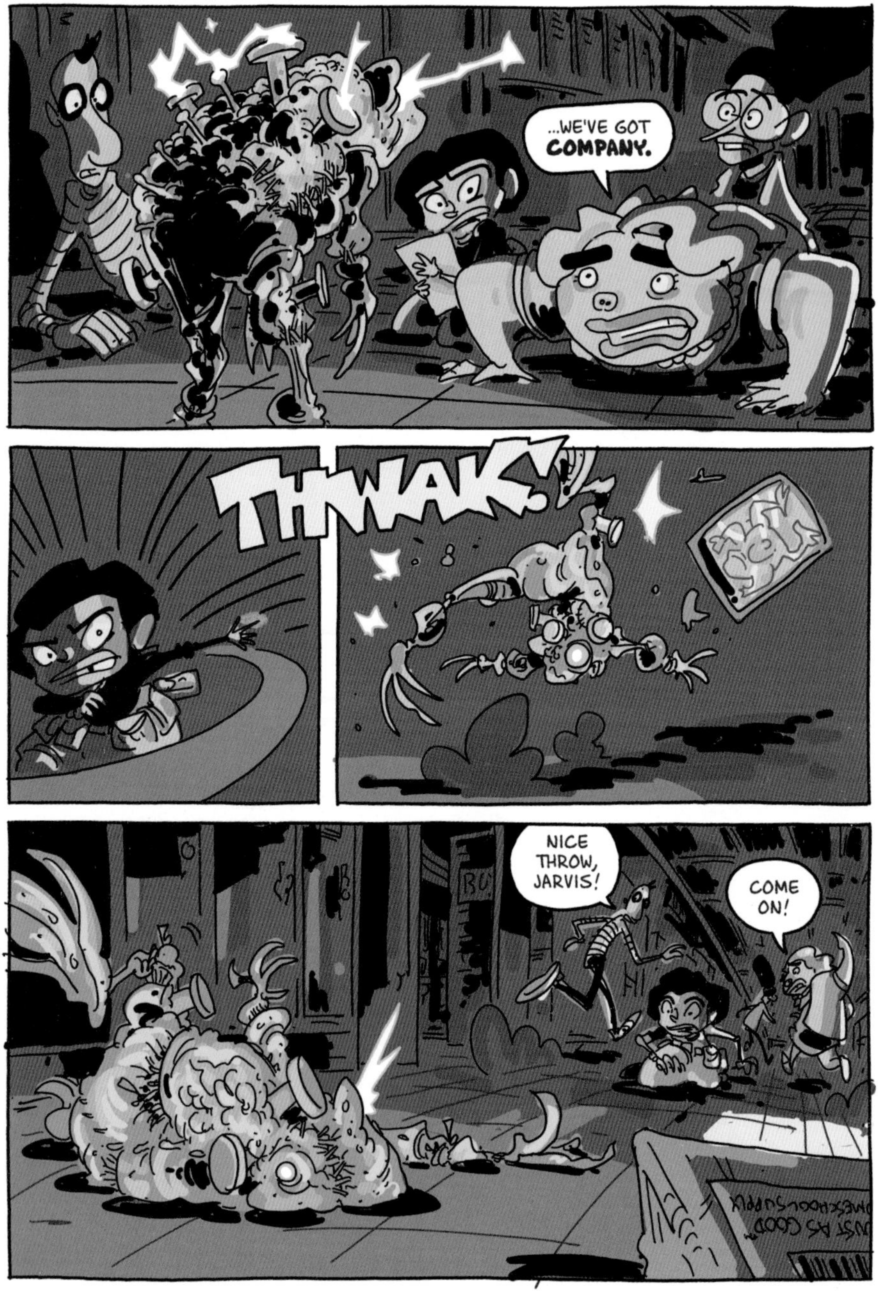
...WE'VE GOT **COMPANY.**
THWAK!
NICE THROW, JARVIS!
COME ON!

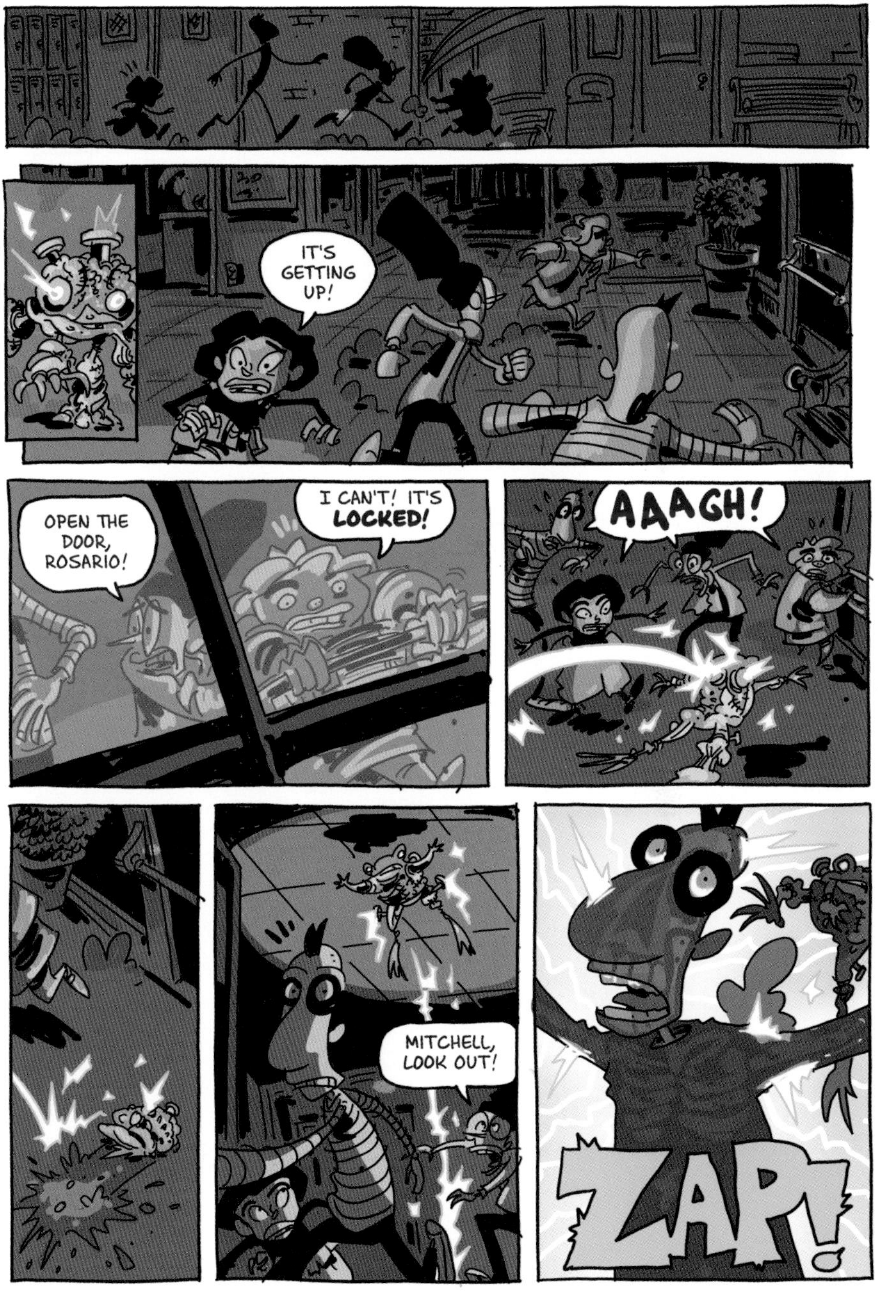
IT'S GETTING UP!
OPEN THE DOOR, ROSARIO!
I CAN'T! IT'S LOCKED!
AAAGH!
MITCHELL, LOOK OUT!
ZAP!

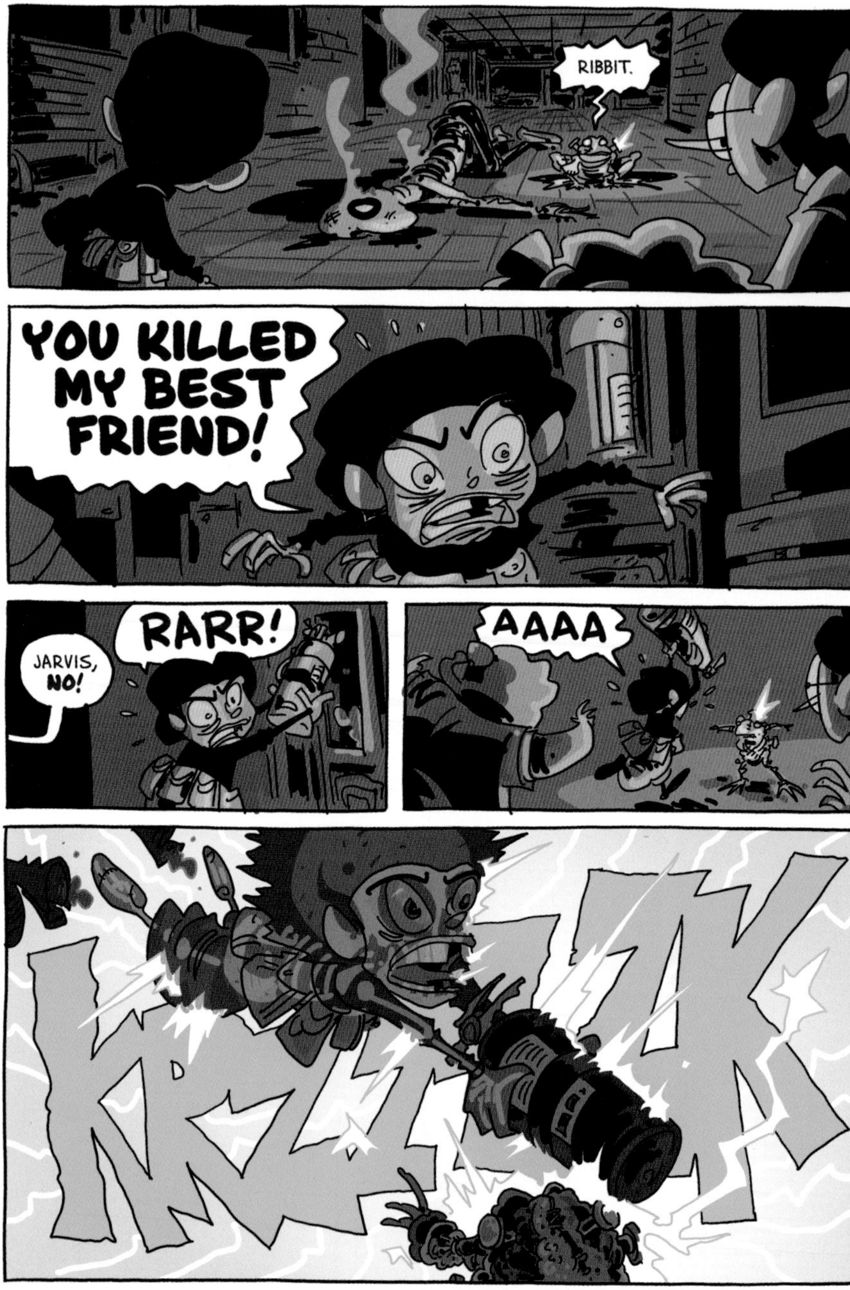
RIBBIT.
YOU KILLED MY BEST FRIEND!
JARVIS, NO!
RARR!
AAAA
KRZZZK

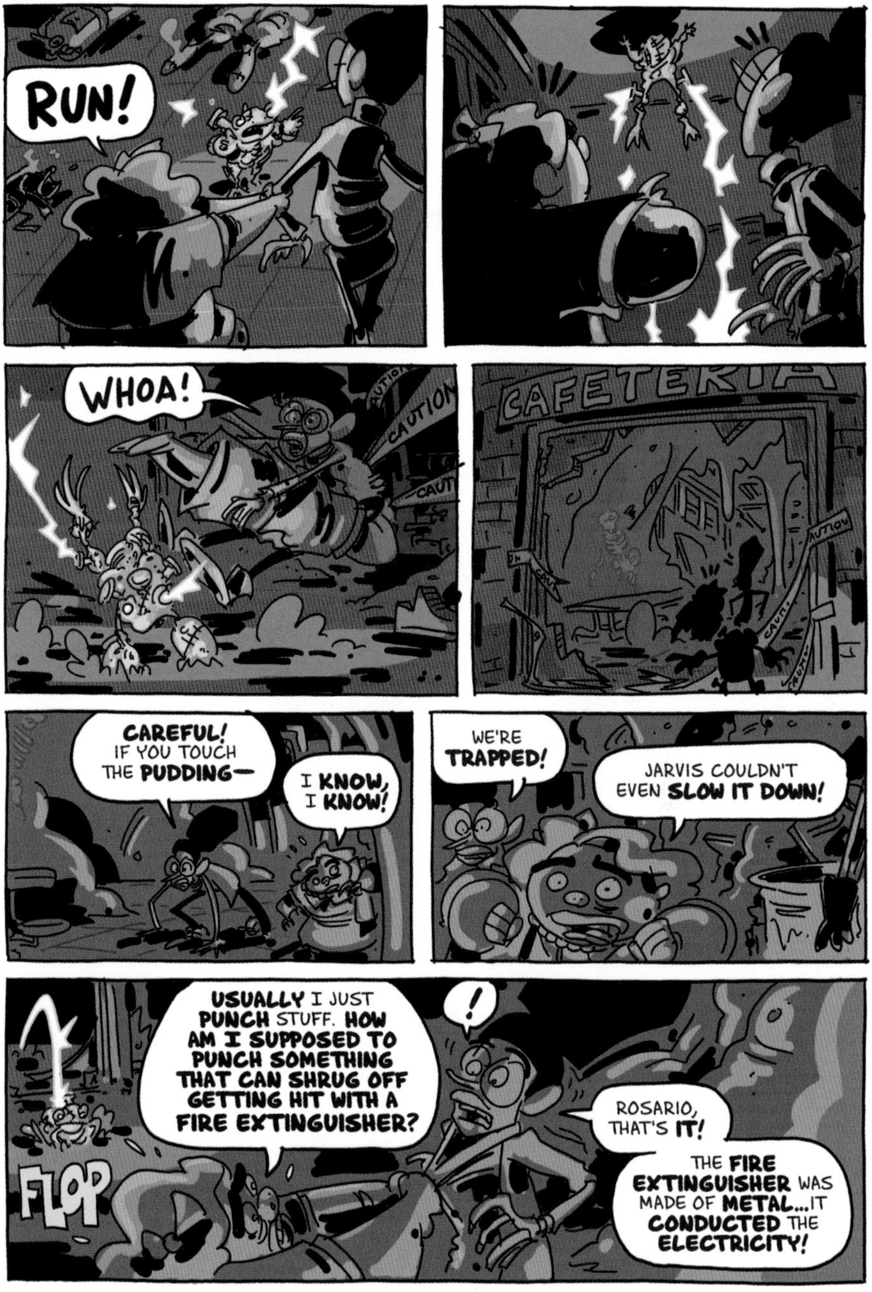
RUN!
WHOA!
CAUTION
CAFETERIA
CAREFUL! IF YOU TOUCH THE PUDDING—
I KNOW, I KNOW!
WE'RE TRAPPED!
JARVIS COULDN'T EVEN SLOW IT DOWN!
USUALLY I JUST PUNCH STUFF. HOW AM I SUPPOSED TO PUNCH SOMETHING THAT CAN SHRUG OFF GETTING HIT WITH A FIRE EXTINGUISHER?
!
ROSARIO, THAT'S IT!
THE FIRE EXTINGUISHER WAS MADE OF METAL...IT CONDUCTED THE ELECTRICITY!
FLOP

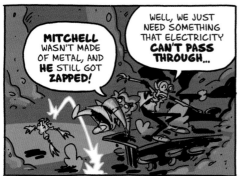

MITCHELL WASN'T MADE OF METAL, AND HE STILL GOT ZAPPED!

WELL, WE JUST NEED SOMETHING THAT ELECTRICITY CAN'T PASS THROUGH...

!

...SOMETHING LIKE MR. PINTO'S RUBBER GLOVES!

CAROL!

USE IT, ROSARIO!

CAROL!

ZAP!

RIBBIT.

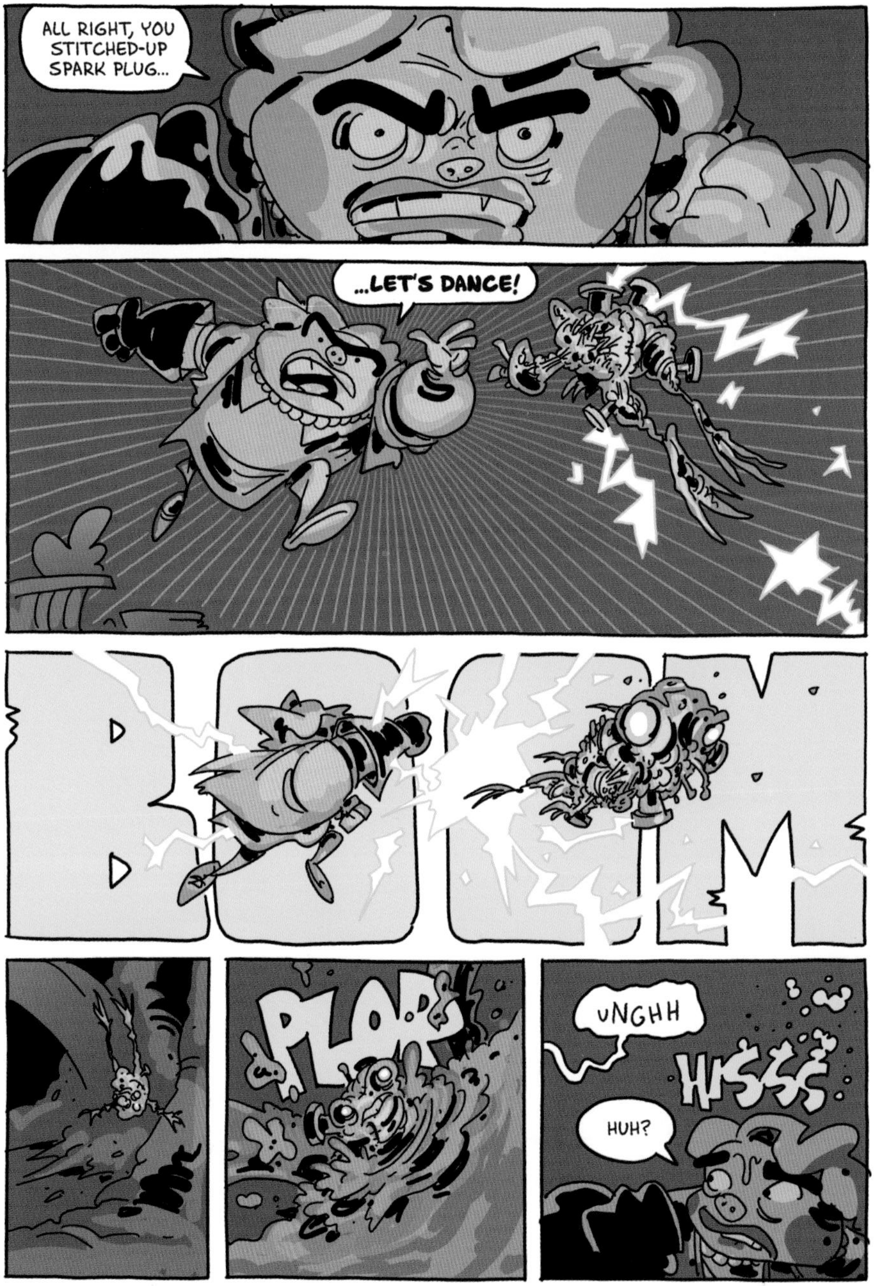
ALL RIGHT, YOU STITCHED-UP SPARK PLUG...
...LET'S DANCE!
BOOM
PLOP
UNGHH
HISSS
HUH?

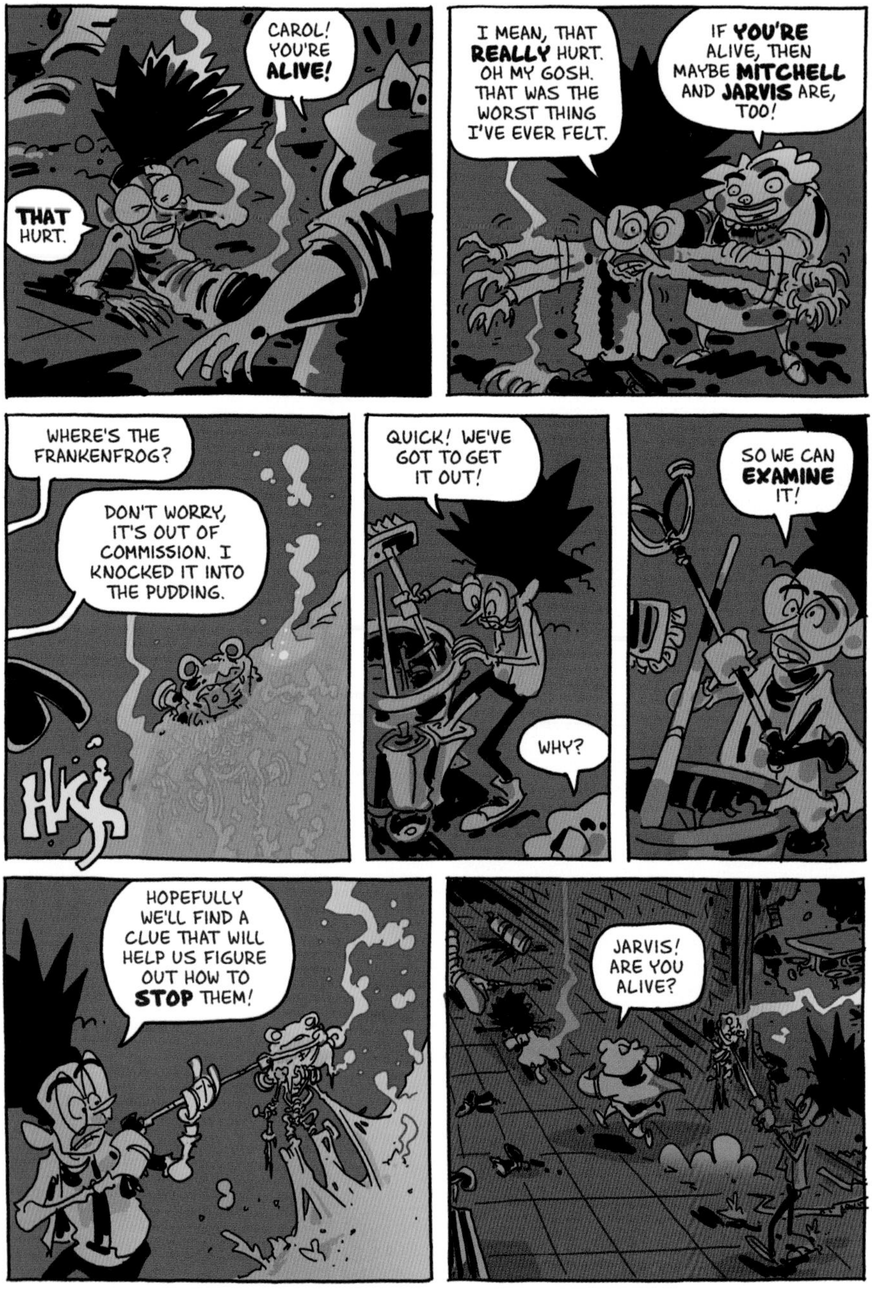
THAT HURT.
CAROL! YOU'RE ALIVE!
I MEAN, THAT REALLY HURT. OH MY GOSH. THAT WAS THE WORST THING I'VE EVER FELT.
IF YOU'RE ALIVE, THEN MAYBE MITCHELL AND JARVIS ARE, TOO!
WHERE'S THE FRANKENFROG?
DON'T WORRY, IT'S OUT OF COMMISSION. I KNOCKED IT INTO THE PUDDING.
QUICK! WE'VE GOT TO GET IT OUT!
WHY?
SO WE CAN EXAMINE IT!
HOPEFULLY WE'LL FIND A CLUE THAT WILL HELP US FIGURE OUT HOW TO STOP THEM!
JARVIS! ARE YOU ALIVE?

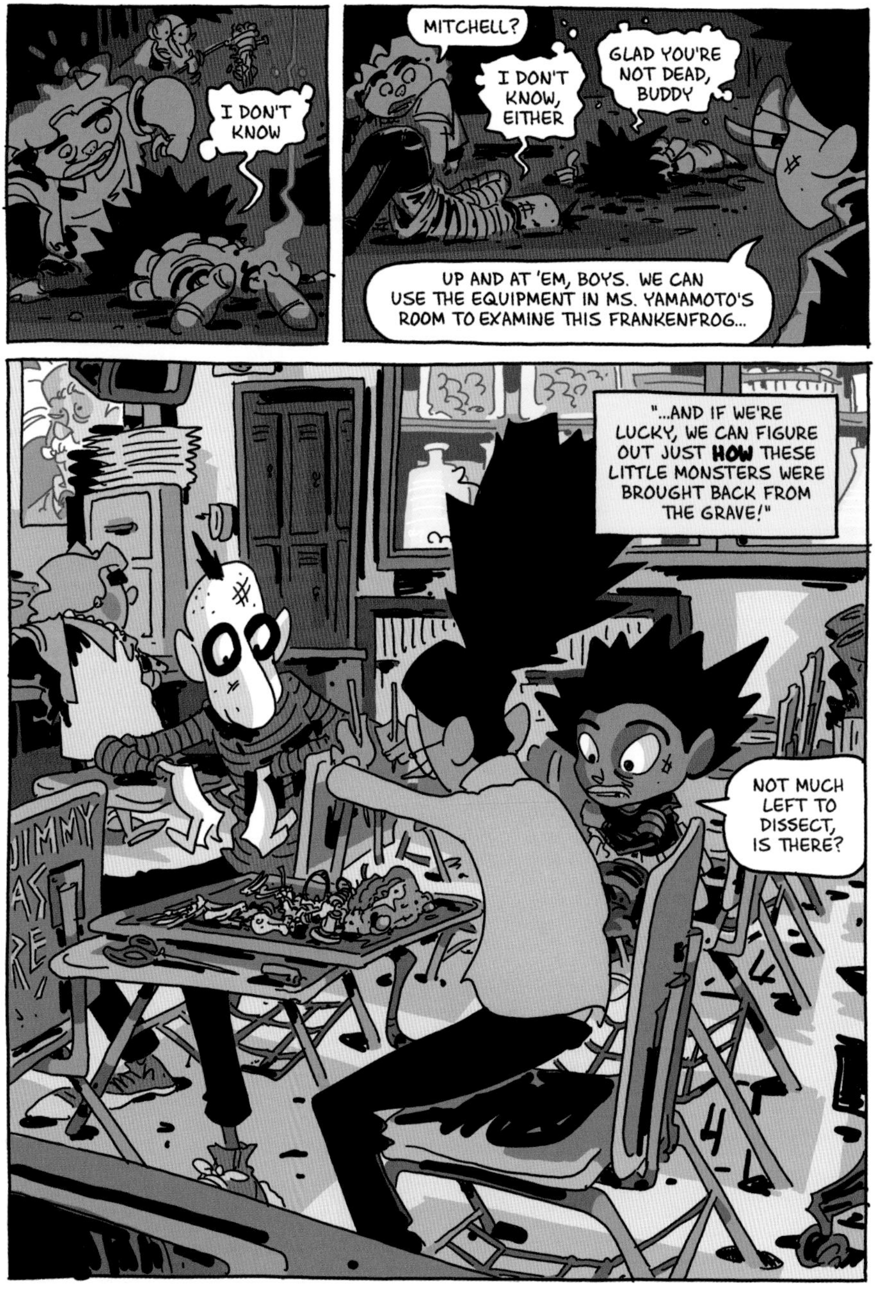
I DON'T KNOW
MITCHELL?
I DON'T KNOW, EITHER
GLAD YOU'RE NOT DEAD, BUDDY
UP AND AT 'EM, BOYS. WE CAN USE THE EQUIPMENT IN MS. YAMAMOTO'S ROOM TO EXAMINE THIS FRANKENFROG...
"...AND IF WE'RE LUCKY, WE CAN FIGURE OUT JUST **HOW** THESE LITTLE MONSTERS WERE BROUGHT BACK FROM THE GRAVE!"
NOT MUCH LEFT TO DISSECT, IS THERE?

THAT DOESN'T MEAN WE CAN'T LEARN FROM WHAT WE STILL HAVE.

LIKE THIS THING. WHAT COULD **IT** BE?

THAT? IT'S A **DYNAMO.**

WHAT'S A DYNAMO?

IT'S A MECHANISM THAT TURNS **ENERGY** INTO **ELECTRICITY.**

I DON'T SEE A BATTERY.

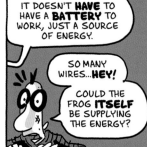

IT DOESN'T **HAVE** TO HAVE A **BATTERY** TO WORK, JUST A SOURCE OF ENERGY.

SO MANY WIRES...**HEY!**

COULD THE FROG **ITSELF** BE SUPPLYING THE ENERGY?

WELL, **SURE,** IF YOU GAVE IT A **JUMP-START** FIRST. THE DYNAMO GIVES THE FROG **LIFE,** AND THE FROG'S ENERGY POWERS THE **DYNAMO,** WHICH KEEPS THE FROG **ALIVE,** WHICH POWERS THE **DYNAMO,** ON AND ON!

RAD.

YOU KNOW, THESE STITCHES SURE ARE **WEIRD-LOOKING.**

THAT'S BECAUSE THEY'RE HOLDING TOGETHER A BUNCH OF DEAD **FROG BITS.**

NO, THEY'RE...

YARNY.

SNIP

ROSARIO, **YOU** KNOW FABRIC LIKE NOBODY ELSE. TAKE A LOOK AT THIS.

OH, **NOW** YOU WANT MY FASHION EXPERTISE? I THOUGHT I WAS JUST AROUND TO **PUNCH** STUFF.

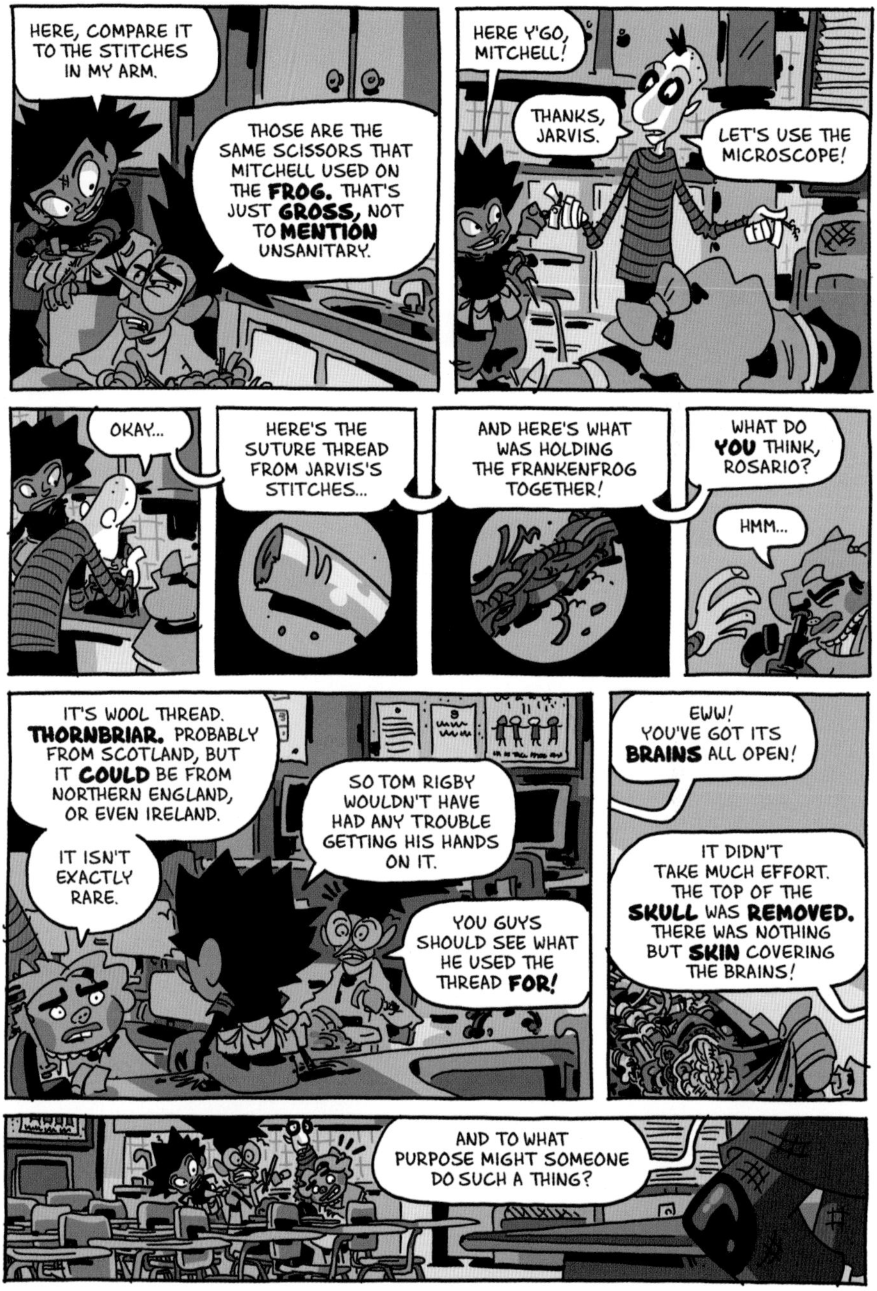
HERE, COMPARE IT TO THE STITCHES IN MY ARM.
THOSE ARE THE SAME SCISSORS THAT MITCHELL USED ON THE FROG. THAT'S JUST GROSS, NOT TO MENTION UNSANITARY.
HERE Y'GO, MITCHELL!
THANKS, JARVIS.
LET'S USE THE MICROSCOPE!
OKAY...
HERE'S THE SUTURE THREAD FROM JARVIS'S STITCHES...
AND HERE'S WHAT WAS HOLDING THE FRANKENFROG TOGETHER!
WHAT DO YOU THINK, ROSARIO?
HMM...
IT'S WOOL THREAD. THORNBRIAR. PROBABLY FROM SCOTLAND, BUT IT COULD BE FROM NORTHERN ENGLAND, OR EVEN IRELAND.
IT ISN'T EXACTLY RARE.
SO TOM RIGBY WOULDN'T HAVE HAD ANY TROUBLE GETTING HIS HANDS ON IT.
YOU GUYS SHOULD SEE WHAT HE USED THE THREAD FOR!
EWW! YOU'VE GOT ITS BRAINS ALL OPEN!
IT DIDN'T TAKE MUCH EFFORT. THE TOP OF THE SKULL WAS REMOVED. THERE WAS NOTHING BUT SKIN COVERING THE BRAINS!
AND TO WHAT PURPOSE MIGHT SOMEONE DO SUCH A THING?

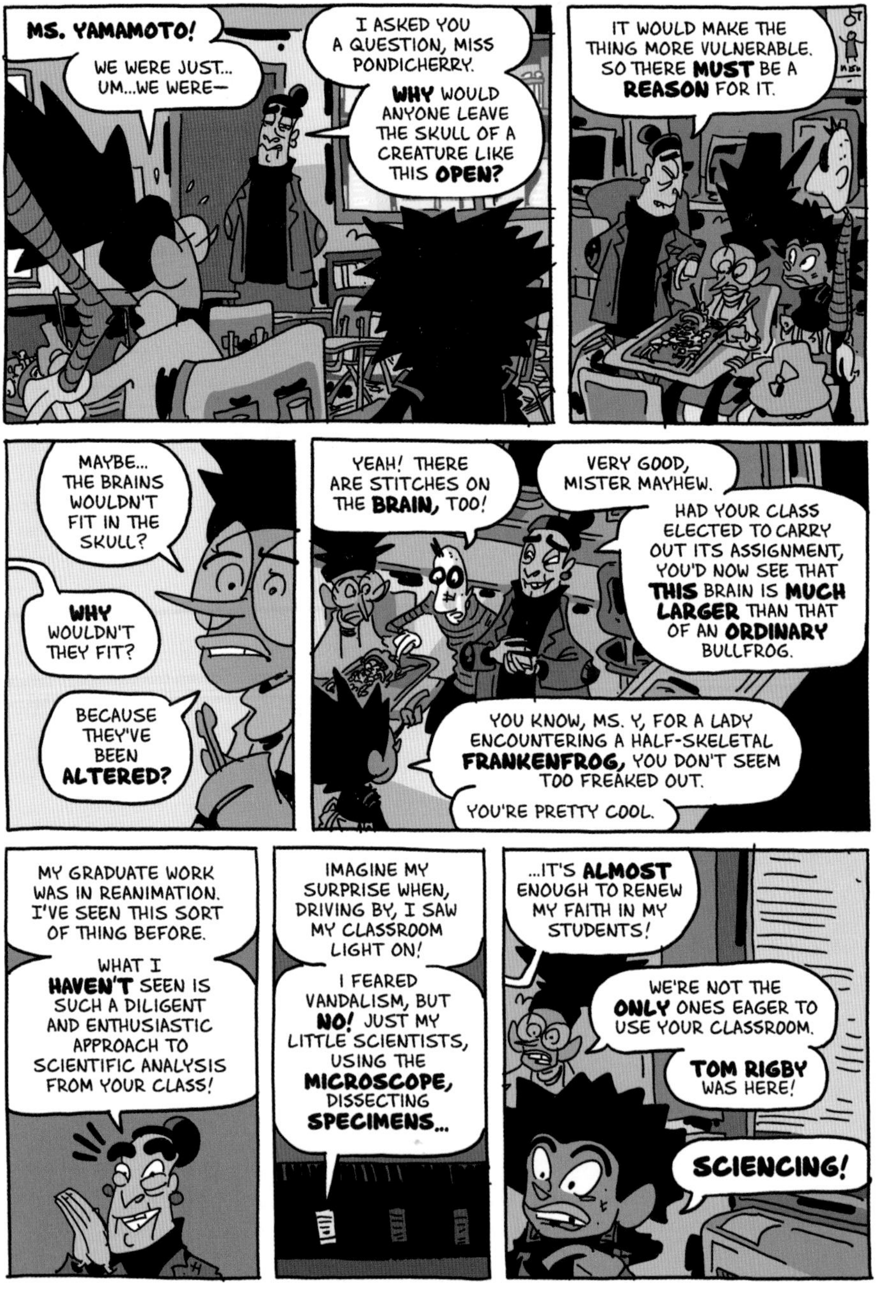
MS. YAMAMOTO!
WE WERE JUST... UM...WE WERE—
I ASKED YOU A QUESTION, MISS PONDICHERRY.
WHY WOULD ANYONE LEAVE THE SKULL OF A CREATURE LIKE THIS OPEN?
IT WOULD MAKE THE THING MORE VULNERABLE. SO THERE MUST BE A REASON FOR IT.
MAYBE... THE BRAINS WOULDN'T FIT IN THE SKULL?
WHY WOULDN'T THEY FIT?
BECAUSE THEY'VE BEEN ALTERED?
YEAH! THERE ARE STITCHES ON THE BRAIN, TOO!
VERY GOOD, MISTER MAYHEW.
HAD YOUR CLASS ELECTED TO CARRY OUT ITS ASSIGNMENT, YOU'D NOW SEE THAT THIS BRAIN IS MUCH LARGER THAN THAT OF AN ORDINARY BULLFROG.
YOU KNOW, MS. Y, FOR A LADY ENCOUNTERING A HALF-SKELETAL FRANKENFROG, YOU DON'T SEEM TOO FREAKED OUT.
YOU'RE PRETTY COOL.
MY GRADUATE WORK WAS IN REANIMATION. I'VE SEEN THIS SORT OF THING BEFORE.
WHAT I HAVEN'T SEEN IS SUCH A DILIGENT AND ENTHUSIASTIC APPROACH TO SCIENTIFIC ANALYSIS FROM YOUR CLASS!
IMAGINE MY SURPRISE WHEN, DRIVING BY, I SAW MY CLASSROOM LIGHT ON!
I FEARED VANDALISM, BUT NO! JUST MY LITTLE SCIENTISTS, USING THE MICROSCOPE, DISSECTING SPECIMENS...
...IT'S ALMOST ENOUGH TO RENEW MY FAITH IN MY STUDENTS!
WE'RE NOT THE ONLY ONES EAGER TO USE YOUR CLASSROOM.
TOM RIGBY WAS HERE!
SCIENCING!

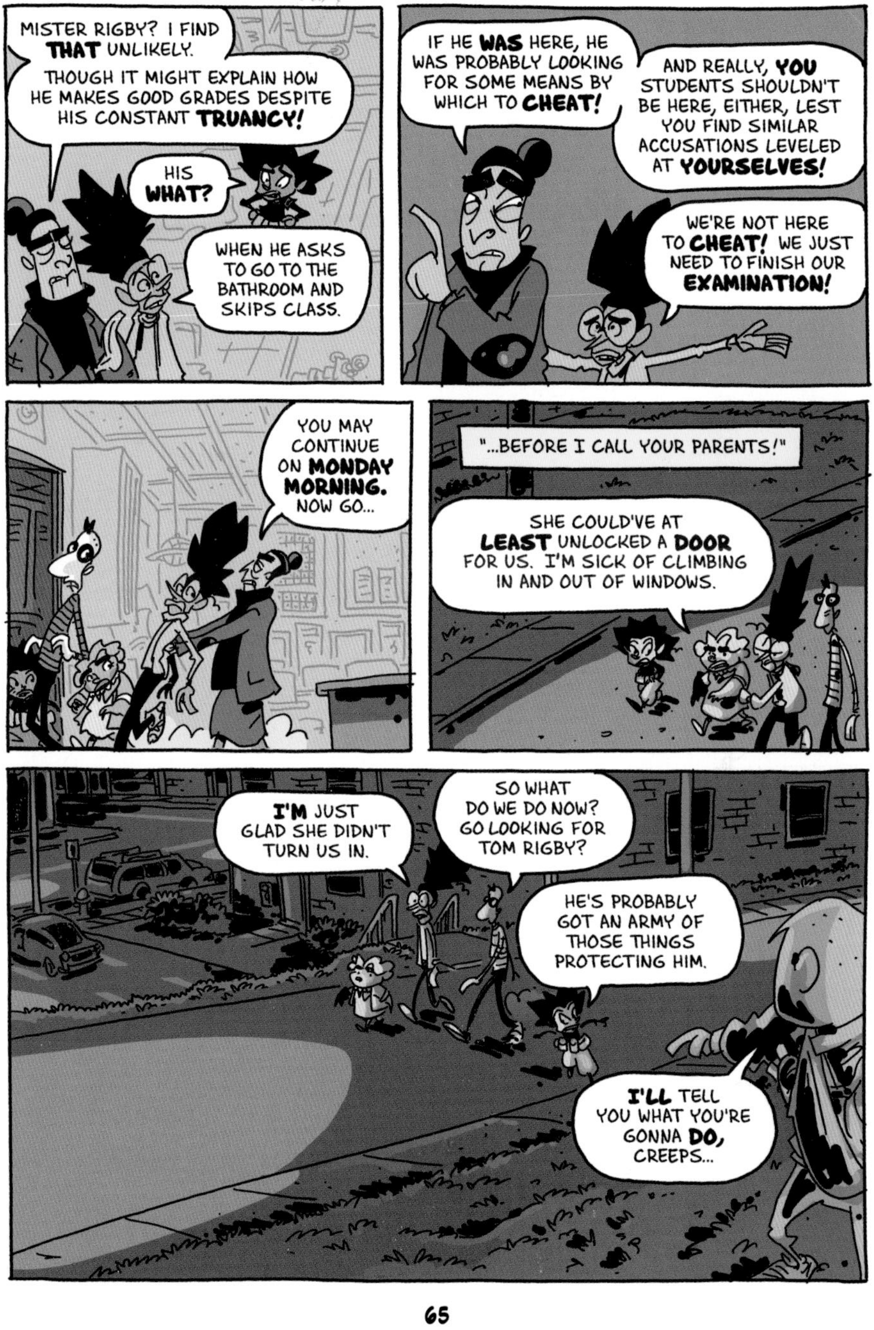
MISTER RIGBY? I FIND **THAT** UNLIKELY.
THOUGH IT MIGHT EXPLAIN HOW HE MAKES GOOD GRADES DESPITE HIS CONSTANT **TRUANCY!**
HIS **WHAT?**
WHEN HE ASKS TO GO TO THE BATHROOM AND SKIPS CLASS.
IF HE **WAS** HERE, HE WAS PROBABLY LOOKING FOR SOME MEANS BY WHICH TO **CHEAT!**
AND REALLY, **YOU** STUDENTS SHOULDN'T BE HERE, EITHER, LEST YOU FIND SIMILAR ACCUSATIONS LEVELED AT **YOURSELVES!**
WE'RE NOT HERE TO **CHEAT!** WE JUST NEED TO FINISH OUR **EXAMINATION!**
YOU MAY CONTINUE ON **MONDAY MORNING.** NOW GO...
"...BEFORE I CALL YOUR PARENTS!"
SHE COULD'VE AT **LEAST** UNLOCKED A **DOOR** FOR US. I'M SICK OF CLIMBING IN AND OUT OF WINDOWS.
I'M JUST GLAD SHE DIDN'T TURN US IN.
SO WHAT DO WE DO NOW? GO LOOKING FOR TOM RIGBY?
HE'S PROBABLY GOT AN ARMY OF THOSE THINGS PROTECTING HIM.
I'LL TELL YOU WHAT YOU'RE GONNA **DO,** CREEPS...

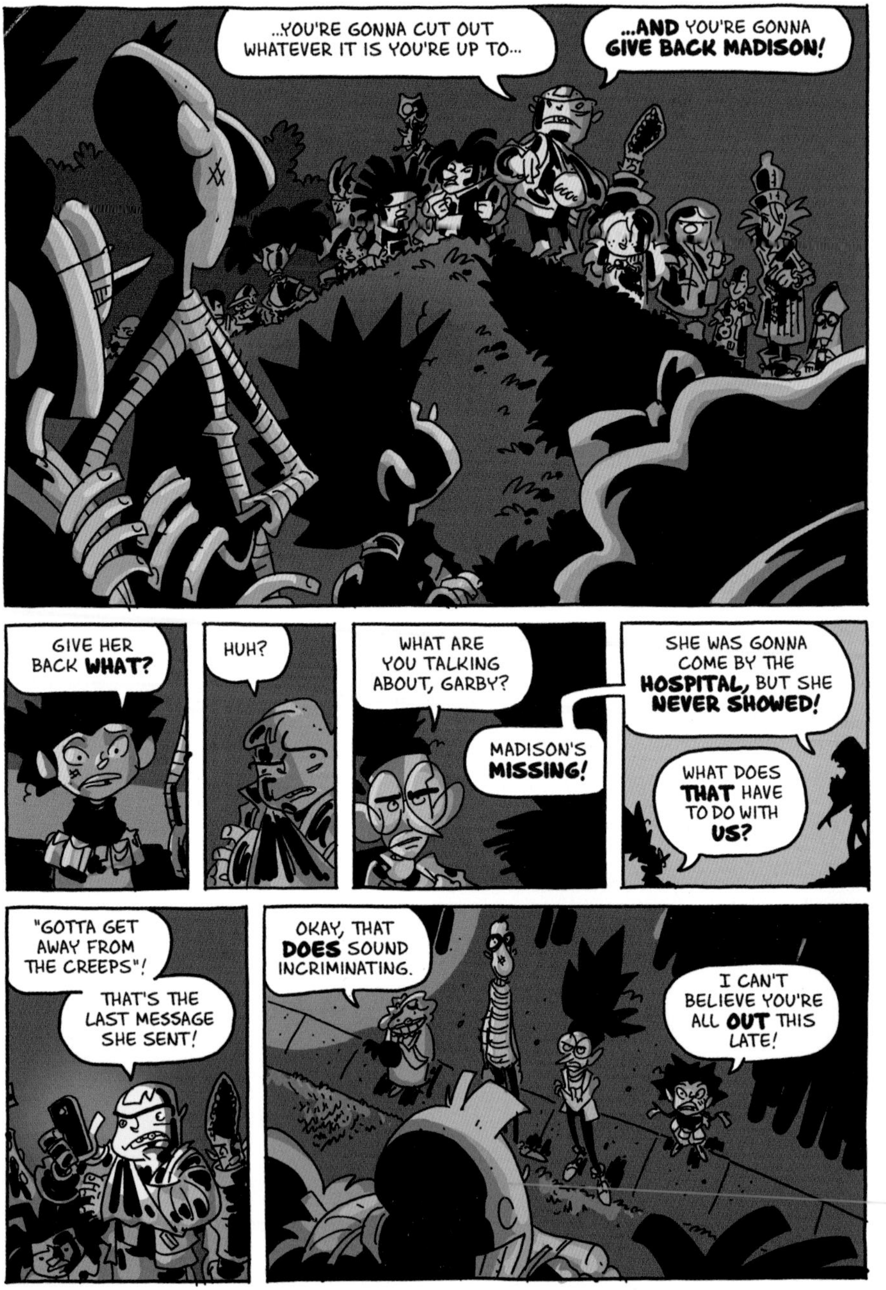
...YOU'RE GONNA CUT OUT WHATEVER IT IS YOU'RE UP TO...
...AND YOU'RE GONNA GIVE BACK MADISON!
GIVE HER BACK WHAT?
HUH?
WHAT ARE YOU TALKING ABOUT, GARBY?
MADISON'S MISSING!
SHE WAS GONNA COME BY THE HOSPITAL, BUT SHE NEVER SHOWED!
WHAT DOES THAT HAVE TO DO WITH US?
"GOTTA GET AWAY FROM THE CREEPS"!
THAT'S THE LAST MESSAGE SHE SENT!
OKAY, THAT DOES SOUND INCRIMINATING.
I CAN'T BELIEVE YOU'RE ALL OUT THIS LATE!

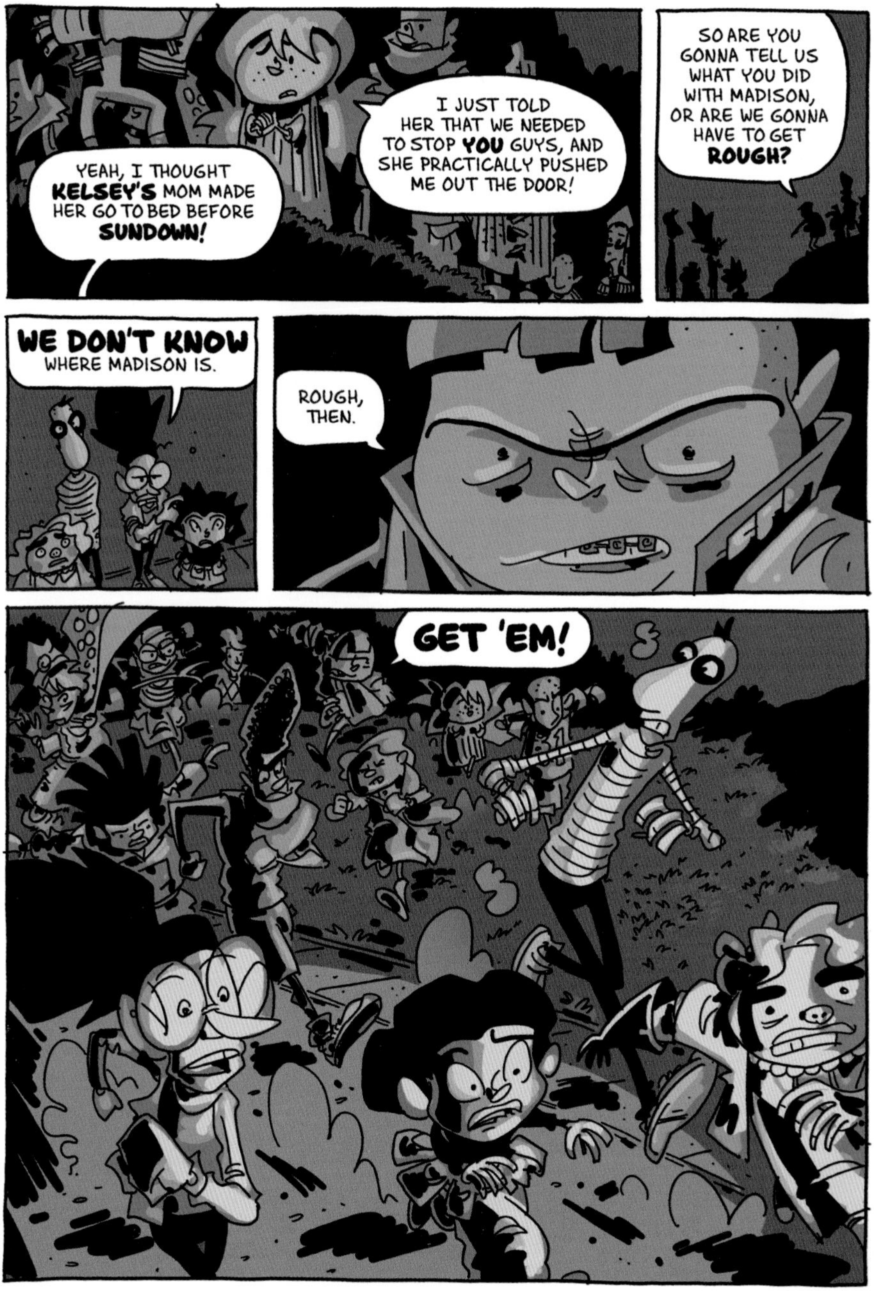
YEAH, I THOUGHT KELSEY'S MOM MADE HER GO TO BED BEFORE SUNDOWN!
I JUST TOLD HER THAT WE NEEDED TO STOP YOU GUYS, AND SHE PRACTICALLY PUSHED ME OUT THE DOOR!
SO ARE YOU GONNA TELL US WHAT YOU DID WITH MADISON, OR ARE WE GONNA HAVE TO GET ROUGH?
WE DON'T KNOW WHERE MADISON IS.
ROUGH, THEN.
GET 'EM!

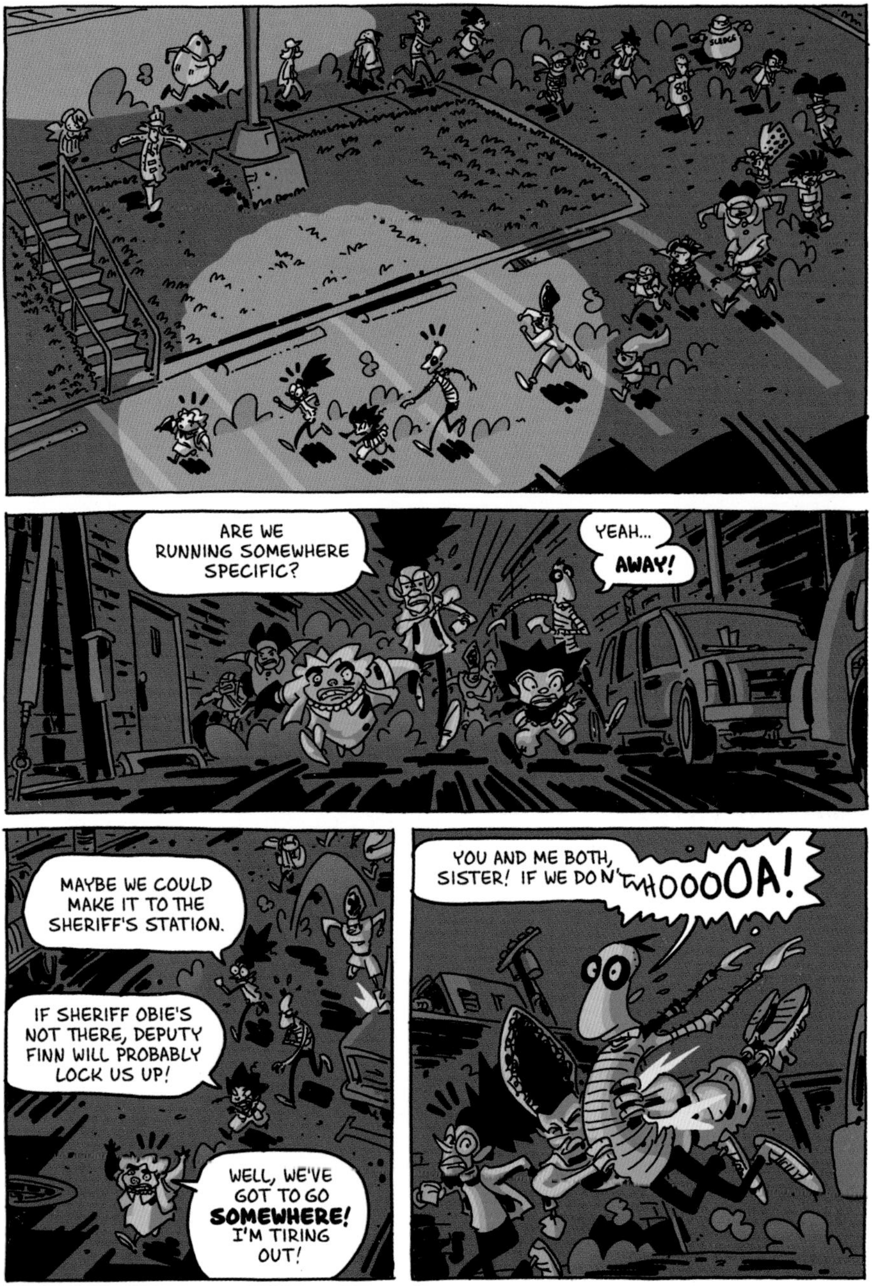
ARE WE RUNNING SOMEWHERE SPECIFIC?
YEAH... AWAY!
MAYBE WE COULD MAKE IT TO THE SHERIFF'S STATION.
IF SHERIFF OBIE'S NOT THERE, DEPUTY FINN WILL PROBABLY LOCK US UP!
WELL, WE'VE GOT TO GO SOMEWHERE! I'M TIRING OUT!
YOU AND ME BOTH, SISTER! IF WE DON'T
WHOOOOA!

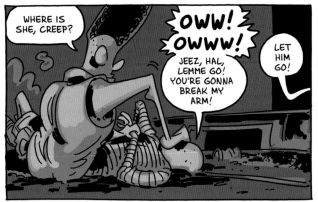

WHERE IS SHE, CREEP?

OWW! OWWW!

JEEZ, HAL, LEMME GO! YOU'RE GONNA BREAK MY ARM!

LET HIM GO!

WE'LL LET **YOU** GO WHEN **YOU** LET **MADISON** GO!

WE **DON'T HAVE HER!**

MAYBE WE NEED TO ASK A LITTLE **HARDER!**

OW! OW!

FRANKENFROGS! FRANKENFROGS!

WHAT'S HE YELLING ABOUT?

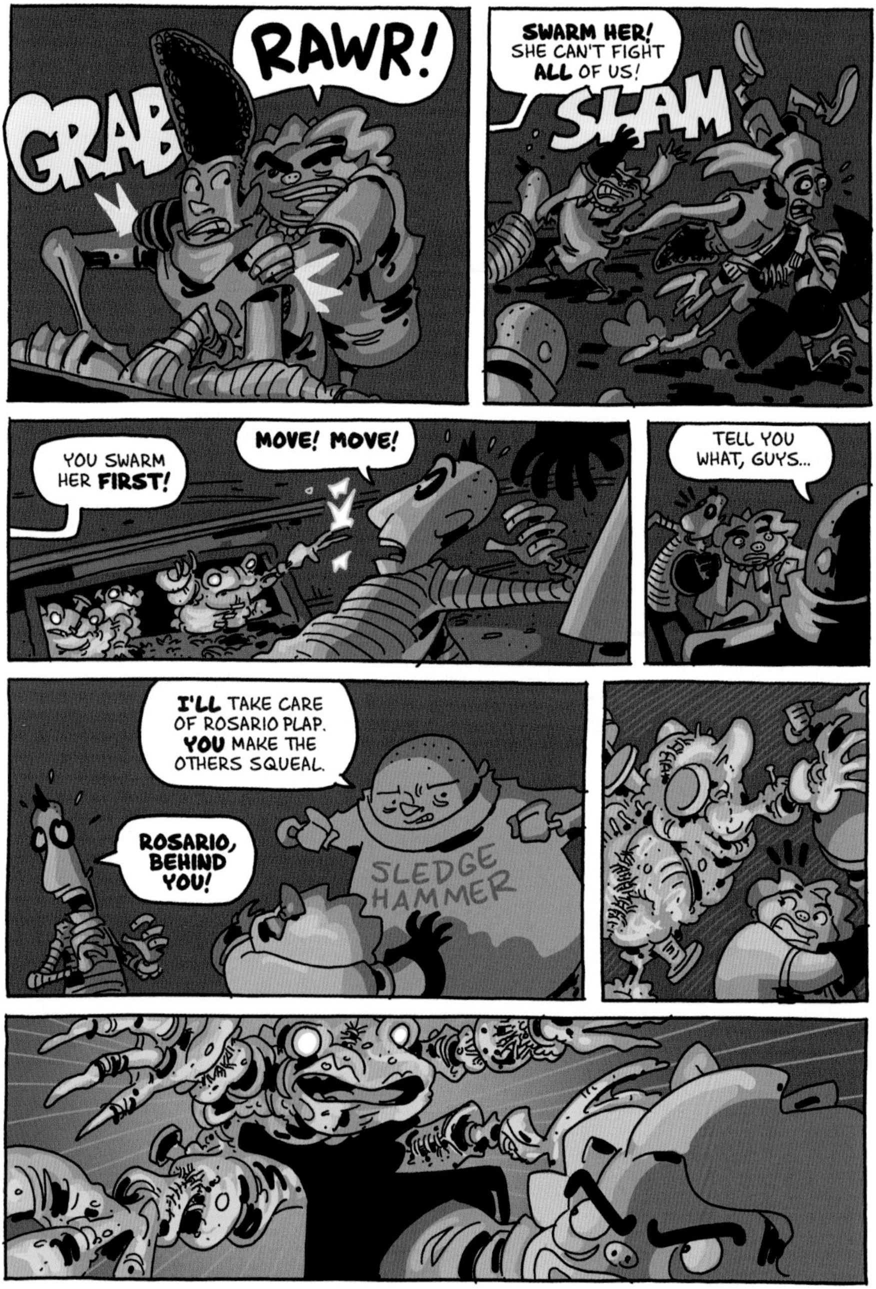
GRAB
RAWR!
SWARM HER! SHE CAN'T FIGHT ALL OF US!
SLAM
YOU SWARM HER FIRST!
MOVE! MOVE!
TELL YOU WHAT, GUYS...
I'LL TAKE CARE OF ROSARIO PLAP. YOU MAKE THE OTHERS SQUEAL.
ROSARIO, BEHIND YOU!
SLEDGE HAMMER

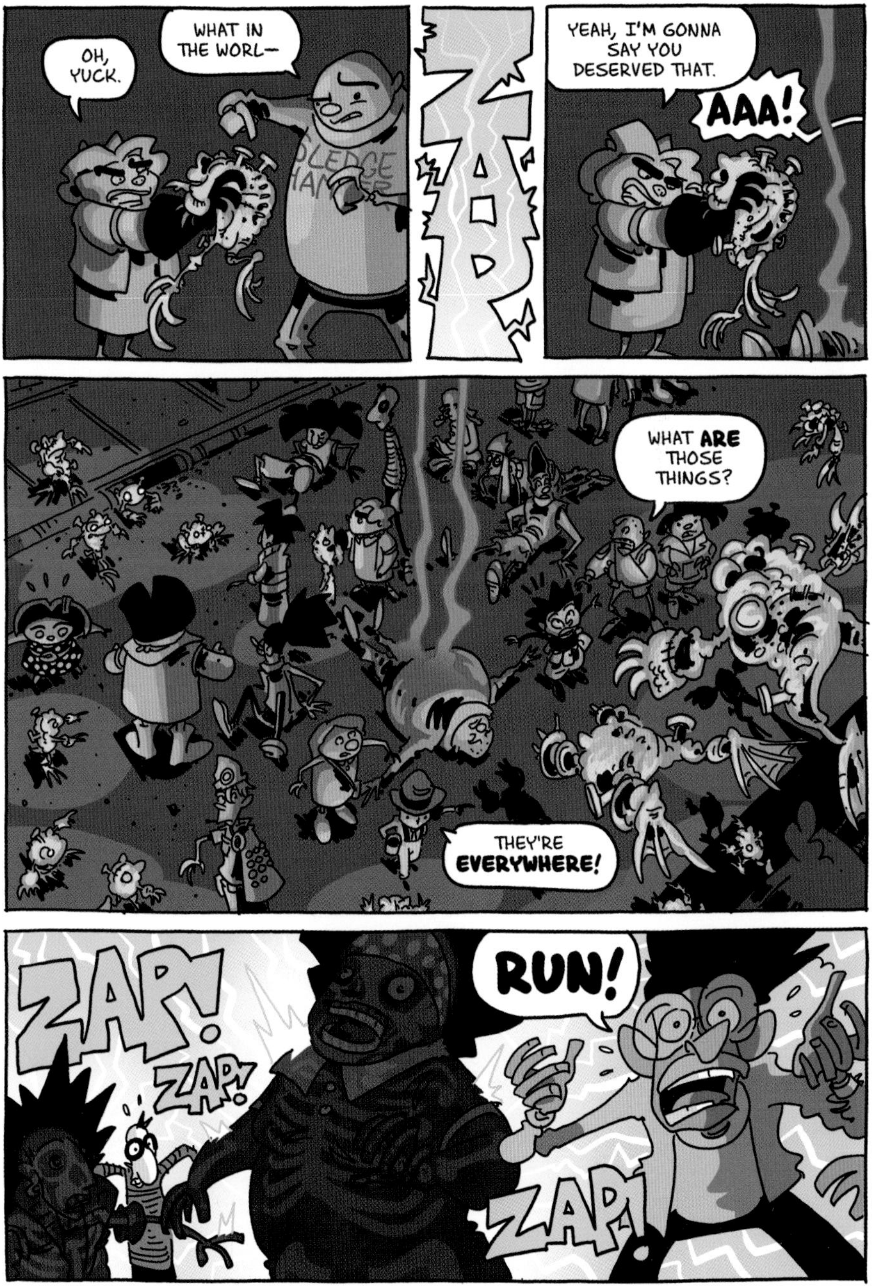

OH, YUCK.
WHAT IN THE WORL—
SLEDGE HAMMER
ZAP!
YEAH, I'M GONNA SAY YOU DESERVED THAT.
AAA!
WHAT **ARE** THOSE THINGS?
THEY'RE **EVERYWHERE!**
ZAP!
ZAP!
RUN!
ZAP!

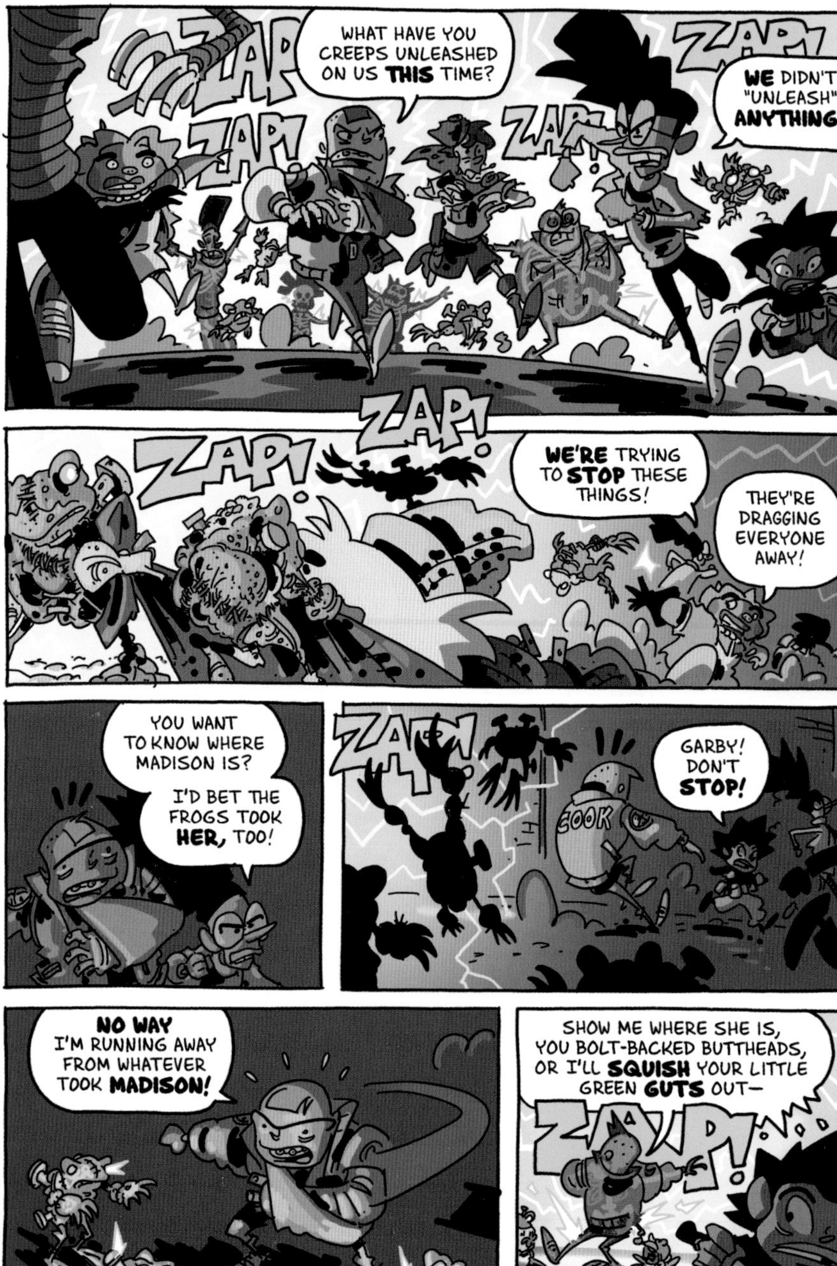
ZAP!
WHAT HAVE YOU CREEPS UNLEASHED ON US THIS TIME?
ZAP!
ZAP!
ZAP!
WE DIDN'T "UNLEASH" ANYTHING!
ZAP!
ZAP!
ZAP!
WE'RE TRYING TO STOP THESE THINGS!
THEY'RE DRAGGING EVERYONE AWAY!
YOU WANT TO KNOW WHERE MADISON IS?
I'D BET THE FROGS TOOK HER, TOO!
ZAP!
GARBY! DON'T STOP!
COOK
NO WAY I'M RUNNING AWAY FROM WHATEVER TOOK MADISON!
SHOW ME WHERE SHE IS, YOU BOLT-BACKED BUTTHEADS, OR I'LL SQUISH YOUR LITTLE GREEN GUTS OUT—
ZAP!...

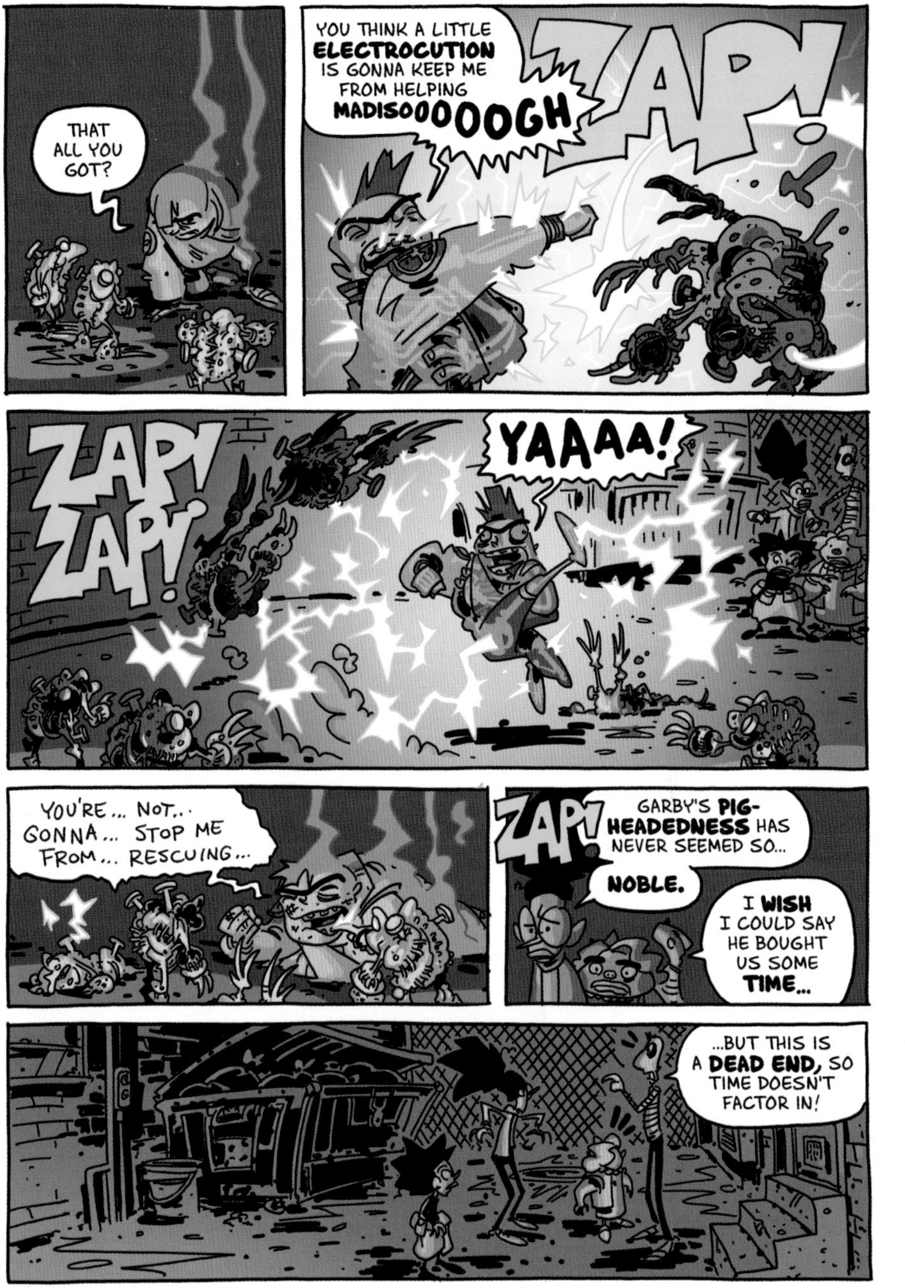
THAT ALL YOU GOT?
YOU THINK A LITTLE ELECTROCUTION IS GONNA KEEP ME FROM HELPING MADISOOOOOGH
ZAP!
ZAP! ZAP!
YAAAA!
YOU'RE... NOT... GONNA... STOP ME FROM... RESCUING...
ZAP!
GARBY'S PIG-HEADEDNESS HAS NEVER SEEMED SO...
NOBLE.
I WISH I COULD SAY HE BOUGHT US SOME TIME...
...BUT THIS IS A DEAD END, SO TIME DOESN'T FACTOR IN!

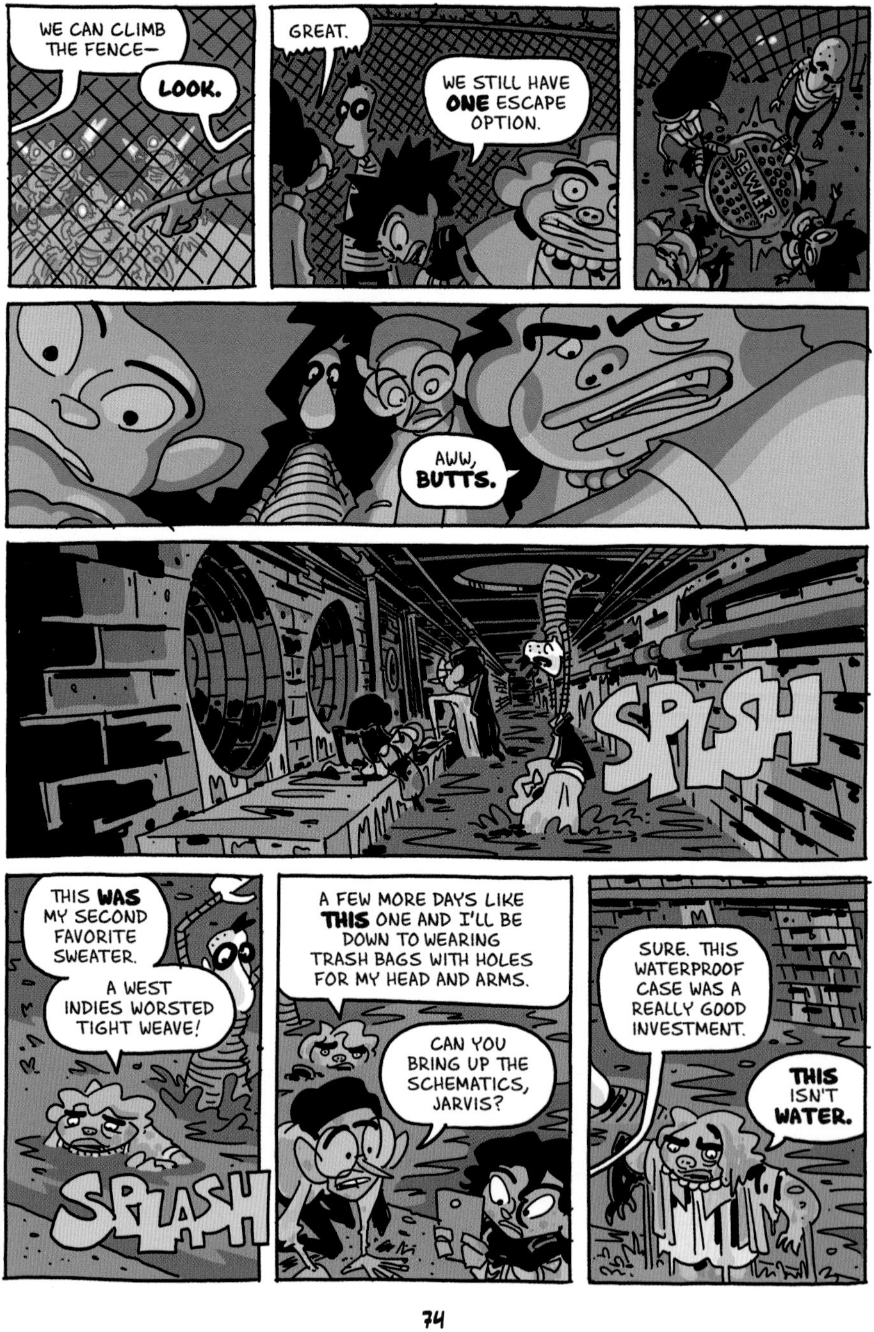
WE CAN CLIMB THE FENCE—
LOOK.
GREAT.
WE STILL HAVE ONE ESCAPE OPTION.
SEWER
AWW, BUTTS.
SPLASH
THIS WAS MY SECOND FAVORITE SWEATER.
A WEST INDIES WORSTED TIGHT WEAVE!
SPLASH
A FEW MORE DAYS LIKE THIS ONE AND I'LL BE DOWN TO WEARING TRASH BAGS WITH HOLES FOR MY HEAD AND ARMS.
CAN YOU BRING UP THE SCHEMATICS, JARVIS?
SURE. THIS WATERPROOF CASE WAS A REALLY GOOD INVESTMENT.
THIS ISN'T WATER.

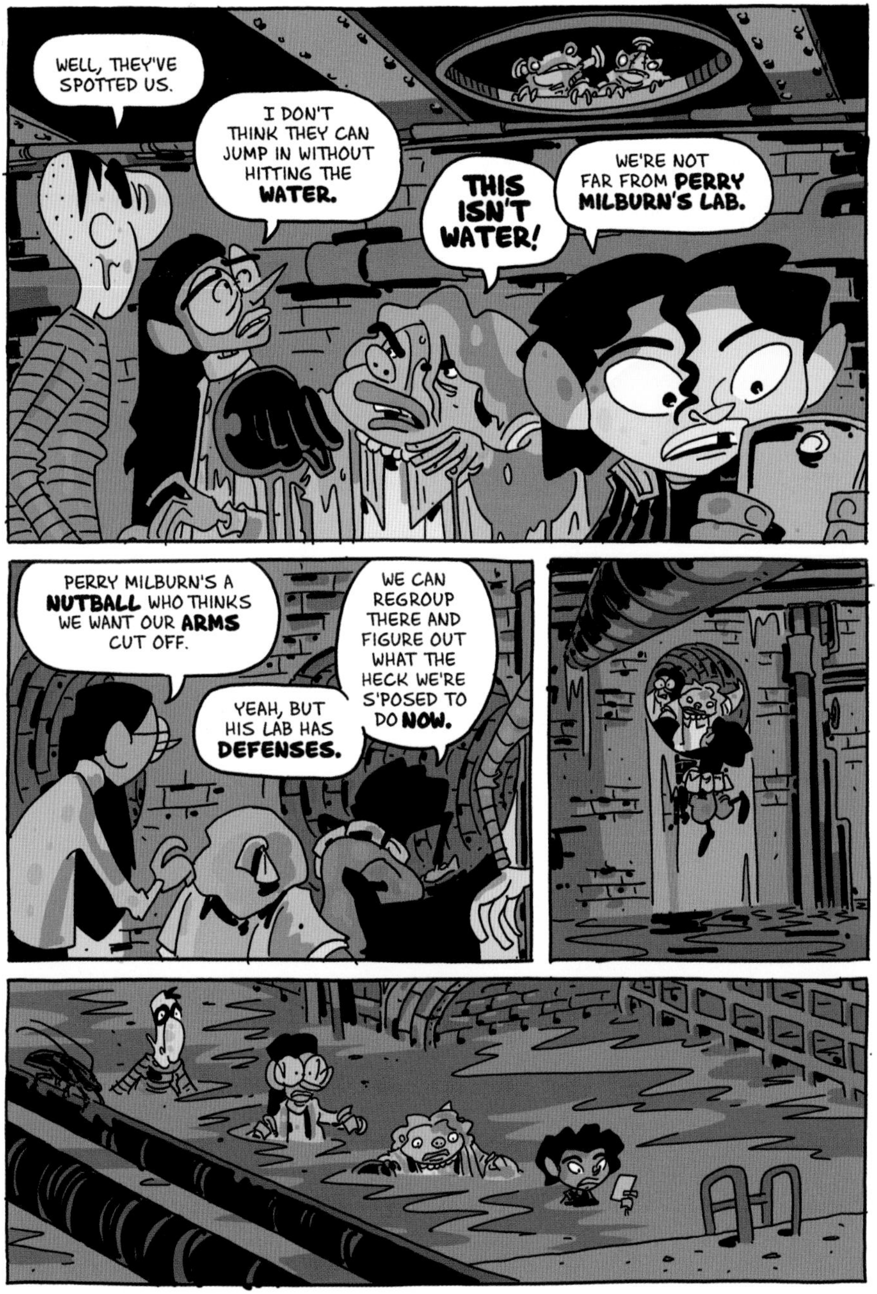
WELL, THEY'VE SPOTTED US.
I DON'T THINK THEY CAN JUMP IN WITHOUT HITTING THE **WATER.**
THIS ISN'T WATER!
WE'RE NOT FAR FROM **PERRY MILBURN'S LAB.**
PERRY MILBURN'S A **NUTBALL** WHO THINKS WE WANT OUR **ARMS** CUT OFF.
YEAH, BUT HIS LAB HAS **DEFENSES.**
WE CAN REGROUP THERE AND FIGURE OUT WHAT THE HECK WE'RE S'POSED TO DO **NOW.**

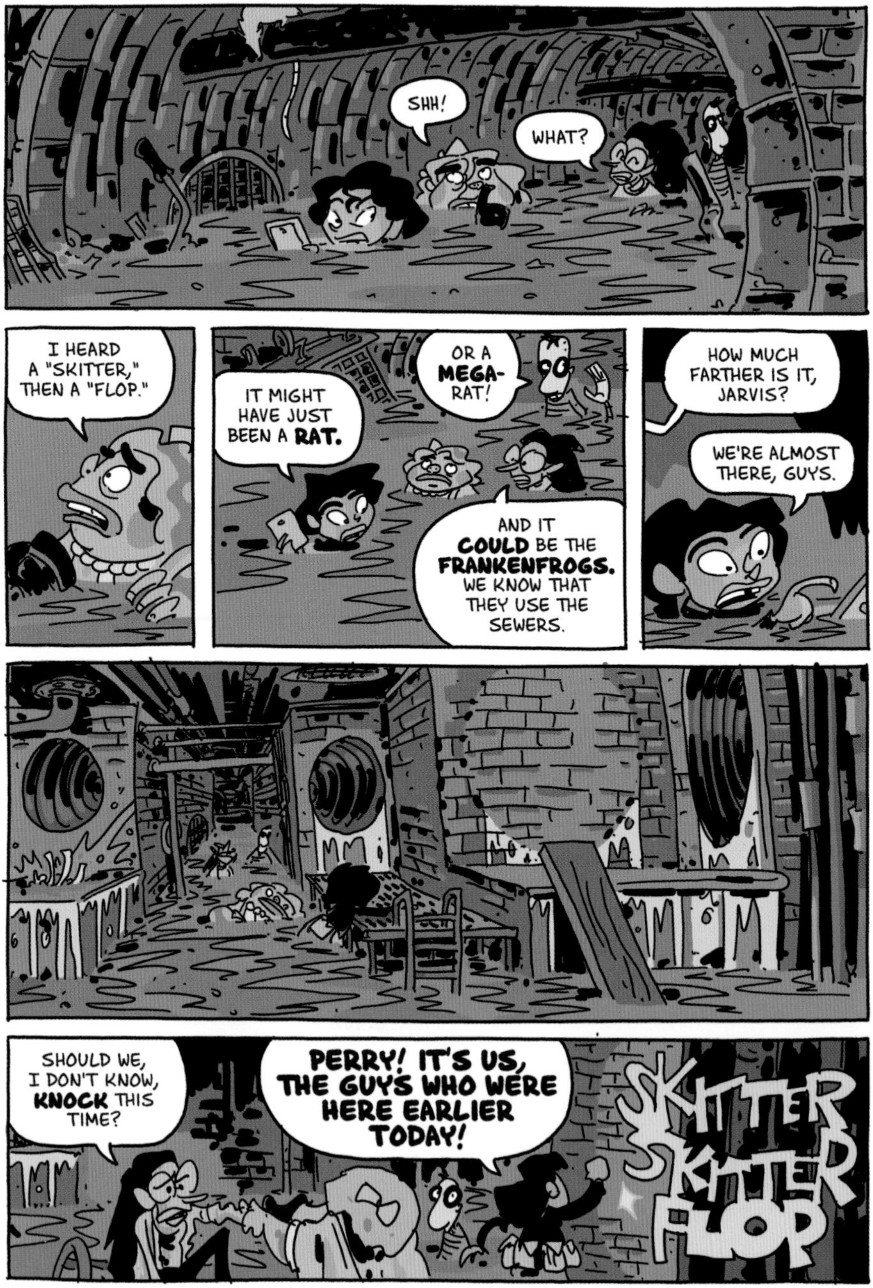
SHH!
WHAT?
I HEARD A "SKITTER," THEN A "FLOP."
IT MIGHT HAVE JUST BEEN A **RAT.**
OR A **MEGA-** RAT!
AND IT **COULD** BE THE **FRANKENFROGS.** WE KNOW THAT THEY USE THE SEWERS.
HOW MUCH FARTHER IS IT, JARVIS?
WE'RE ALMOST THERE, GUYS.
SHOULD WE, I DON'T KNOW, **KNOCK** THIS TIME?
PERRY! IT'S US, THE GUYS WHO WERE HERE EARLIER TODAY!
SKITTER SKITTER FLOP

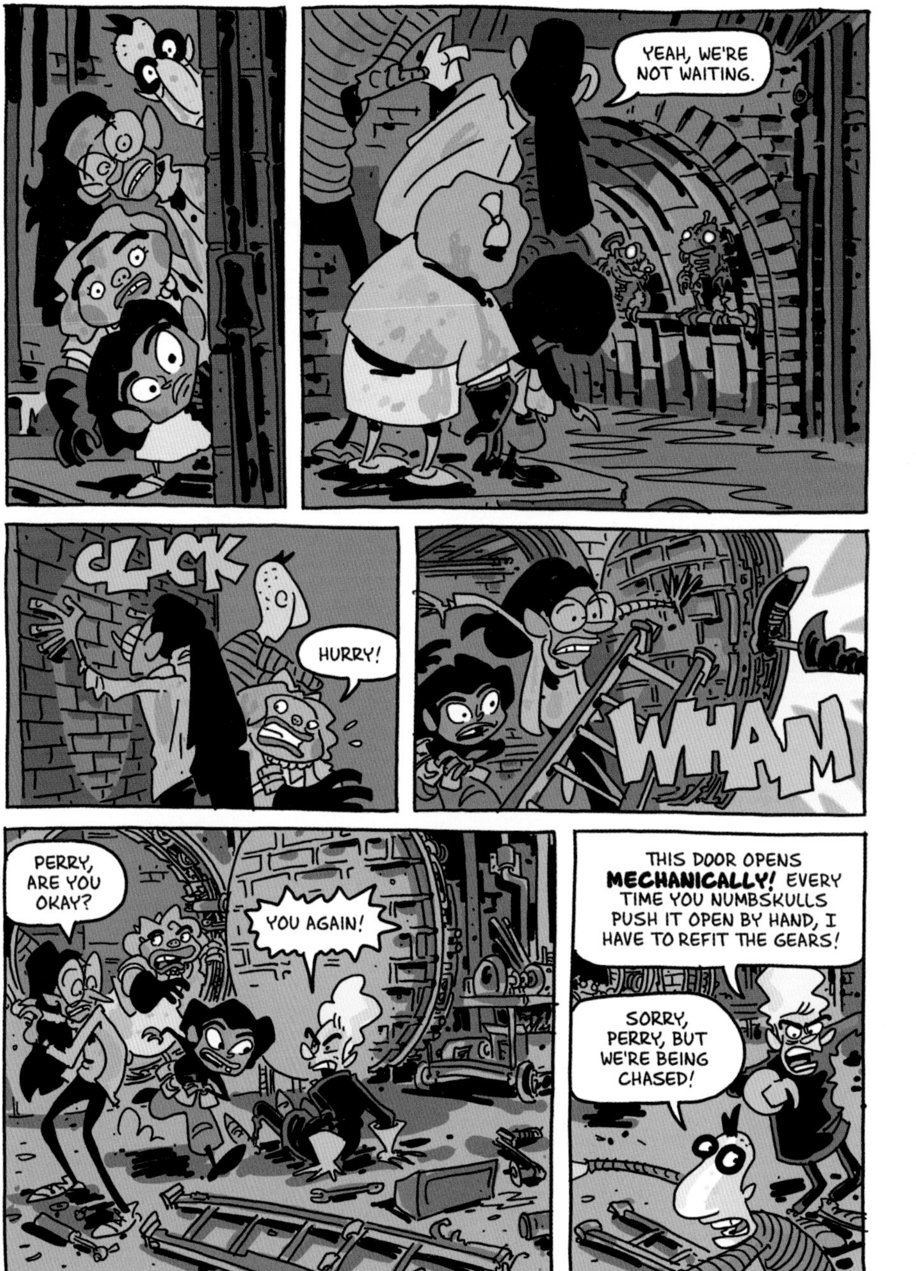
YEAH, WE'RE NOT WAITING.
CLICK
HURRY!
WHAM
PERRY, ARE YOU OKAY?
YOU AGAIN!
THIS DOOR OPENS **MECHANICALLY!** EVERY TIME YOU NUMBSKULLS PUSH IT OPEN BY HAND, I HAVE TO REFIT THE GEARS!
SORRY, PERRY, BUT WE'RE BEING CHASED!

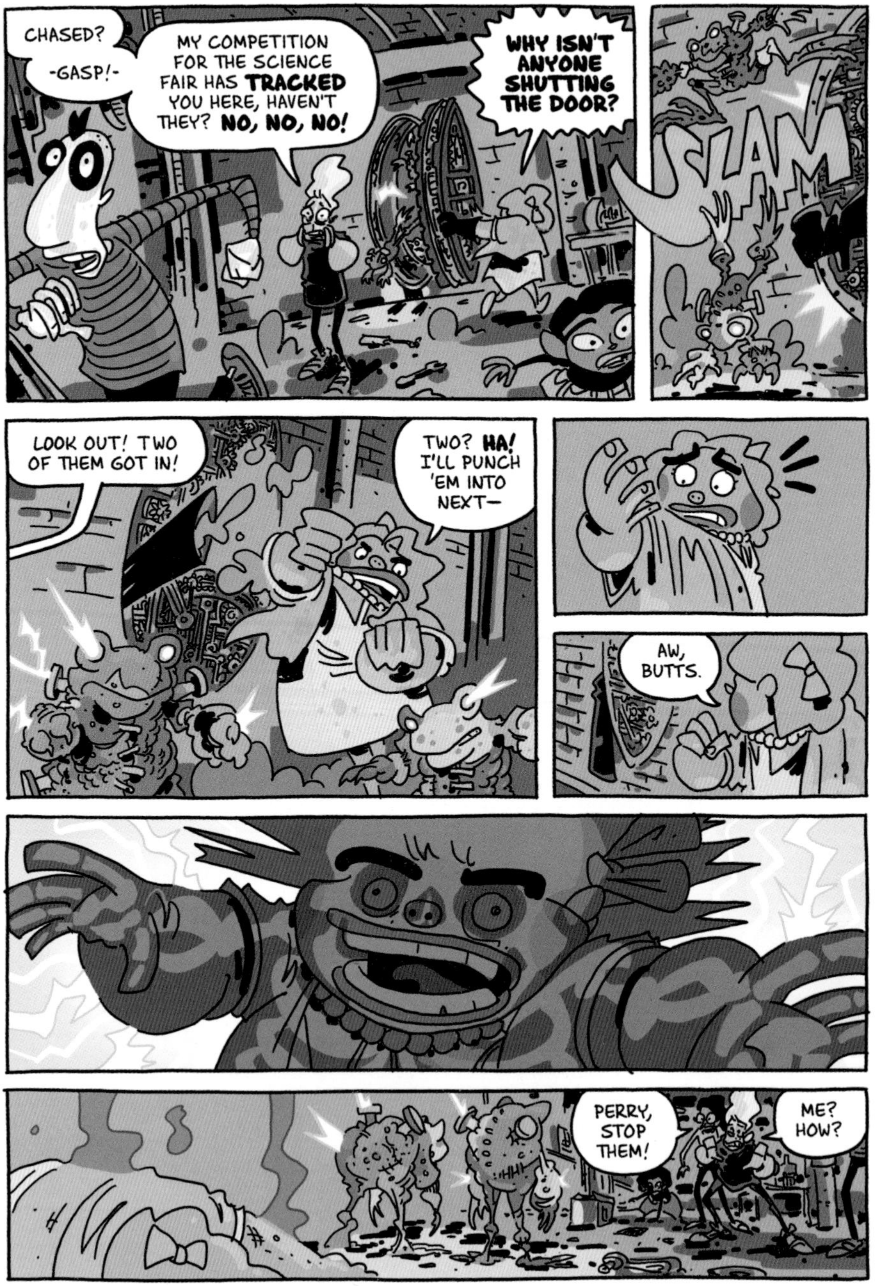
CHASED? -GASP!-
MY COMPETITION FOR THE SCIENCE FAIR HAS TRACKED YOU HERE, HAVEN'T THEY? NO, NO, NO!
WHY ISN'T ANYONE SHUTTING THE DOOR?
SLAM
LOOK OUT! TWO OF THEM GOT IN!
TWO? HA! I'LL PUNCH 'EM INTO NEXT—
AW, BUTTS.
PERRY, STOP THEM!
ME? HOW?

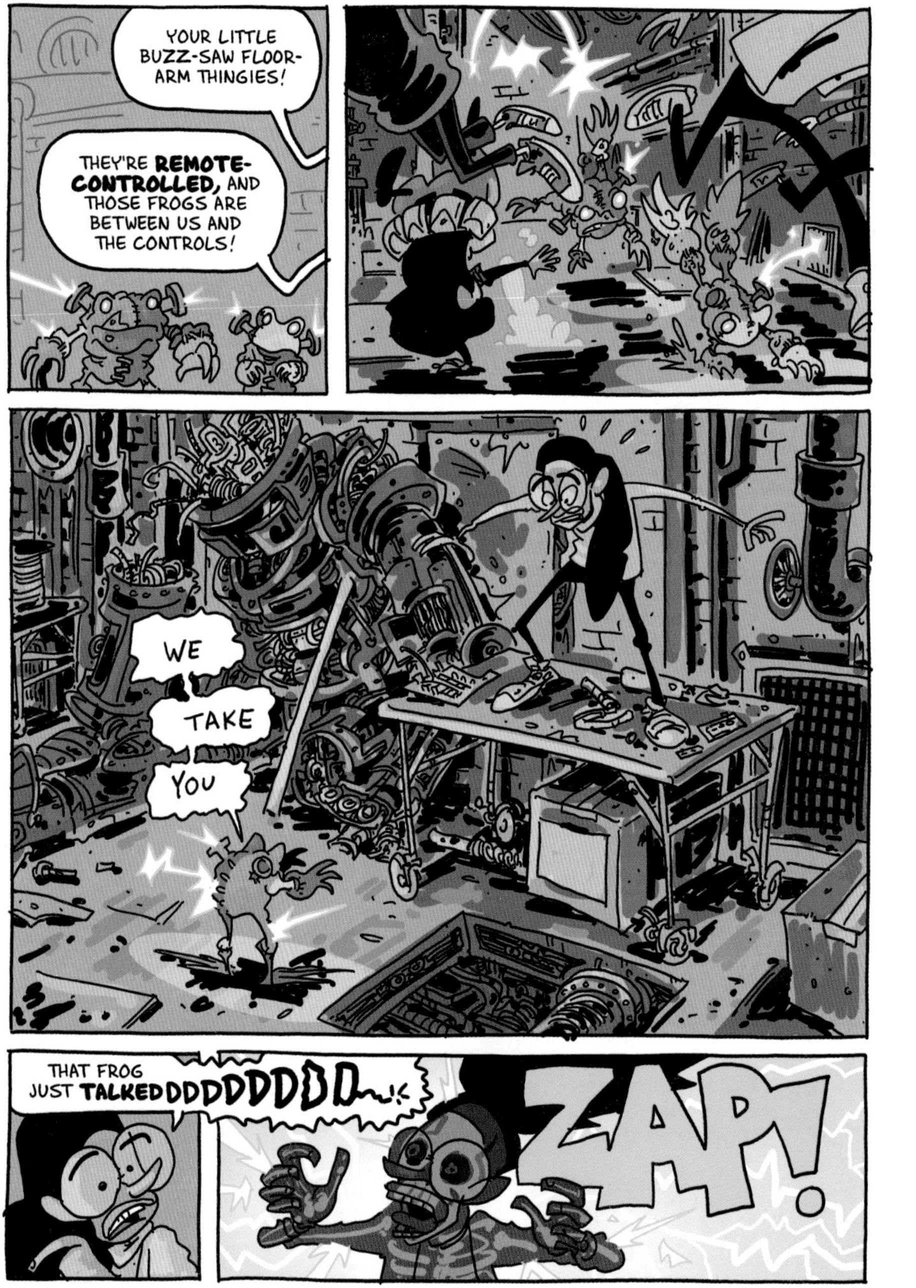

YOUR LITTLE BUZZ-SAW FLOOR-ARM THINGIES!
THEY'RE **REMOTE-CONTROLLED,** AND THOSE FROGS ARE BETWEEN US AND THE CONTROLS!
WE
TAKE
YOU
THAT FROG JUST **TALKED**DDDDDDDD~!¿
ZAP!

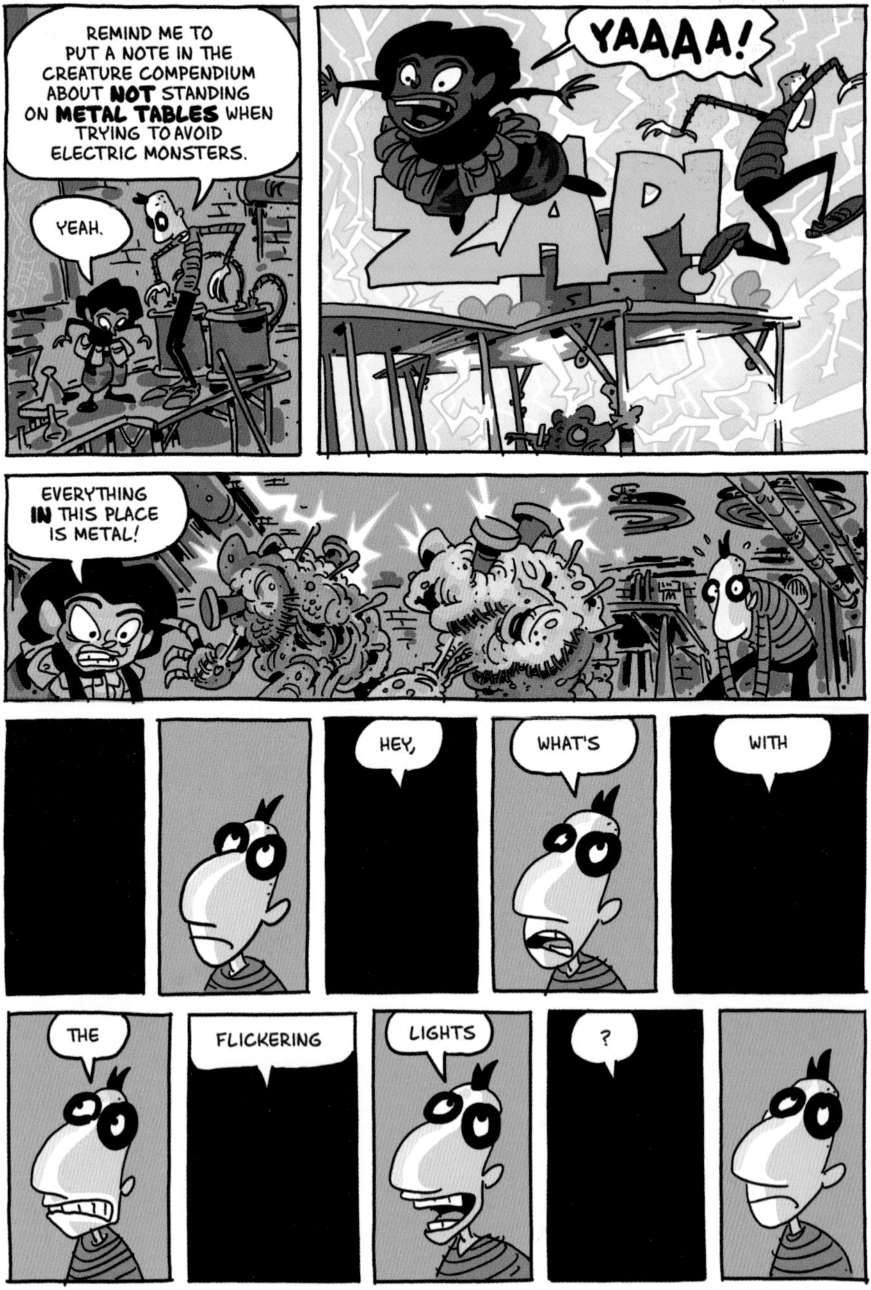
REMIND ME TO PUT A NOTE IN THE CREATURE COMPENDIUM ABOUT **NOT** STANDING ON **METAL TABLES** WHEN TRYING TO AVOID ELECTRIC MONSTERS.
YEAH.
YAAAA!
ZAP!
EVERYTHING **IN** THIS PLACE IS METAL!
HEY,
WHAT'S
WITH
THE
FLICKERING
LIGHTS
?

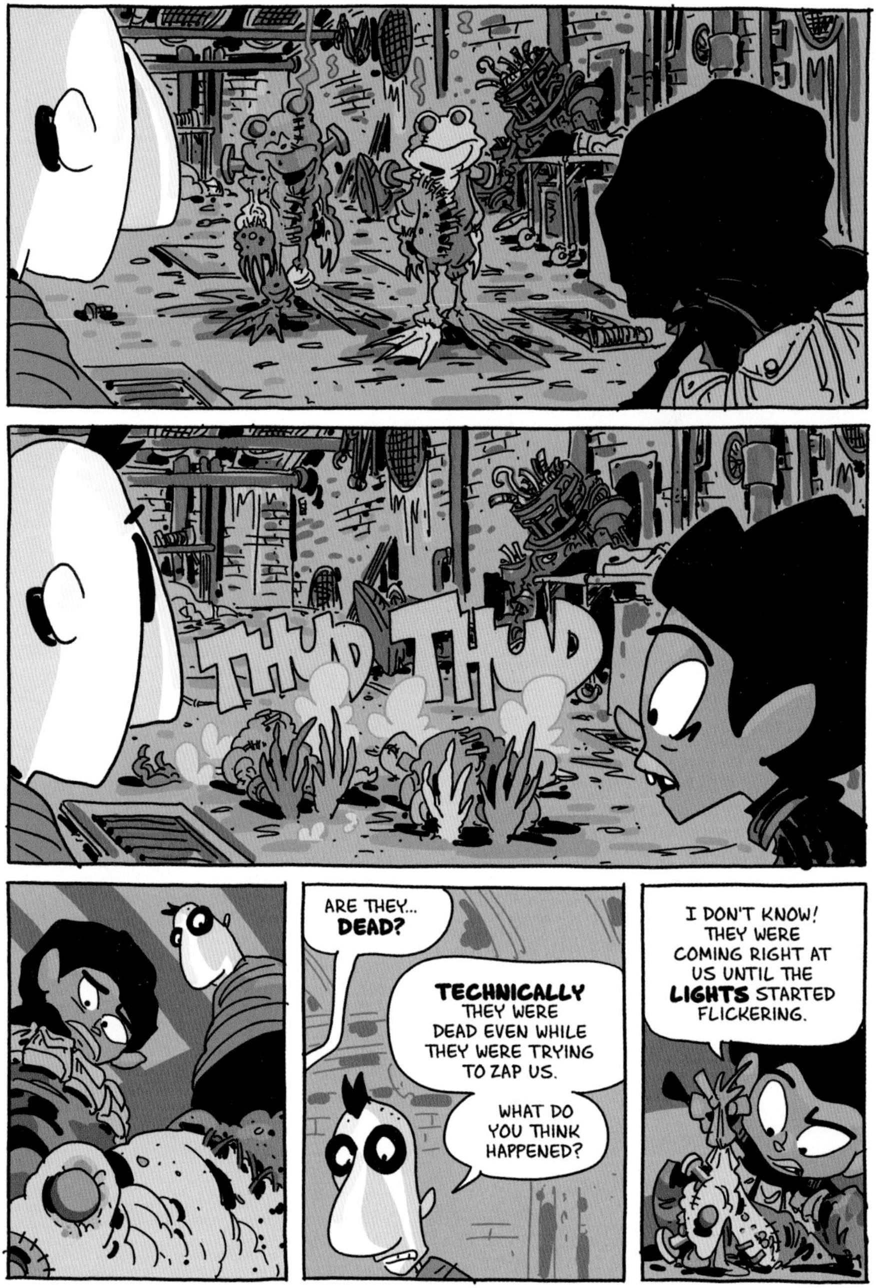
THUD THUD
ARE THEY... **DEAD?**
TECHNICALLY THEY WERE DEAD EVEN WHILE THEY WERE TRYING TO ZAP US.
WHAT DO YOU THINK HAPPENED?
I DON'T KNOW! THEY WERE COMING RIGHT AT US UNTIL THE **LIGHTS** STARTED FLICKERING.

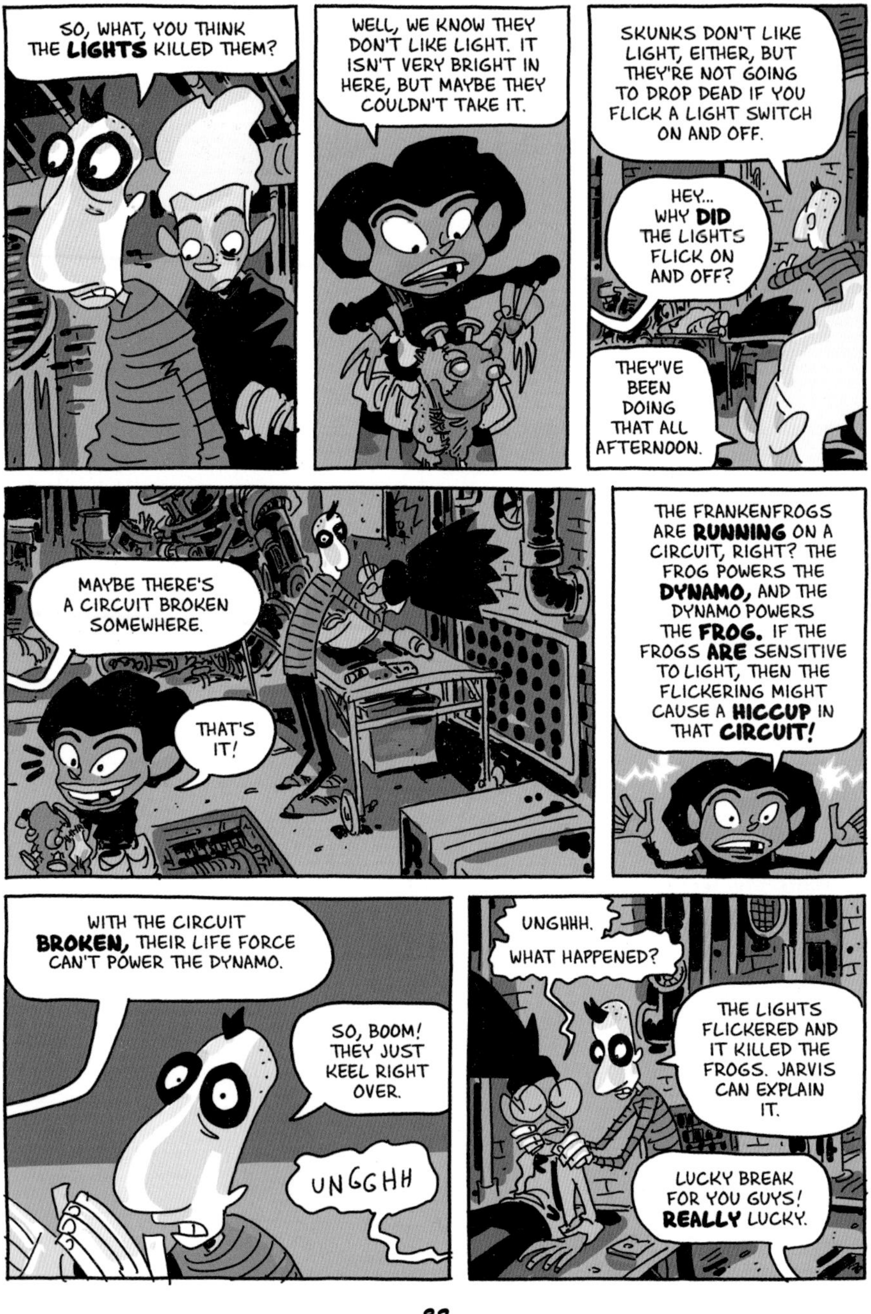
SO, WHAT, YOU THINK THE **LIGHTS** KILLED THEM?
WELL, WE KNOW THEY DON'T LIKE LIGHT. IT ISN'T VERY BRIGHT IN HERE, BUT MAYBE THEY COULDN'T TAKE IT.
SKUNKS DON'T LIKE LIGHT, EITHER, BUT THEY'RE NOT GOING TO DROP DEAD IF YOU FLICK A LIGHT SWITCH ON AND OFF.
HEY... WHY **DID** THE LIGHTS FLICK ON AND OFF?
THEY'VE BEEN DOING THAT ALL AFTERNOON.
MAYBE THERE'S A CIRCUIT BROKEN SOMEWHERE.
THAT'S IT!
THE FRANKENFROGS ARE **RUNNING** ON A CIRCUIT, RIGHT? THE FROG POWERS THE **DYNAMO,** AND THE DYNAMO POWERS THE **FROG.** IF THE FROGS **ARE** SENSITIVE TO LIGHT, THEN THE FLICKERING MIGHT CAUSE A **HICCUP** IN THAT **CIRCUIT!**
WITH THE CIRCUIT **BROKEN,** THEIR LIFE FORCE CAN'T POWER THE DYNAMO.
SO, BOOM! THEY JUST KEEL RIGHT OVER.
UNGGHH
UNGHHH.
WHAT HAPPENED?
THE LIGHTS FLICKERED AND IT KILLED THE FROGS. JARVIS CAN EXPLAIN IT.
LUCKY BREAK FOR YOU GUYS! **REALLY** LUCKY.

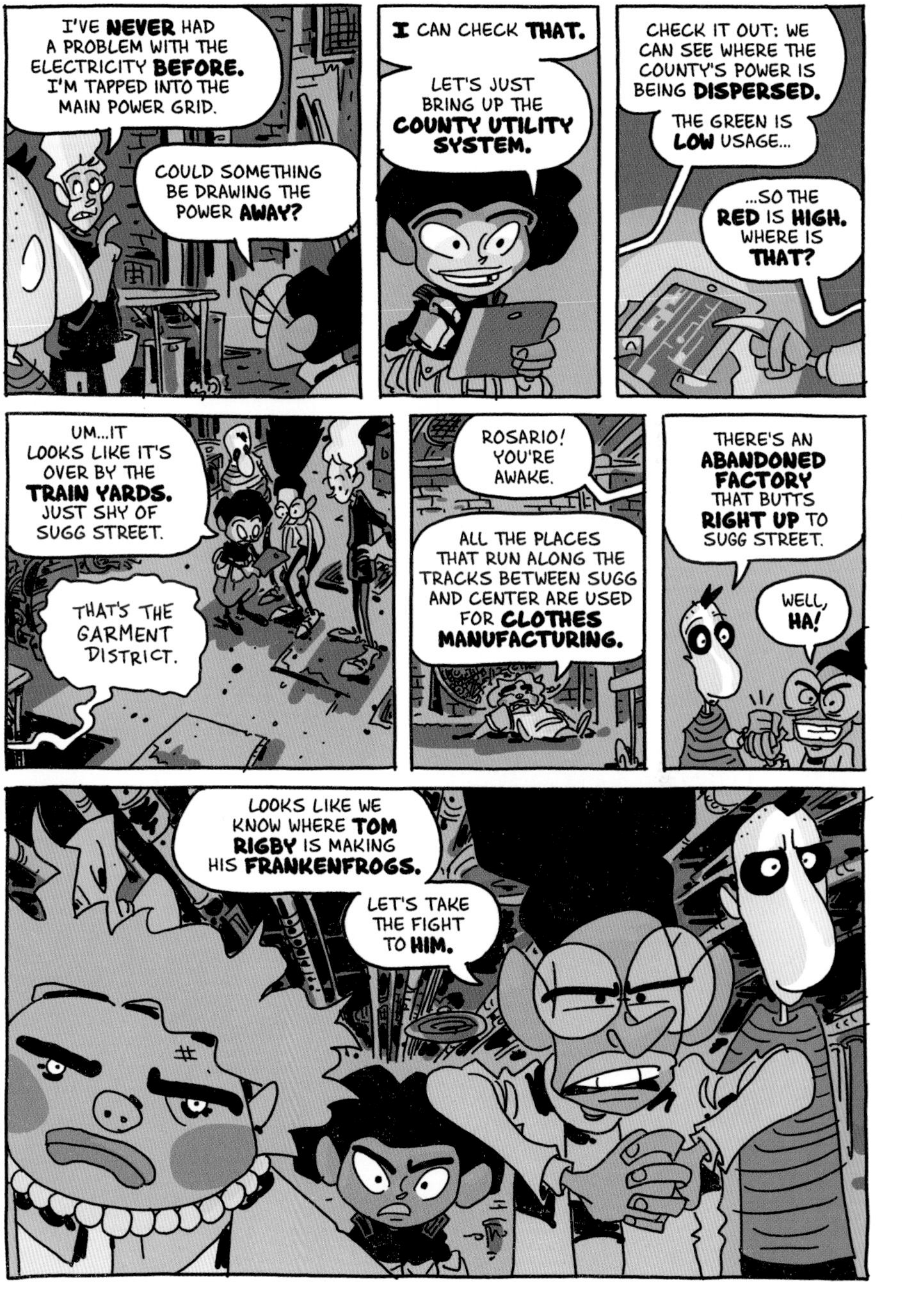
I'VE **NEVER** HAD A PROBLEM WITH THE ELECTRICITY **BEFORE.** I'M TAPPED INTO THE MAIN POWER GRID.
COULD SOMETHING BE DRAWING THE POWER **AWAY?**
I CAN CHECK **THAT.**
LET'S JUST BRING UP THE **COUNTY UTILITY SYSTEM.**
CHECK IT OUT: WE CAN SEE WHERE THE COUNTY'S POWER IS BEING **DISPERSED.**
THE GREEN IS **LOW** USAGE...
...SO THE **RED** IS **HIGH.** WHERE IS **THAT?**
UM...IT LOOKS LIKE IT'S OVER BY THE **TRAIN YARDS.** JUST SHY OF SUGG STREET.
THAT'S THE GARMENT DISTRICT.
ROSARIO! YOU'RE AWAKE.
ALL THE PLACES THAT RUN ALONG THE TRACKS BETWEEN SUGG AND CENTER ARE USED FOR **CLOTHES MANUFACTURING.**
THERE'S AN **ABANDONED FACTORY** THAT BUTTS **RIGHT UP** TO SUGG STREET.
WELL, **HA!**
LOOKS LIKE WE KNOW WHERE **TOM RIGBY** IS MAKING HIS **FRANKENFROGS.**
LET'S TAKE THE FIGHT TO **HIM.**

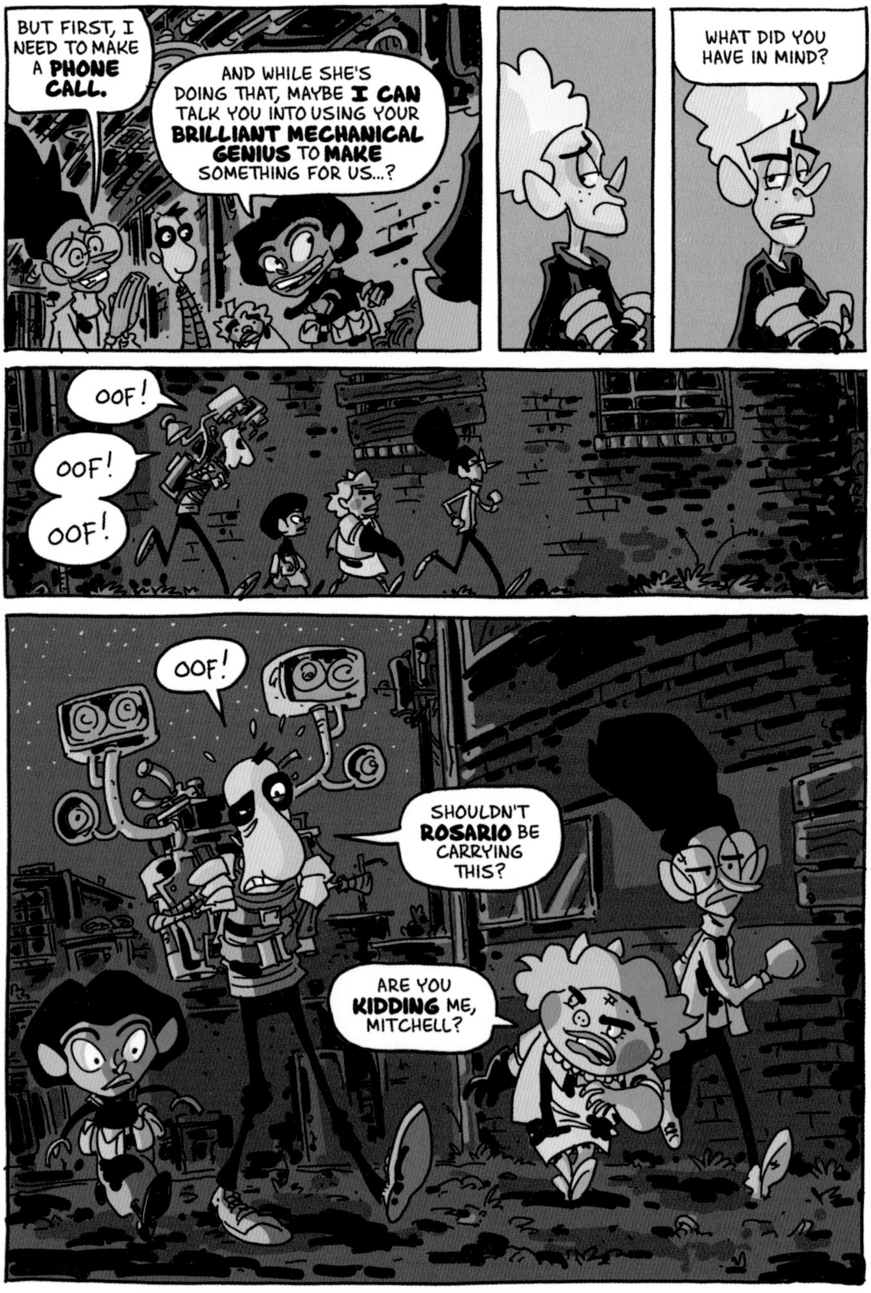
BUT FIRST, I NEED TO MAKE A **PHONE CALL.**
AND WHILE SHE'S DOING THAT, MAYBE **I CAN** TALK YOU INTO USING YOUR **BRILLIANT MECHANICAL GENIUS** TO **MAKE** SOMETHING FOR US...?
WHAT DID YOU HAVE IN MIND?
OOF!
OOF!
OOF!
OOF!
SHOULDN'T **ROSARIO** BE CARRYING THIS?
ARE YOU **KIDDING** ME, MITCHELL?

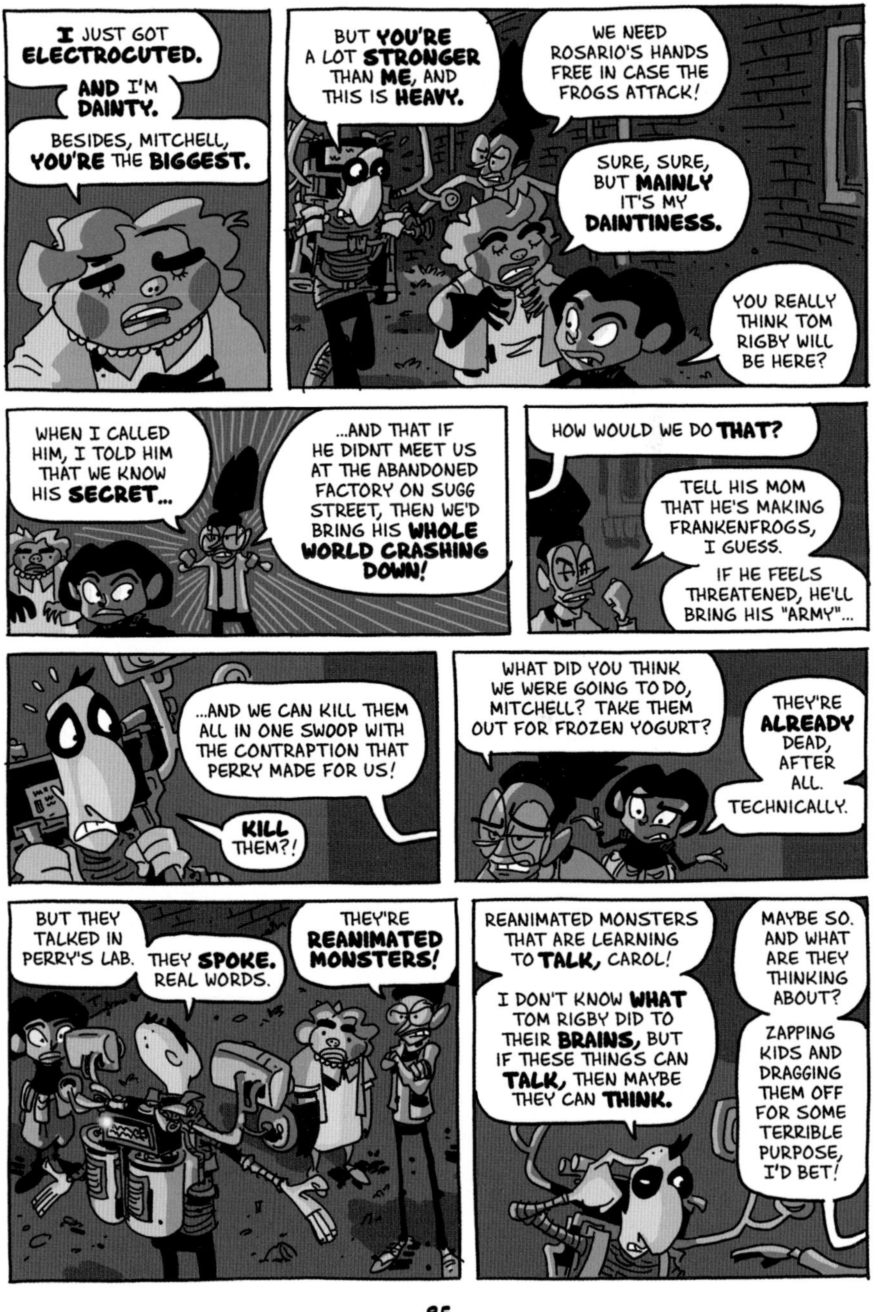
I JUST GOT ELECTROCUTED.
AND I'M DAINTY.
BESIDES, MITCHELL, YOU'RE THE BIGGEST.
BUT YOU'RE A LOT STRONGER THAN ME, AND THIS IS HEAVY.
WE NEED ROSARIO'S HANDS FREE IN CASE THE FROGS ATTACK!
SURE, SURE, BUT MAINLY IT'S MY DAINTINESS.
YOU REALLY THINK TOM RIGBY WILL BE HERE?
WHEN I CALLED HIM, I TOLD HIM THAT WE KNOW HIS SECRET...
...AND THAT IF HE DIDNT MEET US AT THE ABANDONED FACTORY ON SUGG STREET, THEN WE'D BRING HIS WHOLE WORLD CRASHING DOWN!
HOW WOULD WE DO THAT?
TELL HIS MOM THAT HE'S MAKING FRANKENFROGS, I GUESS.
IF HE FEELS THREATENED, HE'LL BRING HIS "ARMY"...
...AND WE CAN KILL THEM ALL IN ONE SWOOP WITH THE CONTRAPTION THAT PERRY MADE FOR US!
KILL THEM?!
WHAT DID YOU THINK WE WERE GOING TO DO, MITCHELL? TAKE THEM OUT FOR FROZEN YOGURT?
THEY'RE ALREADY DEAD, AFTER ALL.
TECHNICALLY.
BUT THEY TALKED IN PERRY'S LAB.
THEY SPOKE. REAL WORDS.
THEY'RE REANIMATED MONSTERS!
REANIMATED MONSTERS THAT ARE LEARNING TO TALK, CAROL!
I DON'T KNOW WHAT TOM RIGBY DID TO THEIR BRAINS, BUT IF THESE THINGS CAN TALK, THEN MAYBE THEY CAN THINK.
MAYBE SO. AND WHAT ARE THEY THINKING ABOUT?
ZAPPING KIDS AND DRAGGING THEM OFF FOR SOME TERRIBLE PURPOSE, I'D BET!

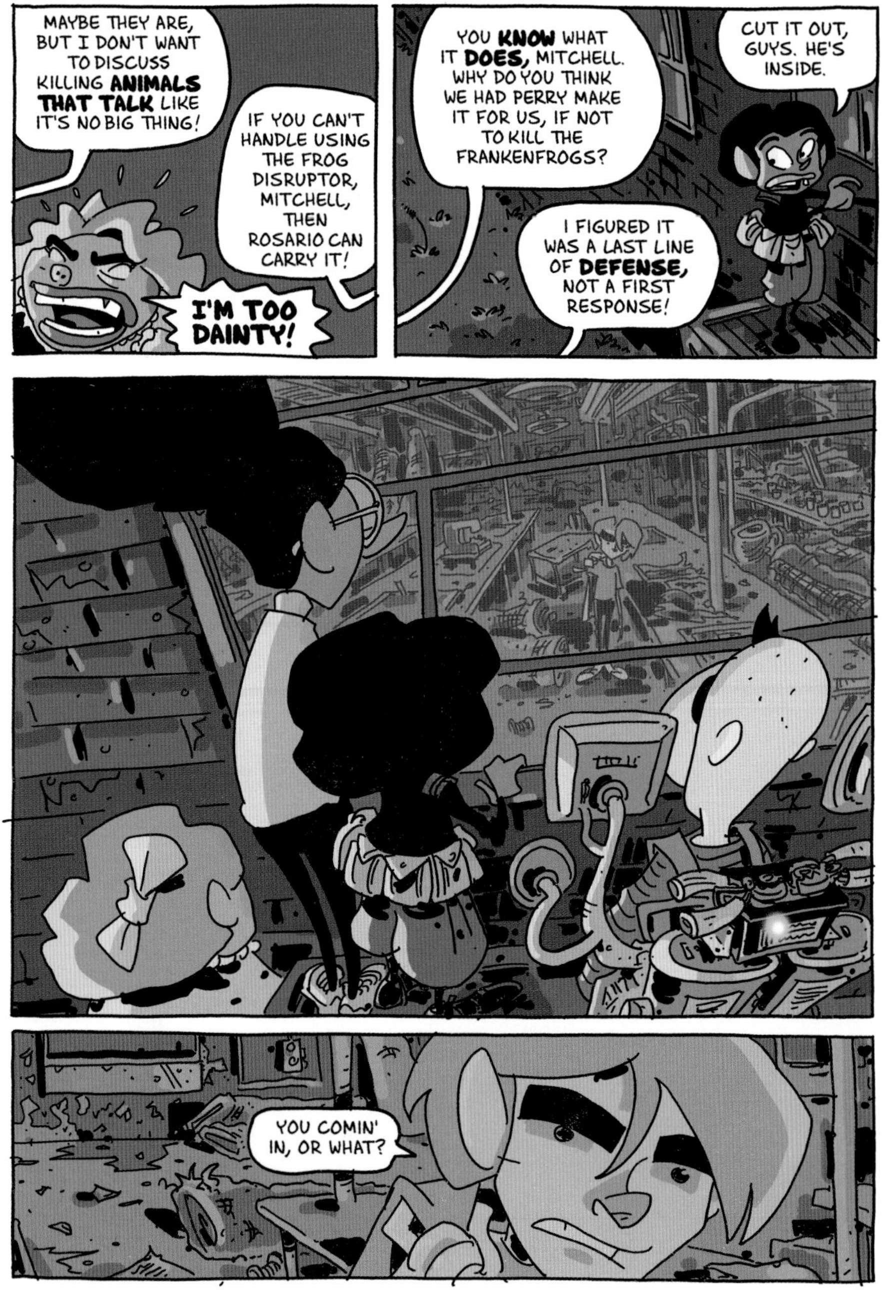
MAYBE THEY ARE, BUT I DON'T WANT TO DISCUSS KILLING **ANIMALS THAT TALK** LIKE IT'S NO BIG THING!
IF YOU CAN'T HANDLE USING THE FROG DISRUPTOR, MITCHELL, THEN ROSARIO CAN CARRY IT!
I'M TOO DAINTY!
YOU **KNOW** WHAT IT **DOES,** MITCHELL. WHY DO YOU THINK WE HAD PERRY MAKE IT FOR US, IF NOT TO KILL THE FRANKENFROGS?
I FIGURED IT WAS A LAST LINE OF **DEFENSE,** NOT A FIRST RESPONSE!
CUT IT OUT, GUYS. HE'S INSIDE.
YOU COMIN' IN, OR WHAT?

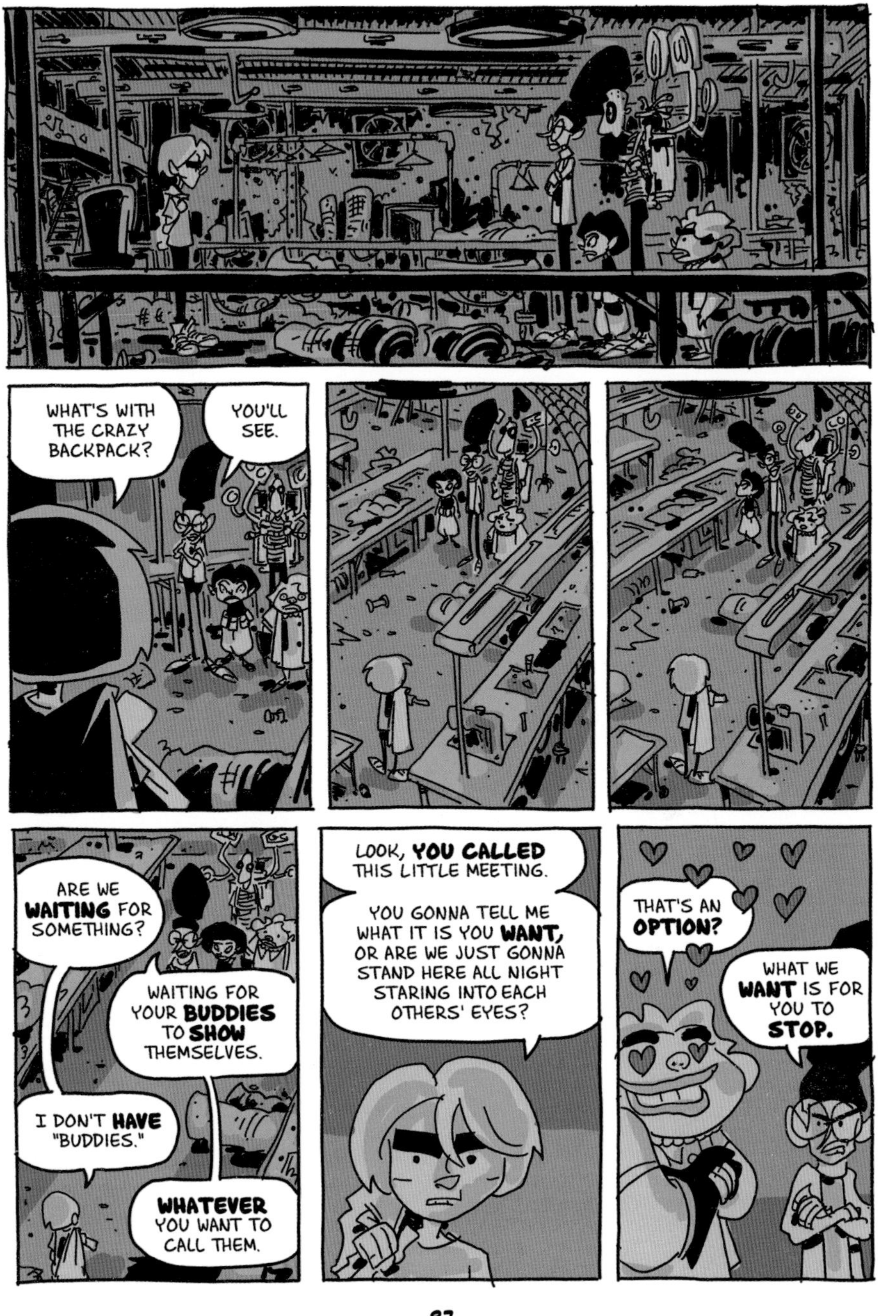
WHAT'S WITH THE CRAZY BACKPACK?
YOU'LL SEE.
ARE WE WAITING FOR SOMETHING?
WAITING FOR YOUR BUDDIES TO SHOW THEMSELVES.
I DON'T HAVE "BUDDIES."
WHATEVER YOU WANT TO CALL THEM.
LOOK, YOU CALLED THIS LITTLE MEETING.
YOU GONNA TELL ME WHAT IT IS YOU WANT, OR ARE WE JUST GONNA STAND HERE ALL NIGHT STARING INTO EACH OTHERS' EYES?
THAT'S AN OPTION?
WHAT WE WANT IS FOR YOU TO STOP.

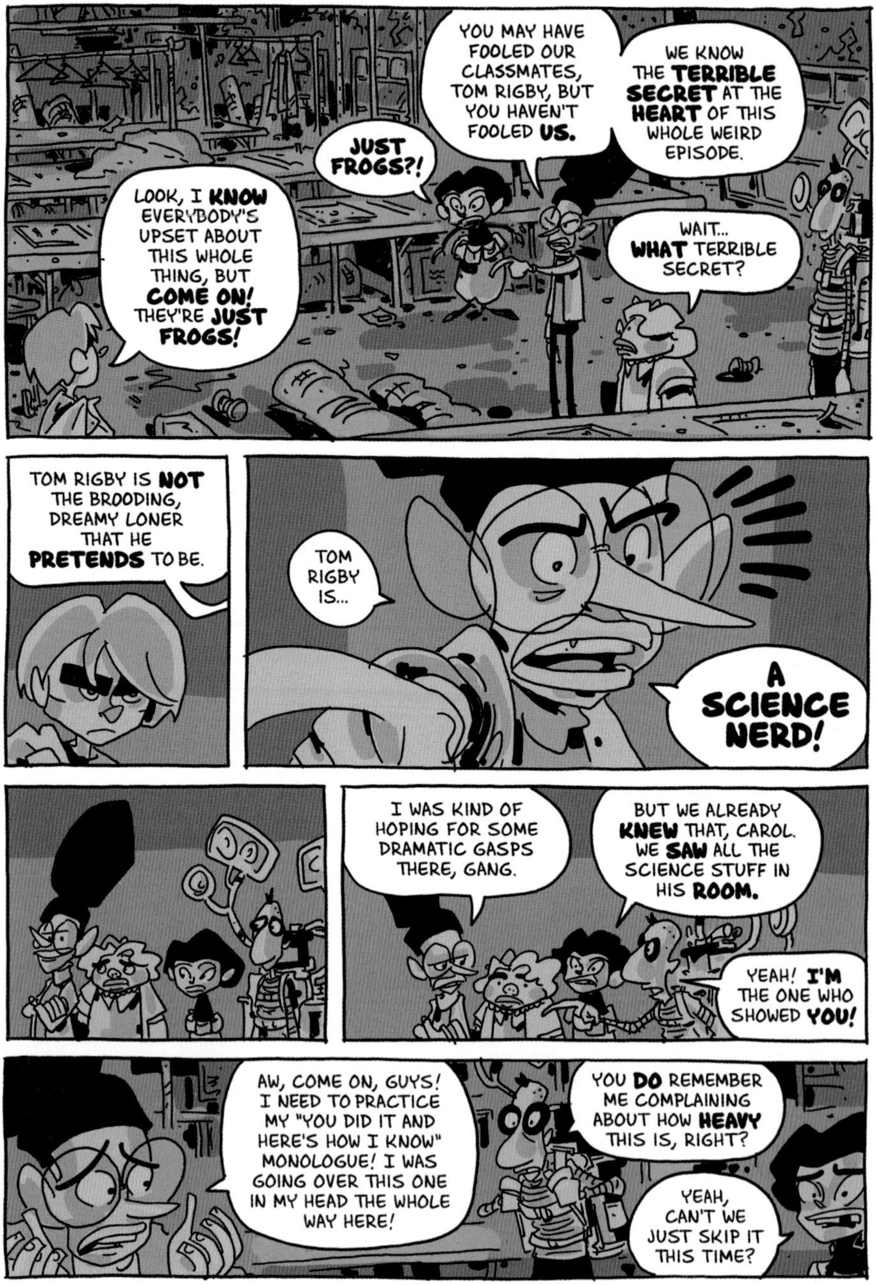
LOOK, I KNOW EVERYBODY'S UPSET ABOUT THIS WHOLE THING, BUT COME ON! THEY'RE JUST FROGS!
JUST FROGS?!
YOU MAY HAVE FOOLED OUR CLASSMATES, TOM RIGBY, BUT YOU HAVEN'T FOOLED US.
WE KNOW THE TERRIBLE SECRET AT THE HEART OF THIS WHOLE WEIRD EPISODE.
WAIT... WHAT TERRIBLE SECRET?
TOM RIGBY IS NOT THE BROODING, DREAMY LONER THAT HE PRETENDS TO BE.
TOM RIGBY IS...
A SCIENCE NERD!
I WAS KIND OF HOPING FOR SOME DRAMATIC GASPS THERE, GANG.
BUT WE ALREADY KNEW THAT, CAROL. WE SAW ALL THE SCIENCE STUFF IN HIS ROOM.
YEAH! I'M THE ONE WHO SHOWED YOU!
AW, COME ON, GUYS! I NEED TO PRACTICE MY "YOU DID IT AND HERE'S HOW I KNOW" MONOLOGUE! I WAS GOING OVER THIS ONE IN MY HEAD THE WHOLE WAY HERE!
YOU DO REMEMBER ME COMPLAINING ABOUT HOW HEAVY THIS IS, RIGHT?
YEAH, CAN'T WE JUST SKIP IT THIS TIME?

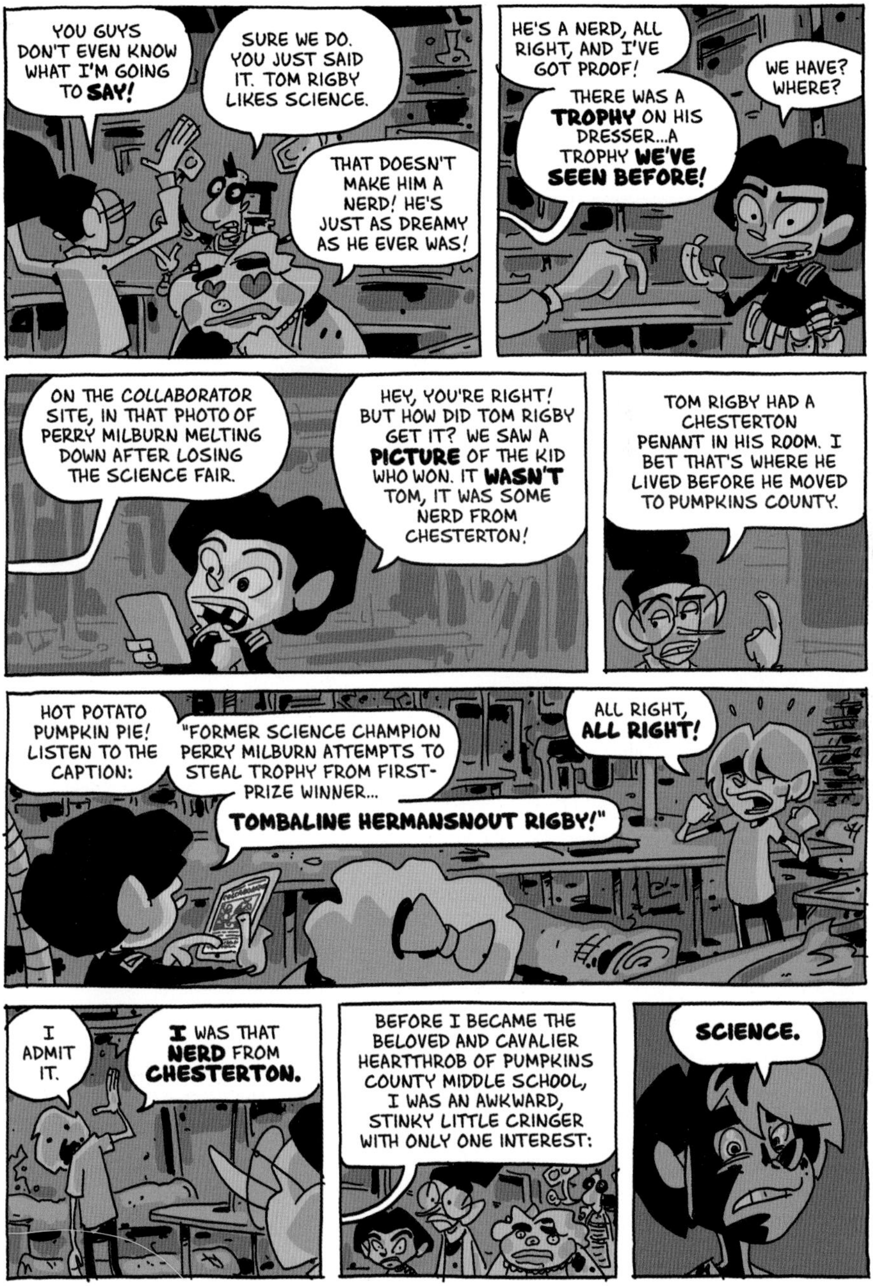
YOU GUYS DON'T EVEN KNOW WHAT I'M GOING TO **SAY!**
SURE WE DO. YOU JUST SAID IT. TOM RIGBY LIKES SCIENCE.
THAT DOESN'T MAKE HIM A NERD! HE'S JUST AS DREAMY AS HE EVER WAS!
HE'S A NERD, ALL RIGHT, AND I'VE GOT PROOF!
THERE WAS A **TROPHY** ON HIS DRESSER...A TROPHY **WE'VE SEEN BEFORE!**
WE HAVE? WHERE?
ON THE COLLABORATOR SITE, IN THAT PHOTO OF PERRY MILBURN MELTING DOWN AFTER LOSING THE SCIENCE FAIR.
HEY, YOU'RE RIGHT! BUT HOW DID TOM RIGBY GET IT? WE SAW A **PICTURE** OF THE KID WHO WON. IT **WASN'T** TOM, IT WAS SOME NERD FROM CHESTERTON!
TOM RIGBY HAD A CHESTERTON PENANT IN HIS ROOM. I BET THAT'S WHERE HE LIVED BEFORE HE MOVED TO PUMPKINS COUNTY.
HOT POTATO PUMPKIN PIE! LISTEN TO THE CAPTION:
"FORMER SCIENCE CHAMPION PERRY MILBURN ATTEMPTS TO STEAL TROPHY FROM FIRST-PRIZE WINNER...
TOMBALINE HERMANSNOUT RIGBY!"
ALL RIGHT, **ALL RIGHT!**
I ADMIT IT.
I WAS THAT **NERD** FROM **CHESTERTON.**
BEFORE I BECAME THE BELOVED AND CAVALIER HEARTTHROB OF PUMPKINS COUNTY MIDDLE SCHOOL, I WAS AN AWKWARD, STINKY LITTLE CRINGER WITH ONLY ONE INTEREST:
SCIENCE.

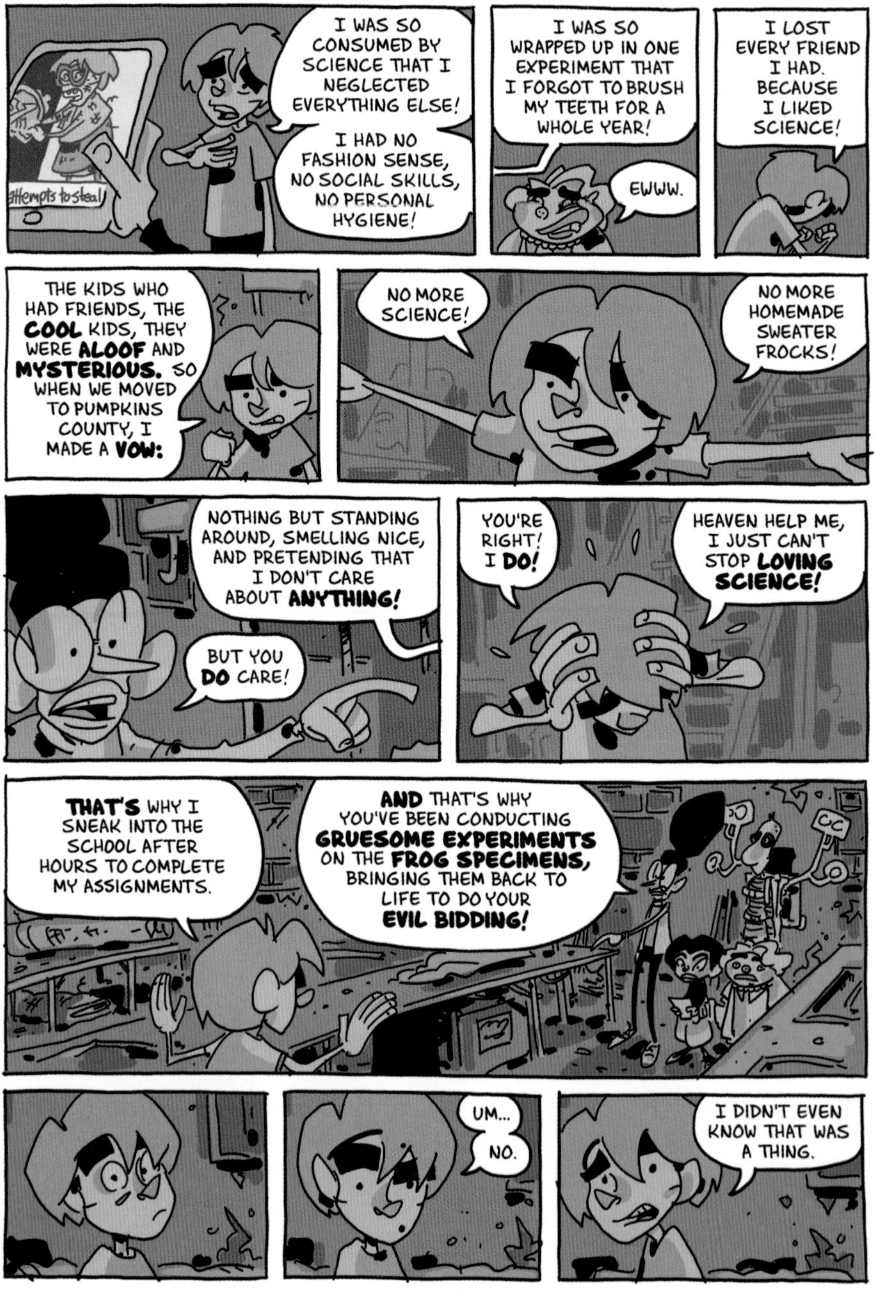
attempts to steal
I WAS SO CONSUMED BY SCIENCE THAT I NEGLECTED EVERYTHING ELSE!
I HAD NO FASHION SENSE, NO SOCIAL SKILLS, NO PERSONAL HYGIENE!
I WAS SO WRAPPED UP IN ONE EXPERIMENT THAT I FORGOT TO BRUSH MY TEETH FOR A WHOLE YEAR!
EWWW.
I LOST EVERY FRIEND I HAD. BECAUSE I LIKED SCIENCE!
THE KIDS WHO HAD FRIENDS, THE COOL KIDS, THEY WERE ALOOF AND MYSTERIOUS. SO WHEN WE MOVED TO PUMPKINS COUNTY, I MADE A VOW:
NO MORE SCIENCE!
NO MORE HOMEMADE SWEATER FROCKS!
NOTHING BUT STANDING AROUND, SMELLING NICE, AND PRETENDING THAT I DON'T CARE ABOUT ANYTHING!
BUT YOU DO CARE!
YOU'RE RIGHT! I DO!
HEAVEN HELP ME, I JUST CAN'T STOP LOVING SCIENCE!
THAT'S WHY I SNEAK INTO THE SCHOOL AFTER HOURS TO COMPLETE MY ASSIGNMENTS.
AND THAT'S WHY YOU'VE BEEN CONDUCTING GRUESOME EXPERIMENTS ON THE FROG SPECIMENS, BRINGING THEM BACK TO LIFE TO DO YOUR EVIL BIDDING!
UM...
NO.
I DIDN'T EVEN KNOW THAT WAS A THING.

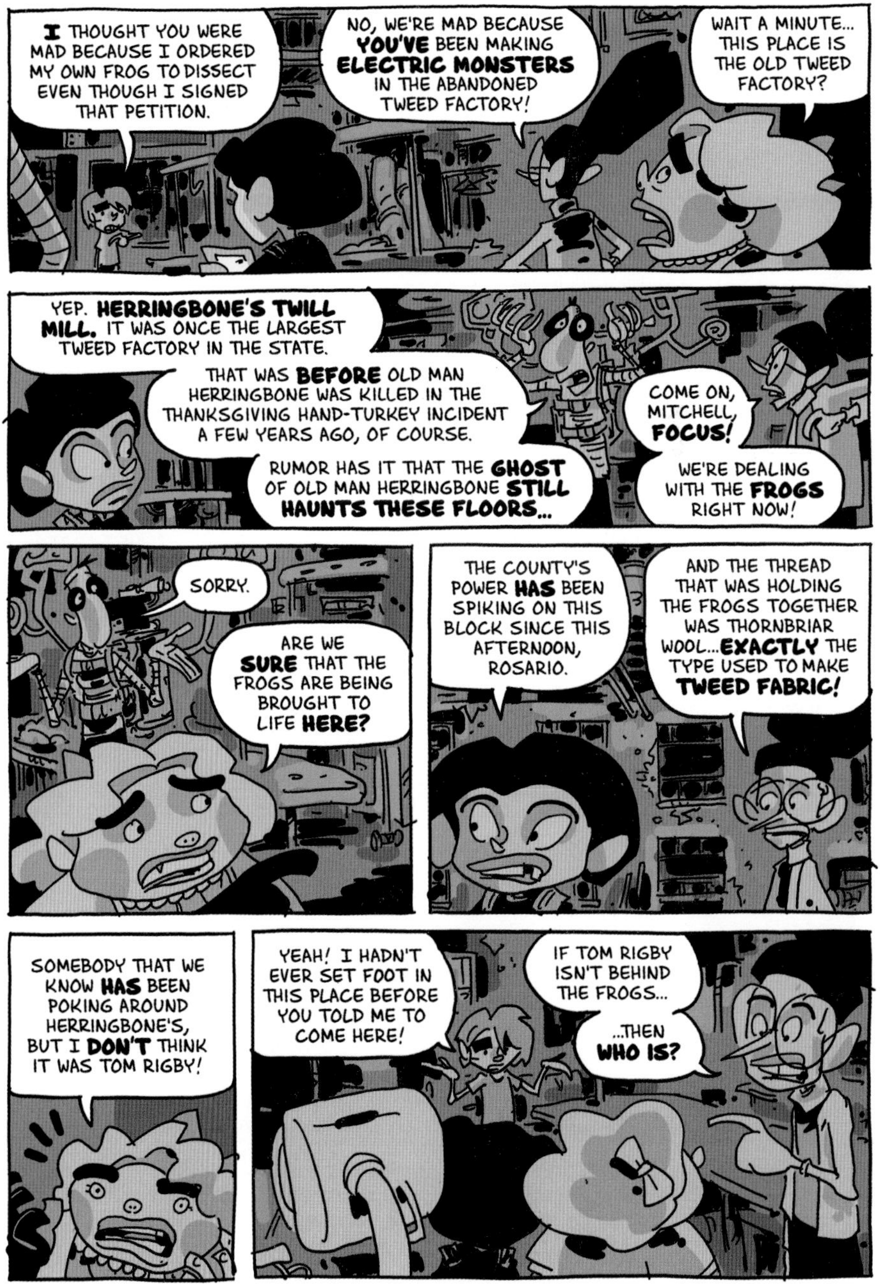
I THOUGHT YOU WERE MAD BECAUSE I ORDERED MY OWN FROG TO DISSECT EVEN THOUGH I SIGNED THAT PETITION.
NO, WE'RE MAD BECAUSE YOU'VE BEEN MAKING ELECTRIC MONSTERS IN THE ABANDONED TWEED FACTORY!
WAIT A MINUTE... THIS PLACE IS THE OLD TWEED FACTORY?
YEP. HERRINGBONE'S TWILL MILL. IT WAS ONCE THE LARGEST TWEED FACTORY IN THE STATE.
THAT WAS BEFORE OLD MAN HERRINGBONE WAS KILLED IN THE THANKSGIVING HAND-TURKEY INCIDENT A FEW YEARS AGO, OF COURSE.
RUMOR HAS IT THAT THE GHOST OF OLD MAN HERRINGBONE STILL HAUNTS THESE FLOORS...
COME ON, MITCHELL, FOCUS!
WE'RE DEALING WITH THE FROGS RIGHT NOW!
SORRY.
ARE WE SURE THAT THE FROGS ARE BEING BROUGHT TO LIFE HERE?
THE COUNTY'S POWER HAS BEEN SPIKING ON THIS BLOCK SINCE THIS AFTERNOON, ROSARIO.
AND THE THREAD THAT WAS HOLDING THE FROGS TOGETHER WAS THORNBRIAR WOOL...EXACTLY THE TYPE USED TO MAKE TWEED FABRIC!
SOMEBODY THAT WE KNOW HAS BEEN POKING AROUND HERRINGBONE'S, BUT I DON'T THINK IT WAS TOM RIGBY!
YEAH! I HADN'T EVER SET FOOT IN THIS PLACE BEFORE YOU TOLD ME TO COME HERE!
IF TOM RIGBY ISN'T BEHIND THE FROGS...
...THEN WHO IS?

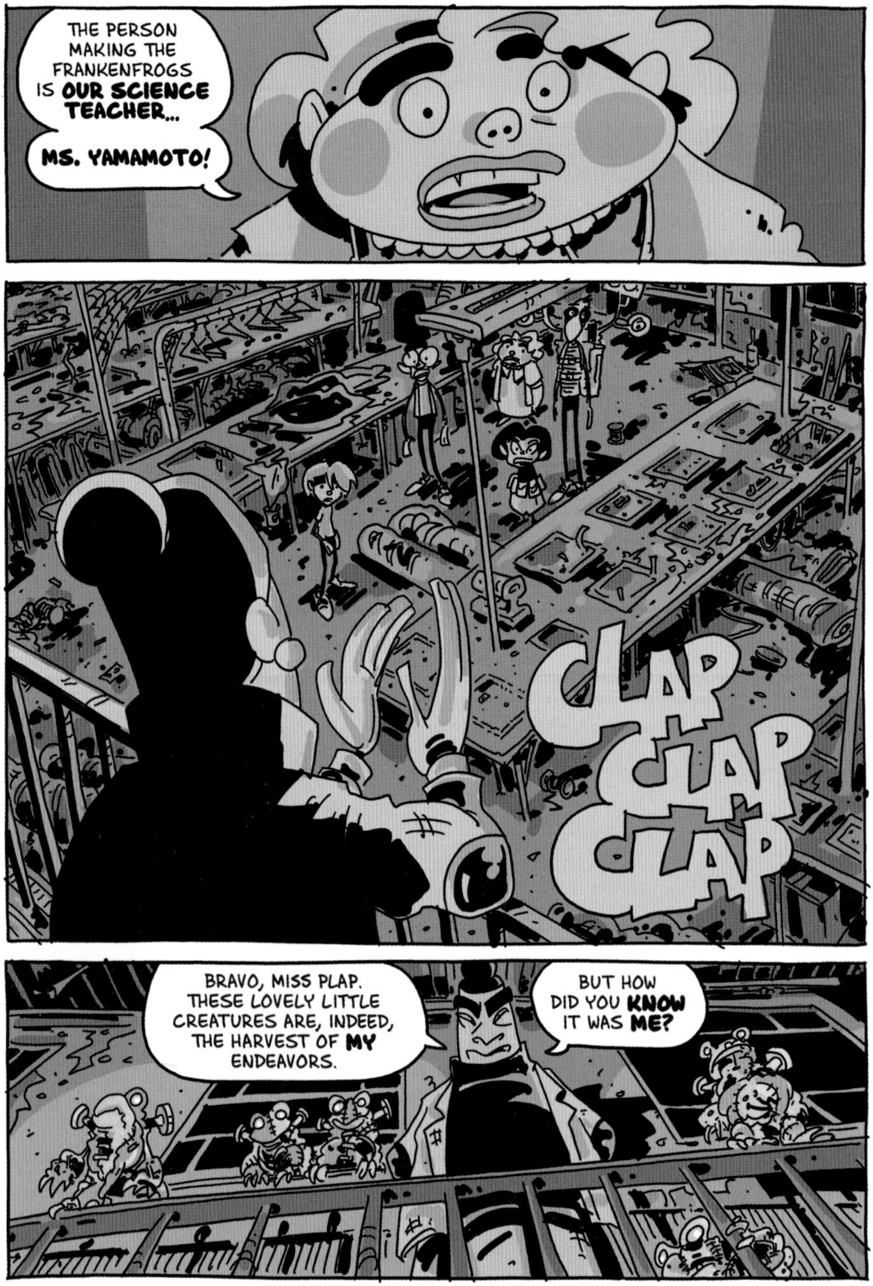
THE PERSON MAKING THE FRANKENFROGS IS **OUR SCIENCE TEACHER...**
MS. YAMAMOTO!
CLAP CLAP CLAP
BRAVO, MISS PLAP. THESE LOVELY LITTLE CREATURES ARE, INDEED, THE HARVEST OF **MY** ENDEAVORS.
BUT HOW DID YOU **KNOW** IT WAS **ME?**

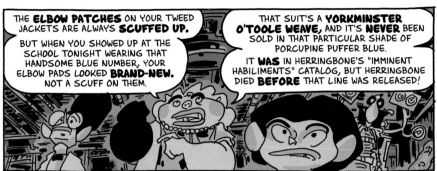

THE **ELBOW PATCHES** ON YOUR TWEED JACKETS ARE ALWAYS **SCUFFED UP.**

BUT WHEN YOU SHOWED UP AT THE SCHOOL TONIGHT WEARING THAT HANDSOME BLUE NUMBER, YOUR ELBOW PADS LOOKED **BRAND-NEW.** NOT A SCUFF ON THEM.

THAT SUIT'S A **YORKMINSTER O'TOOLE WEAVE,** AND IT'S **NEVER** BEEN SOLD IN THAT PARTICULAR SHADE OF PORCUPINE PUFFER BLUE.

IT **WAS** IN HERRINGBONE'S "IMMINENT HABILIMENTS" CATALOG, BUT HERRINGBONE DIED **BEFORE** THAT LINE WAS RELEASED!

THE ONLY PLACE YOU COULD'VE GOTTEN YOUR HANDS ON THAT SUIT WOULD HAVE BEEN HERE, IN THE FACTORY.

WOW, ROSARIO. I DIDN'T KNOW YOU WERE SUCH A GOOD **DETECTIVE.**

WHAT CAN I SAY? I KNOW CLOTHES.

INDEED YOU **DO,** MISS PLAP!

IT'S A PITY YOU COULDN'T PUT YOUR ENTHUSIASM FOR **FASHION** TO A MORE **CONSTRUCTIVE** USE.

BUT **THAT** IS A SHORTCOMING SOON REMEDIED.

ALL RIGHT, MY LITTLE ONES...

GET THEM!

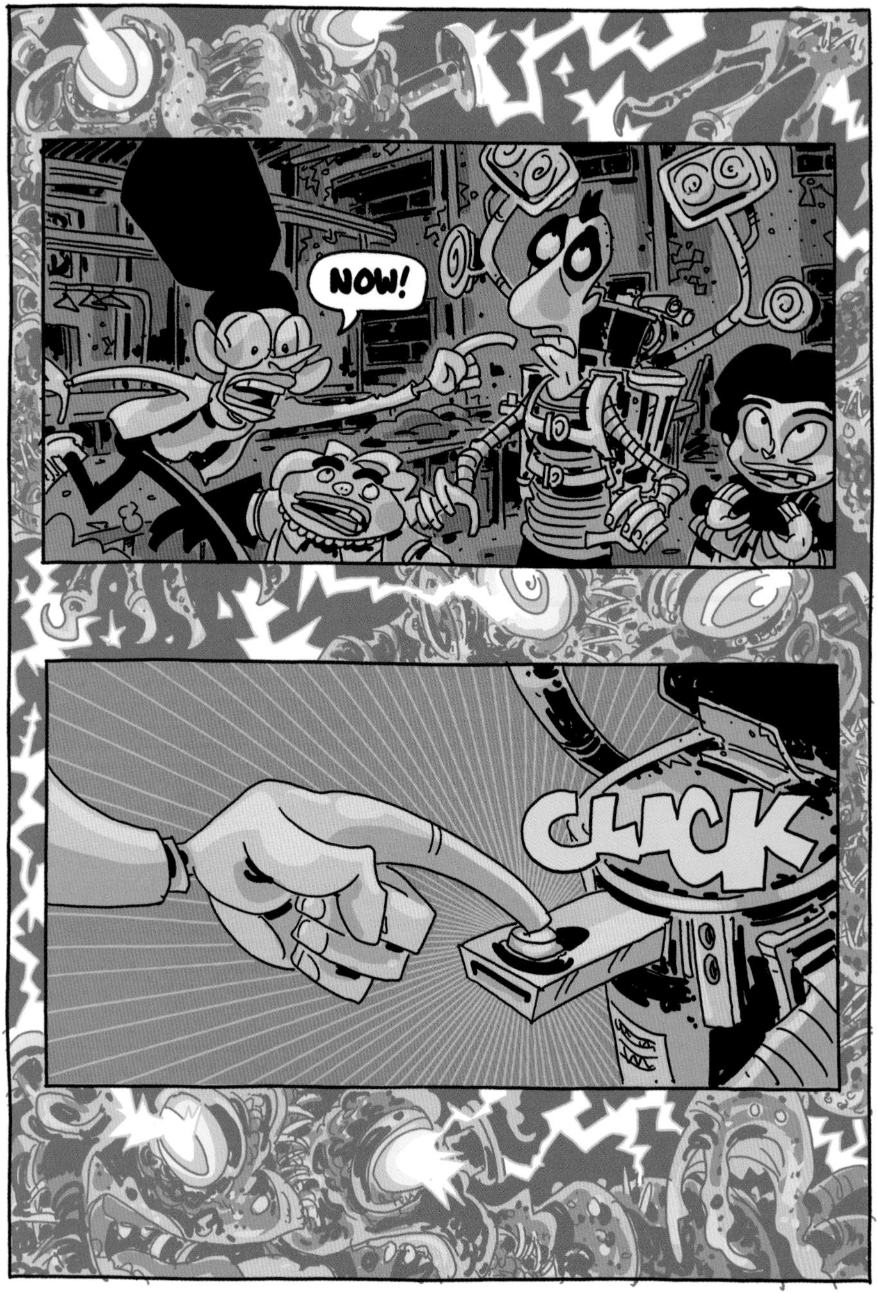
NOW!
CLICK

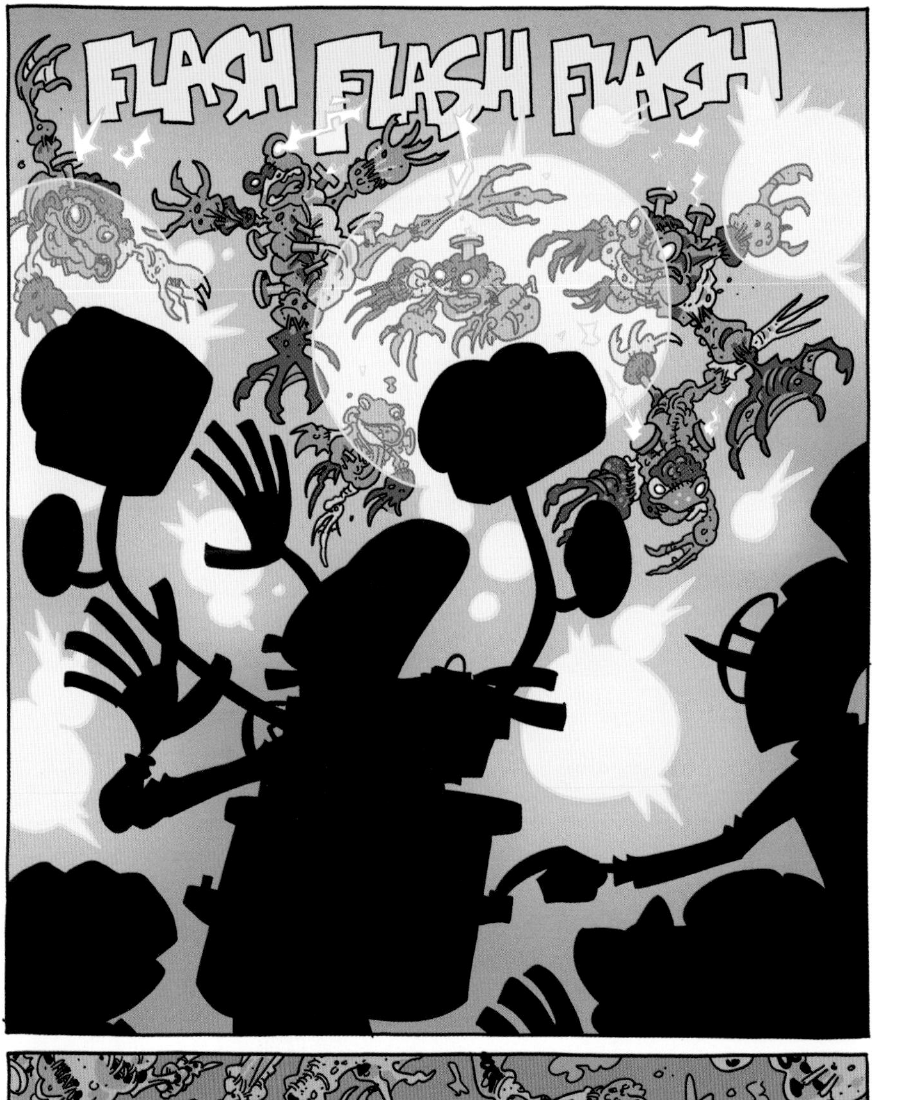
FLASH FLASH FLASH

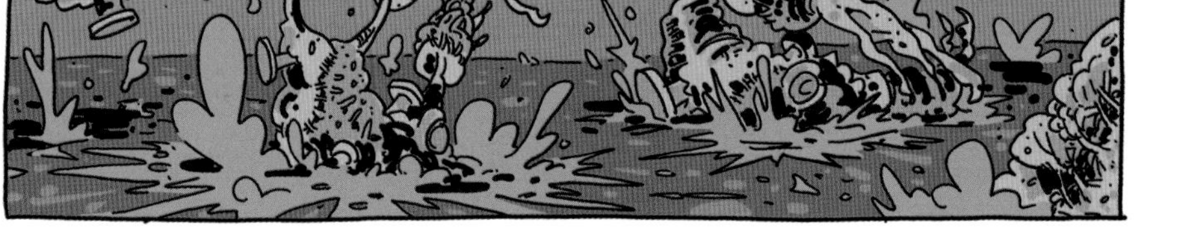

WHAT...

...WHAT DID YOU **DO** TO THEM?

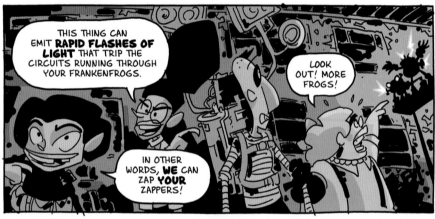

THIS THING CAN EMIT **RAPID FLASHES OF LIGHT** THAT TRIP THE CIRCUITS RUNNING THROUGH YOUR FRANKENFROGS.

LOOK OUT! MORE FROGS!

IN OTHER WORDS, **WE** CAN ZAP **YOUR** ZAPPERS!

DON'T WORRY.

I GOT 'EM.

CLICK

CLICK CLICK CLICK

UM... IT'S NOT FLASHING.

THERE'S A METER ON THE BATTERY.

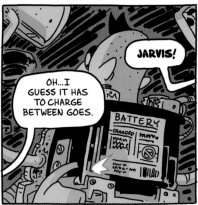

JARVIS!

OH...I GUESS IT HAS TO CHARGE BETWEEN GOES.

BATTERY
CHARGED

GET DOWN!

THUD

WHO NEEDS FLASHING LIGHTS? **ROSARIO** CAN JUST **PUNCH** THEM!

NOT **ALL** OF THEM.

SURE YOU CAN! HOW MANY COULD THERE **BE?**

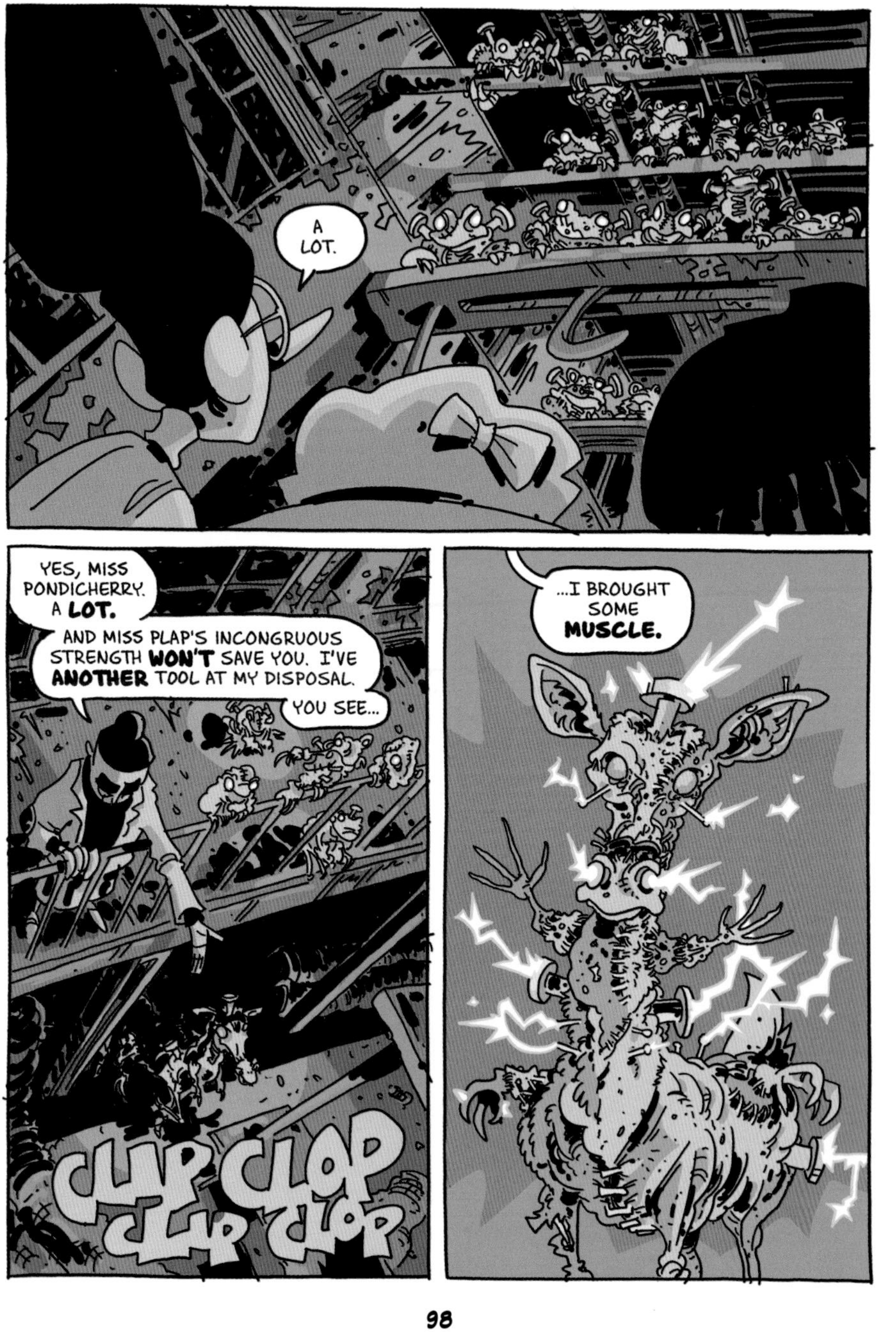
A LOT.
YES, MISS PONDICHERRY. A **LOT.**
AND MISS PLAP'S INCONGRUOUS STRENGTH **WON'T** SAVE YOU. I'VE **ANOTHER** TOOL AT MY DISPOSAL.
YOU SEE...
CLIP CLOP CLIP CLOP
...I BROUGHT SOME **MUSCLE.**

WHAT **IS** THAT?!

THAT IS A LITTLE SOMETHING **EXTRA** THAT I WHIPPED UP AFTER SEEING THAT **YOU** MEDDLERS WERE ON MY TRAIL.

I TOOK A FEW LIBERTIES WITH A DEER THAT DIDN'T **QUITE** MAKE IT ACROSS THE INTERSTATE.

EWW!

A **ROADKILL** MONSTER?

I'M NOT REALLY SURE **WHAT'S** HAPPENING HERE.

IT'S SIMPLE, MISTER RIGBY. THESE LOVELY CREATURES ARE GATHERING UP YOUR **CLASSMATES** FOR ME...

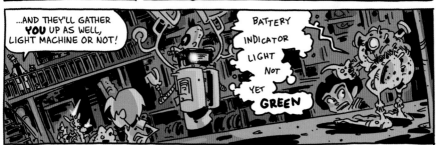

...AND THEY'LL GATHER **YOU** UP AS WELL, LIGHT MACHINE OR NOT!

BATTERY INDICATOR LIGHT NOT YET **GREEN**

THEN **ZAP** THEM BEFORE IT **RECHARGES**, MY LITTLE FROGS, AND PUT THEM WITH THE OTHERS!

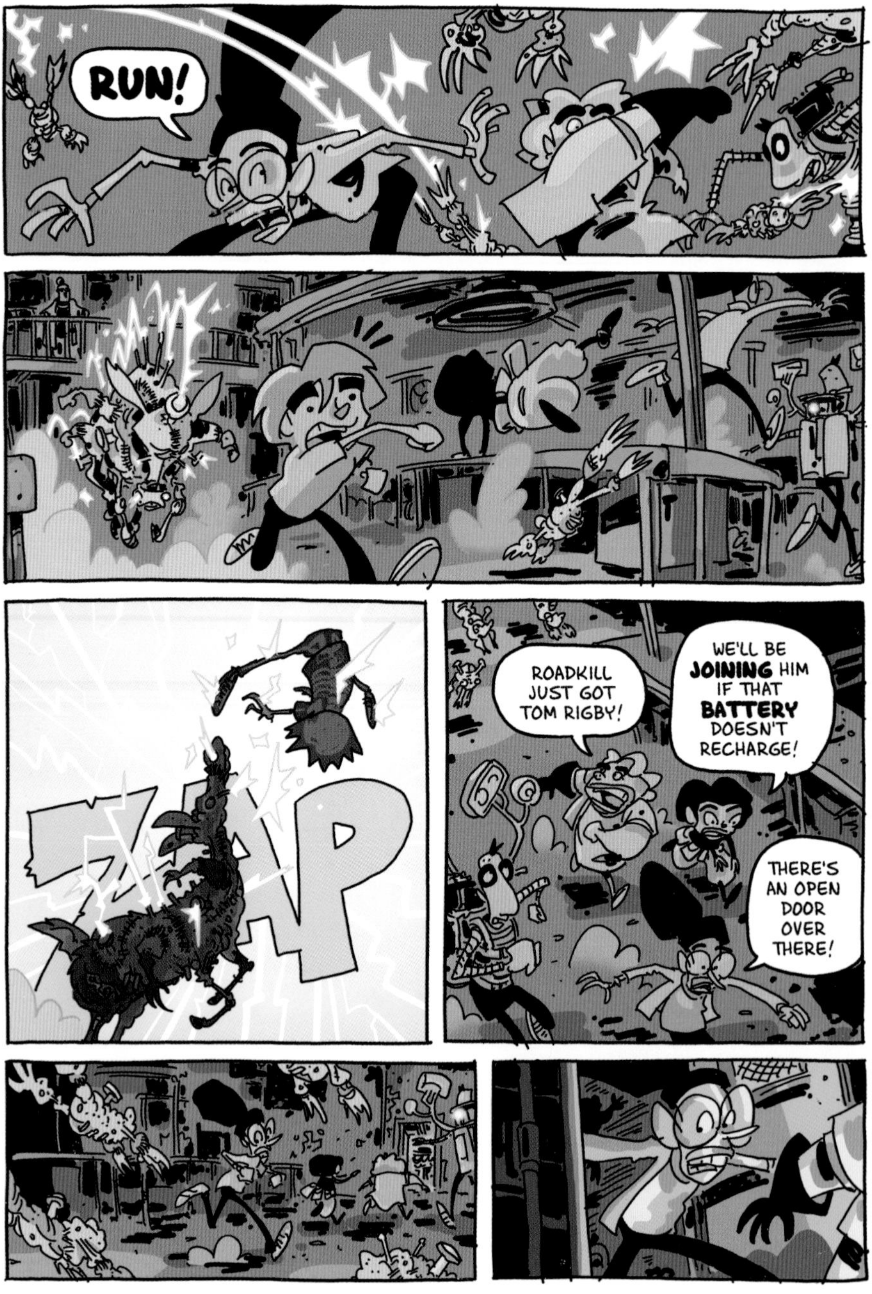
RUN!
ZAP
ROADKILL JUST GOT TOM RIGBY!
WE'LL BE **JOINING** HIM IF THAT **BATTERY** DOESN'T RECHARGE!
THERE'S AN OPEN DOOR OVER THERE!

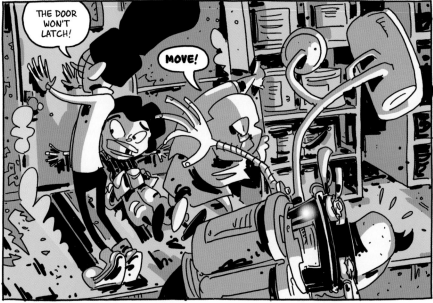

THE DOOR WON'T LATCH!

MOVE!

CRASH

GUYS...

THAT SHOULD KEEP THEM FROM PUSHING IT **OPEN,** AT LEAST.

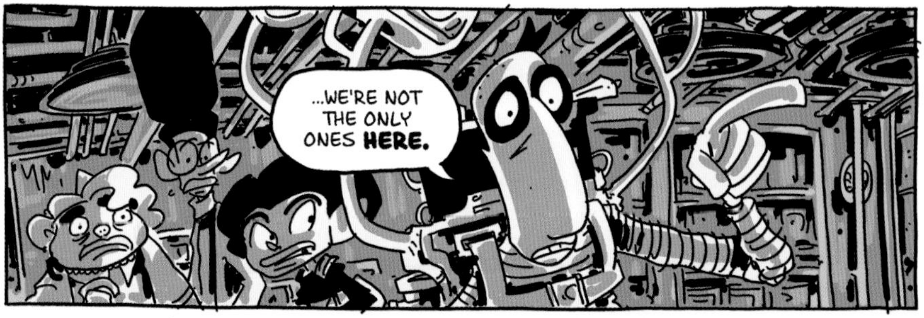
...WE'RE NOT THE ONLY ONES **HERE.**

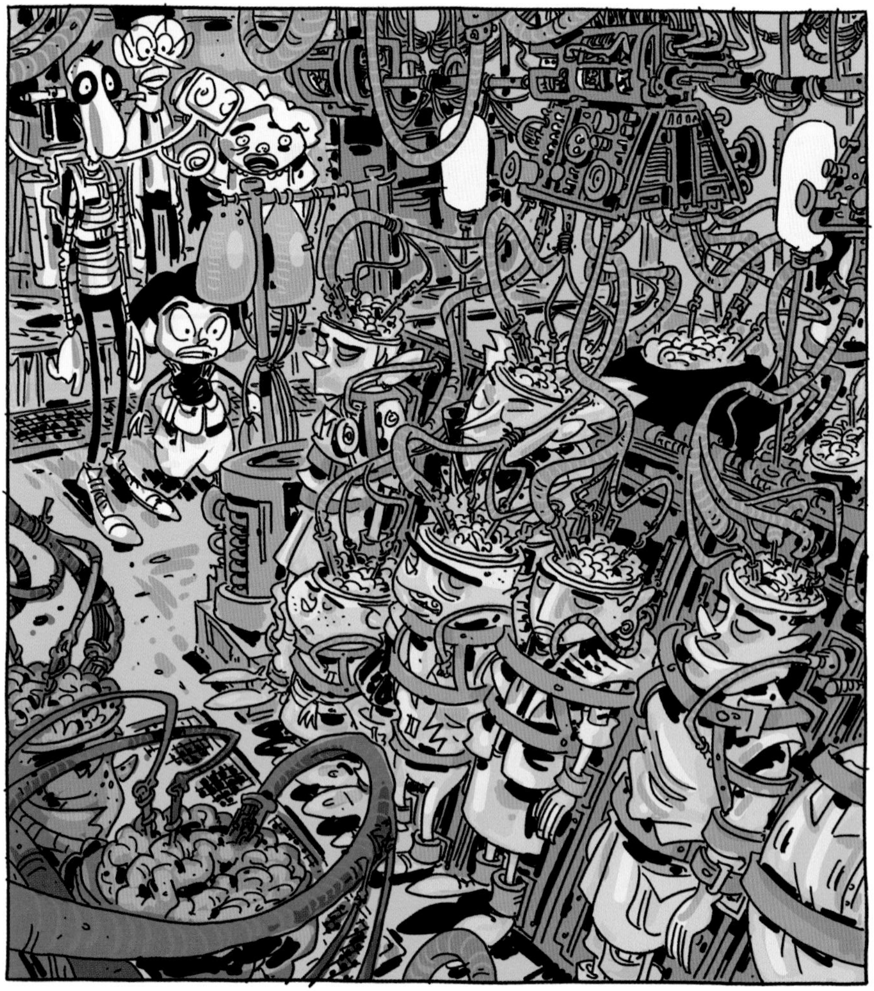

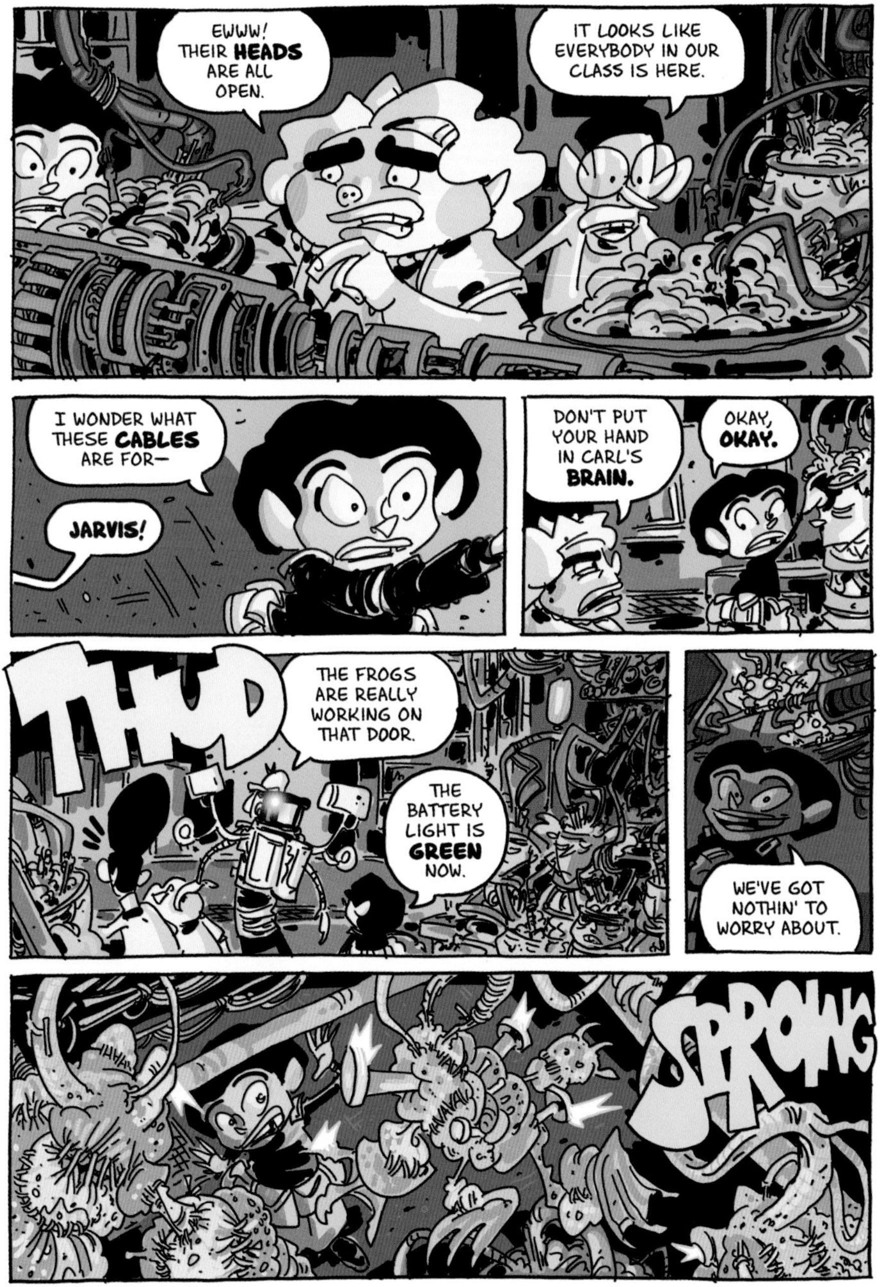
EWWW! THEIR HEADS ARE ALL OPEN.
IT LOOKS LIKE EVERYBODY IN OUR CLASS IS HERE.
I WONDER WHAT THESE CABLES ARE FOR—
JARVIS!
DON'T PUT YOUR HAND IN CARL'S BRAIN.
OKAY, OKAY.
THUD
THE FROGS ARE REALLY WORKING ON THAT DOOR.
THE BATTERY LIGHT IS GREEN NOW.
WE'VE GOT NOTHIN' TO WORRY ABOUT.
SPROING

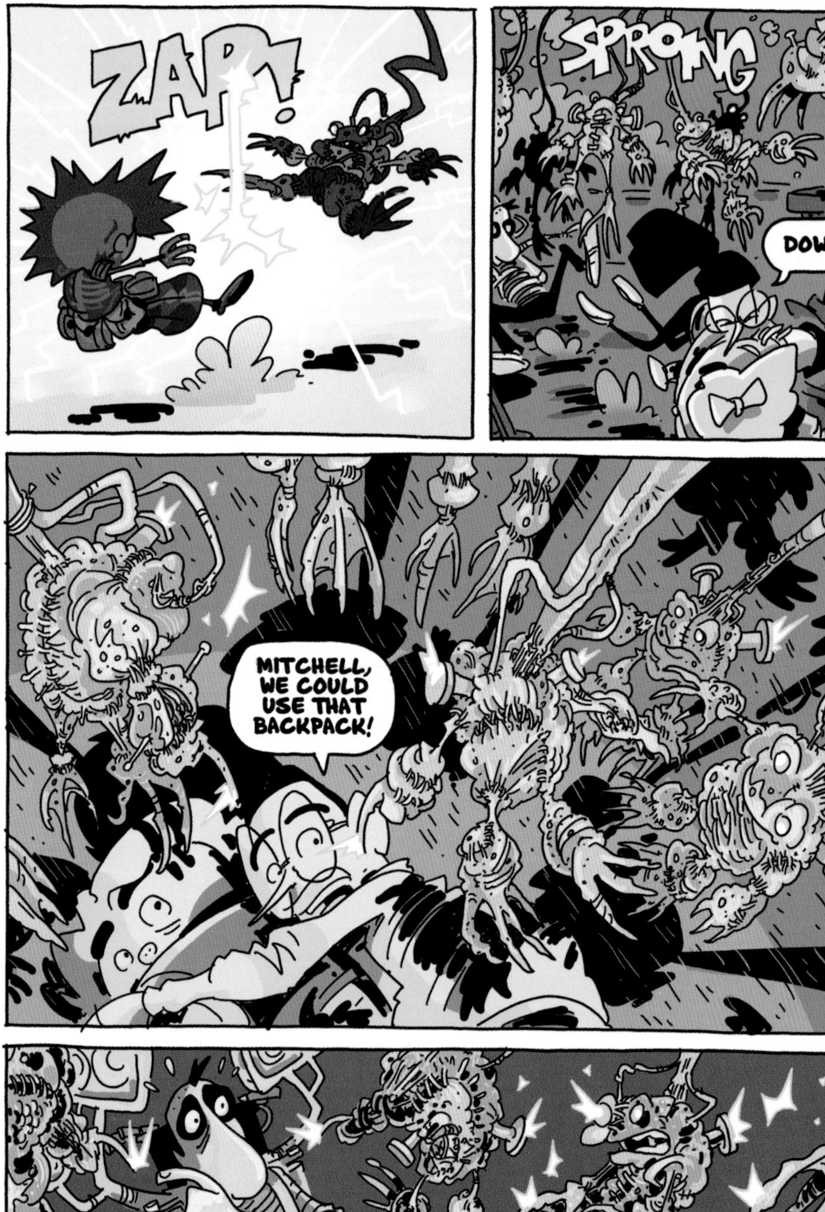
ZAP!
SPRONG
DOWN!
MITCHELL, WE COULD USE THAT BACKPACK!

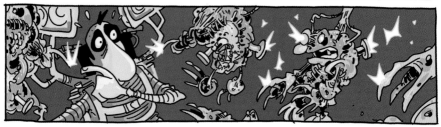

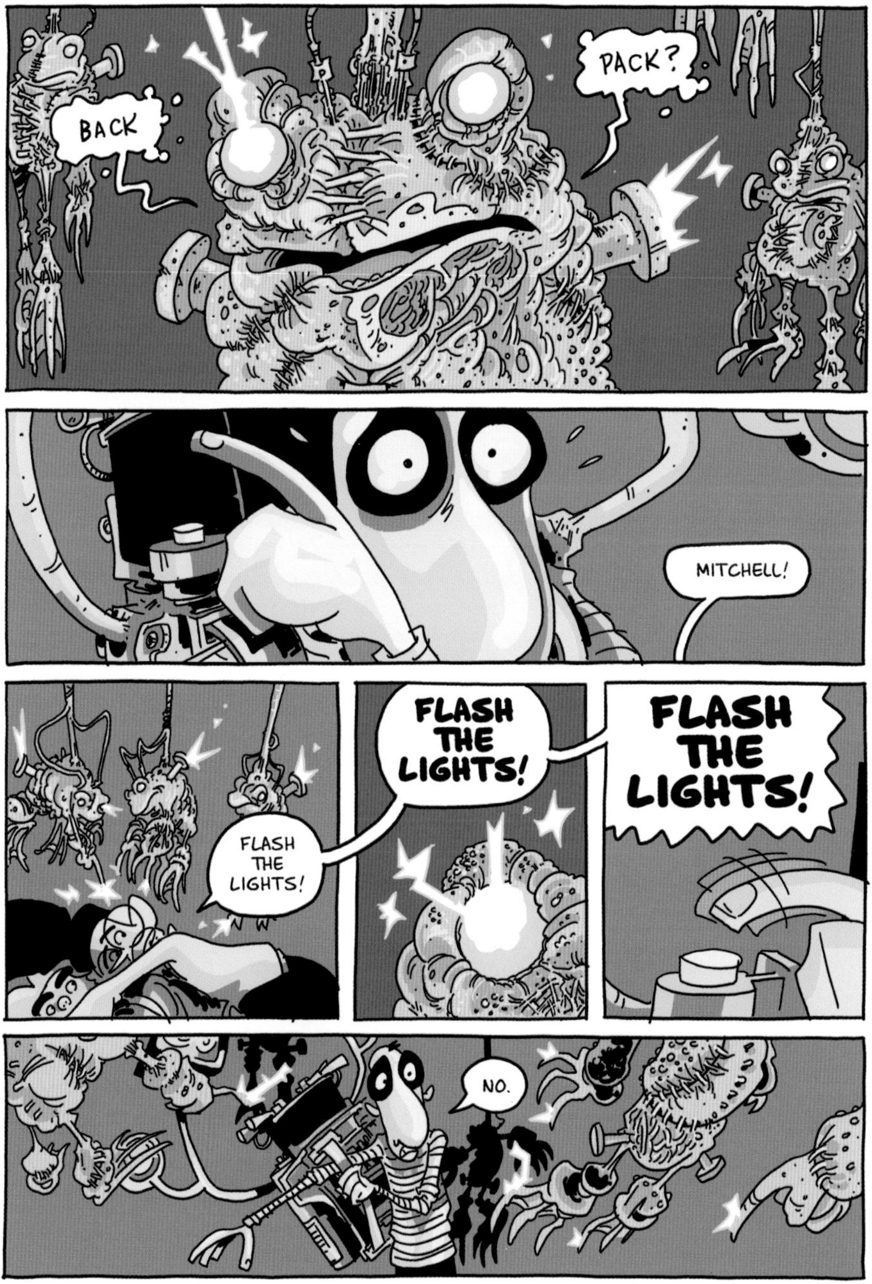
BACK
PACK?
MITCHELL!
FLASH THE LIGHTS!
FLASH THE LIGHTS!
FLASH THE LIGHTS!
NO.

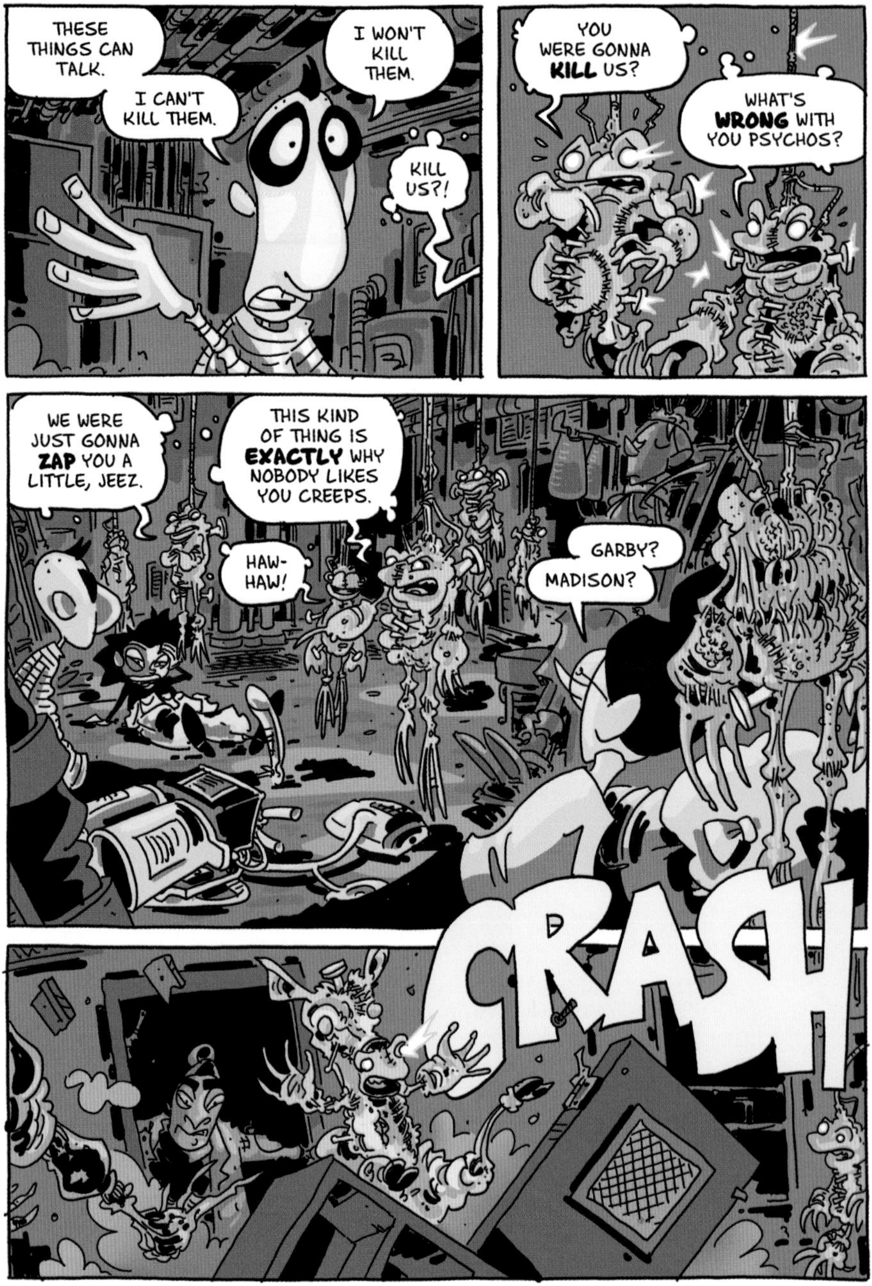
THESE THINGS CAN TALK.
I CAN'T KILL THEM.
I WON'T KILL THEM.
KILL US?!
YOU WERE GONNA KILL US?
WHAT'S WRONG WITH YOU PSYCHOS?
WE WERE JUST GONNA ZAP YOU A LITTLE, JEEZ.
THIS KIND OF THING IS EXACTLY WHY NOBODY LIKES YOU CREEPS.
HAW-HAW!
GARBY?
MADISON?
CRASH

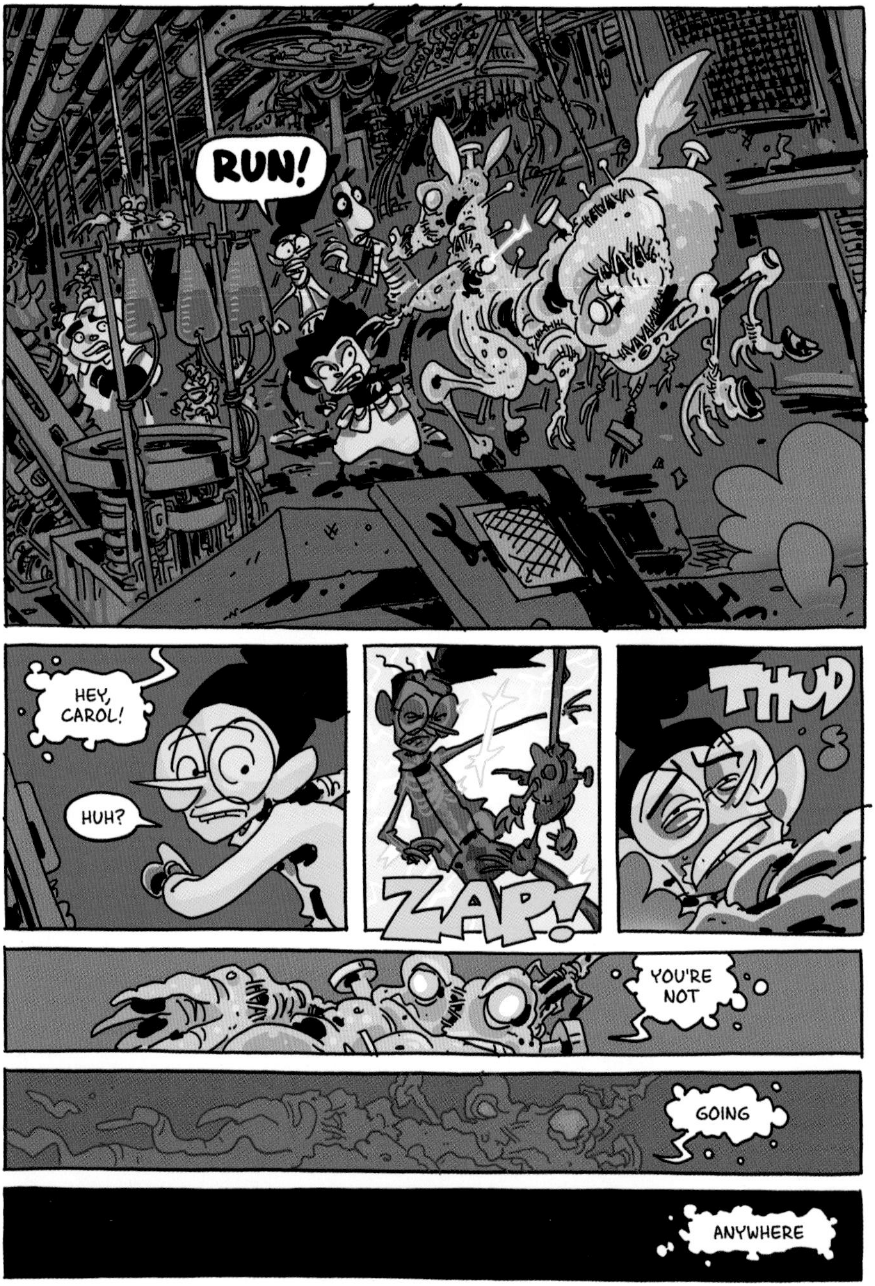
RUN!
HEY, CAROL!
HUH?
ZAP!
THUD
YOU'RE NOT
GOING
ANYWHERE

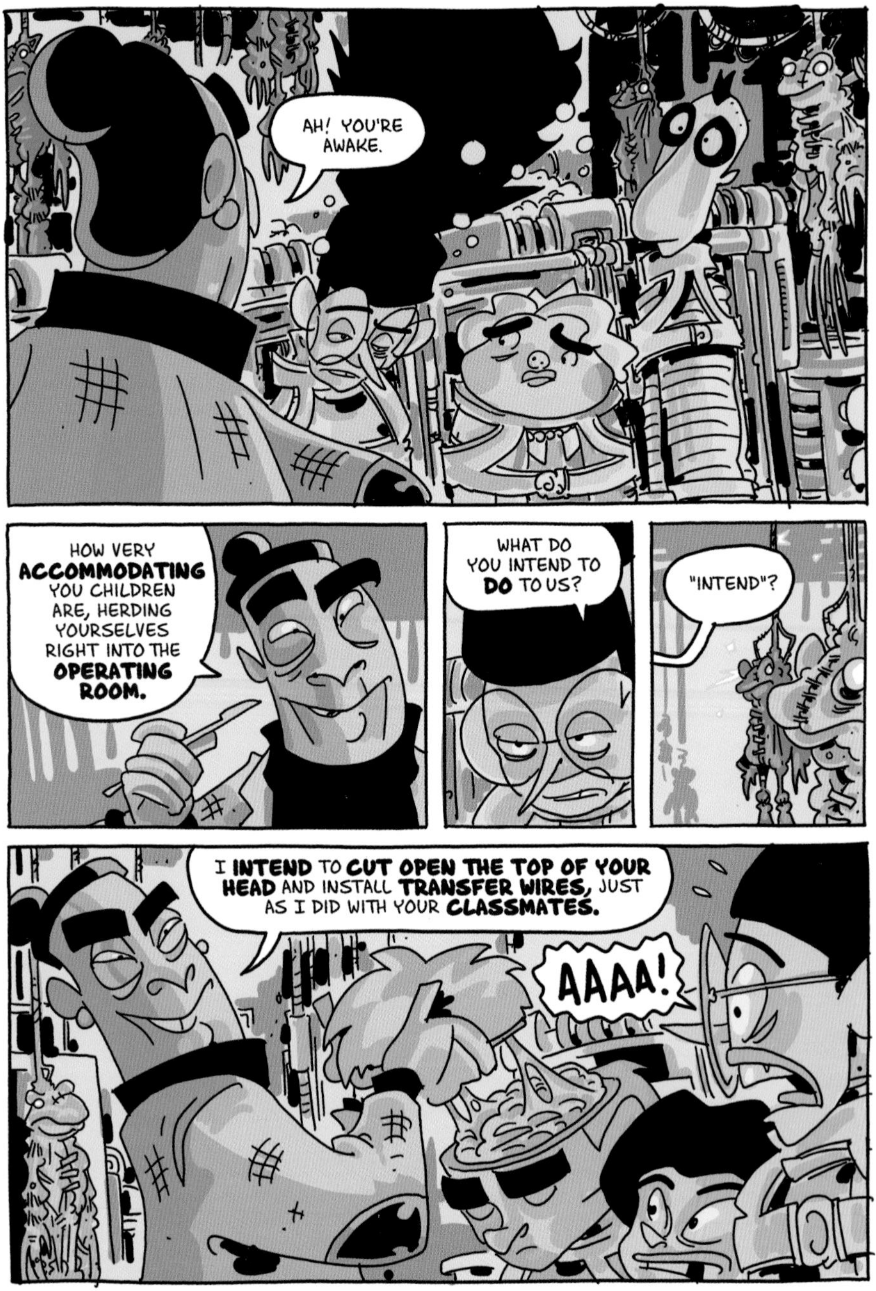
AH! YOU'RE AWAKE.
HOW VERY **ACCOMMODATING** YOU CHILDREN ARE, HERDING YOURSELVES RIGHT INTO THE **OPERATING ROOM.**
WHAT DO YOU INTEND TO **DO** TO US?
"INTEND"?
I **INTEND** TO **CUT OPEN THE TOP OF YOUR HEAD** AND INSTALL **TRANSFER WIRES,** JUST AS I DID WITH YOUR **CLASSMATES.**
AAAA!

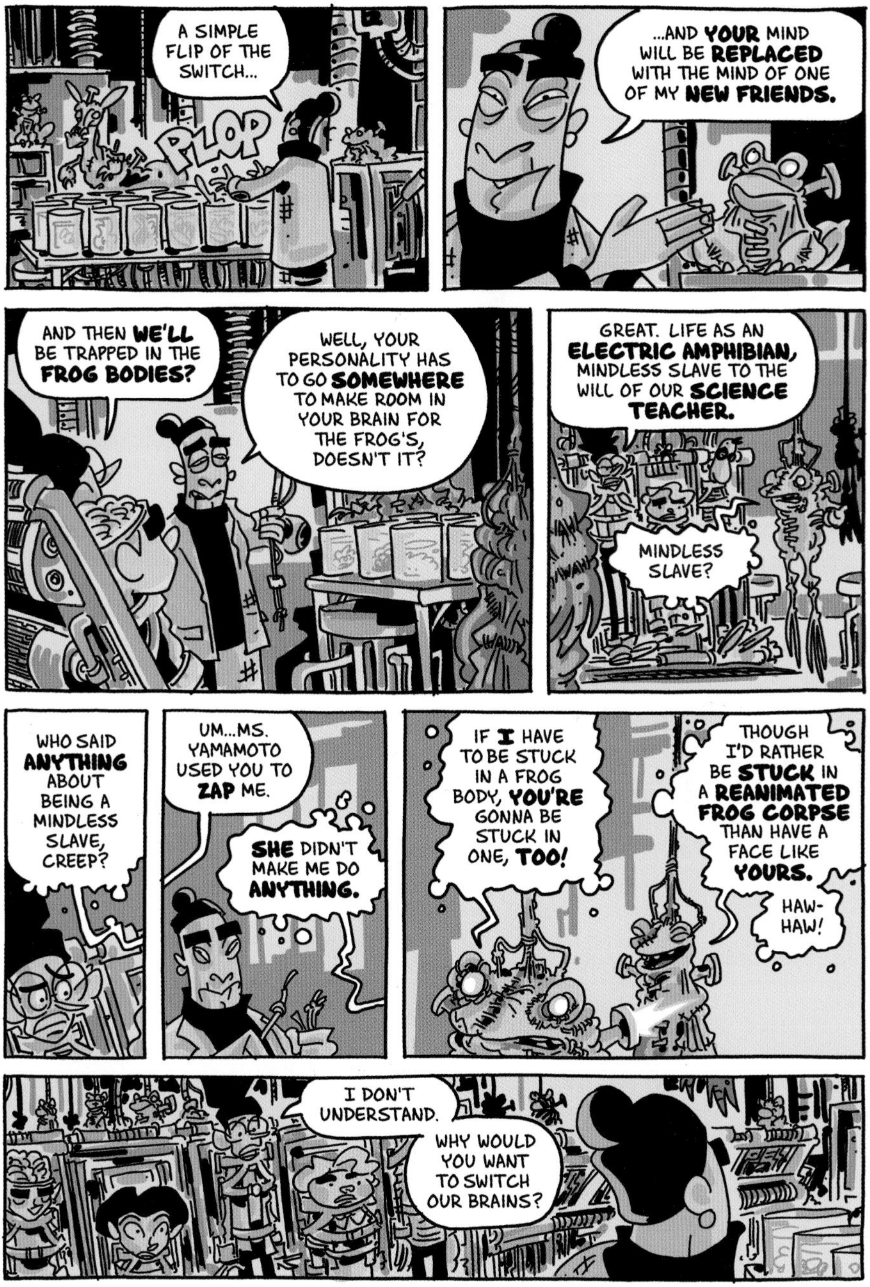
A SIMPLE FLIP OF THE SWITCH...
PLOP
...AND YOUR MIND WILL BE REPLACED WITH THE MIND OF ONE OF MY NEW FRIENDS.
AND THEN WE'LL BE TRAPPED IN THE FROG BODIES?
WELL, YOUR PERSONALITY HAS TO GO SOMEWHERE TO MAKE ROOM IN YOUR BRAIN FOR THE FROG'S, DOESN'T IT?
GREAT. LIFE AS AN ELECTRIC AMPHIBIAN, MINDLESS SLAVE TO THE WILL OF OUR SCIENCE TEACHER.
MINDLESS SLAVE?
WHO SAID ANYTHING ABOUT BEING A MINDLESS SLAVE, CREEP?
UM...MS. YAMAMOTO USED YOU TO ZAP ME.
SHE DIDN'T MAKE ME DO ANYTHING.
IF I HAVE TO BE STUCK IN A FROG BODY, YOU'RE GONNA BE STUCK IN ONE, TOO!
THOUGH I'D RATHER BE STUCK IN A REANIMATED FROG CORPSE THAN HAVE A FACE LIKE YOURS.
HAW-HAW!
I DON'T UNDERSTAND.
WHY WOULD YOU WANT TO SWITCH OUR BRAINS?

-SIGH-

I'M **SO TIRED** OF TEACHING KIDS WHO HAVE NO INTEREST IN **LEARNING.**

THAT **PETITION** WAS THE **FINAL STRAW.**

I DECIDED THEN AND THERE THAT IF I HAVE TO SEE YOUR FACES EACH DAY, THEY'LL BE FACES **EAGER** TO LEARN **SCIENCE!**

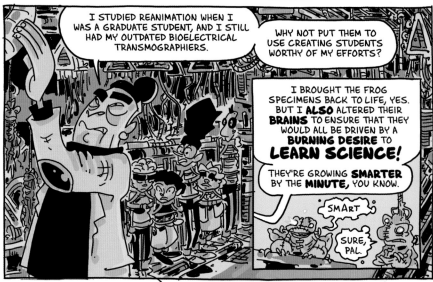

I STUDIED REANIMATION WHEN I WAS A GRADUATE STUDENT, AND I STILL HAD MY OUTDATED BIOELECTRICAL TRANSMOGRAPHIERS.

WHY NOT PUT THEM TO USE CREATING STUDENTS WORTHY OF MY EFFORTS?

I BROUGHT THE FROG SPECIMENS BACK TO LIFE, YES. BUT I **ALSO** ALTERED THEIR **BRAINS** TO ENSURE THAT THEY WOULD ALL BE DRIVEN BY A **BURNING DESIRE** TO **LEARN SCIENCE!**

THEY'RE GROWING **SMARTER** BY THE **MINUTE**, YOU KNOW.

SMART

SURE, PAL.

BUT I CAN'T TEACH A CLASSROOM FULL OF **FROG CREATURES!** SO I SENT THEM OUT TO CAPTURE MY **STUDENTS** TO SERVE AS THE **VESSELS** FOR THEIR **EAGER LITTLE MINDS.**

ALL THAT'S LEFT **NOW** IS TO OPERATE ON YOU TROUBLE-MAKERS, AND MY PLAN WILL BE COMPLETE!

AND WHAT'S GOING TO HAPPEN TO **US?**

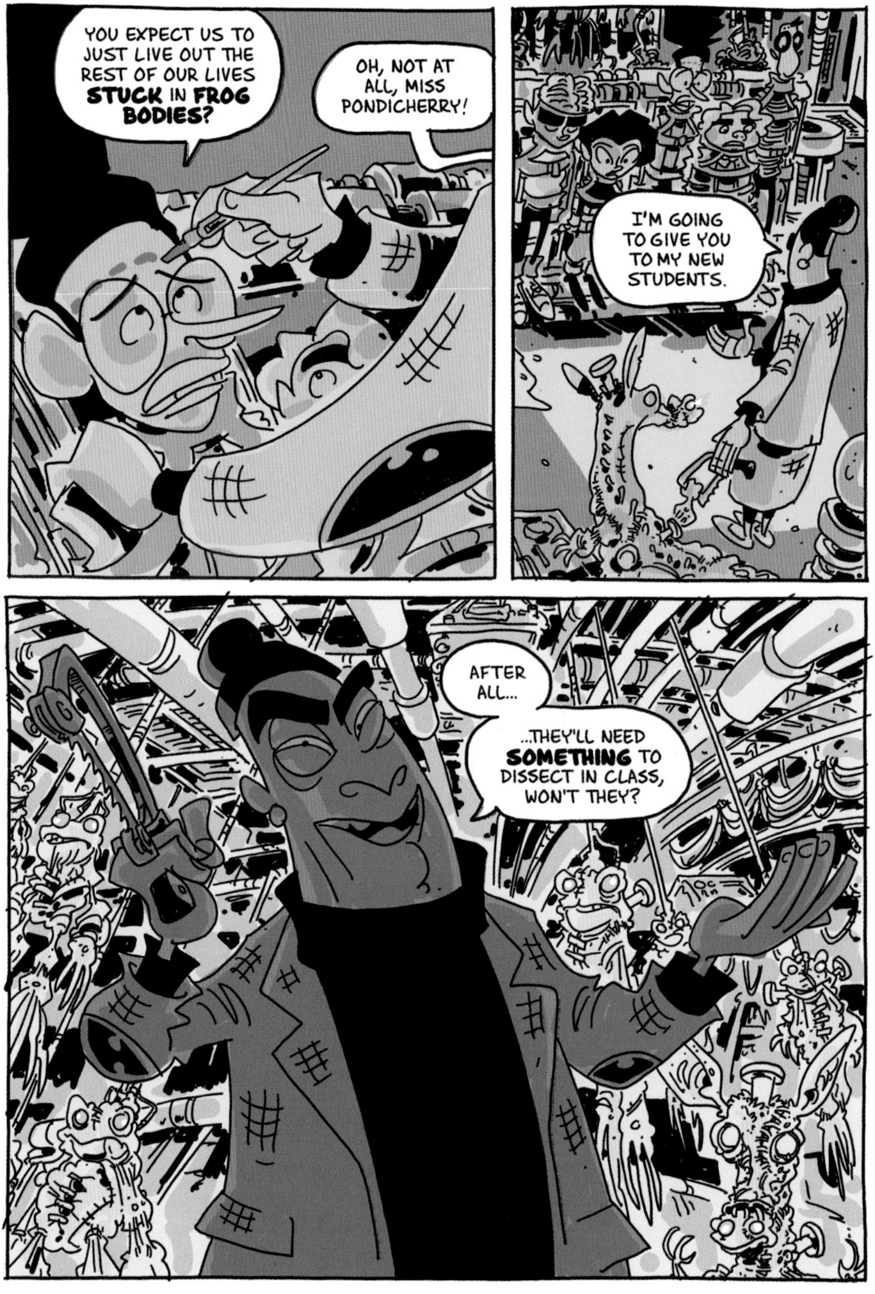
YOU EXPECT US TO JUST LIVE OUT THE REST OF OUR LIVES **STUCK** IN **FROG BODIES?**
OH, NOT AT ALL, MISS PONDICHERRY!
I'M GOING TO GIVE YOU TO MY NEW STUDENTS.
AFTER ALL...
...THEY'LL NEED **SOMETHING** TO DISSECT IN CLASS, WON'T THEY?

I CAN HARDLY BELIEVE IT, MISS PONDICHERRY. AFTER YEARS OF THANKLESS TOIL, I'LL **FINALLY** HAVE STUDENTS **INTERESTED** IN THE MATERIAL I'LL BE **TEACHING.**

BUT, MS. YAMAMOTO...

YOU **ALREADY HAVE** STUDENTS LIKE THAT!

NICE TRY, MISTER MAYHEW.

NO, HE'S RIGHT!

TOM RIGBY IS **NUTS** FOR SCIENCE! YOU SHOULD SEE HIS **ROOM!**

MISTER RIGBY IS A **LAGGARD,** WHOLLY DISINTERESTED IN HIS STUDIES.

NO, HE ISN'T!

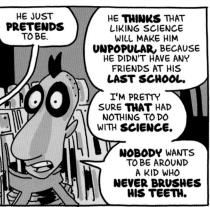

HE JUST **PRETENDS** TO BE.

HE **THINKS** THAT LIKING SCIENCE WILL MAKE HIM **UNPOPULAR,** BECAUSE HE DIDN'T HAVE ANY FRIENDS AT HIS **LAST SCHOOL.**

I'M PRETTY SURE **THAT** HAD NOTHING TO DO WITH **SCIENCE.**

NOBODY WANTS TO BE AROUND A KID WHO **NEVER BRUSHES HIS TEETH.**

HE **SNEAKS INTO THE SCHOOL** JUST TO DO HIS ASSIGNMENTS. **THAT'S** A DEDICATED STUDENT.

AND WHAT ABOUT **CAROL? SHE** USES STUFF WE'VE LEARNED IN CLASS **ALL THE TIME,** FOR OUR **INVESTIGATIONS.**

AND **I** LEARNED HOW TO MAKE **INVISIBLE INK** IN YOUR **CHEMISTRY LESSON!**

I PLANTED A **GARDEN** AFTER OUR SECTION ON **PLANT LIFE.**

ME, TOO!

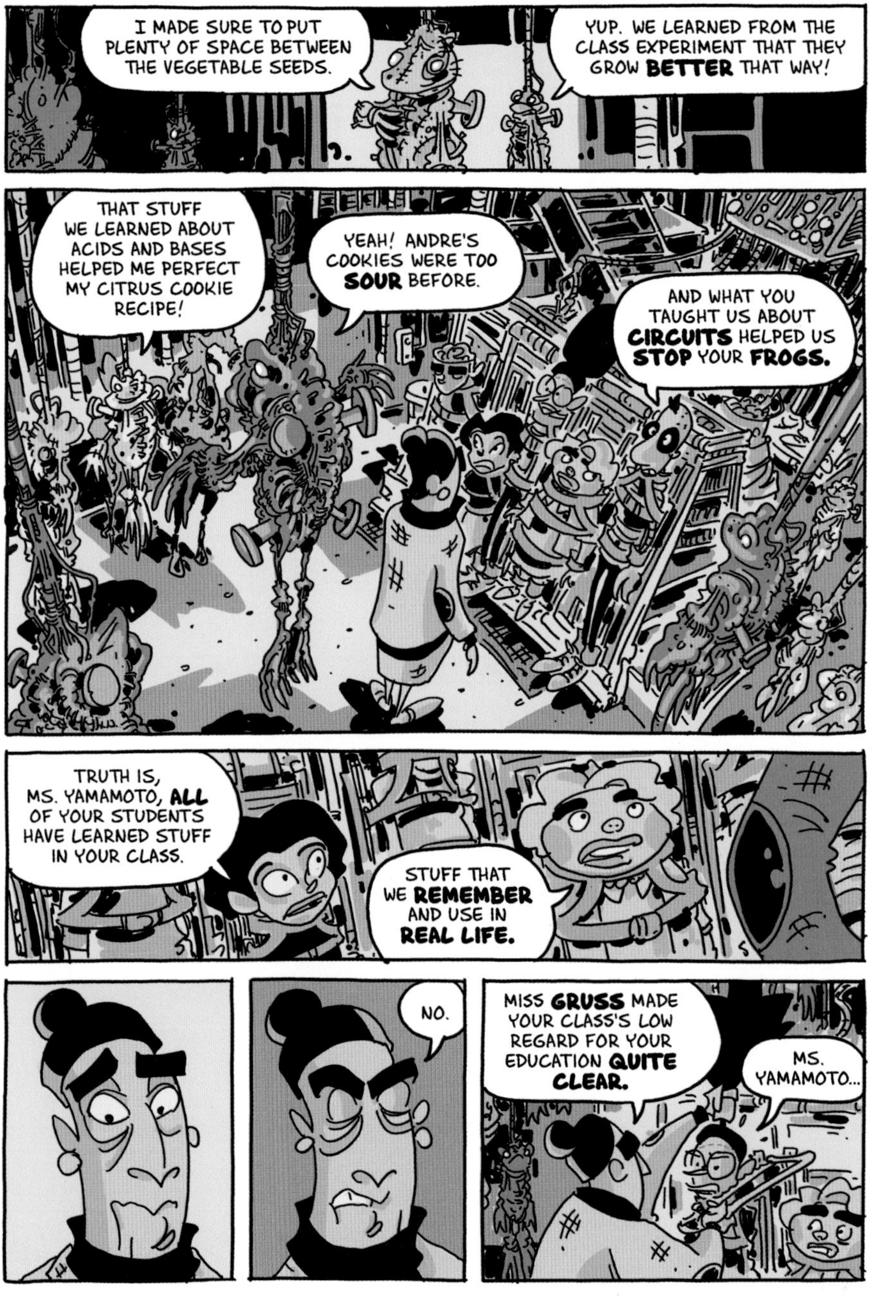

I MADE SURE TO PUT PLENTY OF SPACE BETWEEN THE VEGETABLE SEEDS.
YUP. WE LEARNED FROM THE CLASS EXPERIMENT THAT THEY GROW **BETTER** THAT WAY!
THAT STUFF WE LEARNED ABOUT ACIDS AND BASES HELPED ME PERFECT MY CITRUS COOKIE RECIPE!
YEAH! ANDRE'S COOKIES WERE TOO **SOUR** BEFORE.
AND WHAT YOU TAUGHT US ABOUT **CIRCUITS** HELPED US **STOP** YOUR **FROGS.**
TRUTH IS, MS. YAMAMOTO, **ALL** OF YOUR STUDENTS HAVE LEARNED STUFF IN YOUR CLASS.
STUFF THAT WE **REMEMBER** AND USE IN **REAL LIFE.**
NO.
MISS **GRUSS** MADE YOUR CLASS'S LOW REGARD FOR YOUR EDUCATION **QUITE CLEAR.**
MS. YAMAMOTO...

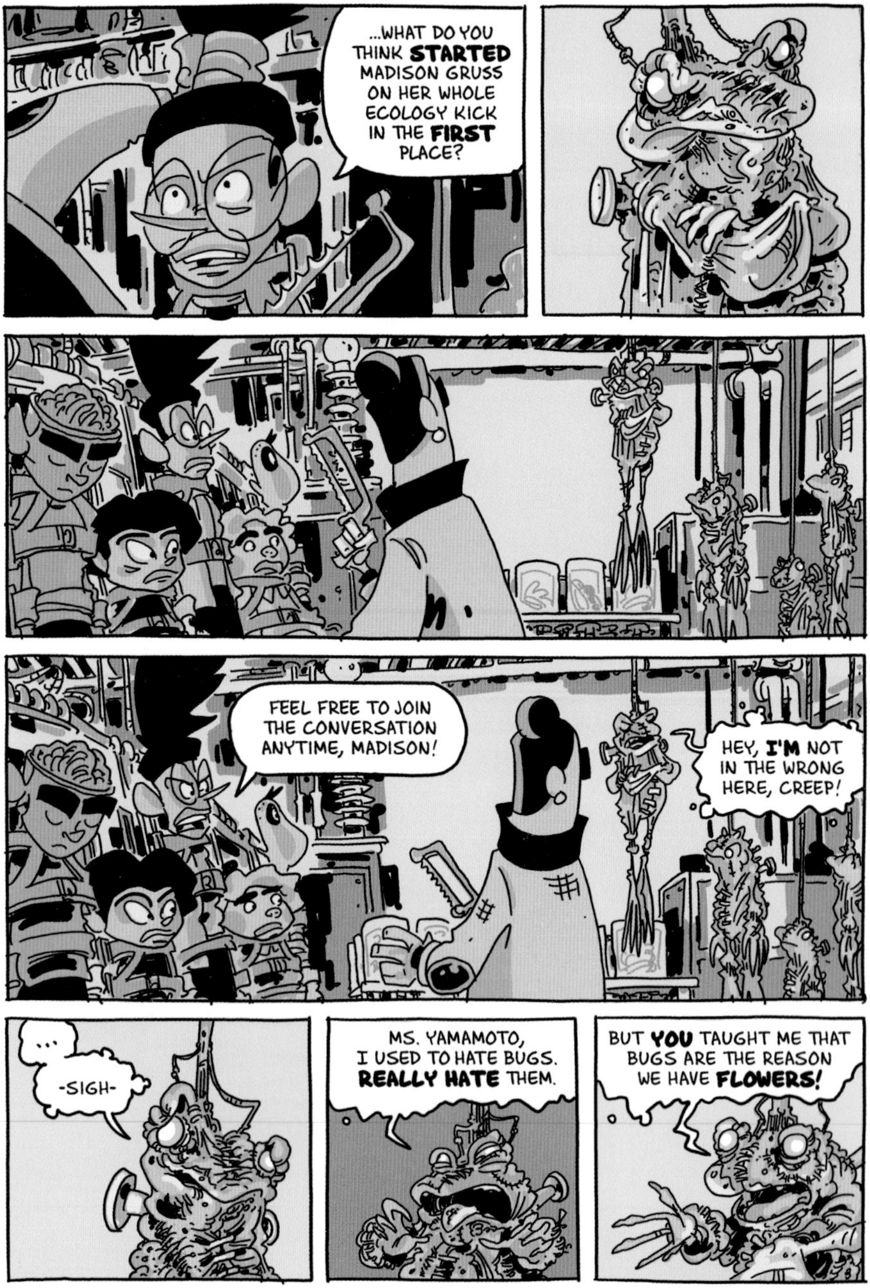
...WHAT DO YOU THINK STARTED MADISON GRUSS ON HER WHOLE ECOLOGY KICK IN THE FIRST PLACE?
FEEL FREE TO JOIN THE CONVERSATION ANYTIME, MADISON!
HEY, I'M NOT IN THE WRONG HERE, CREEP!
...
-SIGH-
MS. YAMAMOTO, I USED TO HATE BUGS. REALLY HATE THEM.
BUT YOU TAUGHT ME THAT BUGS ARE THE REASON WE HAVE FLOWERS!

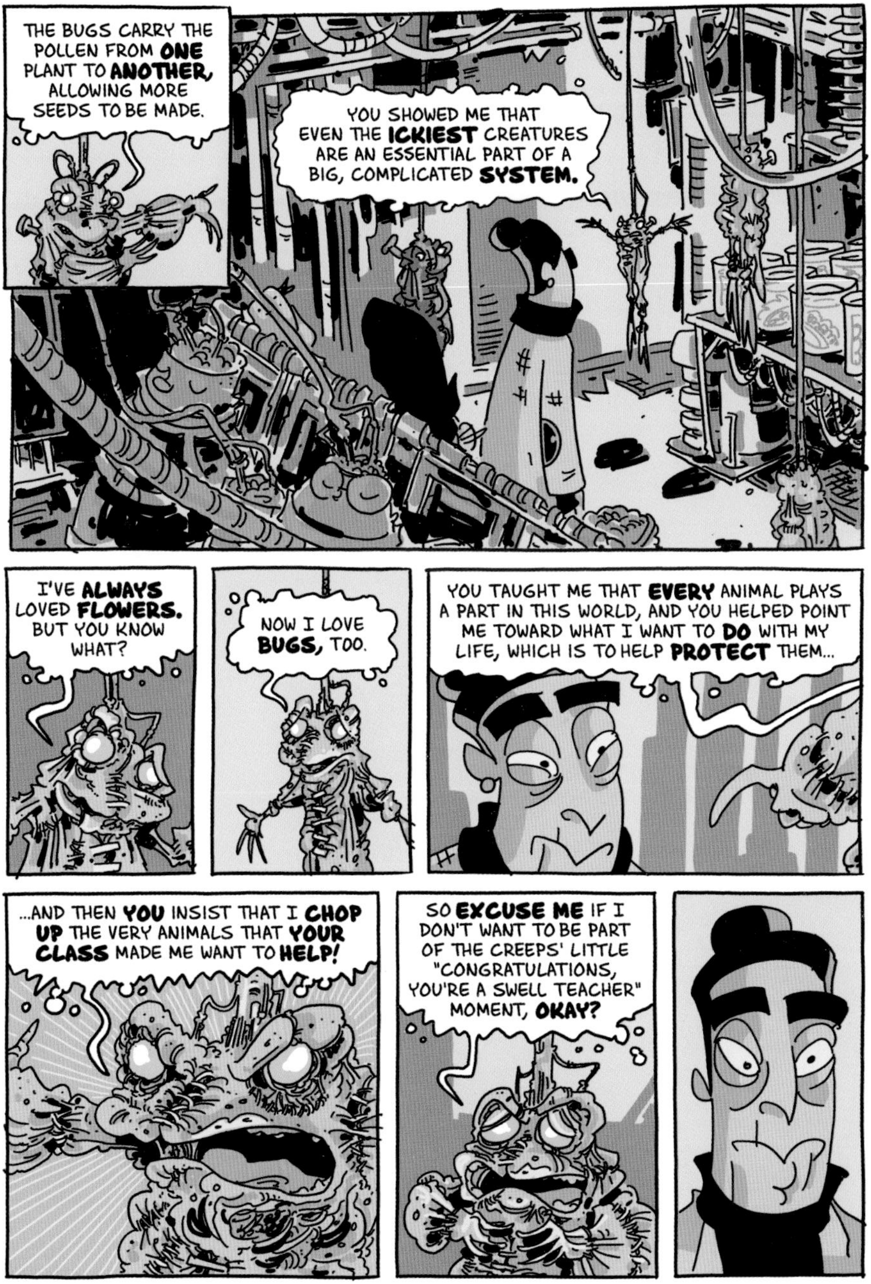
THE BUGS CARRY THE POLLEN FROM ONE PLANT TO ANOTHER, ALLOWING MORE SEEDS TO BE MADE.
YOU SHOWED ME THAT EVEN THE ICKIEST CREATURES ARE AN ESSENTIAL PART OF A BIG, COMPLICATED SYSTEM.
I'VE ALWAYS LOVED FLOWERS. BUT YOU KNOW WHAT?
NOW I LOVE BUGS, TOO.
YOU TAUGHT ME THAT EVERY ANIMAL PLAYS A PART IN THIS WORLD, AND YOU HELPED POINT ME TOWARD WHAT I WANT TO DO WITH MY LIFE, WHICH IS TO HELP PROTECT THEM...
...AND THEN YOU INSIST THAT I CHOP UP THE VERY ANIMALS THAT YOUR CLASS MADE ME WANT TO HELP!
SO EXCUSE ME IF I DON'T WANT TO BE PART OF THE CREEPS' LITTLE "CONGRATULATIONS, YOU'RE A SWELL TEACHER" MOMENT, OKAY?

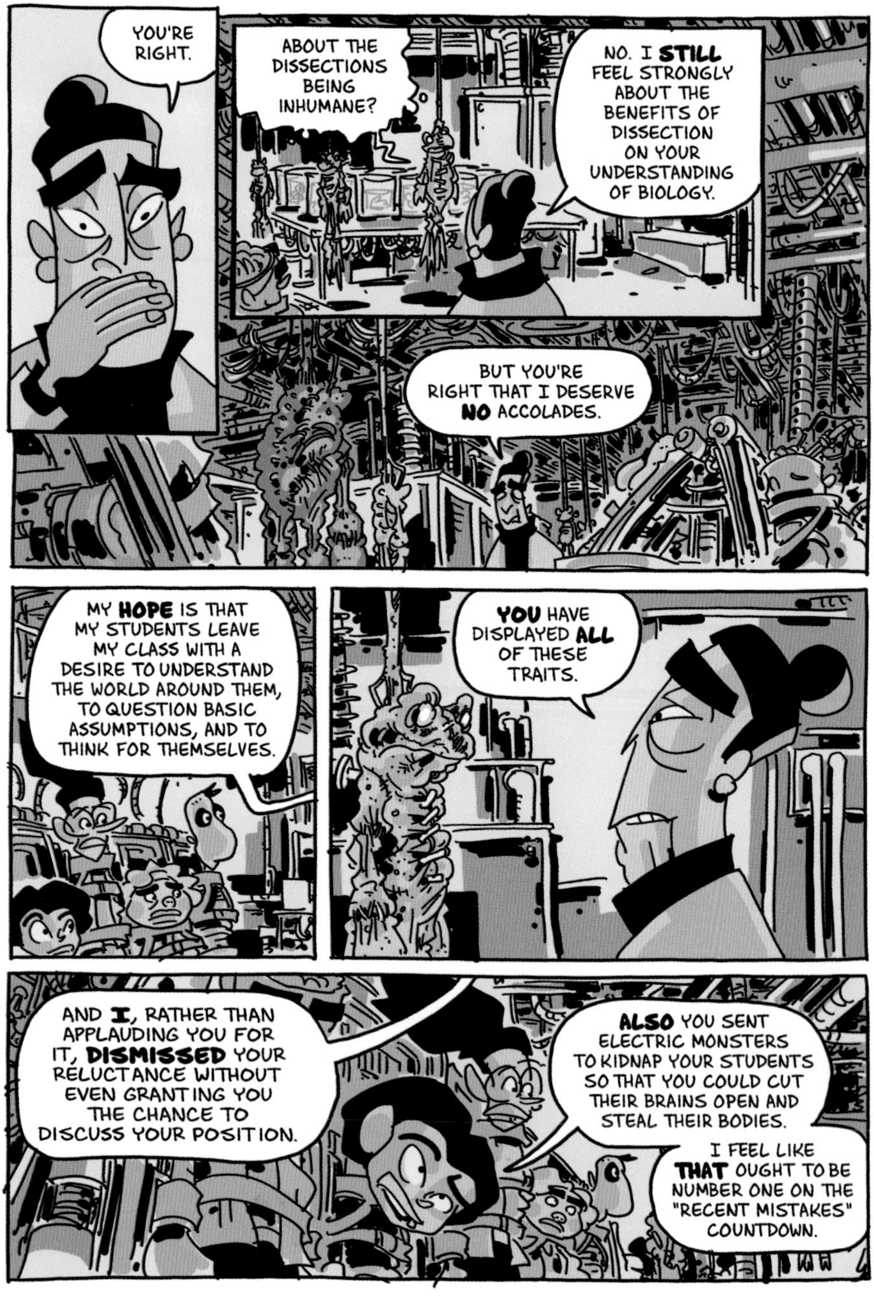
YOU'RE RIGHT.
ABOUT THE DISSECTIONS BEING INHUMANE?
NO. I STILL FEEL STRONGLY ABOUT THE BENEFITS OF DISSECTION ON YOUR UNDERSTANDING OF BIOLOGY.
BUT YOU'RE RIGHT THAT I DESERVE NO ACCOLADES.
MY HOPE IS THAT MY STUDENTS LEAVE MY CLASS WITH A DESIRE TO UNDERSTAND THE WORLD AROUND THEM, TO QUESTION BASIC ASSUMPTIONS, AND TO THINK FOR THEMSELVES.
YOU HAVE DISPLAYED ALL OF THESE TRAITS.
AND I, RATHER THAN APPLAUDING YOU FOR IT, DISMISSED YOUR RELUCTANCE WITHOUT EVEN GRANTING YOU THE CHANCE TO DISCUSS YOUR POSITION.
ALSO YOU SENT ELECTRIC MONSTERS TO KIDNAP YOUR STUDENTS SO THAT YOU COULD CUT THEIR BRAINS OPEN AND STEAL THEIR BODIES.
I FEEL LIKE THAT OUGHT TO BE NUMBER ONE ON THE "RECENT MISTAKES" COUNTDOWN.

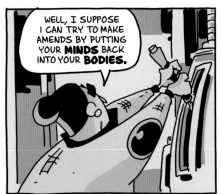

WELL, I SUPPOSE I CAN TRY TO MAKE AMENDS BY PUTTING YOUR **MINDS** BACK INTO YOUR **BODIES.**

CHUNK CHUNK

ZZZZ

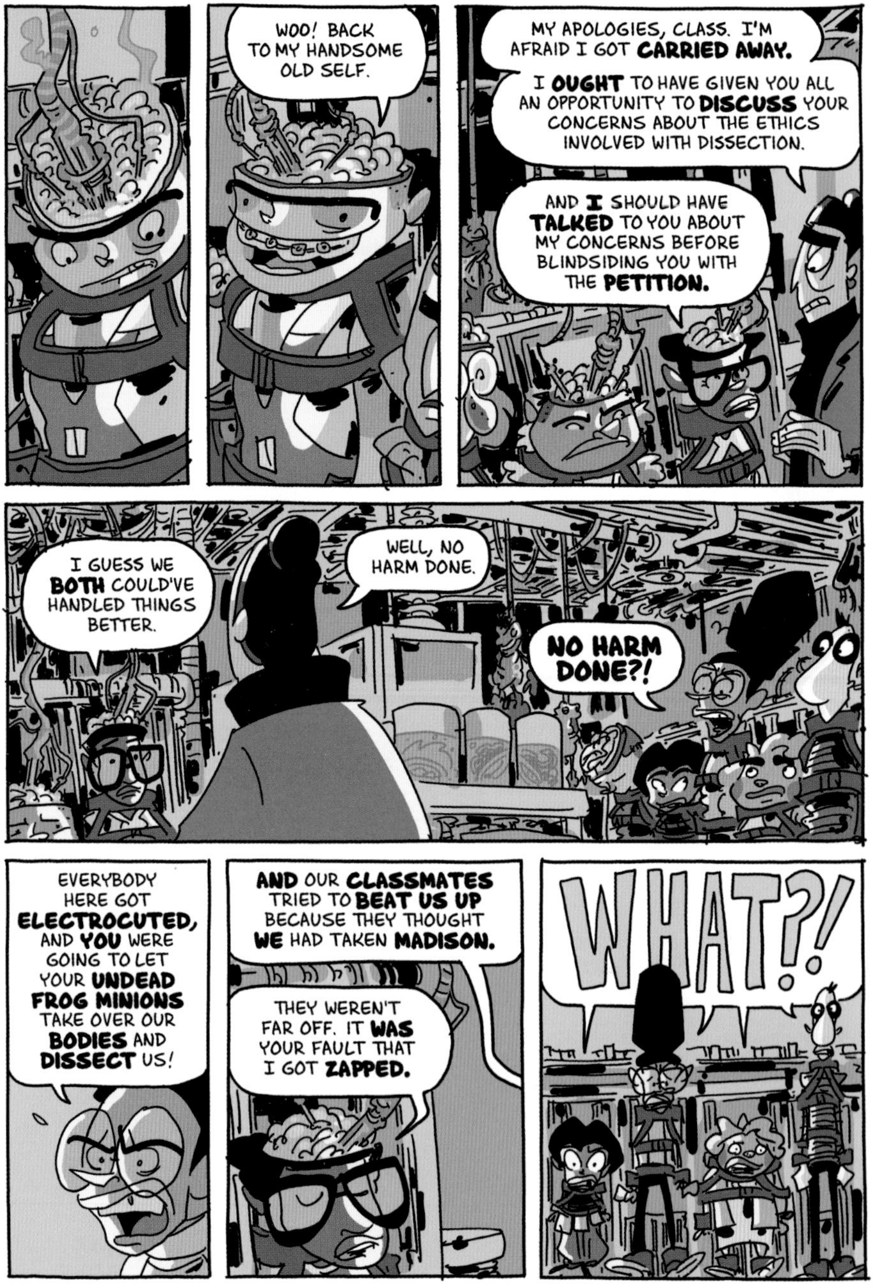
WOO! BACK TO MY HANDSOME OLD SELF.
MY APOLOGIES, CLASS. I'M AFRAID I GOT CARRIED AWAY.
I OUGHT TO HAVE GIVEN YOU ALL AN OPPORTUNITY TO DISCUSS YOUR CONCERNS ABOUT THE ETHICS INVOLVED WITH DISSECTION.
AND I SHOULD HAVE TALKED TO YOU ABOUT MY CONCERNS BEFORE BLINDSIDING YOU WITH THE PETITION.
I GUESS WE BOTH COULD'VE HANDLED THINGS BETTER.
WELL, NO HARM DONE.
NO HARM DONE?!
EVERYBODY HERE GOT ELECTROCUTED, AND YOU WERE GOING TO LET YOUR UNDEAD FROG MINIONS TAKE OVER OUR BODIES AND DISSECT US!
AND OUR CLASSMATES TRIED TO BEAT US UP BECAUSE THEY THOUGHT WE HAD TAKEN MADISON.
THEY WEREN'T FAR OFF. IT WAS YOUR FAULT THAT I GOT ZAPPED.
WHAT?!

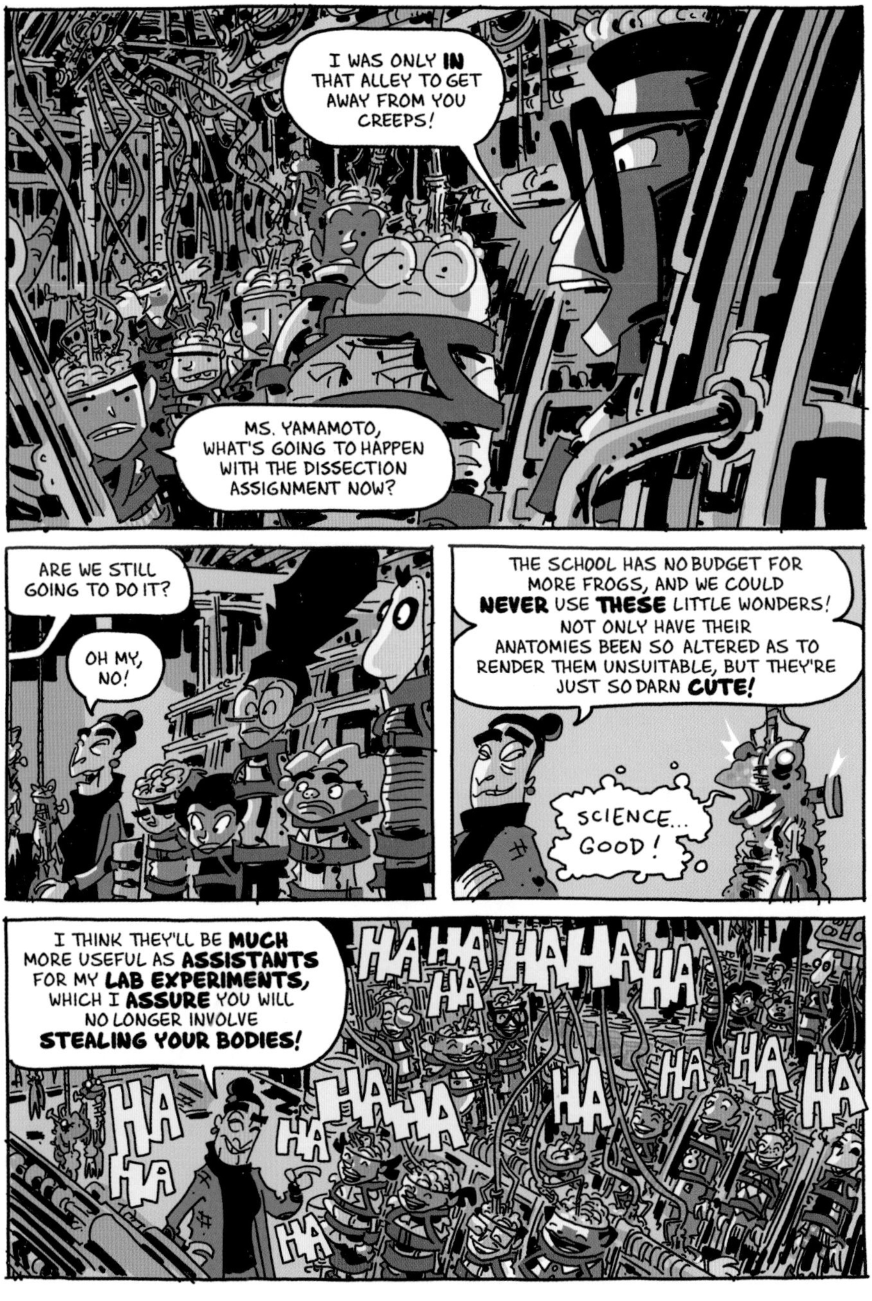
I WAS ONLY IN THAT ALLEY TO GET AWAY FROM YOU CREEPS!
MS. YAMAMOTO, WHAT'S GOING TO HAPPEN WITH THE DISSECTION ASSIGNMENT NOW?
ARE WE STILL GOING TO DO IT?
OH MY, NO!
THE SCHOOL HAS NO BUDGET FOR MORE FROGS, AND WE COULD NEVER USE THESE LITTLE WONDERS! NOT ONLY HAVE THEIR ANATOMIES BEEN SO ALTERED AS TO RENDER THEM UNSUITABLE, BUT THEY'RE JUST SO DARN CUTE!
SCIENCE... GOOD!
I THINK THEY'LL BE MUCH MORE USEFUL AS ASSISTANTS FOR MY LAB EXPERIMENTS, WHICH I ASSURE YOU WILL NO LONGER INVOLVE STEALING YOUR BODIES!
HA HA HA HA HA HA HA HA
HA HA HA HA HA HA HA HA HA HA HA HA HA

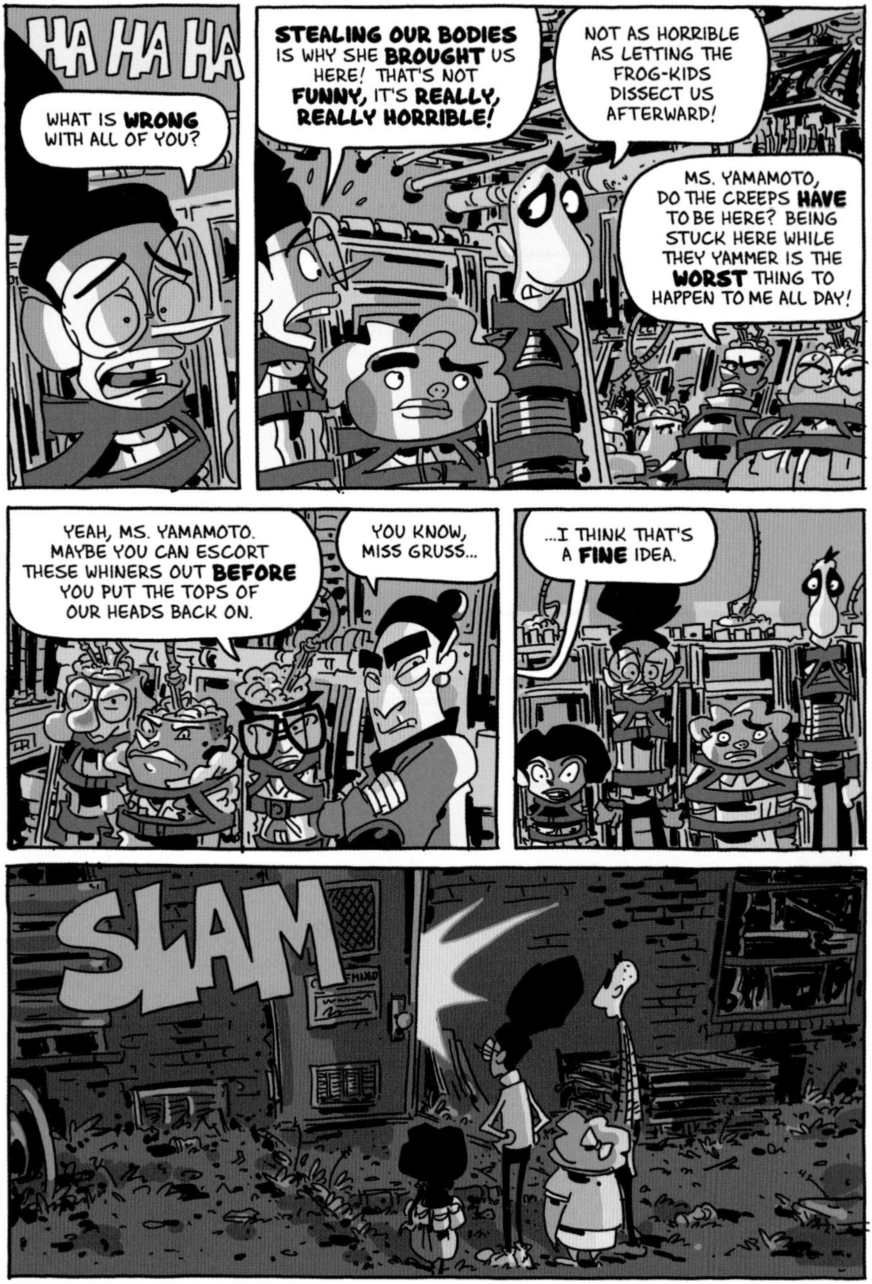
HA HA HA
WHAT IS WRONG WITH ALL OF YOU?
STEALING OUR BODIES IS WHY SHE BROUGHT US HERE! THAT'S NOT FUNNY, IT'S REALLY, REALLY HORRIBLE!
NOT AS HORRIBLE AS LETTING THE FROG-KIDS DISSECT US AFTERWARD!
MS. YAMAMOTO, DO THE CREEPS HAVE TO BE HERE? BEING STUCK HERE WHILE THEY YAMMER IS THE WORST THING TO HAPPEN TO ME ALL DAY!
YEAH, MS. YAMAMOTO. MAYBE YOU CAN ESCORT THESE WHINERS OUT BEFORE YOU PUT THE TOPS OF OUR HEADS BACK ON.
YOU KNOW, MISS GRUSS...
...I THINK THAT'S A FINE IDEA.
SLAM

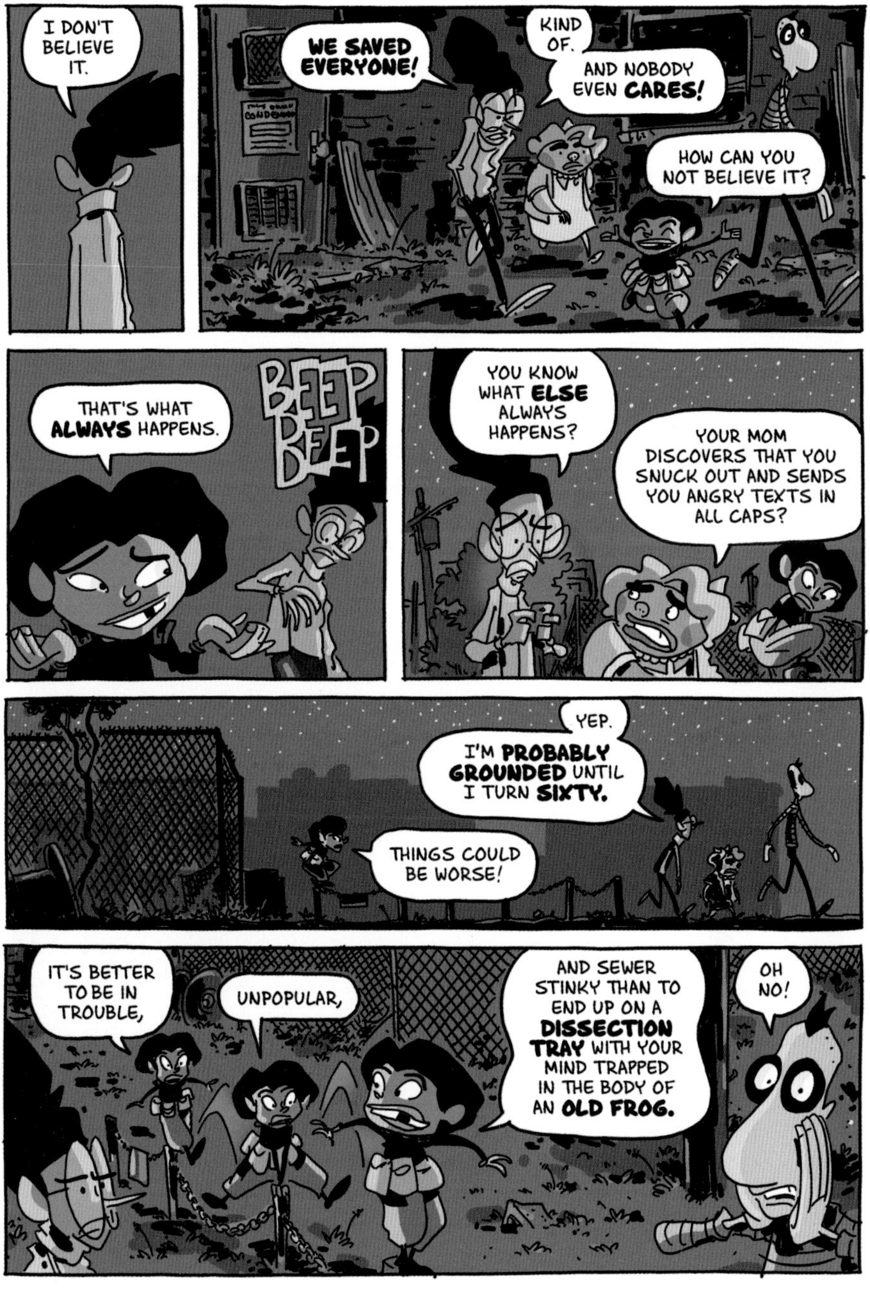

I DON'T BELIEVE IT.
WE SAVED EVERYONE!
KIND OF.
AND NOBODY EVEN CARES!
HOW CAN YOU NOT BELIEVE IT?
THAT'S WHAT ALWAYS HAPPENS.
BEEP BEEP
YOU KNOW WHAT ELSE ALWAYS HAPPENS?
YOUR MOM DISCOVERS THAT YOU SNUCK OUT AND SENDS YOU ANGRY TEXTS IN ALL CAPS?
YEP.
I'M PROBABLY GROUNDED UNTIL I TURN SIXTY.
THINGS COULD BE WORSE!
IT'S BETTER TO BE IN TROUBLE,
UNPOPULAR,
AND SEWER STINKY THAN TO END UP ON A DISSECTION TRAY WITH YOUR MIND TRAPPED IN THE BODY OF AN OLD FROG.
OH NO!

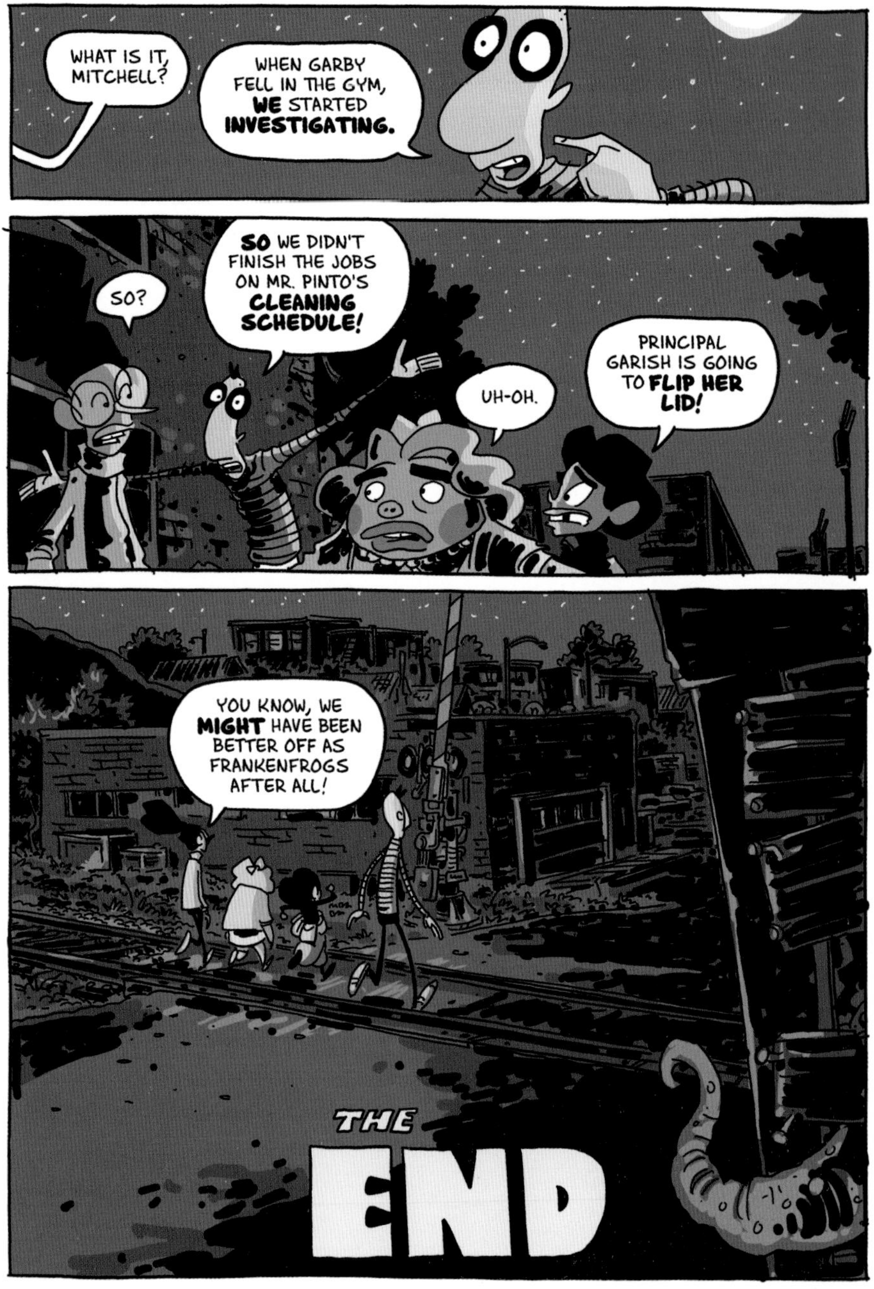
WHAT IS IT, MITCHELL?
WHEN GARBY FELL IN THE GYM, **WE** STARTED **INVESTIGATING.**
SO?
SO WE DIDN'T FINISH THE JOBS ON MR. PINTO'S **CLEANING SCHEDULE!**
UH-OH.
PRINCIPAL GARISH IS GOING TO **FLIP HER LID!**
YOU KNOW, WE **MIGHT** HAVE BEEN BETTER OFF AS FRANKENFROGS AFTER ALL!
THE END

ACKNOWLEDGMENTS

Thanks first and foremost to my wife, Liz, and daughter, Penny, for their patience and understanding during my erratic schedule while completing this book. Liz helped considerably with the book's execution by taking on the task of coloring the main characters throughout, saving me significant time and effort.

Thanks to Charlie Olsen of Inkwell Management, who placed this series with Amulet Books. Charlie has made it possible for me to devote all my work energies toward comics, and that has been a gift of immeasurable worth.

And thanks to everyone at Abrams who had a hand in the launch of this series and the creation of this book in particular, including Charlie K., Erica, Pam, and Carol, who helped to make this book far better that it would have been under my clumsy hands alone.